Joe Macoochee's
Wild Campout Adventures

Joe Macoochee's Wild Campout Adventures

Shirley Ann Wildes

Copyright © 2003 by Shirley Ann Wildes.

Library of Congress Number:		2003095381
ISBN:	Hardcover	1-4134-2503-8
	Softcover	1-4134-2502-X

All rights reserved. No part of this book may be reproduced or transmitted in any form or by any means, electronic or mechanical, including photocopying, recording, or by any information storage and retrieval system, without permission in writing from the copyright owner.

This book was printed in the United States of America.

To order additional copies of this book, contact:
Xlibris Corporation
1-888-795-4274
www.Xlibris.com
Orders@Xlibris.com
20187

CONTENTS

Chapter one: Joe Preparing For His Vacation 11
Chapter two: Ormond Beach Here Joe Comes 20
Chapter three: Joe's Fish Fight At The Park 28
Chapter four: Peace On The Balcony 34
Chapter five: Joe's Restless Night 38
Chapter six: Joe's Stay At Ormond Beach 40
Chapter seven: Mudbogging Joe 47
Chapter eight: Joe And His Lady Friends 54
Chapter nine: Fantasyland Of Wild Riders 59
Chapter ten: The Lonesome Dove Café 68
Chapter eleven: Big Lake Of Okeechobee 73
Chapter twelve: Incidents at Lake Placid 79
Chapter thirteen: Joe Meets Loretta Ann 93
Chapter fourteen: Prairie Camp Supplies 104
Chapter fifteen: Stuck At The Prairie 107
Chapter sixteen: Day Of The Big Dog 110
Chapter seventeen: The Meeting Of Riley 114
Chapter eighteen: Arrival At Camp Prairie 120
Chapter nineteen: Returning To The Dove 124
Chapter twenty: Newsflash About Prison Break 128
Chapter twenty one: Storm From Nowhere 133
Chapter twenty two: Good Day of Fishing 139
Chapter twenty three: Inviting Loretta Ann To Lunch 146
Chapter twenty four: The Walk In The Woods 150
Chapter twenty five: Loretta Ann Returns Home 153
Chapter twenty six: Joe To The Rescue 158
Chapter twenty seven: The Pistol Phone 163
Chapter twenty eight: Joe's Broke Tooth 166
Chapter twenty nine: Dr. Wayne Bojangles 172

Chapter thirty: Appointment At The Dentist's 177
Chapter thirty one: Wet Willie's Water World 182
Chapter thirty two: Joe's Dark Boogery Night 190
Chapter thirty three: The Port-o-let 197
Chapter thirty four: Poison Ivy Itch 201
Chapter thirty five: Coot's Place 204
Chapter thirty six: Back at Camp Prairie 209
Chapter thirty seven: Resting In The Hammock 216
Chapter thirty eight: The Prisoner Capture 225
Chapter thirty nine: The Sheriff's Report 231
Chapter forty: Old Man Dan 237
Chapter forty one: The Mad Boar Gator 241
Chapter forty two: The Old Gator Turtle 251
Chapter forty three: Trip To The Beach 261
Chapter forty four: Floating Far Away 270
Chapter forty five: Home On The Island 275
Chapter forty six: The Sound Of The Waterfalls 285
Chapter forty seven: The Giant Lizard 295
Chapter forty eight: The Cave Explorers 313
Chapter forty nine: The Fish Smokers 320
Chapter fifty: Preparing To Leave The Island 329
Chapter fifty one: Stormy Weather 333
Chapter fifty two: Back To Civilization 337
Chapter fifty three: Oscar Buys Dinner 339
Chapter fifty four: Welcome Home Party 342
Chapter fifty five: Joe's Big-Mouth Bass 345
Chapter fifty six: Scary Movie At The Theater 357
Chapter fifty seven: Hike On The Dike 360
Chapter fifty eight: Farewell Loretta Ann 369
About the Author Shirley Ann Wildes 373

"Joe Macooche"

Joe sleeping away enjoying the Florida sunshine.

Joe lazing around in field by the spillway.

Joe wading through the water looking for lost pole.

Chapter one

Joe Preparing For His Vacation

This is about a young man by the name of Joe Macoochee. He was born in a town called Spicey Town, Virginia. Joe had lived in Spicey Town from the day that he was born. He was a slender, tall young man in his early forties. He had sort of long hair, in which his dad always was after him to get it cut. Joe had liked the hippies from the sixties, and that is where he got his hairstyle. He was told a time or two that he was just too lazy to comb his hair. Joe wasn't too lazy to comb his hair he just wanted to have a little dependence of freedom. This made him feel good about himself I guess. Oh well, I always say to each his own.

It was that time of year that Joe's vacation time came around. This year he was planning to go on a camping trip. He had received some brochures from a friend that used to work with him. He told Joe about a little place in Okeechobee. Ever since Joe was a little boy he had wanted to go camping in the country. He'd always heard how much fun it was to spend time in the country. So when it came time for his vacation he decided he would go down to "The Good Old Sunshine State," of course which is Florida.

Joe always started getting excited this time of year, but

just couldn't help it. Joe had 2 months vacation time built up. Joe liked his job, but he liked his vacation time to. Joe only had a couple of days left on his job so he wanted to make sure he had everything in place, and going accordingly. Joe was almost ready to go. Joe was sitting D.O.R. In other words he was sitting dead on ready, or you could say he was ready to rock and roll.

Joe had a lot of things to do before he could just jump in his car and take off. He had to go by the bank and get some money for his trip. He had to pack up all the clothes, camping equipment, food, and other necessary items he needed for his trip. Joe was planning to check out some other places in Florida on his way down to his final destination spot in Okeechobee.

He could hardly concentrate on the rest of his work he had to finish so he could go home. Everyone at the office said their farewells to Joe, and told him to enjoy himself while he was on vacation. Little did he know, but they were as excited as he was about him getting to go on vacation. You see everyone that worked with Joe really liked him, but they were really glad to get a couple months separation from him. Joe always did his work, but he was somewhat of a klutz in a lot of things that he did. Joe meant well, but it seemed liked he had more bad luck than he had good luck. It seemed that the harder he tried to do things the more everything would go bass-ackwards. Well, Joe was finally finished with all his work so on his way home he went.

As soon as Joe arrived at home he took a shower, grabbed a bite to eat, and then he started packing his clothes for his journey. He had already bought most of the food that he wanted to carry with him. When he got settled in then he'd have the opportunity to do some cooking while he camped out in Florida. He packed his toothbrush, comb, toothpaste, hair tonic, and all the other personal items he thought he'd need. He even packed several rolls of toilet paper in case he was to have an upset stomach and had to use the bathroom quite often. Joe loaded up the charcoal, bar-b-que grill, matches, and starter fluid, along with the ice chest and other stuff he thought he had better carry.

Joe had bought a small tent to put up when he got to the woods so he would have something to sleep in. He also had bought a small cot so he wouldn't have to sleep on the hard ground. He had only been on one camping trip in his whole life, and that was when he was about 5 years old at the time. Joe and his dad had camped out in his back yard. He loved the camp out even if he didn't go anywheres else, but at his home. His dad had to work all the time, and had little time to spend with him. I guess you could say Joe was somewhat of a loner when he was a little boy. He always went to school. He hardly ever missed a day of school in all the years that he went.

Joe grew up, got a job in an office. He has been there almost like a permanent fixture ever since. He lost his dad about 3 years ago. He had lived with his dad up to his last days. He had loved his dad very much.

He always tried to do what he could for his dad since he had always had taken care of him. He never had any brothers or sisters because his dad never got married again. Joe being the only child missed out on a lot of things since he had to stay home all the time. He had a good life as it was though. He just wished that he could have spent a lot more time with his dad. He used to dream of going fishing, camping, and to the football games with his dad like all the other boys got to do with their dads. Joe was thankful that he had his dad around as long as he did.

He decided to get up early the next morning so he would miss all the heavy traffic. He always got up real early to go work because he was always worried that his old stationwagon might break down on the way to work with him one day. He had the car since 1985. It was a big old battlewagon but it had always got him to where he needed to go. Joe doubled checked everything to make sure that he had packed everything he'd need for his vacation. He sure didn't have any idea of what could and might happen to him. He went to bed after he watched the late night news. He wanted to see what the weather would be like the next day. So far it seemed like he would have clear sailing on his trip down to Florida. Joe could hardly get to sleep thinking about all the places he would get to go to. He had all kind of thoughts running through his head. Finally he went to sleep only then he began to dream about everything he had been thinking about when he had went to bed.

Joe got up real early the next morning. He had to make a quick trip by the bank to get some money out of the A.T.M. machine since he forgot to do that the day before. He had did so much packing the day before that he had forgot to go by the bank to get some money for the trip. He was so excited he could hardly concentrate on anything. He brushed his teeth, grabbed a jacket just in case it got too cool on his way to Florida. He stopped by a little fast food stop so he could get a sandwich and a cup of coffee.

As Joe drove along the highway starting on his vacation trip he noticed how strange it seemed that there was hardly any traffic on the highway this time of the morning. Joe had got up at 3:45 a.m. to begin his early journey. He turned on the radio to have some noise to listen to. He never listened to the radio stations much because it was always a rush for him to get to work all the time so he never bothered to ever turn it on. However, he did look at the boob tube once in a while. Joe was approaching the interstate highway he was planning on taking down to Florida, which was I-95. He had sort of planned out a route on a map, which indicated that this highway should be a straight shot down to his vacation spot. As he listened to the news on the radio it seemed the weather was going to be just right. He began to really get down with the music. The more he listened to all the songs the more he thought of what all he'd been missing on the radio in the mornings on his way to work.

Joe was making pretty good time on the road. The cars were starting to get more and more as time went on. He had been driving several hours now and he was just going with the flow. He was glad that everything was going along so smoothly. So far he hadn't a minute's trouble with his old car. He always took care of the old battlewagon because it had been in his family so long. He never had to do any mechanic work on it at all. Of course, it wouldn't have done any good for him to try to work on his car because he was not mechanic smart at all. He always had the service did on his car at the stations in town. He might could change the tire if he had to, but he had never changed any tires on his car because he always had the tire store to do it for him. One thing that Joe did religiously was to keep his car well maintained. His car was in good condition except it wasn't a brand new looking car anymore. That didn't matter to him though because as long as it got him to work faithfully each day Joe was happy. He was as happy as he could be right now because he didn't have to be in any hurry to do anything. He was just cruising along in his old car going down I-95 just taking life easy.

Joe was thinking of the day he left the office where he worked at. He thought everyone was so nice in seeing him off. He knew they would probably miss him when he'd be gone for two whole months. He really didn't know that they were glad they were going to get some peace around there when he left. Joe kept everyone on their toes because he was such a klutz that he caused a lot of accidents to happen, but he didn't ever mean to stir up any trouble.

Joe just wasn't blessed to stay out of trouble. He knew he would have a lot of time on his vacation to get adjusted to his new stay when he arrived in Okeechobee. He hoped to meet some friendly people down there. Joe wasn't too shy when it came to meeting people because he was around so many on his job.

It was almost daylight now. Joe was coming to the Georgia

State line. He decided to stop and take a break. He stopped at a little gas station bought some gas, and went to the bathroom while he was there. He asked the man that was running the station what kind of recreation they had there in his little town, which was by the way called Hootsberry. The little old man told him there was a park there. You can go into the park and take boat trips through the old swamps that joined the Old Ghost's River. Joe thought that sounded like an exciting place he might enjoy going to while he was in the little town of Hootsberry.

He bought some chips, drinks, ice, and some lunchmeat and bread from the man's little station. He thanked the little old man for all the information. The man thanked Joe and told him to have a nice time on his trip since he had mentioned to him that he was on vacation. Joe never did meet a stranger any place that he went. He always took all people to be good at heart like his dad had taught him. He sure missed his dad so much and had hoped one day that he could take his dad on vacation with him, but unfortunately that never happened.

As he drove along the highway he saw the sign that read "Ghost River" 5 miles. He turned on the road once he came to it that read "Ghost River State Park." He found the park without any problem at all. He paid his way to enter the park, and drove around really marveled at what he saw. It was so beautiful there in the woods. The air smelled so fresh, nothing like the stale air that you had to breathe in the big city where he lived. Joe found the place where you could ride in the boats to see the swamps that joined the Ghost River. It sounded kind of spooky, but what the heck. He got into one of the boats with some other people. Everyone seemed excited to be going on a boat ride.

The tour guide began telling them all about the swamps and the river. He told them many years ago there was a lot of Indians that used to live in the swamps and on the river. The guide told them about the disappearance of an Indian

family that was never found. It seemed they just vanished into thin air. The old timers used to talk about the sounds they would hear at night in the swamps that would make the hair on the back of your neck stand straight up.
No one ever knew what could have happened to the Indian family. To this day it still remains a mystery to the people of Hootsberry. Joe thought how sad it was that the family was never found. He forgot about the sad story about the Indians as they journeyed on through the swamps. As they continued on the trip in the little boat everyone began asking the tour guide a lot of questions. The man answered each person's question, and kept telling them all about the swamp. The man would stop now and then, when he came close to an alligator so everyone could get a close up view. Joe saw something in the water besides him. He just wondered what he was looking at in the water. It looked like 2 noseholes sticking up out of the water. He put his hand over the side of the boat and into the water making a rippling sound with his fingers. All of a sudden an alligator lunged for his hand. The guide saw what Joe had done. He hit the alligator with his boat oar, and told him to keep his arm inside the boat unless he wanted to feed it to the gator.
Joe had a close call with the big gator, but didn't really realize what could have happened. Joe didn't think anything about it at all, but he kept his hands to himself like the man told him to do. Joe saw some turtles, snakes, and a few big birds. Speaking of the birds it just wasn't Joe's lucky day because as the big birds flew overhead they let some big bird droppings go which of course landed directly in his face. The people in the boat tried not to laugh at Joe's misfortune, but they couldn't help it.
When the boat ride was finally over he walked around through the park for a while longer. He spent most of the day at the park looking at all the sights there. It was a pretty place there on the Ghost River. Joe kept remembering the

story he'd been told about the Indian family that disappeared, and was never found.

He just wondered if something bad had happened to them, or if maybe they had just moved away. He wished he knew because he just couldn't keep from thinking about the sad story.

Joe walked across a little wooden bridge that crossed a little swamp. As he walked along the path he noticed how beautiful the scenery was there. There were many cypress trees in the swamp that had stumps protruding out of the water at the base of the trees. There were so many white birds in the tops of the trees that the trees were almost white. There was moss hanging from the tree limbs on all the trees. The wind was slightly blowing making the moss sway back and forth from the tree limbs. He had never seen such a beautiful place like this before.

Joe never saw much wild life up in Virginia. It was such a different climate down south than it was in his home state. Maybe that's why everything seemed so different. He had really enjoyed his time there at the park today. He hated that the day had gone by so fast, but he knew he would have to be on his way again. It was getting late so he knew it was time for him to leave the park.

Fell asleep on wood bench in woods. Joe Macoochee

Chapter two

Ormond Beach Here Joe Comes

Joe went back to his car and fixed himself a sandwich, and got a cold drink. He rested about 1 hour then started on the road again. He drove until dark and then stopped at a motel to spend the night. He couldn't see the sights at night so that's why he decided to make the most of it in the daytime. Joe saw some lights that looked like a city ahead so he turned off I-95 at the next exit that came up.

Joe made it across the Florida State line, and stopped to fill up his car with gas so he wouldn't have to stop the next morning. He made it to a little town called Ormond Beach. It was right off I-95. He found a little motel called the Shady Beach Motel, and checked into it for the night. He took a shower, brushed his teeth, and changed his clothes.

Joe thought he would go to a restaurant, and get him a good hot meal before he called it a day. Joe noticed that most of the restaurants all had seafood names. He saw one called Hatty's Crabby Shack Café. He kind of liked the name so he stopped in to see what was on their menu. He went inside, but didn't see many people there. Maybe it wasn't time for supper yet.

All he knew was that he was getting some hunger pains

so it was time for him to eat. He was looking at some different ocean animals on the wall, when a big man came over to where he was and asked him if he was ready to order his food. Joe said, yes I guess I'll have a big glass of sweet tea to start with. He sat down and started to look over the menu that the man had given to him. They had all kinds of seafood on the menu. He thought he would try Hatty's Seafood Platter.

Joe thought the little restaurant was a neat little place. There were a few people sitting there eating their meals when Joe came into the restaurant. As he sat there at his little table Joe saw a jukebox over against the wall. He walked over to the jukebox, and looked over the selection of records that was on it. He decided to play some songs by the Beach Boys. The Beach Boys were a singing group that played a lot of surfing songs back in the 60's. Joe played Surfing U.S.A., Barbara Ann, and The Little G.T.O. song.

As Joe returned to his table he saw a little blonde waitress coming towards his table to wait on him. The big guy that gave him his menu turned out to be the owner of the place. He sure didn't look like a Hatty though. Joe asked the waitress if Hatty was the owner of the café, and the waitress told him that Hatty was the big guy's wife. The waitress told him in a quiet voice the Hatty left on a ride with a motorcycle guy. She called 3 days later and told her husband she wouldn't be back. That was 4 years ago, and the waitress said the big guy was still waiting for her to return one day.

The little waitress was friendly enough, and she talked to Joe while his meal was being fixed. She asked him what brought him to Ormond Beach? He told her he was on his way to Okeechobee, Florida to spend his vacation. He told her all of the things that he wanted to do while he was on vacation.

The waitress told Joe she had went down to Okeechobee 2 years ago to see a cousin that had lived there at the time. She told him that the town was small, but everyone there seemed friendly enough. He told her he thought he'd like the town because he lived in the big city, and it was a rat race all the time. It would be nice for a change to be able to enjoy a place that you didn't have to run like you were going to a fire all the time.

The bell rang in the kitchen for the waitress to pick up his meal. As the waitress sat his plate on the table she told him to enjoy his meal, and asked him if he needed anything else. Joe told the waitress he'd take some more tea, and then he should be in good shape. The waitress just laughed at Joe then went to get him some more tea.

Joe had ordered the seafood platter with all the fixings, and boy it had the fixings. He had never ate any seafood that tasted this good before. He had big jumbo fried shrimp, fried clams, scallops, and crab cakes that came with baked beans, cole slaw, and french fries. The waitress even brought out a cup of conch soup for him to try. Joe thought it tasted good. It would take him a while to finish the big platter of food because there was so much on the platter to eat.

While he sat there eating his food there were some men and women that came into the café to eat. They went over to the jukebox, and played some music. The women started to dance. They were pretty good at the dance they were doing. When the music stopped they went and sat at the table with the 2 men.

The men ordered some beers for them, and they all began to drink away on them. They probably drank 5 beers before they ate anything. They ordered a big plate of onion straw appetizers before their main meal came out. They ate them as quick as they were brought out to them. Joe guessed they were hungry too. The women got up and started to dance again to the music. This time they were looking at him while they danced. Joe didn't know what to do about this situation. He noticed that the men were looking at him, and giving him a dirty look that made him nervous.

He sure didn't want to have any trouble with these 2

fellows because they were a lot bigger than he was. Joe was not a fighter either. He just knew there would be trouble, but the waitress brought out their food and they all started eating their meals. Joe finally finished his food, and got up to pay for his meal so he could go back to his motel for the night. He sure was full, and he told the waitress that he thought he'd have to get her to carry him to his car because he was about to pop. The little waitress told him to have a safe and fun trip. He told her he would try. Joe told her he liked the seafood platter, and it was real good. She thanked him for stopping in, and told him if he was ever that way again to come on back and see them.

Joe walked by the table where the men and women were. The men gave him a dirty look, and he was glad that he was finally getting out of there. He hurried on outside, got into his car, and went back to the motel. Joe was really tired now. He had his belly full, and he was ready to go to bed and call it a day. He watched a little news on the boob tube then he went off to sleep. He was really tired from all the driving he'd been doing so he didn't have any trouble going to sleep at all.

Joe was really sawing logs in his sleep. All of a sudden he was awakened by a loud noise outside his motel room. It had to be a loud noise to wake him up because he wasn't easy to wake up at all once he went to sleep.

Joe opened his door a little ajar. He had no idea of what was going on outside his door. He looked outside, and there were the people that had eaten at the café a few hours ago where he had eaten his supper. He kept watching, but he only saw the 2 women trying to get into their room. He didn't see the men with them this time. He could tell the ladies were having a hard time of trying to get into their room probably because they were half tipsy.

Joe opened his door, and they looked around and saw him. They remembered him right off the bat. They seemed happy to see Joe again. He walked over to their door and asked if he could be of any assistance, and they told him he sure could. He asked them where the key was, and they handed him a key ring with several keys on it. Joe tried each one, but not one of the keys would fit the lock on the door.

It was about 2:00 a.m. and he saw that the women didn't know what they had done with their room keys. The office had closed for the rest of the night, and they wouldn't be able to get another key from the office. He introduced himself to the 2 women. Joe knew they were still a little tipsy from all the beers they had dranked. He asked them where their friends were. The women told Joe they had met the 2 men a little earlier in town at another bar & grill. The men had got aquainted with them and asked them to go eat supper with them. As it turned out the 2 men ended up drinking so much beer that they began fighting with each other, and wound up getting carried off to jail to spend the night.

The women told Joe thanks for his help in trying to get open the door for them. They told him they guessed they would spend the night in their car. Joe told them they could spend the night in his room if they wanted to. The 2 women told him he was very kind, and they ended up spending the rest of the night on his other spare bed. Joe got up the next morning, and told the 2 women he'd see them later. By the way he finally learned that their names were Rose & Mary. They looked kind of sick. Joe felt sorry for them because he knew they probably had a hangover from the night before.

Rose and Mary told Joe thanks for letting them stay there in his room last night. He told them they were welcome. They told him they would go to the office to get another key, and they would be sure to put it in the ashtray of their car so they wouldn't lose it. Joe laughed and told them that was a good idea, but to be sure not to lose their car. They said they wouldn't this time.

Joe told them he'd be back later on if they wanted to sleep in for a while. They told him they would stay one more day then they had to get headed back to their home that was around 150 miles from there. He told them if he didn't see them before they left to be sure to take care of themselves.

Joe left the motel room, and drove into town again. He stopped in and had breakfast at a little run down looking café. It was called Granny's Shanty Shack Café. Joe ordered ham, eggs, pancakes, and hashbrowns. Boy, they were sure good. He cleaned every morsel of food on his plate. He asked the little old lady what kind of recreation there was in Ormond Beach? She told him about the Tomoka State Park that was there. She told Joe that it was a real nice park to see. He got the directions from the little old lady, and went straight to the park without getting lost at all. He stopped at the entrance gate and paid his way into the park.

Joe drove around the park about an hour or two. He found a spot with a little bar-b-que grill and table. The park even had bathrooms close to where he parked his car. This little park was just like being uptown with all the facilities that you need. Joe had brought some frozen meat that he had put in his big cooler before he had left home. It still had plenty of ice on all the meat so he was okay right now.

Joe needed to get another bag of ice for his small cooler so he could keep his drinks cold though. He stopped at the little store that was at the park, and bought a couple bags of ice there so this saved him a trip back to town. He got out and walked all over the park grounds. He saw some statues of Indians there in the park. It was really a nice park. It had all kinds of big tall trees. There were a lot of birds and other animals there. He saw a lot of squirrels and birds there. The squirrels were so playful running up and down the trees that Joe had spent 2 hours just watching them play. He watched the little squirrels getting acorns from the trees, and burying them in the ground at the base of the big old oak trees.

Joe thought it was so comical watching them because the squirrels seemed to be trying to hide the acorns from each other. If one came too close to the other one while they were burying their acorns they would start scolding each other. It was as if each one was trying to tell the other one to go away and leave their stash of acorns alone. There was a bigger squirrel that was putting acorns in the hole in the big oak tree. Joe thought he was smarter because when the winter came the big squirrel wouldn't have to come out in the cold weather to find his food.

He noticed that more and more people were starting to enter the park. Most of the people parked their cars, and got out to walk around the park like Joe did. Everyone seemed friendly because they smiled, and said hello as they passed by him. It was so relaxing at the park he thought. It was really a pretty place to camp at, but Joe thought he'd wait because he would be camping out a lot when he made it to Okeechobee.

Tired and lost Joe Macoochee sits on base of big oak tree.

Chapter three

Joe's Fish Fight At The Park

Poe decided to go back to his car and get out some of the frozen ribs, and get them ready to grill on the bar-b-que grill. He thought he had better start to get some cooking lessons in before he got to Okeechobee because he didn't know what he would get into down there.

Joe put the ribs on the little table. He got out the charcoal and starter fluid. He finally found his matches to light the coals with. Joe wasn't very experienced at cooking, but was ready to give it a big shot. He squirted a lot of starting fluid onto the charcoal bricks. When he threw the lit match onto the charcoal bricks they blazed up fast. Well, he managed to start the fire okay, but he hadn't ever bar-b-qued any meat before.

Joe washed the ribs under the water spigot until they were clean. He salted and peppered the ribs real good then placed them on the grill. He opened a can of corn, and a can of baked beans. He put them each in a pot inside the grill over to the edge so they wouldn't cook too fast. He figured it would take a long time for the ribs to cook so he decided to walk around some more since he had everything under control on the grill.

Joe left the grill cooking his ribs, corn, and baked beans. He only meant to be gone a few minutes. Just as it would happen he would be away a lot longer than he expected to be. Joe was walking along the park shoreline when he saw a man fishing inside the little lagoon. He had been looking at the different types of seashells that had washed up on the shore. Joe walked on over to where he saw the man fishing. He asked the man if he had caught any fish. He was trying to strike up a conversation, but the man was really trying to enjoy his fishing.

Joe wasn't much of a fisherman either. He had only gone on a fishing trip with his dad one time when he was about ten years old. He saw that the man wasn't in a real talkative mood so he started to walk away. All of a sudden the man yanked back on his fishing rod. Joe knew that the man had a big fish on his rod by the way it was bending double. He was getting excited at seeing the man fighting with the big fish. Boy, the man was having a hard time trying to bring the big fish in. Joe stood there looking at the line running out farther and farther as the big fish put up such a struggle to try and get loose from the man's hook.

Joe saw a fish net lying on the ground next to the fisherman's tackle box. He walked over and picked up the net, and started to wade out into the water. Joe thought he would give the man a helping hand, and try to catch the fish in the net for the man. Well, Joe waded out, grabbed the fishing line while the man reeled it in. He spotted the fish getting close to him. Boy, what a big fish it was Joe thought. It must weigh 15 pounds or more. Joe took the net and held onto the long aluminum handle, then he slipped the fishnet slowly under the fish.

Little did Joe realize that he was about to have the fight of his life with a big barracuda fish? He didn't know that salt-water fish all have a mouth full of teeth, but he was about to find out. The poor barracuda fish was putting up a fight for his life. He was desperate to get away. The fish was flopping around in the water so hard that he was bending the handle on the fish net. He was so big that he was hanging halfway out of the fish net. Joe saw that the fish was about to get out of the net so he reached out, and grabbed hold of the barracuda with his bare hands.

When he grabbed the fish he took the hook out of the fish's mouth. That was one of the worst mistakes Joe could have made at that time. You see when he got the barracuda's mouth loose from the hook this gave the fish the opportunity to make Joe a believer. The big fish bit down on his wrist. Boy, Joe knew what the fish felt like being caught at that moment. He wanted to get away from the fish as bad as the fish wanted to get loose from him.

Joe and the fish were really stirring up some waves in the water. There's nothing like wrestling with a big fish, but wrestling him with your bare hands shows you're not too smart especially if they are salt-water and have a mouthful of teeth. If you get my drift then you'll know what I mean. For those that don't then I'll explain that it means he was sort of crazy to have caught the fish with his bare hands to start with. We know, it being Joe Macoochee that's normal for him because he isn't one to stop, and weigh out the options of what could happen. Poor Joe maybe one day he will get on the right track.

Well, he was really battling it out with the big old barracuda fish. He was doing everything he could to get loose from the fish. Joe tried hitting the fish with his other fist, but the fish wasn't about to let loose of him. The fish was fighting for his life, and he wasn't giving up to Joe either.

Joe only could think of one more way that might get the fish loose from his wrist. The only way left was to bite the fish back and this is just what he did. Joe bit the fish right on the top of his head. This caused the barracuda to jump one last hard time. The fish let go of his wrist, and Joe turned loose of the big barracuda. Now the fish had made his escape from death to his freedom. The barracuda you could say was now a free Willy. Joe and the barracuda would both have something in common. Each would carry a big scar from now on.

Well, Joe didn't realize it at that moment, but he had trouble waiting on shore for him. As he waded back to where the fisherman was, Joe knew he was in a lot of trouble. The fisherman saw that Joe was chewed up from the fish, but he wasn't hurt real bad so he was ready for Joe now. Joe tried to tell the fisherman how sorry he was that he let the fish get loose.

However, the fisherman was so furious with him that he picked up a shell and threw it at him. Well, as Joe's luck would have it the big shell that the man threw at him was a conch shell. The conch shell hit Joe smack in the nose. The point of the conch shell stuck in the side of his nose. He had to pull the shell loose from his nose. Well, not only did he have a big bite on his hand now he had a pierced nose. Boy, it wasn't turning out to be Joe's day after all.

Joe's pride was really wounded along with his wrist and nose. He decided right then that it was time for him to return to his campsite. Joe then started walking back to his little camp.

As he got nearer to the grill he could see a thick heavy smoke coming from the grill stack. He ran to the bar-b-que grill, and lifted the big lid up. That's another mistake Joe made at that time. You never lift a lid up to see if there's fire inside because it will blaze up like a fire under a car hood. The fire began to blaze out of control for a few minutes, but he finally managed to get it under control.

Well, he found one thing out for sure. That is if you can't stand the heat then it's time to get out of the kitchen. As for the good meal he was looking forward to eating, it just wasn't meant to be. Poor Joe's ribs were charcoaled blacker than the coals that cooked them. The corn was cooked so much that it was almost popped, and the baked beans were cooked harder than rocks. He knew that it was time for him to go back to town so he could get something to eat. He had to get some medicine to so he could doctor his wounds and his pride.

After Joe cleaned up his mess at the grill, and loaded up everything back into his car. He headed back to town so he could go by the drugstore and buy some alcohol, peroxide, and bandages. It just hadn't been a good day for him at all. Joe meant well as he always did, but as usual everything went bass-ackwards for him. Maybe if he didn't try so hard he wouldn't have everything go in the opposite direction. Joe always kept persevering to go on so that's why he wasn't a quitter I guess.

He found a drugstore in town where he bought everything he needed to doctor himself with. He went back to his room at the motel, and doctored his puncture wounds. Joe's pride was hurt a little from the scolding he got from the man plus the damage the fish caused him. Boy, I must have been stupid he thought. I shouldn't have messed with the man's fish then I wouldn't have gotten bit by the barracuda. Joe was pretty hard on himself, but in a way he was right. Oh well, as they always say experience is the best teacher.

Joe checked out of the motel he'd stayed at with Rose and Mary. He wanted to find one closer to the ocean so he could watch the people swim at the beach. Joe found a big motel right on the beach. His room was on the twelfth floor, and he had the ocean view from his room. There was a little balcony that extended out on the ledge. Joe even had two chairs he could sit in on the balcony. Of course he sat in one chair, and propped his feet up in the other one. He knew he was at the right place now.

The motel he checked into was called "Big Kahuna's Hideout." Joe wished he had found this motel before he had checked into the other one. The motel had two swimming pools, and had the ocean right at its back door. There was a recreation room down on ground floor, and there were pool tables and games to play in there. He had played pool a few times with some of the guys at a party he once attended. He wasn't a party animal so he just didn't have the urge to go much of anywheres at all.

His room had a little kitchenette in it, so if he didn't want to go out to eat, he could fix something there in his room. Joe sat on the balcony for a long time enjoying the cool breeze that was blowing in off the ocean. The sun was out, but it wasn't hot because the breeze was so cool. Joe could taste the salt in the air. He could feel his skin starting to become sticky because the salt air was damp. I guess when the ocean is rough it causes a mist to blow through the air when there is a good breeze.

Joe went back inside his room. He turned on his t.v. but decided to take a shower to get the salt off of his skin. After he finished showering he lay down on his bed to take a nap. He sure needed some rest after the long hard day he'd had. Joe turned on his air conditioning after he closed the door leading out to his balcony. He lay down on his bed, and it was so comfortable. It was only a few minutes before he was dead to the world. Joe had slept for a couple of hours only to be awakened by a nightmare he was having. His nightmare was about the fish he had a fight with. The nightmare was so disturbing to him that he didn't go back to sleep anymore that day until it got dark.

Chapter four

Peace On The Balcony

Joe got up and went outside to his car. He ended up bringing some food up to his room to eat. Vienna sausages and pork and beans were what he ate for his slim supper. He brought up a six pack of sodas so he would have something to drink besides just water. If he wanted anything else to eat later he would cook it since he had the use of the little kitchenette. Joe had all kinds of groceries down in his car that he could fix if he got the urge to cook. After the meal he cooked on the grill he wasn't too sure that he should try cooking anything else. He'd hate to burn something up in the motel. Knowing his luck he would be the one and only person that could make a smoke alarm go off, and not even have any smoke in the room. After he ate his little supper all he wanted to do was just to try to recuperate after his awful day.

Joe saw what he looked like in the mirror when he got out of the shower. He looked like he had been in a battle of some kind. He didn't dare go out on the town all beat up looking because he might end up in some other kind of trouble. He sure wasn't up to anymore bad luck today. After the day that he had, he ended up staying in the rest of the night in his motel room. He just couldn't stand anymore excitement of any kind. Joe went back out on his little balcony to sit. It was dark now, and you could see all the city lights lit up in town. It was lit up all along the ocean around the motels. There were so many lights around the swimming pools that it looked almost like daytime at the poolside.

As he sat there on his little balcony he watched the people swimming in the pools and enjoying themselves. He thought he'd like swimming in the pool, but he didn't have any swim trunks. Joe sure wasn't going swimming in his birthday suit that was for sure. He sat back in his chair so relaxed as he watched the world go by. He knew he had to go in before much longer so as not to fall asleep on the balcony.

Joe just couldn't seem to pull himself away from the balcony because he was enjoying himself so much right at that moment. He looked at all the stars shining in the clear sky. There were so many out tonight that they made the sky light up like a faraway city. Right now he was taking life easy with no problems at all. He was really enjoying himself where he was and he was taking it all in while he could.

Joe sat on the balcony for hours. He sat there listening to the sound of the waves crashing in from the ocean. Everyone on the beach had come in since the waves were getting higher and closer to the shore. That was a wise thing for everyone to do because it was very dark, and there weren't any lifeguards on duty.

Joe had started to get a little chilly from the ocean breeze so he pulled a blanket from his bed to cover with as he went back to sit in his little chair on the balcony. He propped his legs up in the other chair like he had done earlier. Boy he was comfortable once again. It was getting pretty close to midnight, and Joe noticed everyone had left the swimming pools. He saw a man coming out of the motel down on the ground floor to check to see if everyone had left the pool. The man turned off the lights to the swimming pools, and locked the gates behind him.

Well, Joe thought he was by himself on the balcony, but he heard someone on the balcony on the next floor above him. He heard a woman and a man laughing. He saw a man on the balcony beside his. The man walks out, and climbs up on his balcony chair, then leaned over the side of his balcony. Joe got scared for a minute because he thought the man was going to jump off of the balcony. As it turned out Joe saw he was trying to get the attention of a lady on a balcony below his. He was sure glad the man wasn't planning to jump off of the balcony because he sure wasn't up to seeing someone getting flattened like a pancake. After that episode he was at ease once again.

Joe laying down in the field of flowers enjoying his vacation.

Chapter five

Joe's Restless Night

Joe watched television way past midnight then turned it off to go to bed. He tossed and tumbled, but finally went off to sleep. During the early wee hours of the night, he had to get up to use the bathroom. The motel kept the outside lights on all night, but it didn't light his room up much at all. He couldn't find the night switch so he couldn't turn on the lights to see where he was going in the room. His room was very dim so he had to be careful walking around in it.

Joe never thought to bring his flashlight inside from his car. As it went he had to hunt his way to the bathroom. He was still half-asleep, but he did find his way at last. He was unable to find the bathroom switch, but he found the bathtub with out any problem. You see, Joe accidentally fell into the bathtub. As he sat there in the tub he felt around and finally felt the toilet. He held on to the toilet with one hand and then he found the sink. Joe felt around on the wall and finally found the switch to turn on the light.

He used the bathroom, and decided to leave the light on in the bathroom so he would be able to see if he had to get up again. Joe went back to bed, and slept like a log the rest of the night. He would be in for a surprise when he woke up the next morning. He would be in for a little shock of his life especially when he saw himself in the mirror again. Joe looked a lot worse than he had the day before.

When he saw himself in the mirror it instantly brought back his terrible memories of the day before.

Well, Joe tried to move his wrist, but could hardly move it because it was so sore. Then he started sneezing all of a sudden. Boy, he thought that he had sneezed his nose off because it hurt so badly. He felt of his nose, and it was really sore. This was one day that he hoped he could put behind him. All this damage was done because of the fish incident. He had learned one lesson though, and it was about interfering with someone while they are fishing. It can be dangerous to your health, and you can have bad after effects like Joe.

Chapter six

Joe's Stay At Ormond Beach

It was real early in the morning. Joe could have slept late if he'd wanted, but he was so accustomed of getting up early that old habits are hard to break. Well, he got out of bed and began to think of what was going to be on his agenda for today. First thing Joe wanted, was to take another shower so he could start the day off refreshed and ready to go. As he made his way to the bathroom to get showered he looked at himself in the mirror again. Joe thought he saw someone in the mirror other than himself. He was shocked each time he looked in the mirror, and saw his big bruised swollen up nose. Gosh, he looked rough. He looked like he had been run over by a truck.

Joe took an early morning shower then went into town, as bad as he hated to. He dreaded for anyone to see him looking like he did. He wanted first of all to get him something to eat. He knew he'd probably get a lot of stares, but he was a hungry man right now so he would just ignore the stares.

He drove on into town to eat breakfast. Joe stopped in and had a big breakfast at the little café he'd eat at before. He saw the same little old lady that had fixed his breakfast the other morning. She told him good morning, and asked him what the world happened to you son. Joe told her all about his episode from the day before. She laughed then told him he'd better give up his fishing techniques. He told her he guessed he better do that to.

Joe ate all his breakfast then paid for it at the cash register up in the front part of the café. The little lady told him to call her Granny if he wanted to because everyone else did. He told Granny the breakfast was real good then he bid her good-bye. He told her he would try to come by and see her before he left on his trip down to Okeechobee.

Joe decided to stay another day in Ormond Beach then he would start on his trip again. After Joe left Granny's Café, he drove around the town of Ormond Beach. He noticed a lot of old buildings that were probably 150 years old. The buildings looked as if they had been taken care of because they weren't run down looking like most old buildings. As he drove around he saw a sign that read 3 miles to the ocean. He thought he would go to see how it looked, and away he went.

Joe arrived at the inlet of the ocean, which by the way was the Atlantic because it is on the East Coast of Florida. He thought how nice it was there. Joe got out of his car, and started walking out on the walkway towards the ocean. The wind was blowing hard, but as they say there's nothing like a good ocean breeze that can clear the mind. Joe had better stay there all day so maybe the breeze might just clear his brain. There were a few people on the inlet walkway fishing, but he knew not to pay them any attention. After the trouble he got into the other day he wasn't about to bother anyone who had a fishing pole in his or her hands. He learned his lesson the hard way and you can say he chalked that one up from experience.

Joe watched the sea gulls fly overhead and watched them fly down through the air to catch minnows the people threw to them. He was amazed at how they were able to catch the food in mid-air. Joe looked at the blue colored ocean, and thought it was pretty because it was so crystal clear. You could see the bottom in some places that's how clear the ocean was at that moment. He walked to the end of the walkway of the inlet. He watched as some big boats, and freighter ships made their way into the inlet from the ocean. The port wasn't too far from the inlet, and you could see all the other boats that were docked there.

Well, he stood there at the end of the inlet thinking how nice the weather was right at that moment. He was almost tempted to go buy himself some swimming trunks then go swimming. He changed his mind because he wasn't sure if he could swim in the waves on the beach. Joe thought he would just go back to town, and check out the museum he'd passed on his way to the ocean. There would probably be a lot of interesting things to see there. He loved going to places like that where you could see things from the olden days.

As Joe started walking back to his car he felt something grab hold of his ponytail. It turned out to be a fishing lure that one of the fishermen was trying to throw out into the water. When the man tried to cast out his fishing line the fishing lure got caught in Joe's hair. As the man pulled on the fishing lure he yanked it so hard that it got really tangled up deep into Joe's hair. Joe then let out a holler that could have sent chills through a ghost's backbone if they had one. After the man saw what he had done he tried to get his lure out of Joe's hair. No matter how hard he yanked his rod the lure was still tangled up in Joe's hair. The poor man was really nervous at what had happened and tried very carefully to get it out without pulling all of Joe's hair out. As it ended up there was a big wad of hair that came out of his head. The poor man apologized to him several times before Joe left to go to his car. He told the man it was okay, then thanked him for getting the lure out of his hair at last. As bad as the lure was tangled up in his hair he thought he would end up having to get his hair all cut off, but he didn't.

Joe finally made it back to his car. Safe once again he went to the town museum, and went inside to look around.

As he walked through the museum he noticed the musty smell it had. Joe guessed it was because the stuff was so old inside. You could tell the museum had to be very old. The museum had cobwebs hanging from some of the antiques on the walls. He thought it to be sort of eerie looking in a way, but it was a museum that was very well displayed inside.

Joe liked it there because it had all sorts of old antiques that were many years old. There were big old rusty bells, and all different kinds of statues that once were on the front of big ships. There was a shelf that was displayed with many kinds of old plates, bowls, drinking mugs, and other artifacts. There were too many things inside of the museum to try to describe and mention. He looked at some old coins that were inside a showcase that was on display. Joe browsed around the museum for 3 hours. He really enjoyed all the old antiques, and all the old history that was on display there at the museum.

When he left the museum he felt like he had come away with some new knowledge about the oceans past history. Joe just drove around the rest of the day looking at the quaint little town by the ocean. He really liked the little town because it had so much to see. He visited some of the other sights then he looked at his watch. He couldn't believe that the time had passed by so quickly. Since it was getting late he thought he might go grab a bite to eat before he went back to his room at the motel.

Joe went back to Granny's Little Café to get something to eat. He had told Granny he would go by and see her before he left town so he stuck to his word. Granny was still there at the little café working away. She saw him when he came inside the door. She yelled out at Joe to find himself a seat, and she would be with him in just a minute.

Well, he sat next to a window so he could look outside. He didn't have to wait very long until Granny came and took his order. Granny asked him when was he leaving to go to Okeechobee? He told her he'd be leaving out the first thing in the morning. Granny told him to stop back in if he was ever up this way again, and he told her he surely would. Joe ordered the seafood plate again. He really was beginning to like his seafood. He ate all his food then told Granny he would try some of her blueberry cobbler that was on the menu for the day. After he ate everything on his plate along with the cobbler he was too full to move, but he knew he had to get back to his room to get everything packed up for his trip the next morning.

Joe told Granny to take care of herself, and as usual he told her he enjoyed the good meal. Granny told him to behave himself, and not to do anything she wouldn't do. He laughed then told Granny he'd see her later. On the way back to his motel he decided to gas up his car that way he wouldn't have to do it the next morning. He pulled into the little station, pumped his gas then went inside to pay for it. As Joe entered through the door he almost had a heart attack. It really wasn't a heart attack for real, but he had got so scared that he was ready to have one.

Joe had a big snake drop down on his shoulder as he walked through the door. It turned out to be a pet python, but he didn't care what kind it was because he was scared to death of any kind of snakes. The owner of the station laughed, and told Joe that Sammy wouldn't hurt him. Sammy was of course the name of the snake. He told the man that the snake might not hurt him, but it sure could make him hurt himself.

Joe asked the man what kind of food the snake ate, and he told him he fed the snake rats, mice, birds, and rabbits when he could get them. Joe thought to himself, "how sad it was that the little animals had to become food for the snake." Joe knew the snake had to eat to. Well, he didn't stay around very long because he just couldn't stand it if the snake got on him again. He had shivers running up his spine just watching the snake slithering around the man's neck.

Joe arrived back at the motel, and he was glad to be there because he was tired from being on the go all day. He took a shower then sat down in the big old easy chair in his motel room. He watched a movie that was a tearjerker, and after that he watched some of the late night news. He brushed his teeth then drank some water before he went to bed. Joe wanted to get an early start the next morning so as to beat the traffic. He didn't have to have anyone rock him to sleep. He slept through the night for a change. Joe didn't even have to get up to go to the bathroom and that was something unusual for him.

Joe Macoochee asleep on bench in the woods

Chapter seven

Mudbogging Joe

Joe stopped at a little drive-thru restaurant the next morning before he left Ormond beach. He bought himself a sandwich, hashbrowns, and a coke to have for his breakfast. He stopped long enough in the parking lot so he could eat because he didn't like to eat while he was driving. It didn't take him long to gobble down his little breakfast because he had an appetite this morning. He threw his breakfast paper into the garbage then left the little fast food restaurant.

It wasn't quite daylight yet, but it soon would be. As Joe made his way back on highway I-95 he was glad he had got an early start. There wasn't much traffic on the road yet. Joe was making pretty good time so far. He knew he just had to go with the flow of the traffic again. Joe seemed to be cruising along at a good speed, but it seemed to him that everyone else was driving faster today for some reason. Joe was driving at a speed of 75 M.P.H. He didn't care to drive that fast, but he knew he had to keep up his speed, or he would get run over. Everything seemed like it was going along pretty smooth when all of a sudden he ran over something that was lying in his traffic lane. He thought this was going to be the end for him. Whatever it was that he had run over in the highway had caused him to have a flat tire. He tried his best to keep the big old stationwagon under control, but it went careening off the road right out through the woods. Since Joe was traveling at such a high rate of speed his car went a good distance into the woods. He was very fortunate that he didn't total out his car, but as big as his old stationwagon was it might just have bulldozed the trees down. Joe had his seat belt on, but he was holding onto the steering wheel so tight that you couldn't have pried him loose from the steering wheel. If he had got thrown out of his car his hands would have probably come off and remained clutching to the steering wheel.

Well, after Joe got his car stopped he wasn't sure if he should check his underwear to see if he'd messed in them or not. As he got out of his car he checked to see what kind of damage it had received, but all he could see was that he had a flat tire on the front. It was sheer luck for him that he didn't wreck with the other cars on the highway. Joe said a little thank you prayer that he hadn't got hurt from the accident. Well, he started to think of how he would get the car back onto the highway. He had gone so far off into the woods that he didn't know if anyone even saw him flying into the woods or not. He figured he would have a heck of a time trying to get his big old car out of the woods. He knew he had to change his flat tire first before he would even be able to move his car at all. This was a new experience Joe was about to have happen to him. He would learn something else today about his car that he didn't know about. It would be the topic of changing a flat tire.

Well, since Joe hadn't ever had to change a tire on a car before he would soon learn a few things. You see he had always got the service station to do all that for him whenever he had to have tires rotated or changed. Joe had no idea really how to go about it, but he would soon pick up on it real fast. Well, he went to the back of his car, and hunted for his jack and spare tire. He found a lug wrench so he could take the lug nuts off the wheel, but when he tried to get the hubcap off Joe ran into a problem. He tried prying the hubcap off with the smooth end of the lug wrench, but it would not come off. He then went to his car again, found a big screwdriver, and tried to pry it up with it. He pried and pried on the hubcap, but he couldn't make any headway getting it off at all. This little job had Joe Macoochee very puzzled. He never stood and watched the man at the station while he changed the tires on his car, but now he wished he had done so. Then maybe he wouldn't feel so dense like he did right now. Well, he had no choice but to get the flat tire off and the good one put back on. That is if he ever figured out exactly what he had to do.

Joe was a man of much patience, but it was beginning to wear thin now. He finally got an idea that if he could find a piece of hard tree limb that maybe he could put it under the hubcap once he pried the hubcap up far enough. Well, this worked okay for him all except it seemed that the hubcap was trying to pop right back in place each time. He finally got the hubcap up far enough so that he could put his fingers under the edge of it. As Joe put his fingers under the edge of the hubcap to try to pull the hubcap off it grabbed his fingers and almost pinched them off. He was in a terrible situation now because he wasn't able to pull his fingers from underneath the edge of the hubcap. Joe put his feet against the tire, and began to pull with all his might. He knew that was what had to be done so he managed to get the hubcap pulled away far enough so he could get his fingers released from it. Joe then began to bend the hubcap back and forth until it broke in half from all the bending. Boy, what a job that had turned out to be.

Joe finally got the car jacked up high enough so that he could get the flat tire off. Once he managed to do this he got the other one put on without anymore trouble. He tightened all the lug nuts as tight as he could get them then let down the jack. He picked up his car jack and other wrenches and put them into the back of his stationwagon. As Joe was putting away his screwdriver back into its small toolbox he happened to see a little T-shaped tool. He realized the reason he had such a hard time in trying to remove the hubcap. Joe should have used the tool to take the hubcap off of the tire. Joe's make of car had this type of hubcap that was expensive. When the car company made these types of hubcaps they made a special tool to use in order to remove the hubcaps from the car. There was so many that had been stolen the first year so they came up with this new invention. If you didn't have the tool to remove the hubcaps then chances were the hubcaps didn't get stole. Boy, he felt like a real nincompoop.

Joe knew he had to get his car out of the woods and back on the road again. Joe started up his car then tried to back it up. It was then that he realized that he wasn't going to get out of the woods very easy at all. When he backed up he had hit something which turned out to be a log. Joe hadn't noticed it before because he was busy changing his flat tire. Oh boy, how am I going to get out of this mess? He walked around the wooded area where he was. He sure didn't want to have to go any farther into the woods because he was afraid he couldn't find his way back out onto the highway.

Well, it was around 12:00 noon, and it was beginning to get hot inside the wooded area where he was at. Joe looked ahead of his car then decided he would go ahead a little ways so maybe he could turn his car around. He was beginning to perspire now from the heat. He had worn shorts for the day, but it was still hot weather to him. Joe drove ahead about 500 yards when the tires on his car began to spin. He was in a wet area now. He was worried that he would get his big battlewagon stuck, and never be able to get it out of the woods. Well, as the story goes Joe did get stuck. He stopped trying to move his car anymore. He had to try to think of another way to go about getting his car out of the woods. Right now all he was going to do was sit there and think over his situation. The more Joe tried to think the more he seemed to put a strain on his brain. Well, he decided to take a break from it all for a little while. This way maybe he could get settled down once again. This was the first time he had ever been in such a situation like this before, and he hoped it would be the last.

Since Joe decided to rest for a few minutes he grabbed himself a sandwich to eat. He was disgusted right about now so he thought that was the best thing for him to do. He was tired from all the fighting he did in changing the tire. He wasn't a strenuous man to start with. He never had to really exert himself at anything he had to do. Joe really wished right about now that he was a strong weight lifter because that might help him get a lot more accomplished.

Joe opened the tailgate on his car because it was the best spot that he could find to have his so called lunch. He ate a ham and cheese sandwich along with some potato chips. He got a good cold coke from his cooler, and then he sat on the tailgate where he ate his little meal. After he finished his lunch he packed everything back into his car. He knew he had to get the show on the road because he didn't want to be stranded in the woods all night. Joe knew he had a few more hours before nightfall would be there.

As Joe walked around to get into his car he tripped on some vines that caused him to fall to the ground. The vines had thorns on them, and scratched his legs up pretty bad. He managed to get the car backed out of the wet spot, and even got it turned around back towards the direction of the highway. Joe's car was so heavy that he couldn't keep from worrying he might get it stuck again. Well, just as the big old battlewagon moved a few feet forward it started to spin its tires then became stuck in the mud once more. He got out of his car and looked at the back tires to see how deep they had buried up in the mud. He got an idea, but wasn't sure if it would work at all. He found some pieces of tree limbs then put them under the back tire so that he might back up on them. Once he did this he put some more under the front of the back tires so he could get some traction. It worked like a charm. Joe managed to get his car rolling out of the bad spot where the wet mud was.

Before Joe pulled his car completely out of the woods he had to take another break. His one last stop couldn't be helped. Of course this stop was to use the bathroom because during all the excitement he hadn't even thought of it until now. Well, not trying to get down to all the gory details, but he had to do a number 1 and a number 2 if you know what I mean.

Since Joe was still deep inside the woods he decided to

use the bathroom before he started driving on the highway again. He didn't know how far it was to the next exit so he decided to take care of business before he left. Joe squatted down to use the bathroom there in the middle of the woods. While he was in a compromising position he happened to notice that something was slithering between his legs. It was a big snake, and Joe didn't sit still long enough to see what kind it was either. All he could do was to get up and get away as fast as he could from the slithering snake. As you already know Joe was scared of any kind of a snake.

In the process of trying to get away from the snake, he had pulled up his shorts only to discover that he hadn't quite finished doing his number 2. It was bad enough having to use the bathroom in the middle of the woods, and now here he was with no water to wash his hands or anything else that needed washing. Poor Joe, if he didn't have bad luck he wouldn't have any luck at all. Well, he got back into his car, not smelling too sweet if you know what I mean. He started his car up then began to proceed very carefully back to the highway. Joe had made it back onto the highway, and once again was on his merry way.

Joe Macoochee sleeping against big oak tree. Camp in the wood at Prairie.

Chapter eight

Joe And His Lady Friends

Joe was thinking of how good it would feel to be taking a good hot shower right about now. He knew he had to find one soon because he didn't want to have to go around smelling raunchy all day. Joe's incident with the snake had got him into trouble, and now Joe had to grin and bear it until he could get cleaned up again. Joe had made up his mind he was going to find a motel, and get checked into it early. He had to get hygiene once again because he couldn't even stand himself if you get my drift.

Joe finally made it to the exit that was close to Orlando. He turned onto the exit lane, and made his way to the nearest motel he found first. It was nothing fancy, but he knew it would serve his purpose. Joe parked his car, and went to check in at the motel. He noticed that a man was staring at him in a strange way. The man kept looking at him like something was wrong with him. Joe then realized that the man might have got wind of his odor from the little accident he had in the woods earlier. He hurried up and left the office quickly, and found his room. He was never so happy to be in a motel room before.

Joe had to go outside to his car to get him some clean clothes before he got to take his shower. While he was outside some people got out of their car. They were already looking at him kind of funny, but as the lady walked past Joe she said, "Where is that crappy smell coming from?" The man with her told her there must be a sewer leak somewhere. Little did he know how close he was to the sewer smell, but it wasn't a leak. Just as soon as Joe heard the remarks the people had made he took off in a real hurry. He had used all the motel soap that was only a small bar, but he had brought his bar from the car so he would have plenty of suds. Joe had so much soap on his body that it looked as if he was taking a bubble bath instead of a shower. Well, he got all cleaned up and slicked down once again, and he felt really refreshed since he had the chance to get all hygiene once again.

Joe sat down in the chair in his motel room, and turned on the t.v. to catch up on the news and weather. As he sat in his chair he started to think of what he had just went through today. Joe was wondering if someone had actually put a curse on him when he was a little boy because he always was having bad luck of some sort. Well, after he caught up on the news, and since he was all cleaned up he thought he would go find a restaurant so he could get a good hot meal. Joe wasn't going to do much of anything today because the tire-changing job had worn him out. He would just stay in his motel after he got him something to eat. Then he would call it a day. After all he had a very trying day, but he had managed to get through it okay after all.

Joe drove his car to a gas station to fill it back up with gas so he wouldn't have to do it the next day. He checked the motor oil, but it was still full. His car was pretty good on gas and oil for such a big old car. Joe had never abused his old car in any way because he knew he wouldn't be buying a new one anytime soon. Joe didn't think he would ever get his old car paid for. It took a long time, but he paid for the car in full. He had even thought about buying another one, but he just couldn't bring himself to go into debt again. Joe went in and paid for his gas then started looking for a restaurant to eat at. He found a nice restaurant called Lucy

Lou's. He went inside, and found a booth in the corner to sit at. He just wanted something to eat along with some good old peace and quiet. A big hefty looking waitress came over and took his order. She kept giving him the hairy eyeball if you get my drift. The waitress was all smiles when she brought him his meal. He knew she was about to strike up a conversation with him. Joe knew the waitress was fixing to hit on him by the way she was flirting with him. She asked him where he was from, and where he was heading to next? Joe said, he was on a business trip, and was on his way back home.

Joe told the waitress he would be glad to get back home to his wife and kids. She asked him if he was married, and he shook his head yes to her. This was one time he told a bald-face lie, but it was for a good cause. He just wanted to get out of there as fast as he could. He ate his supper so fast that he didn't realize how good the steak and shrimp tasted because he had to gobble it down. Joe paid for his meal then headed back to his motel.

As he stopped at a red light he saw 2 ladies standing on the corner. They waved and smiled at him. Not thinking anything of it Joe smiled and waved back to them. As he was fixing to drive off one of them came over to his car. She asked Joe if he could drop them off a couple of blocks down the road in the direction he was heading. Joe didn't think anything out of the ordinary so he said, "Sure, hop in ladies." They introduced themselves as Gina and Roxy. He asked them where they wanted to get off at. They said for him to let them off wherever he was going to stop at.

Joe told them that he was on vacation, and he was staying at a motel for the night. He pulled up to his motel and stopped his car. Being a true gentleman as he was he got out and opened the door for the 2 ladies. Well, they thanked him for the ride then they walked across the street to a convenient store. Joe went on inside of his motel room. Little did he know that they had seen which room he'd went into?

The 2 ladies bought some beer then walked back across the street to his motel room. They knocked on his door, and Joe came to the door to see who it was. He was surprised when he saw the ladies again. Gina and Roxy asked him if they could come in for a while? Joe thought for a moment before he let them inside. Since he was by himself he could use some company about now, especially the way his day went.

They asked Joe if he'd like a beer to drink. He told them that he didn't drink. They couldn't believe that Joe was for real. They drank the beer they had, and then Gina went back across the street and bought some more. Once again they offered him a beer. Joe saw that the ladies were beginning to start giggling, and starting to have some fun. Well, he thought that just one beer wouldn't hurt so he drank one this time.

Joe didn't like the taste of the beer, but it seemed to get better after the next one. Since he was not a drinker he began to get a little woozy. Joe drank one more beer then he started to get sleepy, and lay down on the couch and went fast to sleep. He woke up the next morning only to find beer cans all over the room. Joe then remembered the ladies drinking them, but he didn't remember them leaving at all.

Joe sure felt bad to because he wasn't use to drinking, and he made his mind up not to try that stuff again. Joe gathered up all his dirty clothes, and then he put them in his car. He decided to take a quick shower before he left the motel to begin another day. Joe happened to see his wallet lying on his car seat. He wondered if he had put it there, but as you can already figure it out he hadn't. He opened his wallet only to find that all of his money had been taken.

The ladies took all his money while he was sleeping, and started to take his credit card, but they figured they couldn't use it at all so they threw it in his seat. They were so taken in by his manners that they even left Joe an I.O.U. note for the $650.00 they had taken out of his wallet. Well, there was another lesson that Joe had learned. It was never to pick up strange women or men, because you never know what will happen next. The 2 ladies were of course regular con artists along with another profession that I won't mention.

Joe realized he could have been taken for everything while he slept, but since he was such a nice guy to them they let him get by easy. They actually felt like they were treated like ladies for once. Well, so much for the experience he had encountered that night. They were long gone now so he'd just have to carry on. Joe left the motel to find another A.T.M. machine at the bank so he could draw out some more money to use for his trip. He made the withdrawal then stopped and ate breakfast. It seemed that he needed to drink 2 pots of coffee that morning to recuperate. He wanted to be in good shape for the rest of the trip. He made sure he went to the bathroom before he left the restaurant so he wouldn't have to make any stop along the way. Joe then paid for his breakfast, and was finally on the road again.

Chapter nine

Fantasyland Of Wild Riders

Joe left the café and got back onto I-95. He drove a few more exits when he saw some signs showing some attractions. He thought he'd check them out to see what all was there. Joe found his way to the attraction called "Fantasyland of Wild Riders." He thought how nice it would be to enjoy a day in the park all by himself. So he decided to stop and have some fun for a change. Joe had to pay his admission to get in at the parking entrance. As Joe parked his car he did at least notice the spot where he parked his car. It was named Frizzy's Forty-Niner's Aisle. He thought this would be easy enough to remember so he didn't even write it down. Joe would just remember the football team that was called the Forty-Niners many years ago.

    Well, there were many little train shuttle cars picking up the people that wanted to ride on into the park. There were a lot of people there already. Joe knew the park would probably be full of people today. It was the weekend, and he was right. He thought he would ride on one of the shuttle trains so he wouldn't have to walk so far. Joe was the last one to get to the shuttle train. He went to hop on the side since all the seats were filled up. He was holding on pretty good until the little shuttle train hit a bump that caused him to loose his footing. Then down went Joe falling off the side of the shuttle train hanging on for dear life. He was afraid to turn loose, but it had to be

59

done sooner or later. Joe let loose of the railing he had been holding onto, and away he went crashing to the ground headfirst.

Joe hit face first and slid on his knees a long way before his body came to a stop. Boy, Joe was sure beat up this time. He'd skinned all the meat off of his kneecaps and a lot from his already damaged nose. There was a man that worked at the park that helped him to the park's doctoring center. They bandaged his knees up with so much gauze, bandage, and tape that he could almost pass as a mummy. He thanked the nurse and man for taking good care of him from the accident he'd had. The staff even refunded his entrance fee, and told him to go enjoy himself for the rest of the day. They gave Joe a ticket that allowed him to eat or drink any place inside the park that he wanted to.

Joe was really happy then. It hadn't been long since he'd had breakfast so he would wait for a while before he ate anything else. He walked around the park for a few minutes then sat down at a table so he could drink a glass of tea he'd got with the ticket. Boy, Joe was ready to go on some of the rides now. He finished his tea then walked over to the roller coaster ride. He'd rode one when he was a little boy with his dad.

Joe didn't get to do much when he was little because his dad was always working. He walked over and climbed into the seat of the roller coaster. The girl in charge of the ride helped him get buckled in securely. In front of Joe was a lady that acted like she was scared to death to go on the ride, but her man friend coaxed her into going on it anyway.

Little did Joe have any idea of what was about to happen to him next? I'm sure that if he had he wouldn't ever have got on to the ride at all. Well, the roller coaster had all the people it could carry, and so on its way it started to go. He was a little nervous now. He was listening at the click, click, clicking, sound the roller coaster made as it started its long way up the track. Finally, Joe looked over the side, and then and only then he could see how high up in the air he was. He was beginning to have second thoughts about this ride because it didn't seem that tall when he was a little boy.

Joe didn't realize at the time how much everything had changed at the parks since he was a little boy either. Well, just at the moment Joe wanted to get off the ride, away went the roller coaster it seemed at a 1oo m.p.h. the poor lady in front of him was hollering so loud he couldn't even hear himself yelling to the top of his lungs. The lady then got sick, and threw up all her breakfast right in Joe's face and all over his shirt and pants. Joe could not believe this at all. He didn't have a real strong stomach, and this wasn't helping him at all. What in the world else could possibly happen to him now?

As soon as Joe got off the ride he headed for the bathroom. Before he got off though, the poor sick lady apologized for throwing up on him. He knew how sick the lady was because he was just about that way himself. Joe found the men's restroom, and went inside to get cleaned up. He looked in the mirror, and was shocked at what he saw. He saw a picture in the mirror that nearly scared him out of his wits.

Joe thought to himself that he looked as if he'd been put through the mill. You can say in a way he was, because of all that had happened to him since he'd been on vacation. Well, Joe took off his shirt, and started to clean himself up. Joe had a mess to get out of his long hair, and out of his clothes. He sure wished he had some shampoo so he could wash all the upchuck out of his hair that the lady had got in it, but unfortunately he had no shampoo.

Joe was alone in the bathroom at the time, but another guy happened to come into the bathroom where he was. The man was staring at him because Joe was standing there in his underwear, since he had taken off his shorts to wash them off too. The guy was sort of muscled up. Joe was beginning to get a little nervous because the guy kept looking at him in a strange way.

The guy asked him what happened to him, and Joe told

the man about his wild roller coaster ride. Joe started to talk to the man who introduced himself as Dick. Joe told him his name. As he continued to talk to the man he continued to wash up. Dick told Joe to give him some paper towels, and he'd wipe the mess out of his hair he'd missed in the back. Joe didn't really think of anything out of the ordinary so he handed the man some paper towels. Dick started wiping the upchuck out of his hair, and then something that the man did next was the straw that broke the camel's back you could say. Dick had made a pass at Joe. He pinched him on his rump. Joe had never had anything happen to him before like that. His reflex was only natural because he hauled off and popped Dick in his kisser before he thought about it. Joe was a straight fellow, and never had an experience like this before in his entire life.

He was upset at the moment, and couldn't really think of how he should act, or what he should do next. Joe did however grab the soap container off the wall, and told Dick to get back and leave him alone or he wouldn't be responsible for what would happen next. Joe told Dick, "no offense, but I don't go that route." Dick told Joe no offense taken. Dick apologized to him then quickly retreated, and left the bathroom in a big hurry.

Well, Joe was once again alone in the bathroom. Now he noticed that he had another mess to clean up now. When he jerked the container off the wall all the soap had spilled all over the bathroom floor. He then grabbed some more paper towels, and then he began to clean up the soap. Joe not thinking clearly took some more paper towels and wet them. He didn't think about the wet paper towels making things worse. Well, after he did this he realized he just added fuel to the fire because he had one bad soapy mess to clean up now. Well as I always said, Joe was like an accident fixing to happen.

He was trying real hard to get the situation under control. Joe thought he'd done a good job, but he didn't think about his tennis shoes slipping out from beneath him like they did when he walked across the floor. I guess it was just his day for stop, dropping, and rolling. He slipped downed so fast on his hind end he hardly realized what had happened. Joe then grabbed hold of the edge of a garbage can he was near so he could pull himself up. Well, what do you think happened then? Well, he didn't land on the floor again, but instead he landed headfirst into the garbage can. Poor old Joe he was in a predicament now. He tried getting a good foothold, but clumsy as he was he fell back against the bathroom wall, and landed his tail perfectly in the men's urinal. With the garbage can still attached to his head, Joe was having a hard time trying to get out of the urinal. He was trying to grasp the side of the urinal to get out of it, but grabbed the handle of the urinal instead. While Joe held on to the handle it broke off into his hand now causing another disaster to have to deal with. He finally got the can off his head only to see water-going everwheres. When the handle had broken on the urinal it also caused the water line to snap thus causing a flood of water that was going all over the floor.

Joe turned around then only to see a man looking him straight in the eyes. This time it was one of the security men that worked in the park. The man was about to have Joe arrested until he finished telling the man what had happened in the bathroom. The security man then saw that Joe wasn't purposely trying to destroy the parks property so he told him to go ahead that he'd take care of the clean up and repairs. The security man actually felt sorry for Joe.

Joe went to the nearest little café in the park, and got himself some food to eat and something to drink. He was glad he got this on the house because he'd had a real bad day at the park already, and this seemed to help him forget about it. Joe's stomach was beginning to growl from him being so hungry. He was having hunger pains now pretty bad. Joe had stopped at a little Mexican café because he loved hot and spicy food. Boy, the food was hot, hot, hot, but he enjoyed every bite of it. Joe just couldn't resist eating Mexican food even if it gave him bad gas and messed up his stomach sometimes. Joe ate and ate until he was about to bust. He decided he would rest for about an hour then he would see if he were up to riding anymore rides that day.

As he got up Joe hadn't realized how sore and stiff his poor body was getting. He'd had more physical activity than he could endure for one day. Joe walked a little ways from where he had eaten the Mexican food and saw a stand that had all kinds of ice cream at it. He couldn't resist having dessert so he ordered up a big waffle with pistachio and blueberry ice cream mixed up in it. Joe had a heaping high pile of ice cream to eat. Boy, the ice cream was so delicious because the weather was getting hotter in the afternoon. Oh, what the heck it was supposed to be hot because he was in sunny Florida. Finally, he finished all the ice cream I mean every last bit of it. He was really full now.

Joe found a sideshow that had all kinds of birds performing with a man and lady. There were cockatiels, parrots, and some smaller birds, and they really put on a good show. The bigger birds wore little hats and little black suits. They rode little bicycles, and played dead when the man acted like he was shooting them with a gun. The bigger birds even whistled a musical tune and talked some. They were really comical.

The smaller birds flew around and around the people's heads in the audience. They bathed in the little birdbaths on the little stage. The little birds rolled over and over when the lady motioned for them to. These were very smart birds in order to be able to do all the tricks they did. Joe really liked watching the bird show. After the bird show was over Joe walked through the park just browsing around looking at the other shows.

Joe walked along and came to a house of mirrors. He thought that would be fun so he went inside following a man and woman ahead of him. He figured this would be a piece of cheesecake to get through the house of mirrors. He didn't think it would be hard at all to be able to find his way out of it. Joe just kept following along behind the man and woman. They stopped at the first mirror they came to. The man and woman were laughing at themselves in the mirror. She was a short heavyset woman, and the mirror made her look like she was thin and tall, and the man looked taller and skinnier than he was already. Joe looked at himself, and it didn't do anything for his macho skinny body either. As they all walked on through the house of mirrors the lady and man were beginning to make fun of how each other looked.

Finally, they came to the mirror that made the lady look like she weighed three times more than what she did. The man made a snide remark of how the lady looked, and she got mad then they left in a hurry, and left Joe in the mirror house by himself. Joe went through the mazes in the mirror house, and was quite amused with what he saw in the mirrors. The one mirror made him look as thin as a piece of spaghetti noodle. One mirror made him look real macho like a muscle man. Well, Joe was getting tired of the mirror house so he decided to find his way out of it.

Joe came to an open room. He thought this was the way out. He started walking towards the door, but it turned out to be another mirror. Joe had walked straight into the mirror so hard that he hit face first, and ended up biting his lip and chipping his front tooth. Well, it sure seemed that his vacation wasn't going to be an enjoyable one. After another thirty minutes or so Joe did finally get out of the house of mirrors. That was because he ended up following some more people out that had come in behind him.

Joe went to the restroom again to check on his busted lip and chipped tooth. Joe thought nothing else bad could possibly happen to him now, but little did he know how his day would go. You could say Joe was like an accident waiting for a place to happen. While he was in the bathroom his stomach began to cramp real bad. Joe thought about all the Mexican food he'd eaten earlier. He was hoping that the food wouldn't tear up his stomach, but how wrong he was again.

Joe washed his lip off and was fixing to leave when in came a couple of men to use the bathroom. Joe said hello to them and was fixing to leave. Just about that time a bad pain hit him in his stomach again. Joe thought he'd better use the toilet before he left. He really hated to have to use the bathroom while someone else was in there, but this was a have to or else. Joe went in and sat down on the toilet seat because he knew he had to take a number 2 if you know what I mean. His stomach was griping so badly that he could hardly stand it. While Joe was sitting there trying to be discreet, and very quiet, there was no way that could happen. He had so much gas from eating all the Mexican food, and there was no way he could be silent.

As he sat there his stomach cramped again, and out came a loud gaseous sound which I'm sure you know what I'm trying to say without out making it sound nasty. Joe was breaking wind something awful when he heard the men in the bathroom begin to laugh. Joe was so embarrassed he didn't think he'd be able to go out of the bathroom until all the men left. Joe couldn't help it, but he knew he shouldn't have eaten so much of the Mexican food. He was now paying for it.

Joe stunk up the bathroom so bad that one of the men said, "Boy, something must have crawled up that guy and died." At that moment Joe could have flushed himself down the toilet because he felt so small. Well, he sat there and waited as long as he could. He sure didn't want to have to face the men after what they had said, but it was time for him to get the toilet flushed so he could get out of there.

As Joe's luck would have it the toilet stopped up and wouldn't flush. Now Joe was in a bad situation. He wasn't about to go out of the bathroom without flushing down everything he'd put into the toilet. The toilet didn't flush everything down the first time like it should have so Joe was beginning to get nervous now. Joe didn't want to keep flushing the toilet in fear that it would run over onto the floor. Well, Joe shouldn't have flushed the toilet again because when he did it ran all over the floor.

Joe could only do one thing now, and that was as they

sometimes say, "is to face the music." Well, since he had made all kinds of music while he was sitting on the toilet he sure wasn't ready to make anymore. Joe grabbed some paper towels and started to clean up the mess off the floor. As bad as he hated to he had to come out of the bathroom with the messy paper towels.

When he went to put it in the garbage can the men stopped laughing, and began to start gagging once they saw what Joe was doing. It didn't take long for all of the men to get out of the bathroom then. Joe didn't want to make anyone sick, but he did think it was kind of funny that the men had such weak stomachs. The more Joe thought about it the funnier it got because the laugh wasn't really on him after all.

Well, he was all alone once again in the bathroom. Joe finally got his mess cleaned up once again. Then he made sure he washed his hands real good before he left. Joe had become quite a clean up man, but he never did get the toilet unclogged. He sure hated to leave such a mess, but he definitely wasn't a plumber. At least he did give it a good try. Maybe the janitor would see the clogged up toilet, and get it unstopped before anyone else came in. It was a dirty job, but someone has to do it. The restroom didn't smell like roses when Joe left, but he did manage to get it cleaned up except for the clog.

Joe walked outside again to find something else to do at the park. It wouldn't be much longer until he had to call it a day because his legs and whole body was beginning to get stove up. In other words he was getting so stiff that he could hardly walk. Joe watched a couple of shows that had boats, porpoises, and other animals in them. He rode on a water ride, and he almost fell out of it. Joe was ready to leave after that. He was tired, and getting stiffer by the minute. He knew it was time for him to leave. It was time for Joe Macoochee to get somewhere safe for his own good health.

Chapter ten

The Lonesome Dove Café

Joe checked into another motel for the night. He went straight in and took a good long hot shower. He bet he wouldn't have to have anyone rock him to sleep tonight. Boy, he didn't realize how tired he was. He'd only been on vacation a few days, and he wondered if he would survive all the time that he had left. Joe was so tired that he didn't go out that night to get anything to eat. Instead he went to his car and got something to snack on. He watched the boob tube (t.v.) until about midnight then he went off to sleep. He went straight to sleep and didn't even wake up during the night at all. The room was comfortable because Joe had the air-conditioning on cool. It had been a pretty warm day, but it was fun even if he had all sorts of accidents.

    Joe woke up early again the next morning. He took another hot shower then went to fill his car up with gas again. He was really hungry so he stopped in at a café and ate a big hearty breakfast. He had eggs, toast, bacon, sausage, and pancakes topped with a big heap of strawberries and cream. Joe finished eating then paid for his breakfast. He used the bathroom before he left the café because he didn't want to have to make anymore stops until he got to his vacation town of Okeechobee.

Joe got into his stationwagon, and was heading on down to Okeechobee. He was what you could say was Okeechobee bound. He was sure hoping that it would turn out a lot better for him down there than it had anyplace else. It just seemed that Joe had the devil on his tail. He should make it to Okeechobee in about 2 or 3 hours that is if anything else didn't get in his way. He had his radio on listening to the news and weather. According to the weatherman it should be a pretty week ahead so Joe thought that was really nice.

Joe enjoyed listening to the music while he was driving. It helped pass the time on his trip down to Okeechobee. He was making good time today. He arrived in the little town of Okeechobee in 2 hours and 10 minutes. Joe was sure glad to be there at last. He thought how nice it was that he was in a small town now. He thought that he would drive around for a while, and find out where the motels and cafes were located.

Joe really liked Okeechobee from what he saw of it so far. It seemed a lot different than the big city that he lived in. He surely wouldn't get lost here. Joe stopped in at a motel at the south end of Okeechobee. It was called the "Chobee Inn." He took in his suitcase since he was planning to spend a couple of days at the motel.

After he settled into his room he wanted to go back to town. Joe went back uptown and drove around some more just kind of pinpointing the little place. He drove by a little café called The Lonesome Dove Café. It was a nice looking little place so he thought he'd go inside and check it out. Joe went inside and thought this had to be his type of place. It was a nice little café on the inside. It had some pictures of some Nascar racecar drivers on the wall, and other nice paintings such as Burt Reynolds, Princess Diana, and some Indian paintings. There was a life like stand up portrait of one of the famous race car drivers which matter of fact was Joe's favorite driver. Of course, you know it was Dale Earnhardt better known as "The Intimidator." Yelp, this seemed to be a nice place so far.

Well, as it turned out there was a pretty little waitress that came to wait on Joe. She greeted him with a big smile. She introduced herself as Runt. Joe asked why she was called Runt, and she told him that was her nickname her mom and dad gave her when she was a little girl. Joe thought she was really cute because she wasn't bigger than a half-pint.

Joe asked what the house specialty was. She told him that they had the best jumbo burgers you could ever eat. She told him that everybody loved the jumbo burgers, but they had a lot of different things on the menu. Joe ordered one of the burgers along with some french fries and cole slaw. He had ordered a large glass of sweet tea to drink. When Runt brought out the large glass of tea his eyes got real big because it was a jumbo glass of tea instead of a large glass that he had always been accustomed to getting. He drank some of the tea and thought it was the best sweet tea that he'd ever drunk before.

Joe was really surprised when he got his jumbo burger, french fries, and cole slaw because he wasn't sure if would be able to eat all the food that was piled up on his plate. He started to eat his meal and boy was it good. He was sure glad that he'd stopped here. Joe was almost through eating when Runt came back out and asked him if he needed anything else. Joe told her thank you, but he wouldn't be able to eat another bite because he was filled to the gills.

While he was still eating his meal, a big man came into the café and sat down. A lady came from the kitchen, and sat at the table with the big guy. The big guy nodded his head at Joe and said hello to him. The big guy introduced himself as J.R. Hughing. He introduced the lady at the table with him as his wife Dee-Dee Hughing. She was one of the chefettes that cooked there in the café.

Joe began talking to Runt, J.R., and Dee-Dee. He told them he had come to Okeechobee to spend the rest of his vacation time that he'd had left. Joe talked to them about the café and had asked who owned it. Runt told him her mom and dad owned it. She told him Dee-Dee and herself was the top-notch chefettes there that did all the cooking.

Runt told him that her parents' names were Shirley and Donald. She told Joe they had a septic tank business also that kept them busy all the time. Joe told them that was an unusual combination of two businesses. Runt told him that her mom and dad always told everybody that they could catch them coming and going. In other words they would feed them then they would have to service their tanks whenever it needed to be pumped. Joe laughed at what she said, he told her he would like to meet them before he went back home. Runt told him she would tell them about him. Joe asked her who won all the trophies on the shelf at the café. She told him the trophies were her mom's and dad's. She told Joe that her mom and dad both were stock car drivers. He thought that was amazing they both raced stock cars together.

Joe really enjoyed talking to his new friends that he had made at the café. J.R. asked him what was he going to do while he was in Okeechobee on vacation? Joe told him that a friend had given him some brochures on fishing, hunting, and camping that he'd got when he came down to Okeechobee a couple of years ago.

Joe asked J.R. what all was there to do here. J.R. told him there was quite some good fishing in the big lake. He asked J.R. what was the name of the lake he was talking about, and J.R. told him it was named after the town of Okeechobee. He told Joe that Lake Okeechobee was the second largest fresh-water lake in the world. He also told Joe that it had some of the biggest bass, turtles, catfish, and alligators that there were in the United States. J.R. told Joe the town of Okeechobee was once called "Tanti Town" then the people changed it to Okeechobee. It was named an Indian name at one time.

J.R. told Joe that's why they have people coming in from all over the country to vacation there in Okeechobee. He told Joe he'd caught some big lunkers out of the lake himself. Dee-Dee told him about the 15 pound catfish that she almost lost, and that reminded him of the fish that he'd lost for the fisherman a couple of days ago in Ormond Beach. Joe still had the fresh fish bite and the fresh shell-pierced nose from the conch shell that the fisherman had thrown at him piercing a hole in his nose. That's an experience that Joe would never forget, and would tell his children about it one day if he ever happened to get married.

J.R. told him that Donald and Shirley had a camphouse out in the woods north of town. Joe asked where it was at, and J.R. told Joe that it was at the Prairie. Joe asked if the Prairie was bare, or if it had much wooded area there. Dee-Dee told him that it had a lot of wooded land out there for hunting and camping. Runt told Joe there were some canals that had some big fish in them, but most people out that way went fishing at the river. Joe asked what the name of the river was, and Runt told him it was the Kissimmee River. Joe asked her how to spell it. She told Joe, and he pronounced it as the Kiss-A-Me River. They all laughed, and told him everyone pronounced it wrong the first few times they tried to say it. Joe didn't mind them laughing at him because they made him feel right at home.

Joe drank another glass of tea, and thanked them all for the information. He told the girls everything was delicious and he'd see them later on. Joe thanked J.R. for telling him about the lake and town. He hated to leave in a way because this was the first place he really felt at home at. He was certainly coming back here again for his next meal. He left the Lonesome Dove, and drove back to town.

Chapter eleven

Big Lake Of Okeechobee

Joe decided to drive down to the lake to see what it looked like. It was exactly how J.R. had described it. It was just like Joe imagined it was. It was a pretty sight to see. Boy, he could hardly wait to see how big a fish he would be able to catch here. With his luck it would probably be wishful thinking. Joe found a tackle shop and stopped in to see what kind of tackle they had there. He bought a few rubber worms, top water plugs, hooks, and a nice rod and reel to fish with. He bought his fishing licenses to because he sure didn't need to get a fine or go to jail for fishing illegal. He loaded up his fishing tackle into his car, and then left the little tackle shop.

Then Joe went back to the motel to rest for a while. He sat there in his motel room and planned out the next day's schedule of events that he'd be doing. Joe then took a shower, watched t.v. then took a little nap. After he woke up, he went back out and cruised around the little town. As he drove along he thought how easy it would be to make a little town like this home. It wouldn't take much for Joe to fall in love with this place at all.

Joe started thinking how nice it would be to live in a place where there wasn't a rat race going on all the time. He even thought how nice it would be if he lived here because there were a lot of friendly people, and he wouldn't have to travel so far to go to work. Why heck fire, Joe might even meet some nice girl and settle here from now on. Joe thought that of course, was just a dream because he wasn't really a lady's man. He only dated a couple of times because he was into the work-a-holic stage of his life. It seemed that everyone was that way now days. The cost of living is so high that you have to work all the time just to get by anymore. Joe thought it didn't hurt to dream though.

Joe drove down to the lake again, and got to watch the sun go down. That's something you don't get to see in the city because of all the smoke and tall buildings that seem to always block the view. Of course, if you get the chance you can drive way out into the country and if you're lucky you might get to see the sun go down. As he sat at the lake enjoying the scenery he saw some people catching fish from the pier. Joe remembered not to interfere with the people, or else he could be in hot water. So he just remained in his car enjoying the scenery. It seemed so peaceful as he sat there in his car just relaxing and taking life easy at the moment.

Joe began watching the seagulls and other birds flying around all over the place. He saw some kids playing and running about enjoying themselves. He thought how nice it would have been if he had got the chance to be like that when he was growing up as a small boy. After it had got too dark to see anything he did like the other people, and left the lakeside.

Well, Joe drove on back to the motel, and took a shower. He was planning on not going out anymore that day, but he sat there thinking about the good meal he'd eaten earlier at the Lonesome Dove Café. The more he thought about the jumbo burger the hungrier he got. Well, nothing more for Joe to do, but to get up and go back to the Dove, and eat his supper there. When he walked through the door at the café he was surprised to see the same people there that he'd met earlier that morning. There was Runt, Dee-Dee, and J.R. all sitting at the same table together. They all said hello, and told him to come and sit down with them at their table. Joe was really surprised that they would even remember him at all. He really felt flattered and surprised that they asked him to sit at their table with them.

Joe never had the opportunity to hang out with anybody before because he always went home from work, and stayed there until time to go back again. He did occasionally go to town on the weekend to buy a few groceries and necessities that he needed around the house. Everyone that worked with Joe liked him well enough, but never took the time to hang out with him. He seemed kind of odd to them all.

Well, Joe looked at the menu and wanted to try everything on it, but knew he couldn't eat that much though. He ended up eating some catfish fingers, baked beans, french fries, and cole slaw. At first he didn't know what catfish fingers were. Joe was sure that catfish didn't have fingers, but he'd heard of walking catfish before so you never know. He asked Runt what catfish fingers were, and she laughed and told Joe it was the catfish taken off the bones of the fish and cut up into strips. That made the catfish taste that much better when he got them to eat. Joe felt kind of dumb at times, but he guessed everybody feels that way at one time or another.

He ate his meal in a hurry. That was one bad habit that he'd picked up working at the office. You only had 30 minutes for lunch, and that's why you ate fast or, you didn't eat much at all. Well, he really felt right at home at The Lonesome Dove with all his newly found friends. Joe talked with everyone for a while, then paid for his meal. He then decided he'd go back to town, and check out some of the stores. After he bid everyone good-bye once more then he left. He was as full as a tick that had just fell off a dog. That was a little expression that his dad used to use, and it was always funny to Joe and it had meaning to it also.

As Joe was driving back into town he saw a bunch of black and white cows in a pasture next to the side of the highway. It was almost completely dark, but he stopped his car to take some pictures of these funny colored cows. His camera had a flash on it so he would be able to get some pictures of the cows even if it was a little dark. He'd seen cows that were solid-colored before, but he never had saw any with black and white spots. As Joe got closer to the cows he couldn't believe how tame they were. The cows came right up to him, and were chomping on the grass they were eating. He was petting one of the cows on her forehead. As he stood there petting her she let out a big old cough. As you can imagine Joe wound up on the wrong end again because the cow coughed up her grass on him. The chewed up grass flew out of the cow's mouth and landed right on his cheek. Since he had just finished eating his supper this made Joe a little queezie at his stomach, and he knew it was time for him to be out of there.

Of course, these were dairy cows, and they were tame because they are milked two times a day. They get fed twice a day so they are use to being around people. Joe took some more pictures then started on his way back to town. He couldn't believe how different it was down here in Florida, and all the different sights there were to see than there were in the city that he lived in. He was really enjoying himself more and more. Well, back to his motel room he went and watched t.v. until 11:00, then off to bed to call it a day. He thought he would get up early the next morning, and go fish a little while at the big lake.

Joe woke up about 6:00 a.m. the next morning. He brushed his teeth, combed his hair, and got dressed so then he went to the little drive-thru restaurant to get himself something quick to eat. Joe didn't have much else to do so he went back to the tackle shop at the lake to see if they were open yet. The lady there told him they had been open since 5:00 a.m. She told him they opened early because the bass fishermen wanted to be out on the lake fishing before daylight.

Well, Joe bought a bait bucket and some minnows because he had already bought some artificial bait there already. He thought he would try his luck fishing at the lake. He walked out on the pier where the other people were. He put some bait on his hook and started fishing. Believe it or not he actually caught 5 speckled perch, but threw them back into the lake because he didn't have any place to put them right now.

Well, Joe was feeling pretty good about himself now so he loaded up everything then went back to his motel room for a while. He got showered and cleaned up once

Joe hunting for fishing pole that got pulled into the water.

again. He was getting bored sitting at the motel so he went back to town. Joe just drove around the little town for a short while, but then returned to his motel room again. He knew he would have to make some plans of what he was going to do because he didn't want to keep driving around all the time. He wanted to get into some sort of action somewhere. Afterall, he was down here to enjoy himself. He just had to find out where the happening places were. He knew he had to go get gas in his car again because it was getting low on fuel. He pulled into a little station that wasn't too far from his motel. Joe went inside the little station to pay for his gas and he noticed a map of Okeechobee on a rack next to the cash register. He thought it might be handy if he bought one to look at because it would help him find his way around the little town. Well, Joe found the park in the middle of town, and went to sit at one of the tables so he could read what was on the map he'd just bought. He spread the map out on the table, and looked over it very carefully. There were different kinds of recreation on the map that he wanted to check on to see if he wanted to do any of them. There was the old Tanti Schoolhouse he would like to go see. It sounded interesting to him because he liked anything that had any kinds of antiques that he could look at. Joe noticed there were helicopter rides that he could go on, but he didn't care that much for heights. He always liked to keep his feet flat on the ground. He had an experience as a kid that was probably the cause of his height fright. He had climbed up a very tall tree when he was only five years old, and couldn't get himself back down. The more he tried to come down from the top of the tree the tighter he held onto the tree. His dad ended up getting the firefighters to go up a ladder and bring him down again. After that Joe never tried to climb another tree. Well, he hadn't realized it, but he had stayed a long time in the park looking over his map. Joe knew he had to get organized on his plans because he only had so much time left to do everything that he wanted to do.

Since it was getting late he knew that he'd better get ready to call it a day so he would be ready to go gung-ho tomorrow. Joe went to his car and got some canned fruit to snack on before he went to bed. Sometimes he had a snack at night instead of eating a big meal. After he finished his fruit snack he took a shower then he lay on the little sofa that was in his motel room. It was getting late, and it was quiet at the motel where he was staying. It seemed peaceful this time of the night to Joe. He watched a little television, but went off to sleep with the television on. When he ate anything at night he would get really sleepy. He woke up around 2:00 a.m. then got up turned off the t.v. and went back to bed again. He went right off to sleep again with no trouble at all. Joe had a good day today so maybe that's why he slept so well.

Chapter twelve

Incidents at Lake Placid

Joe woke early the next morning. He took an early shower so he'd be fresh for his day's adventure. He drove into town, and stopped to eat breakfast at a little fast food restaurant. After he'd ate he thought he would see the sights in the little town of Okeechobee. He knew there probably wasn't that much to see there, but he liked the little town so far. Who knows there's no telling what you might find there in the little town? One thing for sure, it was a lot different down here in Florida than it was in Virginia.

As he drove around looking at the town sites he noticed some road signs that read Lake Placid 34 miles to the west. Joe thought that he would like to see where this place was at, so away he drove on his way to Lake Placid, which was another small town. Joe had no idea where he was going, or what kind of place he would end up at. All he knew was there is a town of Lake Placid 34 miles from Okeechobee.

Joe drove along at a slower speed today which seemed nice. He didn't have to run in the rat race with the other cars like he did back home. This part of the country was a lot different than he'd seen before. It was open pastureland with many cows on it as far as the naked eye could see. As Joe drove on he noticed a field that had different colored plants growing on many acres of the land. He saw a sign that read Davy's Caladium Farm Company. He still didn't know what a caladium was. He would ask someone what a caladium was when he stopped. Maybe it was a type of vegetable he didn't know about. Joe thought how different the elevation over this way was. He noticed that Lake Placid had a lot of hills there. It was a lot different compared to Okeechobee. If there were hills in Okeechobee he hadn't seen any so far. It was a nice and peaceful ride for him. He had all day today to just mess around. He wanted to take in as much scenery as he could while he was down in Florida on his vacation. Joe saw a lot of white birds in the colored fields as he passed by. There must be a lot of insects there in the fields for them to feed on he thought. Joe knew this must be farming country over around Lake Placid because he saw a big field of what looked like corn, and vegetables growing there. Joe also saw some orange groves that had a lot of fruit on the trees. It's strange how each state differs, but each one has it own little surprises I'm sure. He saw a sign that read Lake Placid 2 miles. It was just a skip and a hop from Okeechobee to Lake Placid he thought. It was a pleasant little ride over there. He hardly passed any cars on his way over to Lake Placid so he didn't have much traffic to contend with. That was what he liked about the trip because it was such an enjoyable ride.

  Joe finally made it to the little town of Lake Placid. He drove all through the little town looking to see what he could see. He saw that all the buildings in town had Muriels painted on the walls. It reminded him of the Lonesome Dove which had a Muriel of a wildlife scene painted on the inside wall, which really was beautiful. The drawings on the buildings in Lake Placid were really pretty too. He thought that whoever painted them had a real God given talent. He couldn't draw anything at all. He couldn't even draw a perfect circle. Joe didn't like trying to look and drive at the same time because he might end up having a wreck. So he pulled over and parked his car, and walked down the streets admiring the paintings. There were paintings of farm scenes, old timey men and women from way back when. He could see how the olden days might have been by looking at the different paintings on the walls. He was amazed as he studied the paintings on the walls. It seemed to him that each painting had a certain special meaning to it.

    Joe walked around at least 2 hours checking the different sights out in the little town. Well, it was getting pretty hot outside so he thought he would find a drink box and buy himself a coke. As he walked down the sidewalk he saw an old drugstore. He went inside to look around. It reminded him of the old one they used to have back home in Virginia. Joe saw that they had a counter to sit at like he remembered seeing in a store when he was a little boy. Of course, that was back in Virginia many years ago, and now he was a grown man. He sat down on one of the stools at the counter, and began to read what the drugstore had to eat and drink. He could remember his dad taking him into the old drugstore and buying him a thick milkshake and licorice candy. Joe could almost taste the shakes as he sat there remembering the good old days.

    He saw several different kinds of milk shakes so he ordered one. Joe ordered a pineapple milk shake to drink. As he sat there on his stool drinking his shake he asked the lady that waited on him what caladiums were? She told him that caladiums were a decorative plant people planted around in yards, around houses, and around office buildings. The lady told Joe they have a caladium festival every year there in Lake Placid. She told him it would be there again in 2 weeks, and she told Joe he should come to it because it was really beautiful how they displayed all the caladiums. He told the lady he might come over to it since he was on vacation. She asked him if he was staying there in Lake Placid, but he told her he was vacationing in Okeechobee. He told her he was staying in a motel right now, but he is planning on camping out in the woods somewhere in Okeechobee.

    The lady told Joe it was a nice little town and that she had lived there for 4 years before she moved to Lake Placid. Joe told her he really liked what he had seen of it, and he'd only been there a couple of days. The lady asked him how long was he on vacation, and he told her he had 2 months this go around. Another customer came in so she had to go wait on him.

When Joe finished his milk shake he started to leave the drugstore, and the lady told him to be sure to come back again, and not to forget the festival. Joe told her he would try to come and see it. He walked around the little town a while longer. He noticed the stores were built close together like they were in his hometown. The buildings were built completely different to what they were in Virginia. He had noticed down here in Florida most of the roofs were flat, but up there most buildings had pitched rooftops. Up there, the snow might cause the roofs to cave in if they were flat. He thought he would build a house with a tin roof like the one at the Lonesome Dove. That was one of the first things that Joe had noticed about his favorite little café. It was a lot different from what he had been use to seeing back home.

He walked through some of the little stores in Lake Placid, but didn't buy anything. He saw some different stuff he would like to have, but he thought if he came back over again he'd buy them then. Today he was just being a typical person on vacation. Little did Joe know what was to come about a little later on in the day? Joe at this moment was a perfectly normal person that was enjoying the sights of this little town.

As he walked along the sidewalk looking into the windows of the stores he saw a reflection of a tall building. It stood tall like the buildings in the city where he lived. Joe was wondering what a tall building like that was doing in Lake Placid. He was so curious that he got in his car then drove over to where the tall building was. The tall building turned out to be the lake Muriel Tower. The tower was very tall. Joe parked his car in the tower parking lot. He walked inside the little building at the base of the tower. It was a little shop that had all sorts of gifts that you could buy there. You had to buy a ticket to ride an elevator up to the top of it. He thought at first that he shouldn't go up on the tower because he was so afraid of heights. Soon he changed his mind and up, up, and away he went after he paid his fee to go up. Joe stepped inside the elevator then pushed the button to close the elevator door. When the door closed the elevator began moving slowly towards the top of the tall tower. The little elevator made a sudden jerk that scared Joe. It seemed that the elevator was trying to come to a halt. The elevator was moving slow, but it managed to take him to the top of the tower. When the elevator stopped he waited for the door to open. It seemed to take a longer time than it should for the door of the elevator to open up Joe thought. Maybe the elevator didn't get used that much so that was why it seemed to be a little sluggish.

Finally the door of the elevator opened wide. As he stepped out of the elevator he was amazed at the spectacular view of everything you could see from the top of the tower. You could see all the lakes, orange groves, and the little town of Lake Placid so clearly from the top. What a pretty little town, Lake Placid was. Joe stayed at the top of the tower, and looked through the binoculars that were mounted on a post for everyone to look at the countryside with. It was a spectacular view. Joe could stay up there all day enjoying the view from the top of the tower.

Joe saw a little platform at the very top of the tower. It had steps leading up to it. He walked up the steps, and when he got to the little platform he saw that it was much higher in the air. There were only rails to hold on to, and it seemed spooky to Joe because there wasn't a wall around him like there was when he was on the floor below. He saw a sign that had Crow's Nest written on it, and since he wasn't a crow and couldn't fly Joe went back down the stairs immediately. He stayed up on the tower enjoying the view for a long time. There were a lot of people that came up on the tower with Joe, but they didn't stay up there very long. He didn't pay much attention to the other people. He just kept looking at the sights in the distance from the tower. He had stayed longer than he realized, but he was enjoying himself so much. Well, Joe decided to head back to Okeechobee since it was getting late into the afternoon. He took one last look at the little town below through the binoculars before he left.

Joe got into the elevator to go back down to the ground floor. As he entered the elevator and closed the door he pressed the button to take him down to the ground floor. The door closed then the elevator started on its way down the tower. All of a sudden the elevator started to jerk and shake then it came to a complete stop. Lo and behold, the emergency bell began to ring. It was so loud that Joe thought it would bust his eardrums. When the bell began to ring it was so loud that it scared him. He hoped there wasn't much wrong with the elevator because he was hanging a long way up in the air. Joe sure didn't want to be in an elevator and have it to fall to the ground. He didn't want to be a statistic that wound up getting flattened out like a pancake from falling to the ground because of an elevator that went awry. He knew something just wasn't right at that moment. He knew he had to remain calm though because he was the only one there in the elevator, and it wouldn't do him any good to have a panic attack.

Joe saw the emergency phone, but thought the elevator would only be stuck a minute or two. Well, he waited a few minutes to see if the elevator would start moving again, but it didn't. He picked up the telephone to use for such emergencies like this. He rang and rang and rang the operator, but no one answered his call. Joe was beginning to get a little worried now because he was alone in the elevator by himself. As he waited for someone to answer his call he thought he might as well sit down on the floor until help came. Joe wished he hadn't taken the trip up the tower then he would be on the ground where he belonged to be. His feet would be flat on the ground instead of dangling on a wire like a trapeze artist walking on a tight rope.

Well, he kept trying the operator, but still he couldn't get an answer at all. Joe looked at his watch and it was 2:15 p.m. he hadn't eat any lunch yet, and his stomach was letting him know because it was starting to growl real loud. He sat there thinking what would he do if he had to stay there all night. Surely someone would notice that the elevator was stuck, and yet maybe he might be locked up for a long time there in the elevator.

Well, nothing would have it, but at about that time Joe knew it was time for a nature break. When he got nervous he would always have to use the bathroom. What in the world could he do now? He sure didn't want to have to use the bathroom there in the elevator because it would be really embarrassing if someone came along, and saw that he had went to the bathroom there. He kept trying to reach the operator, but didn't have any luck. Well, in the meantime his kidneys felt like they were going to pop. Joe kept saying to himself I'm not going to use the bathroom over and over, but the more he said it the worse he had to go. He didn't want to have to do it, but he didn't have a choice. Finally, Joe couldn't wait any longer so he had to do the unthinkable. He got in the corner of the elevator and took a wee-wee. Whew, what a relief that was. He was glad that the elevator door didn't open while he was using the bathroom because he wouldn't have been able to come out of the elevator. Joe would have been too embarrassed if anyone had seen him using the bathroom especially in the elevator. It was just one situation that couldn't be helped. It was beyond his control. There's an old saying that goes like this, when you gotta go then you gotta go, and that's the way it is.

Joe was really nervous about the situation he was in now. He was unsure about the telephone. He began to wonder if it even worked on the other end of not. He was beginning to be impatient now, and that wasn't one of his traits. The ringing bell was getting on his nerves because it was a steady ringing that just wouldn't quit. Now he was a very patient person most of the time, but this was one time he was beginning to lose his patience. He looked at his watch again now it was 3:45 p.m. Joe now wondered if the tower would close at 4:00 p.m., or if it stayed open later. He knew lots of businesses closed at a normal hour.

Joe was a little worried that he wasn't able to contact anyone on the phone. He wondered why someone hadn't tried to reach his beckoning call for help. He knew that someone should surely hear the ear piercing sound of the emergency bell ringing on the elevator. That was the warning to let them know that someone needed help.

He only hoped that someone down there in the tower office knew something was wrong, and was trying to get the situation under control. Well, he decided to try pushing the open door button to see it would do anything, but nothing happened.

Joe knew someone should surely hear the emergency bell on the elevator ringing because it was about to drive him up the wall. Well, since the sound had gotten on his nerves so bad he decided to tear the end off of his shirt so he could make himself some plugs for his ears. Joe had to bite the end of his shirt with his teeth since he hadn't put his little knife back into his pocket. He felt like a dog chewing on his shirt at that moment, but knew if he could tear his shirt to get the cloth for his ears it would be worth every minute he had to chew on it. He did manage to get a little hole gnawed in the shirt big enough that he managed to tear the shirt with his fingers. Once he got the piece of shirt torn off he immediately plugged his ears, and it worked like a charm. Now he could barely hear the continuous ringing of the bells.

All Joe could do now was just to sit and wait. Joe was beginning to feel like he was the only person in the world by himself. He had no one to talk to except himself, and he had no one to hear him when he wanted to complain. Since he couldn't make any contact with anyone, all he could do was to think about getting out of the disabled elevator. While he sat there waiting he started to hum a little tune as he often did when he got really nervous about something. Joe couldn't believe that he'd been stuck so long inside the elevator and that no one had tried to contact him at all. He wasn't sure if he would get out today or tomorrow. He started to think of how he'd seen it done in the movies, and he was seriously thinking of going through the roof of the elevator in order to escape. Well, the more he thought about it, he began to wonder how he'd be able to reach the top of the ceiling. He wasn't a jolly green giant so he wasn't about to get out that way. If he had another person there with him, he might get out by standing on their shoulders then get out through the ceiling. Oh well, so much for that idea. Since he was the only one there he would just have to wait till someone could get him out. Joe stood up then began to walk around and around inside the little elevator getting no place fast. After he did this for a while he became tired, and he knew he was just wasting his energy and not accomplishing anything.

He knew he might as well just sit down on the floor and be calm about this whole situation because he wasn't going anywheres, at least not now. He sat there resting patiently, and finally the telephone rang. Joe jumped up and said hello. The operator asked him if he was all right. Joe told her he was fine, but please hurry up and get the elevator working so that he could get out of there. The lady told him to stay calm, and she would get him help soon. Joe thanked her then he hung the phone.

Thank goodness, at least they knew that he was stuck there, and they would get him out soon. Well, Joe started watching his watch go from one hour to another. The time was dragging by slowly. He realized that it was getting late because his stomach wouldn't let him forget. He was really hungry now. He sat there thinking of how awful it would be to be stranded on a deserted island with no food or water. Joe tried to think of something else more pleasant, but the thought of something to eat just came popping back into his head. He wished he could quit thinking about food, but that's how your mind works when you're in a terrible predicament. It probably seemed to Joe that it was the end of the world until he got the phone call from the lady downstairs. Now he was feeling a little better knowing that it would only be a matter of time before he was free to go again.

While he sat there waiting he knew he had to head back to Okeechobee before it got too late. Joe decided before he left town the first thing he'd do when he got out of there was he would find a café and get something to eat and drink. He hoped the people at the tower got him out pretty soon. He didn't want to be stuck there all day because his bathroom situation wasn't good at all. He knew it wouldn't be much longer before Mother Nature called on him again, and this time it wouldn't be the nice way. He knew that by the way his stomach felt that it wouldn't be much longer until something had to give, and oh how Joe dreaded the mere thought of what he might have to do. If it came to this he thought he would never be able to live down the humiliation that it would cause him.

He sure didn't want to have to use the bathroom again in the elevator, but that's the breaks that sometimes happen to you in life. Well, what Joe wanted didn't count because what his stomach was letting him know was that his time was near again. Well, as it happened he had to use the bathroom again. This time it was to do a number 2 if you know what I mean. Poor Joe was bound and determined not to go to the bathroom again. He would try to hold it, if at all possible.

Well, it had been 21/2 hours since the lady has spoken to him. He just couldn't figure out why they couldn't get the elevator up and moving again. He sure hoped that they hurried up because he had enough shame today. Man, oh man, what would he do if he started using the bathroom in the worst kind of situation? He shuttered to even think of that at all. First of all he didn't have any toilet paper, and second of all it wouldn't be too sanitary at all. Then third of all if it came down to the situation of it all he'd probably be caught in action or you could say that he might get caught with his pants down. That would be one of the worst things that he would have ever had to do in his life. Joe would rather take a whipping than to have to use the bathroom again there where he was at. He was getting all tore up again because he didn't have any control over his situation.

Joe's mind had all sorts of things going through it. It would be his luck the news media would be there at the tower doing a news flash about the man stuck in the elevator. Then whenever he did get to come out of the elevator he would end up making the headlines of the nightly news knowing his luck. The headlines would probably be on the front page and read something like this, "The man who had to wait but couldn't." He could just see his name splashed on the front page of the newspaper. Well, he kept hoping that nothing like that would happen. He was beginning to become desperate of thinking how much longer it would take the tower people to rescue him. Joe realized that he might as well try and keep cool, calm, and collective at this moment. He had to get grip of himself, but it was easier said, than done.

Joe sure didn't want anyone to see him go to pieces just because he got trapped in an elevator. Boy, he was wondering if they would even be able to get this thing up and running again. He had seen movies on t.v. where people had been trapped in elevators a couple of days. This made Joe shutter to even think of something like this happening to him. He'd read where an elevator had fallen to the ground floor before the people had been able to be rescued. He'd saw where they had to climb through the top to even be able to get to the people so they could rescue them. He wasn't sure if he'd be able to climb out of the roof if he had to or not. Right at this moment Joe wasn't too sure of much of anything at all. He sure wanted to get out of this darn elevator though. Joe was even having second thoughts of having to ride up another elevator at his work place. He might just take the stairs from now on even if it took him an hour to get to his office floor. Joe thought of how much exercise he'd get by going up the stairway, and he thought of how tired he'd probably be. At least he would be getting somewhere if he walked the stairs. Well, what can you say, Joe was sure to have a good stroke of luck happen to him somewhere along the line? It just had to happen sooner or later.

Joe sat there waiting when all of a sudden he had a bad gas pain in his stomach. Oh no, it was the time of the day when he had to do you know what. Well, he had made up his mind that he wasn't going to use the bathroom again no matter what. As it went Joe couldn't hold it any longer. He had to go and that was all there was to it. He really felt bad at having to use the bathroom again, but he would have felt worse if he had to use the bathroom in his pants. Well, Joe couldn't hold it back any longer he had to do the unthinkable thing that just couldn't be helped.

Well, as he sat there using the bathroom in the corner of the elevator he was trying not to think about what he had to do. The next thing that happened was going to be the most embarrassing moment that Joe would probably ever have happen in his entire life. Well, I reckon you probably already have it figured what happened to him next. Yelp, just as he began using the bathroom the elevator door opened, and lo and behold, there sat Joe. He'd got caught with his pants down. Poor Joe jerked his pants up quickly, and ran out the door. He was really embarrassed at that moment. He could have crawled through the eye of a needle at that moment in his life, but as usual he managed to survive another embarrassing ordeal. Joe got out of the elevator as quick as he could. It just happened that the elevator had stopped directly where a doorway was at so he didn't have to climb out of the top of the elevator. The man that had gotten the door open asked him if he was okay, but Joe didn't take time to answer the man. He just wanted to be outta there.

Joe didn't stay around to answer any questions of what had happened either. He knew there were a couple of reporters there because they came towards him with a pencil and paper in their hands. He left the scene at the tower really fast. He had made it back to the parking lot where his old car was parked. He was sure glad to see his old stationwagon once again. He got in it and took off like a greased streak of lightning. Joe was really relieved that he got out of that situation not being the topic of the evening. So much for that thought because he had another surprise coming. He drove on back to Okeechobee to his motel. He was really stressed out about how his day had turned out. He took a good long hot shower to try and relax after all the unfortunate incidents he'd been in today. He didn't go to a restaurant to get him anything to eat. Instead he went to his car, and found something to eat that would get him by until the next morning. He turned the t.v. on, and started watching a movie that was a love story, and it ended up that the girl in the movie died. He didn't know it was going to be a tear-jerking movie like it was. It was so sad that it brought tears to his eyes even if it was only a movie. Joe watched the late night news before he went to bed only to see a story on it about the mysterious man trapped in the elevator in Lake Placid. It had shown him almost running to his car making a fast exit from the tower. The news said the name of the man at this time was unknown. His picture on the video was clear enough that anyone that saw him running away knew who he was. He didn't really care because the article didn't tell of all the details that had happened in the elevator, and to him it was a relief.

Loretta Ann

Chapter thirteen

Joe Meets Loretta Ann

Joe decided it was time for him to go check out the Prairie to try to find a good spot to go camping at. After all that's what he came to Okeechobee for was to go on a camping trip so he could enjoy the outdoors for at least another month. As he left the motel and drove in the direction of the Prairie he just couldn't resist going by the Lonesome Dove to eat again. That little café was beginning to be his second home. He just felt so much at home there with all his newly found friends. Joe saw that everybody that he'd met there was still there just working away as usual. He ordered himself another one of his favorite jumbo burgers with fries and some baked beans. He even ordered a side order of that good cole slaw that Runt made from scratch. That was the best cole slaw that he had ever eaten before.

Since Joe's ordeal from the previous day had sorta short changed him from getting a good hot meal he would make up for lost time today. He knew he was at the right place at the right time now so he was going to make the best of it. Joe wasn't going to leave the Dove hungry that was for sure because he was planning to have dessert after he finished the rest of his meal. He sure liked the food here in Okeehobee. It was what you called down home cooking. That was right down his alley to because he hardly ever got a meal as decent as this when he was at home. He just wasn't a big cook when it came time for him to fix for himself. He just ate light most of the time.

Joe waited patiently for his food to get fixed. When he saw Runt coming out of the kitchen bringing him his big plate that had the jumbo burger and fries on it, he was getting as excited as a puppy would when he was about to be fed. As he got his meal he sat there eating on his big old hamburger. He was in hog heaven right then. As Joe munched away on his food he noticed a lady that walked into the café by herself. She sat at the booth across from him. She looked over at Joe and sort of smiled at him. He had a mouth full of hamburger that showed as he nodded his head at her and smiled back trying to be friendly. While he sat there eating his meal he noticed the lady was still staring at him. He thought she might be watching him the way he was eating because he was so hungry that he wasn't using his manners like he should.

Joe just tried to ignore her while he ate. It was then that he thought she was giving him the eye because she kept giving him a little smile. He would just smile back not really knowing what to do just then. Finally, he decided to speak to the lady. He introduced himself to her. She told Joe her name was Loretta Ann Perkins. Then she gave him a real big smile then. He noticed at that moment that Loretta Ann needed to have a lot of dental work done on her teeth. She was pretty shy and all she knew to do was just sit there and smile at Joe. Loretta Ann really didn't know what to talk about to Joe. She started talking away to Runt when she came out to take her order. Runt could break the ice with anyone it seemed. She could probably get a person that was sleeping to talk in their sleep if she wanted to. She asked Loretta Ann what she wanted for lunch today, and she told Runt she would have a jumbo cheeseburger with all the fixings. When Joe heard this he was wondering where this little skinny lady would put that big of a meal.

He noticed Loretta Ann wore thick black rimmed glasses. He was beginning to check her out like she had him. After

Runt took Loretta Ann's order he saw Loretta Ann looking at him once more, but she didn't say anything. Joe didn't want to be rude so he began to talk to Loretta Ann for a while. When he said something to her it seemed that she was at ease then. He could tell she was bashful, but soon she was talking up a storm to Joe. She talked to him like they had been friends for a long time. They were hitting it off with each other pretty good. Joe had now met himself a lady friend.

Now Loretta Ann probably wouldn't win any door prizes, but neither would Joe. One thing that he had been taught was that you don't judge a book by its cover. After all, Joe had been told and taught by his father, that beauty was only skin deep. His father taught him that it's what comes from a person's heart that makes the person who he or she is. He asked her if she was from Okeechobee? Loretta Ann told him yes, that she was born and raised here. She told him she lived in Florida all her life, and hadn't been very far from Okeechobee at all. She told Joe that she had never been out of the State of Florida either. He and Loretta Ann were really enjoying each other's company.

The two of them struck up a good conversation with each other. He told her that he came to Okeechobee to do some outdoor camping in the woods. Joe told her that he was planning to camp at the place that was called the Prairie. He asked her if she knew anything about the camping area called the Prairie. Loretta told him that she knew a little about the place he was talking about, but had never been out there. She told him that she knew a lot of people that had been out to the Prairie hunting and fishing, and she thought that she might go out there one day herself.

Runt brought out Loretta Ann's jumbo meal. Loretta Ann told her thanks, and then Runt asked Joe if he needed anything thing else to eat or drink. He told Runt she could bring him another glass of sweet ice tea and some peach cobbler that he'd saw on the menu. When Runt brought his tea and cobbler to his table she asked him what was he up to today. He told her he was going out to the Prairie to find a place to go camping at. He told Runt he wanted to enjoy himself, and do a lot of things before his vacation time ran out.

Runt then started telling him about the camp that her mom and dad had out there. It sure sounded like a good place to camp. After she told him about the camp she told him her parents probably wouldn't mind if he camped out there at their lot. She told Joe that she would probably see them later on today. She told him that if she didn't get to see them she would call her mom and dad to see if it would be okay for him to stay out there. Joe told Runt that was real nice of her to do that for him.

He was getting a little excited now just thinking about his next adventure. He started talking to Loretta Ann again since Runt had to go back to the kitchen to answer the phone. When Runt answered the phone it was her mom. She asked her mom what time they would be off work, and her mom told her they would be home shortly.

Joe and Loretta Ann were still talking to each other, and were still hitting it off pretty well. He asked her if she'd like to ride out with him to the Prairie if she wasn't doing anything else that day. She told him she was off work for the rest of the day so she might take a ride out there as long as he was coming back to town before it got too late. He told her he wouldn't be gone but a couple of hours or whenever she got ready to come back. Loretta Ann thought that Joe seemed to be a nice enough guy so she said she would ride out there for a little while. He told her they wouldn't stay gone very long. Loretta Ann finished eating her meal, and waited until Joe was ready to go.

Runt came back to where Joe was now sitting which was at Loretta Ann's table. She told him that her parents were on their way home from a job they were doing around the lake. She told him to wait around a few minutes, and he'd get to meet them. Joe told her he'd sure like to meet them. He had heard so much about them that it seemed like he knew them already.

They each paid Runt for their meals. They sat there talking about different things, and it seemed that they had a lot in common. He was really enjoying himself sitting there with Loretta Ann. They were really having a good time talking about all the different things here in Okeechobee. She told him what all there was in the little town of Okeechobee. He bet she could she could tell him the history too if he asked.

They even got on the subject of where Joe lives and works at. He really seemed relaxed with Loretta Ann. She was in a way much like him. She didn't go out with anybody, but she did have a job in which she worked at 5 to 6 days a week. Loretta Ann worked at cleaning people's houses, and sometimes cleaning up offices for some business people that she had known for years. All she ever did was go to work then usually back home unless she had to go to the stores or post office to get her mail.

Joe told Loretta Ann that he didn't go much of anywhere when he was at home because of having to get up so early to go to work. He was a homebody also. He thought how nice it was to be able to carry on a conversation with a lady like Loretta Ann. He was really starting to take a liking to her.

They kept talking a while longer after they had finished their lunch at the Lonesome Dove. Runt's parents hadn't come out there yet so they decided to head on out to the Prairie. They took his car out to the Prairie to see what all was out there. Joe had told Runt he'd be back before they closed. Maybe by then her parents' would be home, and he would get to meet them. She told Loretta Ann and Joe to behave themselves, and she'd see them later. Loretta Ann was blushing after Runt told her and Joe to behave themselves. Joe's face even turned a little red to. They told Runt they'd see her in a little while. Runt smiled then waved a little goodbye to them.

Joe and Loretta Ann left the Lonesome Dove to head for the Prairie. As he and Loretta Ann drove along the highway they were very quiet towards each other. You can say that they were at a loss for words I guess. Finally, Loretta Ann broke the ice and began talking away a 100 miles per hour. I reckon she was a little nervous since she drove off with a perfect stranger you might say. It seemed to her that Joe was a nice guy at the time she was talking to him at the café. He seemed normal enough, but now a days you just can't be too careful. Well, finally Joe got a few words in edgewise, and the two of them became relaxed with each other again like they had known each other for all their life.

They finally came to the highway that they had to turn on to get to the Prairie. Loretta Ann told Joe he'd probably get to see some wild animals because she'd heard everyone talk about how many wild animals there were at the Prairie.

The way everyone talked it seemed like a place that was out of a storybook in a way. They drove on for probably another 25 miles then they saw the sign that pointed them in the direction of the Prairie. When they left the highway where they had to turn at they had to turn onto a dirt shell road. The road was so bumpy that Joe didn't think that he would be able to drive on it. His old stationwagon car was so long that it just wanted to spin sideways when he tried to go a little faster. Loretta Ann started to laugh, and the way she laughed it made him start to laugh too. Loretta Ann had got so tickled that she could hardly catch her breath. She was practically in hysterics from all the laughing that she was doing. Joe could hardly see because he was laughing so hard that his eyes were slap full of tears from laughing at her. He and Loretta Ann were having the blast of a lifetime at that moment.

Joe kept mashing down on the gas petal making his old car go swerving all over the road because he and Loretta were having such a great time at that moment. Well, as they came to the end of the road they had to turn either to the left or the right. He asked her which way did she want to go, and she told him to go to the right. So to the right they turned and drove along a real sandy dirt road. Boy, they would be in deep crap if they got stuck way back there on the backside of the Prairie.

Joe and Loretta Ann had no idea what they would be into if they did. He had started slowing down once they came to the sandy road that looked so bad. He managed to go around the sand bed okay. Well, Joe and Loretta Ann were both surprised when they saw a big buck deer jump in front of them while they were driving slowly along on the dirt road. Joe was amazed by a big old deer he saw. The big deer just stopped still in the middle of the road and looked at them. Joe then stopped his car, and watched to see what the deer would do next. Well, the deer was pretty used to seeing a lot of people driving around out there all the time so he walked to the edge of the road and began to eat the grass. The deer didn't pay anymore attention to Joe and Loretta Ann.

Joe had wished that he had brought his camera, but as it always happens he forgot and left it in his motel room back in town. Oh well, he thought he'd be back later so maybe he'd get to see some more wildlife to take pictures of when he came back out to go camping. Joe and Loretta were really enjoying themselves together. He was thinking that Loretta Ann was his kind of girl. The both of them were having quite a good day.

Joe asked her if she was going with anyone or if she was involved with anyone. Loretta Ann told Joe that she wasn't interested in anyone, and really didn't have the desire to be committed to anyone at this time. Well, he thought that he hit a sore spot at the way she sort of cut him off short on that subject, so he changed the conversation to something else real quick like.

He started talking to her about the Prairie after that. He asked her if she had ever heard anyone talking about camping out there at the Prairie, and she told Joe that she hadn't. She told him she knew they went hunting and fishing, but didn't know where or if they had camped there or not. She told him she hadn't ever been out there until now, and she hadn't gone camping that much. She told him she was glad that she finally got to go out to see what it looked like though. She told Joe it would be a nice place to camp because there was so much wooded area there.

They were really amazed at all the wild life that they were seeing out there at the Prairie. They saw 5 or 6 squirrels playing in the tops of the tall old oak trees. They saw 2 otters in an old pond next to the road jumping and diving in and out of the water. At first Joe thought that the otters were some types of beaver, but Loretta Ann laughed and told him that they were black otters. Well, he was a little embarrassed and felt a little dumb just about then. Joe slammed on brakes and told her to look at the big turkeys at the edge of the woods, by the big old hammock of trees. Joe counted eight hen turkeys in the bunch. There were a couple of big gobblers, and just like a typical male they were strutting their stuff in front of the hen turkeys. The hen turkeys seemed to not be paying much attention to the gobbler turkeys at all. The hen turkeys were too busy feeding on the grass, and scratching around looking for bugs to eat. They must have watched the turkeys for 15 or 20 minutes, then decided to drive on and see what else they could find out there to look at.

It was really a quiet peaceful place out there. You wouldn't think anyone lived out there at all, but there were a few homes that had been built out there. He told Loretta Ann it must be nice to be able to live in peace and harmony in a place such as this. She agreed with him about how nice it was, and she told him she'd like to have a place out like this one-day.

Joe drove along on the dirt road they were on, and they came to the end of it because it wasn't a thru road. He told her they would drive around on some of the other roads, and check them out to see if they could find any good camping spots. He told Loretta Ann that he was coming back out when he could find out where the best place to go was at. When he talked to Runt again at the café maybe he would know if he would be able to use her parents camp. If only he could be so lucky.

He told her that he wanted to go fishing in some of the ponds that they passed. When he got his camp all set up he would take in some fishing then. He told her if she would like to she could come back out there with him one day before he had to go back home. He asked her if she liked to fish? She told him she liked to fish, but never caught much when she went fishing. Loretta Ann smiled real big at Joe, and said she might just take him up on his invitation. After all, she was having a pretty good time herself even if she didn't want to admit it. Joe was glad that she said she might come back out with him.

He was so glad to have someone to talk to, and was really glad that Loretta Ann was taking time to get to know him to. Joe saw a raccoon crossing the road in front of him, and he slowed down as not to scare it off. Just about the time he was ready to speed up and go, Joe saw 4 little baby coons coming up from the side of the road. They were following their mama, but she wasn't hanging around for them to catch up. Joe and Loretta Ann waited to see if she would keep going and leave them behind, but the mama coon finally stopped and waited on them. The raccoons were heading towards a big old pond. It was pretty hot so he thought they were probably going to get some water to drink from the pond. Loretta Ann told him she knew the animals had to love it here in the woods because they had plenty of places to hide if they had to.

Joe never saw so many animals in the wild before. It was really exciting to him because he never got out at home like he has since he's been on vacation. He knew he had been missing out on a lot of things by just staying home all the time, but back in Virginia he didn't have that much drive to want to go anywheres because he was usually too tired from working so much. Well, Joe looked at his watch and it was already 6:30 p.m. he told Loretta Ann that they better head back to town so he could get all his stuff ready so he could come back camping.

He went back by the Lonesome Dove Café and went inside to see if Runt's mom and dad had made it in yet. Runt told Joe they had already came and gone, but would be back the next morning. He told her he was coming back out the next day so he would stop by then, and maybe he could catch her parents before they went to work. She told him to come out early because they always got an early start to go to work. They did this before it got too hot during the day.

Joe told Loretta Ann that he really enjoyed the afternoon with her. He thanked her for helping him find the Prairie. She told him she enjoyed her day out there with him very much. She was really glad that she finally got to go see the Prairie too. They both said good-bye and they would get together again before he had to go back home. It seemed the two of them were suddenly attracted towards each other in a funny kind of way. Well, as Joe started to leave the cafe' he told everyone goodbye and that he'd see all of them later on, then he headed on his way back to town to his motel room.

Well, after Joe made it back to the motel room in town he grabbed him a snack to eat. He then took a long hot soak in the bathtub. Joe just lay soaking in the tub of water thinking of the great day he and Loretta Ann had together. It was such a good day that he couldn't stop thinking of it. Nothing drastic happened to him so that was one thing he had that went his way for a change. Loretta Ann Perkins, "What a nice girl she seemed to be." That was all Joe could think of the rest of the day. If I didn't know better I'd think that he had become quite fond of Loretta Ann, and he'd only known her for a few hours. Do you think it might be love at first sight? Sometimes things happen that way. Naw, it's probably all the attention that Joe had received from the opposite sex that day. He was just a little rambunctious I guess. Here he was, all alone so any attention he got he took it all in.

He had met a nice girl named Loretta Ann Perkins. She seemed like she could be his type of girl. Joe thought she was somewhat like him in a way. She seemed kind of shy and quiet like him, but that was okay though because he did seem to have a little interest in Loretta Ann.

He decided to stay at the motel for the rest of the day. He watched some t.v. and just reared back and rested the remainder of the day. Joe sat back in his easy chair thinking of what he was going to do the next day. Well, he watched some more t.v. until 11:00 P.M. then turned in for the night. He got up early the next morning to go eat breakfast at the "Dove." Finally he got to meet Shirley & Donald. They are Runt's mom and dad. Surprisingly enough he got to talk to them for a couple of hours before they had to go out on the job. You see they own a septic tank business along with the café to so they sort of set their own schedules. Runt introduced Joe to her dad, and he shook hands with Joe. Shirley told Joe she was glad to meet him. She told Joe just to call her the "Doody Lady" because she is always in a world of it. Joe laughed and said, "that's about the way it goes." Now he understood why they called her that. Of course, Doody goes along with the type of business they are in. Joe liked Runt's parents. So far he had liked everyone he'd met here in Okeechobee.

He had told Shirley & Donald about wanting to camp out before he goes back home and back to work. They told him to go ahead and make his camp out on their property at the Prairie if he wanted to. They told him he could stay up there the rest of his trip if he wanted to because it was okay with them. Joe thanked them for letting him use their camp. He was thrilled to death that someone would actually let him stay on their property. Especially him being a perfect stranger to them. Well, they told Joe they had to get the old ball rolling, and they'd see him around later on. They told him to enjoy his stay in the woods, and then off to work they went.

Joe wanted to eat breakfast before he left. He didn't know he had such an appetite today. He ordered himself a big breakfast to eat. Joe was in misery by the time he ate all of his breakfast. He had ordered a big stack of pancakes with blueberries and whipped cream. He also ate sausage patties, bacon, and hashbrowns. Joe would weigh 500 pounds if he didn't slow down on his eating. He just had nervous energy and couldn't help himself I guess. He knew one thing for sure he wouldn't go away hungry when he ate at "The Dove." Runt always piled his plate up with food every time he ate there.

Joe sure felt like this was his home away from home here in Okeechobee. Joe noticed that the people here sure were friendly unlike they were back home. It was a totally different atmosphere all together. It was an atmosphere that he really enjoyed being in. When Joe finished his breakfast he paid for his meal. He told everyone he'd see them all later. He was on his way to start his wild camp out. When he said this he had no idea of how wild it would be. He knew he had to have a few things that he'd ran out of so he would have to go back to town before he went to the Prairie.

Chapter fourteen

Prairie Camp Supplies

Joe went back to town to buy some groceries from the Bubby Lubby's Grocery Store. He bought the rest of the supplies and groceries that he needed for his camping trip.

Joe bought some cans of beanie weenies, potted meat, and other items to fix sandwiches with. He bought a case of cokes and plenty of junk food to pig out on too. He didn't figure he'd be cooking too much since he'd be by himself out there at the Prairie. Joe did buy some more spare ribs to try to grill again since he burnt the last ones he cooked to a crisp. He was bound and determined to have some good tasting ribs just one time to eat. Of course, he went a little wild on buying groceries because by the time he finished buying them he'd spent over $300.00 for the groceries. Oh well, one thing for sure he sure wasn't about to go hungry.

Joe went back to the motel room to pack up all his stuff he'd taken out of the stationwagon. He got everything back in the car. After he paid his motel bill he then left and drove around town just killing a little time before he took off for the Prairie. After he had driven pretty much all around town he headed on his way to set up his campsite. Joe had driven around Okeechobee enough now that he pretty much had his bearings of where he had to go in the little town.

    It was a bright sunny morning, and the wind was blowing enough to make the day enjoyable. Joe didn't have to be in any hurry so he just took his time on his way out to the Prairie. Afterall he was on his vacation, and he wasn't supposed to have to be hurried up like he was when he was at home. As he was cruising along in his old battlewagon he started thinking of what he would do once he reached the camp. He planned on setting his tent up and getting everything in place once he reached the campsite. Joe knew he would be in a different environment when he got to the woods so he wanted to make sure everything was so-so as to speak.

    Since Joe would be camping out by himself in the woods he wouldn't have to have a set schedule on anything he did. He could get up late if he wanted to, or he could just relax all day long if he desired to do so. He sure hoped he would be able to find the camp okay once he got to the Prairie. He could pretty well find his way around when he was on the road traveling. Well, he had got lost a couple of times, but always found his way back in the right direction.

    Joe was listening to his radio, and sort of jamming out as he cruised along the highway. He started singing along with the music on the radio. He had the station on one of the Oldie Goldie radio stations. He thought he was back in the sixties at that moment listening to all the good old rock and roll music. He even heard songs he hadn't heard in many years since he was a young man. The music made Joe feel like he was a teenager again.

    Joe came to the little road that turned off the main highway that went towards the Prairie. He loved it in the country and out in the woods. He wished he lived in the country away from the city, but unfortunately he didn't. As it was he wasn't too far from his job, but he still had to fight the traffic everyday when he went to work. Being close to his job was convenient because he didn't have to drive a long way like some of the people had to do that worked at the same place with him.

Sometimes when he went to work in the morning it would be so crowded on the highway. There would be big traffic jams especially when an accident happened on the way to work. The traffic would be snarled, and trying to get to his job sometimes was really frustrating.

Chapter fifteen

Stuck At The Prairie

Joe was getting closer to his destination point. He turned at the little sign he came upon that read the Prairie. It had another sign under it that read Peavine Road 10 miles. Joe thought that was where he was heading so he was going in the right direction so far. He drove on going slow because he wanted to take his time sight seeing. Joe thought out there at the Prairie was really in God's country. It was so peaceful and it was so pretty out there in the woods. It wouldn't take too much to convince Joe to buy him a place in the country. Matter of fact no one would even have to twist his arm at all to get him to live in the country.

Well, Joe looked at the little map that Runt had made for him to follow to get to her parents' camp. He was to turn on the 10-mile road then go to the west 7 miles. It showed 2 little bridges to cross before he got to the road he would have to turn off on to go to the camp. He started noticing that the little dirt road he was on was beginning to get real sandy. The road had big ruts in it. He started not to go any further. He thought that maybe he would be able to get through because his car was so heavy. He thought that it might go through the ruts without any problem.

Well, he made it through the first 2 sandbeds without any trouble, but the third one was the one that he got his car stuck in. Joe was almost through the sandbed when his car started to spin its tires. He thought, "what will I do if I get stuck way out here in the middle of nowhere?" Well, Joe was fixing to find out. His car spun all the way down to its rear end. He was really in a fix now. Here he was stuck, and he had no idea how far it was to the Wildes camp.

Joe sat there in his car about an hour before he decided that no one would be coming by. He figured he'd better start hoofing it, if he wanted to get his car out before nightfall. Well, Joe started his country walk to go find help if he should be so lucky. One thing he was fixing to get was his daily exercise. He walked for probably what turned out to be an hour. He still saw no houses or anyone in sight.

The only thing he saw or came across was 2 big black wild hogs. He was walking along the side of the road because the road was hard to walk on because it was so sandy. As Joe got close to the hogs they jumped up and ran right past him straight to the pond at the edge of the woods. The hogs scared the daylights out of Joe. He saw them hit the mud at the edge of the pond, and then they lay down in the mud as if they were in a hog pen. The hogs were startled as bad as he was when they saw him. The black hogs blended right in with the mud. These hogs were what you'd call piney-wood rooters. He was lucky that the wild hogs didn't try to catch him. I guess they were too interested in the mudbogging they were doing in the pond.

Well, Joe was looking everwheres after he walked up on the hogs. He sure didn't walk up and surprise any other animals. There was no telling what all was in the woods running wild. He hoped it wouldn't be much longer until he could find some help. He sure didn't want to have to walk back to town. At least he was lucky enough to have some cold drinks and water in his car in case he got thirsty. He also had plenty of food to eat if he got very hungry.

Joe had walked about 3 miles from where his car was stuck. He came to one of the little bridges that he remembered on the little map that Runt had drawed for him. He stopped at the little bridge crossing and rested for a little while. As he sat down on the cement edge of the bridge he saw some big fish swimming in the water. The water appeared to be shallow. He would have given a hundred dollars to be able to catch a big fish like he saw swim into the culvert near the bridge. It looked like a giant black catfish, and it looked like it might weigh 30 pounds or more.

    Joe had heard of catfish getting really big, but he had never saw one that big until now. If only he had his camera. He would have been able to get a picture of the hogs, and of the big catfish. Well, maybe he would get the chance to take some pictures of the wildlife once he got settled in to his camp. Joe sat and rested a few more minutes then he began to walk on his way to find help again. He was beginning to get warmed up from the heat now. It was a lot cooler earlier, but the wind seemed to stop blowing. Joe took his shirt off because he began to perspire a lot. He wasn't ammuned to the hot sun at all. He didn't know it, but if he wasn't careful he'd get sunburned real easy because he looked like a glow stick. Joe was as white as a ghost was because he never got the chance to get out in the sun very much back home.

Chapter sixteen

Day Of The Big Dog

As Joe walked on he began to whistle. That was something that he hadn't done in years. He was surprised that he could even whistle at all since he hadn't puckered up in years. Joe was making good time as he walked along. Finally, he came to a driveway that led up to a house. Man, he was glad to see there was someone that lived out this way afterall.

Joe walked up the driveway towards the house. As he got closer to the house he didn't see any vehicles in the yard. He guessed the people must be at work. Joe walked up to the door and knocked on it real loud. He stood there listening to see if he could hear anyone inside, but there was no one home.

As Joe turned to walk away and leave he heard something coming around from the side of the house. As he saw what it was he panicked and ran as fast as he could. For what Joe saw was a big black rockweiler dog. He knew the dog would make hash out of him if he stopped long enough for the dog to get hold of him. All Joe knew right at that moment was he had to run for his life. He would be in for trouble if he stopped and let the dog attack him.

Joe was running as fast as he could possibly run. He

didn't take time to look back behind him at all. He was too afraid that if he did he would get caught for sure. Joe could hear the dog growling and barking as he was running behind him. The big dog was close on his heels. He could actually feel the dog's breath on his heels. Joe knew he had better tighten up and run faster or he would get turned into dog meat. He was tiring out from the running, but knew he couldn't stop. Joe saw a big tree at the edge of the road and was able to shimmy up it, but before he made it all the way up the dog caught his foot. The dog hung onto his shoe pulling it off his foot. Joe was lucky that his foot wasn't in the shoe.

All he could do was watch as the dog lay under the tree gnawing away on his shoe. The dog seemed to enjoy slobbering all over Joe's shoe. The big animal was chewing his shoe to pieces. Finally, the rockweiler got up and went back towards the house with poor old Joe's shoe in his mouth. The dog had himself a trophy, which was his shoe. He knew he had been real lucky that time.

Joe was glad that it was his shoe instead of his foot. He could always buy another pair of shoes, but not another foot unless it was an artificial one. He wanted to keep his original parts as long as he could. That is, he wanted to keep his whole body in tact forever because right now everything seems to be working okay.

Whew, Joe had managed to escape the jaws of the rockweiler for now. Man, he was so tired from the physical exertion that he felt like he would fall out of the tree at any moment. It was so hot that Joe thought he might just pass out from the heat. He was really hot now because he had to run quite a ways to get away from the dog. Thank goodness, he was able to escape from being mauled to pieces by the ferocious animal.

He just sat there in the tree trying to catch his breath again. He wasn't coming down out of the tree until he was sure that the dog had gone back to the house. Well, he looked at his watch, and it was already 2:45 p.m. Joe couldn't believe it was that late, but it was. Well, he waited for about an hour then he decided to climb down out of the tree.

He managed to get rested up while he waited for the coast to clear. That is, he wanted to make sure the dog had gone away without any if's, and's, or but's. Joe had cooled down a little, but he was sure thirsty at that moment. He thought how good it would be to be able to put a bottle of cold water up to his lips and be able to drink it. Well, that was one thing he didn't have to worry about right then because that wasn't about to happen. He would have to wait until he went back to his car, or if he got lucky enough to find someone that would be kind enough to give him something to drink.

Well, Joe didn't see the dog anymore so he climbed down from the tree. He started to walk again to see if he could find some help. If he couldn't find someone to help him pull his car out of the sandbed then he would have to walk back into town. Joe hoped and prayed he would be able to find someone to help him. It was a long, long, way to have to go by foot. He didn't know if he would even be physically able to walk that far or not.

As Joe was walking along he noticed he still had one shoe left on his foot. He really felt stupid because here he was walking down the road with one shoe on. Joe was sure glad he noticed it in case someone had come along. They would think he was really off balance for sure just walking around in the woods with one shoe on his foot.

Joe took off the shoe he had left, and carried it on his hip by tying it to his belt loop. He was keeping it in case he might need it for an emergency. Boy, the sand was so hot that Joe had to walk through the grass on the side of the road. He might have to put his shoe back on if he didn't get away from the hot sand. The shoe would serve some purpose if he had to do this. At least he would be able to keep one foot cool.

As it happened he made it to the second little concrete structure. It had water running under it so that was when Joe stopped to hang his feet over the side to cool off his feet. Oh, the water felt so refreshing to his hot feet. He hadn't realized how hot his feet had gotten from walking in the sand. He thought his feet would burn up before he got out of the sandy road.

Joe knew he surely had walked 5 or 6 miles by now. He was about to give up and go back in the direction of his car. He was going to rest a few minutes more then walk a little ways farther. Then he would turn around and go back to his car if he didn't see anyone soon. Well, Joe was so thirsty he was almost tempted to drink the water flowing under the structure. He was so thirsty he could drink a pond dry he thought. The longer he sat there with his feet dangling into the water the lazier he became. It seemed like he was getting thirstier and thirstier as he sat looking at the water.

Since Joe had his feet in the water on the south side of the structure he thought he would go to the other side and take a tiny swig of water to keep his mouth from being so dry. The water was clear looking enough, and it was flowing steadily. So he took him a couple swallows of water from the canal. Joe knew back in the olden day that was how the pioneers did. Surely he would be okay. Besides, the water looked real clear and clean.

He drank some of the water thinking that it wasn't half-bad at all. The water tasted so delicious because he was so thirsty. After Joe drank a lot of the water he wasn't thirsty anymore. Well, the water had seemed to hit the spot until he saw something floating in the water upstream from him maybe a hundred yards or so. Joe had to get up to go see what it was. It was close to the edge of the bank in the water. As he got closer to it he could see that it was an old dead cow. It was at that moment that Joe Macoochee turned green as a gourd. He started heaving so hard that he lost all the water he had just drank. He was a sick joker right now because he had drank the water that had a dead cow laying in it. Joe knew it was the thought that had made him so sick, but now he didn't know if he would get really sick from the water he had just drank.

It was at this moment that he wished he had remained thirsty instead of doing like Adam and Eve when they became tempted and ate the forbidden fruit. Joe knew one thing for sure, and that is that he wouldn't drink out of a canal anymore no matter how thirsty he was. Well, he was sick from seeing the cow, but he would get better he hoped.

Chapter seventeen

The Meeting Of Riley

Joe left the structure to walk on his way once again. This time Joe's luck changed. He hadn't walked maybe a couple of blocks when he saw an old man outside in his yard. There was a mobile home there so he knew he had found civilization once again. Joe yelled out to the old man. The man told him to come on up to his house. Joe then yelled out and asked the man if he had any dogs that would bite. The man told him his old dog was too lazy to bite anything except dog food out of a can.

Joe slowly walked towards the old man. As he got closer to the man he saw the man was working on his jeep. He introduced himself to the man. The old man told him his name was Riley. He asked Joe if he was broke down or if he was just taking a hike. He told Riley that he had got his stationwagon stuck in the sandbed a few miles back down the road.

Riley told him he had to finish putting oil in his jeep then he would see if he could pull him out of the sandbed. Joe thanked him and asked if he had a water faucet outside somewhere. Riley told him there was a faucet in front of his trailer. He thought Joe wanted to wash his face off because he was hot. When he saw him drinking the water like he was thirsting to death he told Joe he would fix him some ice water to drink. Joe told him that was okay because he just wanted to get a drink of water.

He thanked Riley for offering him some cold water. The old man told him he knew how it was to be thirsty and not be able to get something to drink. He told Joe many years ago he had went hunting with some of his buddies. They each had gone off by themselves to see if they could bag a deer or hog. As it went 2 of the men got lost for about 8 hours. One of the men happened to be Riley. He told Joe he hadn't carried a canteen of water with him at all. He told him he thought he would die if he didn't get something to drink before much longer, but he managed to survive until he was found.

Joe told Riley he had drank some of the canal water on his way which wasn't too far from his house, but found the dead cow in the water. Then he told how he upchucked the water he had dranked because he saw the dead cow floating in the water. Riley laughed then told him he would have upchucked his water to if he'd saw the cow in the water he'd just got through drinking. Riley told him he had seen the cow a few days ago. He thought someone must have shot and killed her. Riley told him he had to be careful drinking water out of ponds and canals because of the spray that gets put into them. Joe told him he would never drink water out of anything unless it came out of a faucet, bottle, or pump of some kind. He told him the cow was his lesson. Riley just laughed at Joe then told him he guessed that would be a good enough excuse not to drink water from a canal. The water might look good and taste good, but you know it's what you can't see that can definitely make you sick. Joe agreed with Riley one hundred percent.

Well, Riley finished up with his little jeep. He cranked the jeep up and let it sit idling long enough to make sure it had picked up the oil in the motor okay. After he had everything checked out he told Joe to climb in, and he would take him to pull his car out of the sandbed. Joe hopped into the jeep, and saw real quick like that he'd better hang on. The old man drove the little jeep like he was going to a fire or some kind of an emergency. Joe noticed that they were fixing to cross the little bridge structure, and he saw that Riley wasn't going to slow down so he held on that much tighter to the windshield of the jeep. Joe sure hoped the windshield didn't come off in his hands because he wasn't about to let go of it at all.

As they went across the little bridge in such a hurry he just knew they would probably flip over into the canal, and someone would find them both drowned. Well, they made it across the first one without any trouble, but they still had another one to cross. As it turned out they made it across the other bridge without any problems at all.

Joe had hoped that the old man was a good driver, but now he knew Riley could drive okay. He wasn't about to turn loose of the dash and the outer edge of the windshield because he knew already what would happen if he fell out and hit the ground. Joe still had his knees tore up from the accidental fall he'd had at the park in Orlando.

Well, it didn't take too long to get back to the place where his car was at. They did make it back all in one piece without having a wreck believe it or not. Joe's car was stuck to the housing, and he wondered if Riley's jeep would be strong enough to pull his big old car out. Riley and Joe got out of the jeep then looked under the front of his car to see how bad it was buried up in the sand. Luckily it had room to get a chain hooked to it so it could be pulled out. Well, Riley told him to hook up the chain to the front end of his car, and he'd lock in his wheels on his jeep so he could have four wheel drive.

Riley yelled out to him to see if he had the chain hooked up to his car. Joe waved at him to back up. As Riley started to back up to get the slack out of the chain he told Joe to stand back just in case the chain broke. He stepped back from the car about fifteen feet so he would be out of the way. Riley had the slack out of the chain, and pulled away on the chain trying to get his car out of the sand bed. The car wouldn't budge an inch. Riley yelled out and asked him if he took the car out of park, and Joe told him he hadn't. Riley told him to crank his car up and to put the gearshift into neutral. Joe did as the old man told him to do.

Riley started to pull against the chain again, but he couldn't seem to move the big car at all. Riley told Joe he would have to try to snatch against the chain to get the car to move at all. Joe told him to go ahead and do what he had to do. Well, as Riley jerked against the chain several times the old car began to move a little bit. Riley told Joe he would give the chain one hard last jerk and his car would probably come out of the sand. Joe told him to go for it.

Well, Riley did give the chain one last hard jerk, but the car didn't come out because Joe's bumper came off, and went flying through the air towards him. Riley saw what had happened and stopped the jeep immediately. Riley asked Joe what he hooked the chain to. He told him he hooked the chain around the bumper. Riley told Joe no wonder the bumper came off because he should have hooked the chain to the frame of the car.

It was at that moment that Riley knew Joe didn't know much about getting a car unstuck. He kind of felt sorry for Joe in a way. Oh well, maybe Joe would remember the next time if he happened to get in that type of situation again. Riley took off the chain and hooked up a snatch rope he'd had inside his jeep so he then hooked it to the car's frame himself because he didn't want to tear anything else off of Joe's car. Riley asked Joe to get in his car, and put it in gear once again. Joe managed to do this without any problem. Riley told Joe to give the car some gas when he snatched against the rope because the rope would stretch then tighten back up.

Riley took off real fast to make the rope stretch then stopped and held his brakes so the jeep wouldn't go backwards. Joe on the other hand mashed the petal to the metal and came spinning on out of the sandbed when the rope began to contract and tighten up. Joe thought the stretch rope was real neat because he'd never saw a rope work like this one did. Well, you've got to understand that Joe lived quite a protected life, and never having to deal with anything like he had been dealing with since he had been on vacation was quite understandable. He was learning more and more even if it was the hard way.

Well, Joe was happy as a lark to have his car out of the sandbed so he could be on his way to find the little camp he was suppose to stay at. He asked Riley how much he owed him for pulling his car out of the sandbed, and the old man told him you don't owe me one red cent. Joe thanked him for his help, and Riley told him he might have to help him out one day. Riley told him he was sorry about pulling his bumper off of his car, but Joe said don't worry about it because it was my fault that I hooked the chain up to the wrong place.

Well, Joe loaded up his bumper into the back of his old stationwagon. He told Riley his car looked customized without his bumper on it. He told him it sort of looked like a mean machine.

Riley laughed and told Joe to stop by and see him when he got situated at his camp. He told Riley he would do just that. Joe had mentioned to him that he was camping out there at the Wildes Camp for about a month or so. Riley told him he would enjoy himself especially after he came away from the city life. Joe told him he could stay out here in the woods and not go back to the city at all. Riley said I know exactly what you mean because I lived in Miami once. That town was a mad house and was getting worse everyday. I came to Okeechobee from Miami 23 years ago and have been here ever since. I haven't even gone back to Miami at all. Okeechobee is my home now, and you couldn't even root me out of here if you tried. Joe said, yelp I'm becoming attached to the little town to.

Joe thanked him once again for his help. Well, he had his bumper loaded up in his stationwagon, and he wasn't stuck anymore so now he was ready to start on his way towards the camp again. Hopefully this time he would make it okay. He now had something else he could jot down in his memory book about his vacation experience. Joe could just about write a book on what happened to him in such a short time. If only he survives then the story would be one with a happy ending.

Joe asked Riley if he would like a good cold bottle of water or maybe a cold soda to drink before he left, but the old man told him no thanks he didn't care for anything right now. They each told one another good-bye then left to go their own separate way. Joe followed Riley as far as his house then he had to go a few miles more before he finally reached the camp.

As he drove along the road towards the camp he thought how lucky he was to have met Riley. He thought Riley was quite a nice old man. Most people wouldn't take the time to help you out of a jam like he had helped him out of. Joe knew there were a few people left that would go out of their way to help you. He had been lucky so far because he had been in several scrapes where someone had given him a helping hand. Thank goodness for the help he received or he might not have made it this far.

Chapter eighteen

Arrival At Camp Prairie

Joe was glad when he finally made it to the campsite where he would be staying until his vacation came to an end. He wanted to get most of his camp set up today, but since it was getting so late he thought he might sleep in his stationwagon the first night. He would have plenty of time tomorrow to work on getting it set up like he wanted. Joe walked around and looked the little campsite over undecided where he would put everything. Well, he didn't have to do it all in one day. Like they say, Rome wasn't built in a day.

Joe looked at his watch and lo and behold it was way past time for lunch now. Since it was so late he ended up eating a sandwich and some beanie weenies along with some tater chips. He opened himself a good cold can of soda to drink with his little meal. It wasn't anything fancy, but it filled his empty stomach up.

Joe got out his little canvas chair from his station wagon, and rested in it for a while. He thought he would unload his camping gear then assemble it tomorrow since he would be out there all day. He had packed up enough gear to stay in the woods for 6 months or longer. He grabbed every blanket, pillow, and bedding he had at home. One thing for sure was that Joe wouldn't have to sleep uncomfortable.

Joe put himself a blanket and some pillows up in the front seat of his car. Since it would be too dark to do much else he wanted to be sure he had his bed fixed. He was plum tired out from all the running, walking, and physical exertion he'd been through today. He would sleep like a baby tonight that was for sure.

After Joe got tired of sitting in the canvas chair he got up then started to look for wood to build a campfire with. He was able to find a lot of wood so he stockpiled it to one side. He wouldn't build a fire tonight, but he would the next night and every night after that. Joe was so tired he went on to bed. He would get up early the next morning, and get started on everything he had to do. Joe piled up inside his car then it wasn't long before he was dead to the world. He was completely worn out from the day.

Joe Macoochee gathering up oak fire wood for campfire

It was a cool night so he slept in comfort his first night in the woods. He did however get up to get something to drink during the night though. After he drank a bottle of water he went back to bed then he didn't get up for the rest of the night. Joe slept like a baby.

Well, the morning came and it was a new day again. Joe got up early to start his day. It was really chilly to him when he first got up to walk around. It was probably because there was so much fog that the dampness made it cool to him. The dew was heavy and the trees were dripping moisture from their limbs. It was almost as if it had sprinkled rain during the night. It seemed eerie to Joe at first when he saw the fog. It was like a scary movie with all the fog because you could barely see 5 feet ahead of you. While he walked around in the fog he remembered the movie he'd seen a long time ago about a spooky creature in a swamp. It was real foggy, and there were some teenagers that had their car break down in the middle of nowhere. They had left their car to walk for help then got lost in the foggy swamp. The creature caught 2 of the teenagers, and luckily the other 2 managed to get away.

Joe knew it was only a movie, but he still got the creeps thinking about it. He couldn't do much until the fog lifted so he went back to his car then laid back down. He went back to sleep, and slept 3 more hours. This time when he got up it was a clear day with no fog in sight. Joe felt more at ease now since he could see what he was doing. He had a chance now to look around to see exactly where he was, and where he wanted to pitch his tent that he would be sleeping in.

Joe saw a nice spot under some big old grandfather oak trees. He spread his tent on the ground after he picked up all the sticks that were scattered under the tree where they had fallen to the ground over time. He was a happy camper now because he was finally getting everything to come together. His tent went up without a hitch. Next he would have to get his bedding put inside, and get everything fixed up inside of his tent.

Joe sat his little canvas chair inside of his tent so he could sit in it if he didn't wanted to go right off to bed. He also had a couple of chairs that he sat near the place where he'd be building a campfire on a regular basis. He wanted to be sure he was better organized here in the woods than he was at home. He planned to do his grilling near the water pump so he would have access to the water if he needed it in a hurry. I guess he wanted to be able to put out a fire should he have one.

Joe seemed to learn something new every day. That usually was from one of his mishaps that he would have. They always say that experience is the best teacher, and sometimes I believe it is. After he finished setting up his camp, he then decided to go to the Lonesome Dove to get him a bite to eat. He wanted to let Runt know that he had made it out to the campsite okay. He thought that everything looked up to par so he left on his way to go eat him some lunch.

Joe was getting hungry now so he was kind of in a hurry to get to the Dove. When it came time to eat he didn't let any grass grow under his feet. When he was a little boy he never had to be called to the supper table twice. He was there willing and waiting to feed his face whenever it was chow time.

Chapter nineteen

Returning To The Dove

Well, Joe just couldn't wait until he got to the "Dove" again to eat. As he turned into the driveway of the café he couldn't believe at how many cars were parked in front of the café. He had never seen that many cars there before. Maybe it was because he wasn't there at lunch at the right time. Joe saw there was a full house there, and wondered if he would be able to find a place to sit. He noticed they were real busy so he went and sat down at the booth in the corner that was empty.

Runt yelled for him to make himself at home, and she would be there in just a minute to take his order. Runt brought him out a menu and took his drink order which was a jumbo glass of sweet ice tea. She told him she would give him a minute or two to look at the menu. Joe ordered a 16-ounce T-bone steak with potato salad, cole slaw, baked beans, and rolls. He sure hoped it wouldn't take too long to get his meal because his stomach was letting him know it was hungry because it began to growl. His stomach worked like clockwork. It always let him know when it was time to eat.

Joe sat there at his booth watching Runt and her Granny running around from customer to customer. Little old Granny was helping clean the tables, and she filled up everyone's tea glasses and even took some orders that had to be cooked. Boy, Joe had never seen the little café this busy before. He guessed that he was just there at the wrong time. Finally, after Runt & her Granny had everyone's food out to them she came over to talk to Joe for a minute.

He told her he had spent the night at the Prairie last night, and had just finished setting up camp. He told Runt to be sure to tell her parents that he would be up there camping in case someone saw him up there. He sure didn't want to get shot or locked up for trespassing. He knew how funny people were about their property now days. He gave her his order then she went into the kitchen to prepare it for him. As he sat waiting for his meal he saw Dee-Dee coming out of the kitchen in a fast trot carrying two big plates of food over to a table that had six people sitting at it. He watched her as she took off to the kitchen again. It wasn't just a few seconds until she came out with more plates to go to the same table again. Finally after her third trip she had everyone's food to them, and they all seemed to get really quiet because they were feeding their faces. Joe knew Dee-Dee hadn't seen him come in because she would have stopped to talk to him. He knew they all were busy as bees.

Joe finally got his meal and ate it in a hurry because the day was going by so fast. He wanted to get back to the Prairie before dark so he could double check to see that he had everything in order. If he got back before it got too late he wanted to ride around and look at the other part he hadn't been able to check out yet. Joe noticed there were a lot of prison guards there in the café. He asked Runt if there was a prison nearby. She told him to look across the cow pasture in front of the café, and he wouldn't be able to miss it. She told him that was the big house over there. He told her he hadn't noticed it there before.

Joe had hoped that he might get to see Loretta Ann at the café, but she didn't eat at the cafe' everyday. He asked Runt when she brought him some more tea if she had seen her lately, but Runt told him Loretta Ann hadn't been in since she was there with him. She told him, "You like her don't ya?" Joe's face turned blood red because Runt had embarrassed him. He blushed really easy especially when a female kidded him. Joe told her Loretta Ann was all right he guessed. Runt laughed, then had to go wait on another customer. She went to Joe's table to see if he needed anything, but he told her he couldn't eat or drink anything else.

She told him that Loretta Ann worked all the time too, and stayed pretty much to herself. He told her that he sort of liked Loretta Ann because she seemed like a nice girl. Joe told Runt that he was pretty much of a loner himself. She smiled at Joe and told him that he might have something in common with Loretta Ann. He sort of blushed and told her, we might just have something in common.

Loretta Ann at Lonesome Dove Café

He asked Runt if she knew where Loretta Ann lived at, and she told him that she knew just about where she lived at in town. Runt told Joe if he wanted to go by Loretta Ann's house she would find out exactly where she lives and she'd be glad to show him where it's at. She told Joe that Loretta Ann lived in East Okeechobee somewhere behind the post office. He got a big smile again and told her that he would like it if she could help him find Loretta Ann's house. She told him to let her know when he wanted to go by there, and she would call Loretta Ann and let her know.

Joe got up paid for his lunch then told everyone at the café he'd see them later. Well, he was so full he wouldn't have to eat another meal today. He already felt like he had gained 3 0r 4 pounds since he'd been on vacation. He probably got it from eating so much at his favorite little café. He told Runt he was going back to the Prairie to ride around, but might have to take him a nap first.

Runt told him to be careful, have fun, and to behave himself out there in the woods. He told her it was real foggy at his camp this morning, and it was kind of creepy to him. She snickered and told Joe not to let the Satscwatsh get him out there in the woods. He wasn't sure who Satscwatsh was so he had to ask. She told him what a Satscwatsh was. He started laughing and told Runt that's probably just someone playing a joke dressed up in a furry suit. He really wasn't too sure about that either. He would probably keep the Satscwatsh creature on his mind since she told him about it. Joe didn't want to think of anything that would make him nervous. You see he wasn't a real brave soul to start with. He never had any reason at all to be scared of anything before so he hadn't really worried about anything bad ever happening to him. Little did Joe know what was in store for him down the road. He had a lot of things that would change his life forever more I'm sure.

Chapter twenty

Newsflash About Prison Break

Well, he got in his old stationwagon and headed on his way to the woods. Joe was listening to his radio while he was driving. He was really relaxed and cruising on down the road. He was listening to the local radio station when a news flash came over the radio. The newsflash was about an escaped prisoner that had escaped from the big house there. Joe thought to himself how strange it was that a prisoner had escaped because he was just talking to Runt about the prison before he left the café a little while ago. He remembered seeing all the guards at the café so that might be why so many were there at the time. He hoped they caught the prisoner before he got too far away. Joe figured the prisoner probably had already skipped town by now. He knew they wouldn't wait around if they were trying to get away. He had seen where there were several prison breakouts up north, and it seemed they all managed to get to another state when they broke out. He sure hoped that everyone would be safe from the prisoner that broke out. The radio said the prisoner was very dangerous, and could possibly be armed.

Well, Joe forgot all about the news once he made his way back to the Prairie. He found his way back without getting lost in the woods. It was getting late in the afternoon, and he wanted to be sure he got to his camp before it got too dark. Joe made himself at home once he got to Shirley and Donald's camp. He was glad to be back there. He drove his stationwagon to the camping spot that was under the big oak tree. Joe really loved the peace and quiet.

Joe had his camp set up pretty good so he didn't do anything else to change it around. He saw some squirrels running around in the top of the trees. He knew the little squirrels weren't too wild because they came down on the ground about 5 feet from where he was standing. He figured that Shirley and Donald probably fed the animals here on their lot because there were feeders in 3 or 4 places around the camp.

Joe noticed that one of the squirrels didn't have but 3 feet. He felt sorry for the little squirrel because he sat there with his front leg shaking. A hunter probably shot the little squirrel, or it could have been another wild animal that had perhaps tried to catch the little squirrel for food. The little squirrel didn't let his missing foot keep him from running all over the place because he was up a tree in a flash when another squirrel ran after him.

Joe thought how sad it was that the little hurt animals didn't get doctored when they got hurt. It has to be rough living as an animal in the woods. He thought how terrible it was in a way because some animals probably starved to death if they were hurt too bad, and they wouldn't be able to find food to eat. He forgot about his sad thoughts when he saw a couple of squirrels fighting with each other. He then saw that the little creatures could pretty much take care of themselves.

Joe took some oak wood he had gathered up earlier and piled it up to make a campfire later on. He wanted to leave one burning all night long so that he would be able to get up during the night in case he had to take a nature break. It wasn't long till it would be dark so he just stayed around the camp. He thought he might get up early the next morning and scout around some.

He decided to start his campfire, and sit around it till he went to bed. Joe thought he had better get his old flashlight to keep in his tent because it would help him to see a little. His batteries were real weak in the flashlight and he expected them to go dead at anytime, but if he had to use his flashlight at all every little bit of light would help. Boy, he couldn't believe that the day had gone by so fast. They always say time flies when you're having fun. Well, he did have a pretty good day for a change.

Joe went to his car to get him something to snack on before he turned in for the night. After he got his campfire burning real good he did heat up a can of pork n' beans, and roast some weenies. He cut 2 palmetto fans then trimmed off all of the fan part to make him a stick to put the weenies on. He got out his jug of tea he'd bought, and then he got a big glass of ice to pour the tea over. Joe knew he shouldn't eat anything else after he had eaten so much at the "Dove," but he didn't have much else to do so he ate again.

Joe was really enjoying himself right about now. After the beans and weenies got done he sat back and got comfortable. He had his plate piled up high with the beans. He cut his weenies up then put them into the beans therefore making him some beanie weenies. They sure were good eating he thought. He guessed he'd worked up quite an appetite because he ate 2 plates of beanie weenies instead of one. It seemed to Joe that he was eating a lot more since he'd been on vacation. Oh well, you only live once he thought.

Well, Joe really did over do it this time, but it was too late to cry over spilt milk now. He knew he shouldn't have eaten again, but to his agony and pain he did. Boy, he sure was suffering now, but he told himself if he got over this bloated feeling he wouldn't ever pig out like this again. Well, Joe just sat in front of the campfire and thought how bad he felt after he gorged himself so much. He sat up another hour then got washed up and went to bed. He laid down on his little cot bed. It was pretty comfortable, but of course it wouldn't be as comfortable as his bed at the motel.

As he lay there on his little cot he began listening to all the sounds the animals were making in the woods. He guessed the animals liked it at night because they could get away from harms way better than they could during the day. Joe listened to the night sounds, and forgot the stomachache he'd developed from all the food he'd eaten earlier. It was sure a dark night out and that's probably why the woods were so noisy tonight. All the little creatures were out and about. He heard some hoot owls hooting back and forth to each other and some other birds singing, but couldn't see them so he couldn't tell what kind they were. Joe thought to himself that there's no telling what at this moment is lurking in the woods that he was unable to see. Oh well, as long as they didn't mess with him he was okay.

Gathering dried cabbage tree fans to start fire for camp

Joe Macoochee sleeping against log covered up with cabbage tree fans in the woods.

Chapter twenty one

Storm From Nowhere

Joe noticed the wind was blowing nice and cool. He lay there watching the tree limbs sway back and forth as the wind blew gently through the woods. The cabbage tree fans made a noise brushing against the other trees. It was a nice peaceful moment and a pleasant night.

Joe was so much at peace right now that he dosed off to sleep. He had been on the go all day long, and he was pretty much tuckered out. During the night about 3:00 a.m. he was awakened by a loud clap of thunder and lightning. It was so loud that he thought it was a gun being shot close by. As Joe got his eyes opened, and finally got his senses to working he realized what was going on. Oh, it's just a little thunder he thought, but boy was he wrong.

As he lay there listening to the weather it began raining so hard you couldn't hear yourself holler. The wind was blowing harder and harder. Joe thought his little tent would be blown away at anytime. As the rain kept coming down in droves his little cot began to get soaked from all the rain that began to pond on the ground.

He had heard someone at the café talking about how they really needed rain there in Okeechobee. It hadn't rained there for months.

The lake was really way below normal for this time of year. He thought they must be farmers because of the way they were talking. Joe overheard one of the men say if they did get a lot of rain again it would probably get pumped out of the lake again into the ocean. He thought that maybe the rain would help some by filling up the ponds in the woods that had gone dry.

He didn't mind the rain, but he sure didn't like the wind and lightning. He just hoped he wouldn't get struck by the lightning because it was getting worse. Joe's little cot was saturated with water so he got up and sat in his little canvas chair he'd put in his tent. He was lucky he did that because that's where he'd spend the rest of the night.

As Joe sat inside his little tent, the weather wasn't letting up at all. He was beginning to get worried so he decided he'd better go get in his old stationwagon so he'd be out of the weather. Well, he made a run to his car, but he was surprised when he got to it. There was a real big limb that had broken off the big oak tree, and it was lying directly on top of his car. He tried to open his door, but the tree limb covered the top and sides of his car because it was so humungus. He pulled and tugged at the tree limb, but couldn't get the limb to budge at all. He knew he'd have to wait until morning to see what kind of damages had been done to his car and campsite.

Joe ran back to his tent to try to figure out what he should do. He felt like a drowned rat. He didn't feel comfortable at all being wet so he took off his clothes. He began to squeeze the water out of his shirt and shorts. He lay his clothes on the back of his little canvas chair so they would get dried. Once again he sat down in his little chair to try to finish the night out. As he sat there he began to feel something biting his feet and legs. He took his flashlight and shined it on his feet only to see a bunch of mosquitoes landing on them. Boy, Joe had never seen so many mosquitoes at one time. The biting mosquitoes swarmed him like a bunch of bees. The one difference is that bee's sting a lot harder than the mosquito's bite. Either way one insect is as bad as the other one.

The city Joe lived in didn't have all the insects like Florida does because it was a different kind of climate. He grabbed the sheet from his cot, and covered up from head to toe with it. He looked like a deceased person covered up with a sheet like they do when you're in a morgue. Joe did manage to camouflage himself from the little biting suckers so he did at least get a little more shuteye before morning came. He felt like a pincushion from all the bites he'd got from the mosquitoes.

The weather was really bad the rest of the night. Joe didn't think the thunderstorm would ever go away. He'd never been outside in such bad weather as he'd been in during the night. He sure would be glad when it got daylight so he could see what he was doing. Oh, well Joe did manage to survive the stormy night without any more bad luck. He finally went back to sleep, and when he awoke again it was daylight. He noticed the mosquitoes had all disappeared and he didn't miss them at all.

Joe put on some clean clothes after he bathed the next morning. He put on another pair of shorts to wear for that day. He looked at his legs and arms because he saw little red spots that looked like the measles. Joe then looked at himself in the mirror only to see a lot of little red dots all over his face. One thing for sure you could see he'd been attacked by the mosquitoes.

Joe had to find his bottle of alcohol. It wasn't the drinkable kind because he didn't drink which was good. He took his bottle of rubbing alcohol then rubbed it all over his body because the bites were beginning to itch really bad. Well, after he got dressed he began to access the damage the thunderstorm had done. He saw a lot of tree limbs lying all over the place. He just stood looking at the giant one that had fallen on his stationwagon. He couldn't believe his eyes because the limb was as big as a medium sized tree.

Joe saw that his windshield was cracked on the passenger's side of the car. He began to pull at the limb on top of his car, but couldn't budge it. He climbed up on the hood of his car, and grabbed hold of the limb trying to pull it off. Joe tugged and tugged at the limb, but instead slipped down on the hood of the car. He wasn't strong enough to pull the limb off so he had only one other choice.

The other choice was to get inside his car somehow. It looked as if he would have to break the back window to get inside. He had locked the tailgate of his car, and since the keys were left in the ignition he had to break out the back window. Joe found another piece of tree limb that was big enough to break out the back window. He had to hit the window 4 or 5 times before he finally got the window to break.

If the tree limb hadn't been so humungus he would have been able to get in through the doors. As it was the tree limb hung over the whole top and sides of his car. It was a wonder that his car hadn't been demolished from the giant limb falling on it. His car was so big and long so that was probably why it didn't receive more damage than it did.

Joe managed to get inside of his car through the back door that he broke the window out of. He cranked his car up then tried to move it. He was really worried because the tree limb was so big. When he started moving his car he thought he would be able to make the limb fall off by gassing his car backwards, but it didn't move an inch. He then drove his car forward faster, but the limb still didn't fall off. The ground was still wet from all the rain so he couldn't get up much speed because his tires wanted to spin on the wet ground. It was too wet for his car to get any traction to gain any speed.

He sat there a few minutes thinking his situation over. The only thing he could decide on that made any sense was to get out on the road so he could get up to a fast speed. He was sure the limb would fall off then.

Well, Joe made it out to the highway then he began to pick up speed going down the road. He had gained up to a speed of 65 M.P.H. in his car, but the limb just wouldn't fall off. He started to swerve back and forth on the road, but the limb just wouldn't let go. It was as if the limb had become very attached to the old car. Joe felt plum stupid with the tree limb on top of his car. He could imagine how dumb he looked with it on top of his car. If anyone saw him they would think that the tree fell on the right spot. That spot was right on top of the dummy inside of the car.

He stopped his car, and pulled onto the side of the road. He looked both ways down the highway then turned his car around in a 360 degree circle, but really you could say he just spun a donut. As Joe began to spin his car around in a circle he did see the limb begin to move. Well, it took him 4 donuts round and round before the limb finally fell off. He was sure relieved when the limb fell from his car.

When the limb toppled from the top of his car it fell on the side of the roadside into the ditch. He was lucky that time. He had thought about trying to cut the limb up for firewood, but he had plenty back at the camp plus it would have taken him all day to cut the limb up by hand.

Joe was sure glad the limb fell off because he didn't want to drive his car into town with a big tree limb on the top of it. Everybody would probably call him the "Tree Man." After he got the limb to fall off his car he returned to his little camp. He knew if anything crazy would happen it would definitely have to happen to him.

Joe pulled his wet mattress off his little cot, and leaned it against a cabbage tree. There was a little dry spot next to the tree so maybe the mattress would have a chance to dry out during the day. Afterall, it would be another hot day so it shouldn't take long for the heat to dry out the mattress. Joe at least hoped it would get dry before nighttime. He knew he would have to dry everything that was on the ground inside of his little tent. It was hard to believe that so much rain had fallen last night. Well, he made it through one rainstorm, and the tent didn't fall so he did at least do a good job of setting it up.

Joe opened the door of his tent to let it also dry out because the water had saturated the ground. He had a lot to do to get his little camp organized again, but he could do that later on because he had other things he wanted to do today. He had a light breakfast this morning. Once he finished eating then he was well on his way to start enjoying more of his vacation time. Joe fired up his little camp stove to heat up some water to make a pot of coffee. He ate 3 sweet cinnamon rolls for his breakfast. That was a light breakfast for him this morning. He wanted to scout around all day, and he didn't want to be too full or he'd not get much of anything done.

Chapter twenty two

Good Day of Fishing

Joe's scouting turned out to be a fishing trip for the day. He decided to go fishing this morning. He gathered his fishing rods and poles up then put them into his old car. He went fishing at the Kissimmee River that was a few miles from his camp. When he made it to the river he parked his car next to the bridge so that he wouldn't have to carry his fishing equipment very far. Joe made sure he had everything close at his fingertips so he didn't have to get up and about much once he got into his fishing time. He fixed himself up a little spot to fish at under the bridge. It was out of the hot sun, and it seemed cool enough there in the shade. There were a lot of cars and big semi-trucks that kept going over the bridge, but he really didn't pay them much attention.

Joe sat back in his little canvas chair, and was quite comfortable. He managed to get all his poles and rods baited up for the fish. As he sat there relaxing, and waiting for the fish to bite his bait he saw one of his corks move. Joe's cork bobbled a little then went under the water real fast. He pulled back his pole, and hung into a good-sized fish. He had the hook set in the fish. While he was trying to bring in the fish he'd hooked first, he then had another fish to get on his second pole. Oh man, Joe thought how am I going to get both these fish in without tangling up my lines? Well, believe it or not he did manage to somehow bring in the 2 fish without tangling up his poles.

The first fish that Joe had hung on his pole turned out to be a big old channel catfish. He weighed about 5 pounds. He took out his old flimsy pair of pliers from his back pocket, and somehow managed to get the hook out of the catfish's mouth. The second fish was a speckled perch, and a good-sized one at that. He put the catfish and the speckled perch on a fish stringer then tied the stringer to one of the pilings of the bridge. Once again he baited up his hooks to see if he could catch more fish.

Joe sat back in his little canvas chair, and bingo he had another fish on his line. He was happy that he was doing so well today on his fishing trip. Well, this was strange for him to have such good luck, but as luck has it he kept catching fish for another hour. He almost caught his limit of fish, which in Okeechobee is 50.

Joe decided to go back to camp so he would have plenty of time to clean his catch. He was going to cook fish today for sure because he would have the fresh catch of the day. He finally loaded up all his fishing tackle and poles then he took his stringer of fish, and put them all in a 5-gallon bucket with some water so they wouldn't die before he could get them back to camp. He knew if he didn't put them in water that he would have a hard time of getting the scales off them. He would have to skin all the catfish with his pliers because as you know catfish don't have scales they have skin.

The day was beginning to get real warm, and Joe thought how good a big old glass of sweet ice tea would taste right at that moment. However, he would have to settle for either a coke or a bottle of cold water until he got back to his camp so he could fix some tea. He drank a cold bottle of water, and it seemed to hit the spot. It's better to drink water anyways.

My dear Soldier Men & Women
 I want to tell you all I love you and appreciate all you do for our country and people. Because of all that each of you do we have a great country. Everyday you make a sacrifice by being there in other places and countries serving your country and doing your duty. All of you are truly my heroes. I'm sending you my crazy book that I wrote. Maybe you can get a laugh and have some joy while you are all away from home. I thank you all from the bottom of my heart. Wish I could meet and thank each and everyone of you. You all are in my heart and prayers. Hurry on home, God Bless all of you, take care of yourselves.

    Your Friend in Okeechobee,
    Florida Shirley Wildes

P.S. I'm disguised as Joe and my daughter is disguised as Loretta Ann. She's a beautiful girl and has taken up modeling. If you'd like to write please do so.
  Shirley Wildes
  P.O. Box 1146
  Okeechobee, Fl.
   34973-1146

Taking life easy Joe does his favorite hobby of fishing.

Joe fighting with the big fish at the Prairie.

Fishing and thinking about his Loretta Ann.

Joe concentrating on fishing. Waiting for the Big One.

As Joe made it back to camp he parked his car close to the table next to the well. He took his fish off of the fish stringer then put them in a pan full of water. He lay some newspaper on a piece of plywood he found at the camp so he could clean his fish. Before he started cleaning his fish he took some pictures as evidence that he was not telling a big fish tale about catching a lot of them. He would have proof he could show to everyone when he got back to Virginia, but that still might not convince them that Joe was the one that had caught the fish. He must have taken 15 snapshots before he put away his camera. He would have them developed when he went back into town.

Joe started cleaning all his fish, and it took him quite a long time to clean them because he had caught so many. He was proud of his catch let me tell you. He didn't have much of anything go right his way very often, but today it seemed as if he might just have another normal day afterall.

It was one of those times that Joe wished he had a cell phone of his own. If he had one now he wouldn't have to go to the phone booth to call Loretta Ann. He had to call his sweet Loretta Ann to tell her of his fishing excursion. At least to him it was an excursion. He really took everything to heart. He was a serious person when he went about doing something. So to him he had just came back from a great fishing trip.

Joe finished cleaning his last fish, and was glad that it was the last one because he was getting tired. He packed all his fish on ice then went to the little store to get some more ice. He wanted to keep his fish iced down until he got ready to cook them. He had thought about going to one of the stores in town and buying a little refrigerator that would run off his car battery in his car. He probably could buy an adapter to plug into the lighter if the refrigerator didn't have an adapter plug. That would sure be handy to have a little refrigerator then he wouldn't have to keep buying so much ice.

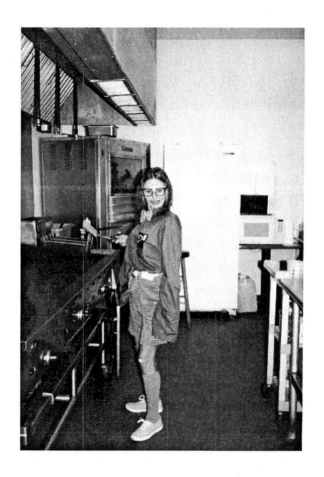

Loretta Ann at Lonesome Dove Café

Chapter twenty three

Inviting Loretta Ann To Lunch

Joe finished everything at camp then went to the little country store. Joe called Loretta Ann from a phone booth at the little country store that was close to the Prairie. He told her that he'd just got back from fishing at the river, and that he had caught a lot of fish. She told Joe that was good that he caught so many. He told her to come out later on today, and he'd fry up the fish, and she could eat out there at the camp with him. She told him she would be glad to come out later on, and if he wanted her to she would help him cook. Joe told her he would wait on her since she was his guest. He told her he'd start cooking when he went back to camp. She told Joe she would be out there around 5:30 because she didn't get off work until 4:30. Joe told her that would give him time to get everything ready to eat.

Joe started telling her all about his stormy night. She told him that was probably why he did so well fishing because after a storm the fish usually bite well. He told her how the wind had blown the big tree limb onto the top of his car. He told her that the limb had also cracked the windshield when it fell, but he had to break the back window out to get into his car because of the size of the limb. The limb covered the sides and top of his car so he couldn't get his doors open.

Loretta Ann told him they only had a little rain there in

town. She told Joe she could see it lightning, and heard it thundering out towards his way. Joe told her he thought that then and there he should have had a cell phone in case something had happened. Joe asked her if she knew a good place to buy a cell phone at in Okeechobee? He told her that after last night he made his mind up to get one because there's no telling what could have happened there in the woods. Joe told Loretta Ann he would buy a phone in a couple of days.

Loretta Ann told him she would show him a good place to buy one at when he was ready. She told him there was a place in town called C.M.A. which stood for "Call Me Anytime." Joe thanked Loretta Ann, and told her he appreciated all her help. He told her he could have used a phone a couple of times already. He told her he sure wanted to be prepared just in case something did happen. Loretta Ann told him that was a good idea having a phone because you never know what can happen. Joe said "yelp, there's a lot of truth in that."

He told Loretta Ann that he slept in his little canvas chair because his cot got drenched from the rain. He told her it was raining so hard that he couldn't even get into his car to spend the night. She couldn't help but laugh at him because he was putting so much expression into telling her what had happened the night before. Joe told her that was a night he'd always remember for the rest of his life. He told her that he'd never been so glad to see when the sun came up and when it was finally daylight there at his camp. He told her he didn't know whether a tornado was coming or what. Joe told her that was the worst weather he'd ever been in during his lifetime. Loretta Ann told him it was beginning to be that time of year when the weather got stormy with thunderstorms, tornadoes, and hurricanes. He told her he could do without all that kind of excitement.

Well, Joe told her he'd let her go and he'd see her at 5:30. He told her he would go back to camp so he could start getting everything ready, and for her to hurry on out as soon as she could. She told him okay, and she would be there as soon as she got through with everything she had to do. When Joe arrived at camp he got the cleaned fish out of the cooler, and salted and peppered them. He put the grease in his frying pan so he could fry some potatoes. Joe peeled 8 potatoes because he wanted to make sure he had enough cooked when he and Loretta Ann sat down to eat. After he finished peeling the potatoes then he rinsed them off, and sliced them up for frying. Joe decided to cook a pot of grits to go with the rest of the meal. He put some baked beans in a pot and spiced them up with bar-be-que sauce, onions, and bacon. He wanted everything to be just right for his lady friend Loretta Ann when she came to eat lunch with him. Joe started frying the potatoes, and started another pan with grease in it to fry the fish in. He put corn meal on the fish along with some other seasonings he'd bought to cook with. Boy, he just hoped that she would be able to eat his cooking.

Joe made a gallon of sweet tea, and put it on the ice he'd bought from the little store. He had everything under control so far. As he let the fish, potatoes, and beans cook he started setting the little eating table with plates, forks, and napkins. Joe wanted to be prepared when he had Loretta Ann there to eat. He wanted everything to be just right for the moment. He finished cooking everything then put it under the little camp cook stove so it would stay warm till she got there to eat. It was good timing on his part because Loretta Ann had made it a little earlier than she had expected.

Joe told her to be seated, and he'd put it on the table. Loretta Ann really loved all the attention that Joe was giving her. She had never been treated this nice before especially by the opposite sex. Of course, Loretta Ann hadn't been one to date or go out so that could be the reason I guess. She told Joe she would be glad to help him if he wanted her to. He told her to just sit back, and let him wait on her. Believe it or not, that's just what Miss Loretta Ann did.

After Joe got everything on the table they just sat there eating their dinner, each one enjoying each other's company. They talked about what day they would go to the phone store so he could get him a phone. Joe asked her if she would like to go out to eat that afternoon when he comes into town? Loretta Ann told him she would really enjoy going out to have dinner with him. He asked her if she cared for anything else to eat or drink. She told him she couldn't eat or drink anything else. She thanked him for inviting her out to lunch. Joe said, "Anytime my little Dovie." Joe's face turned real red because he had shocked himself by calling her that, but she just smiled her big smile at Joe.

Well, when they finished their dinner then they cleaned the table off, and covered up the leftover food. Joe asked Loretta Ann if she wanted to carry some of the food home with her, but she told him she wouldn't eat anything else today. She told Joe the meal was delicious, and the fish were real tasty. She thanked him for having her out to his little camp, and for cooking such a nice meal for her.

Chapter twenty four

The Walk In The Woods

Joe asked Loretta Ann if she'd like to go for a little walk before she had to go back into town. She told Joe she could go for a little while but she had to get back early enough to carry her May Day to do her shopping. She told him everyone had known May Day for so many years that they all called her little May Day. She wasn't really related to her, but she was like family to her anyways. Joe told Loretta Ann he could wash up the pots and pans when he came back from his walk with her.

As they started on their little walk through the woods they both started telling each other about themselves. Before they realized it they had walked quite a ways from the camp. As they walked through a little hammock they both stopped dead in their tracks. They couldn't believe their eyes at what they both were seeing. Right there in front of them a few yards ahead was a mama black bear with 2 baby bear cubs. The little bear cubs were playing and rolling around on the ground. The mama bear was climbing up a tree. As Loretta Ann and Joe walked a little closer they saw that the mama bear was getting ready to rob a beehive that was in a big hole in the tree. They could see the bees flying around the outside of the tree. They thought it was funny that the bear was brave enough to try to get the honey out of the tree. As the saying goes a bear loves honey, that must be true because this bear was bound and determined to get the honey. Joe told Loretta Ann that the mama bear was probably hungry, and maybe she wanted to feed her cubs some honey to. It seemed that at that moment the bear cubs didn't have a care in the world because they were having fun playing.

As the mama bear made her way to the honey, the bees began to circle her because they knew she was after their hive. Before the bear knew it the bees had began to swarm and sting her. At first she only had her mind on the sweet taste of the honey, but as the bees became angrier she had to make a quick exit from the tree. As the bees followed and stung the bear they began to bite and sting the baby cubs as well. Poor little bear cubs they were innocent bystanders.

The mama bear with her bear cubs ran off through the bushes trying to get away from the bees. Joe and Loretta Ann thought the best thing for them to do since the bees were already mad was to get away from their territory before they came after them. Well, as it happened they didn't get away fast enough because Loretta Ann had a bee to fly into her hair, but managed to get it out before it stung her. She shook her head then the bee flew out of her hair straight for Joe along with several other bees. Well, Joe wasn't so lucky, he slapped at the bees therefore making them more hostile than they were already. You should never slap at a bee because they will become very aggressive towards you.

Well, he wound up getting stung on his lip and on his nose. It could have been a lot worse, but the bees flew back towards their hive. They didn't want to lose their honey so they were on guard to protect the hives, and their queen bee. Well, Joe and Loretta Ann managed to get away without more damage from the bees. They knew they were lucky this time for sure. Well, Joe's lip and nose started to swell up really big from the bee stings. Loretta Ann asked Joe if he was allergic to bee stings, but he told her he didn't know. He told her that he'd never had a bee to sting him before. She asked him if he had any meat tenderizer back at camp, and he told her he thought he had brought some from home when he'd packed up his groceries. She told Joe when they made it back to camp she would doctor him up. Joe smiled and told her he would be glad to be her guinea pig.

The two of them started walking back to camp. They were still talking up a storm as they walked along through the woods. Loretta Ann told him she didn't know there were any bears left in Okeechobee because she hadn't saw any until now. She told him that when she was little she heard her Grandpa talk about hunting bears when he was a young man. That was when Loretta Ann told him we never know what lurks out there in the woods. When she said this he told her he just hopes there aren't any Satscwatsh lurking in the woods like the one Runt was talking about. He told her if he met up with a booger like that then he'd be out of there before it made him hurt himself.

Joe started telling her about his neck of the woods up in Virginia. He told her that there were a few bears left up in Virginia where he lived. Joe told Loretta Ann that he didn't hunt because he never had anyone to go hunting with, and that he'd probably wind up getting lost if he went by himself. Besides, he had never even fired a rifle or gun in his entire life. He wasn't a hunter, but he did like to fish though. That was his favorite sport, and he enjoyed it very much. Even though he hadn't been fishing that much.

Chapter twenty five

Loretta Ann Returns Home

Well, Joe and Loretta Ann had made it back to camp, and it was time for her to leave. Before she left she drank a cold bottle of water, and told Joe she hated to leave good company, but she had to head on back to town. Once again she thanked him for cooking her dinner and inviting her out. He told her he would call her later on that evening. Loretta Ann told him she'd be waiting to hear from him.

As Joe walked Loretta Ann to her car, she gave him a little kiss on his cheek. They both turned so red that you'd be able to see them both glow in the dark. Loretta Ann had surprised herself by giving him a peck on his cheek. Joe smiled at her and told her to be careful, and not get lost on her way out of the woods. Loretta Ann told him she wouldn't leave the main road so she would be okay. He told Loretta Ann goodbye then watched her as she drove away going back to her home.

Joe washed up all the pots and pans before he stopped for the day. He put the rest of the leftover food inside his cooler in which he would probably eat on the next day. He threw the fish bones into the garbage, but took the leftover scraps and threw them onto the ground next to the edge of the woods. This way if some of the little critters wanted to eat them they would have something to eat, and not get choked on the bones. After Joe finished cleaning up his little kitchen he called it a day.

Joe took his bath then listened to his little radio for a while. He had a nice day today so he was going to go to bed early. He had enjoyed his fishing trip, and he enjoyed Loretta Ann coming to eat dinner with him. He thought that he was one of the luckiest men in the world right at that moment in his life. He couldn't be any happier than he was right now.

Joe hoped that she made it home safe. He decided he would go into town the next afternoon so he would call Loretta Ann to let her know. He went to bed that night thinking about how he liked it here in Okeechobee. He had made more friends here than he'd made back home. It seemed like everyone here was family to him. Joe didn't like to think of having to go back home. He was more at home here in Okeechobee. Another thing is that he realized he was falling for Loretta Ann. He thought she liked him a lot to.

Joe lay there thinking of something that his dad had once said to him. He told Joe that in good time he would find the right young lady, and when he did he'd better hang in there and not let her get away. Joe's dad told him that's what he did and he didn't let her get away. His mother must have been one of a kind because his dad talked about her like there weren't any other women in the world. He hoped he found someone like that. Joe wished that his dad was still living because he could sure use some advice from him. Well, he went off to sleep, and was dreaming away. Joe was dreaming about Loretta Ann kissing him on the cheek. He dreamed that was the beginning of a new relationship. If only Joe could be so lucky.

Well, Joe's peaceful sleep didn't last that long because he was awakened by a loud crashing noise. He shined his flashlight towards the direction of the noise. There he saw his ice chest turned upside down. He went over to pick it up when he saw 4 big raccoons sitting there by his ice chest enjoying the fish he had leftover. They were really helping themselves to the free meal. Joe startled the raccoons by yelling at them trying to scare them off. The raccoons bowed up like they were going to attack him. Joe stepped back a few steps, and the raccoons started eating again not paying any attention to him. The raccoons weren't really that wild because they always ate the corn out of the feeders that Donald put in them for all the animals to eat.

Joe knew one thing and that was the raccoons didn't like being disturbed while they were eating. He was like that himself because he didn't like to be interrupted while he was feeding his face either. Joe backed away slowly to leave the raccoons in peace so they could eat. He knew they would probably leave and go back to the woods once they got their bellies full. He wanted to be careful around any wild animal because there's no telling what they could be capable of when they become scared or cornered up.

Joe wasn't about to take any chances because he had always heard that raccoons carried rabies, and if they bit you then you could get the rabies to. He sure didn't want to get the rabies like a mad dog. The raccoons made a growling noise when he started to walk away from them. Joe then left them there to eat the rest of the food because he knew they must be hungry to get into the ice chest. He built a fire so he could sit and watch the raccoons eat, but they soon left when the fire began to burn really bright. He picked up the ice chest, and cleaned up the mess the raccoons had made. Joe sat by the campfire a little while longer then went to bed.

Joe lay there in his little tent listening to the hoot owls making their hooting sounds up in the trees. He enjoyed hearing the sounds that the owls were making. He began to hear all the other night birds singing in the tops of the trees. Peace and serenity was what Joe was enjoying right now. It was only a few minutes and he was fast asleep again. This time he only woke up once more during the night. That was when a tree limb broke and fell onto the ground. Joe got up to see what it was and then returned to bed again.

Joe woke up a little later than he usually did the next morning. He felt well rested once he got to go back to sleep during the night. He got up then washed his face, brushed his teeth, and finished grooming himself to go to town. He drank a can of juice, and ate a little cake for his light breakfast that morning.

Well, he had to stop by the little store to call Loretta Ann to let her know he would be coming into town today. He decided to stop in at the Dove to see how everyone was doing. Joe hadn't saw anyone from there in a few days, and he missed seeing them. He might even grab him one of those big burgers while he was there to.

It was still early, but he wanted to ride down to the river before he went into town. Joe also wanted to look at some property that he saw on his way back to camp the other day. When he had gone fishing he saw a couple of for sale signs, but didn't take the numbers down.

Joe stopped at the place where he had gone fishing, and he noticed the river was rough today. The wind was blowing quite hard but it wasn't that hot yet. Joe thought it would probably rain today because he wanted to spend the day in town hanging out with Loretta Ann. Afterall, he didn't have that much time left on his vacation. He still had a few weeks left, but to Joe that wasn't enough time to get all he wanted done accomplished. He drove on a little farther past the river to look at the property he'd saw that was for sale. It had a lot of trees on it, and on the sign it read 10 acres for sale. Joe took the numbers down, and thought he would call the people that had it for sale later on.

He also had several other things he wanted to do while he was in town. He had to buy some more ice and drinks. Joe left to go back by his little camp. He stayed around a little while then he headed on over to the little store to see if he could get Loretta Ann on the telephone. He called her house, but only her answer machine picked up. He left her a message that he would see her at 4:00 today. He decided to go grab him a bite to eat at his little café before he went on to town.

Chapter twenty six

Joe To The Rescue

As Joe was driving along on his way to the Dove he noticed a dairy cow next to the fence in the pasture by the highway. He saw that the cow was hung up in the fence, and was struggling to get free. Joe stopped his car, and immediately got out to try to free the cow from the barbed-wire fence. He also noticed that the cow was trying to have her baby calf. Joe knew he had to try to help her out of the fence somehow. He noticed the cow was having a difficult time so he had to see if he could help her. He wasn't an animal doctor, but he'd saw a cow have a calf on an educational t.v. program one time before.

Joe stood there at the fence trying to figure out just what to do. He didn't want to startle the cow, but he knew he couldn't leave her there tangled up in the fence trying to have her calf. He went to his stationwagon to see if he had any kind of pliers that he would be able to cut the wire with. Well, Joe in fact had a small pair of cutters, and he might be just able to get them to work. It might take a while with such little cutters, but surely he would get the job done.

As he started to climb over the fence he hung the seat of his shorts on the barbed-wire fence. Joe tried to get loose, but the more he tried to free himself from the wire the more entangled he became. He was hung up there on the fence trying to think of a smart approach to his situation, but couldn't come up with anything except to tear a big hole in his shorts. It was either he'd have to do that, or he'd have to take his shorts off, and that wouldn't be too good of an idea at all.

Well, while the poor cow was there tangled up in the fence, she would have to wait a little longer for Joe to be able to help her. He was all tied up at the moment to, but that wasn't anything out of the norm for Joe. After he managed to free himself of the wire, he did help get the cow untangled from the barbed-wire fence. Joe however had a large torn place in the seat of his shorts, but he could get another pair in town when he went by the store.

Once he got the cow freed from the fence she lay down on the ground to give birth to her calf. Joe knelt down by the cow to try and calm her down while she tried to have her calf. He rubbed the old cow on her neck, and tried to calm her down by talking to her. He petted the old cow, and said, "Okay girl everything will be alright." Not that the cow actually understood him, but it did seem to calm her down. The cow knew Joe meant her no harm because he was petting her with a kind hand. He waited there with her for 1 hour and a half then finally out popped the calf. He sort of got queezie at his stomach when this happened. It didn't bother him seeing it happen on t.v. but it got to him in real life. The next thing that happened was really comical in a way, but you wouldn't really believe that it happened. Joe got dizzy headed then passed out cold.

Well, as it went the old cow finished cleaning up her baby calf after she got to her feet. The cow then hobbled over to Joe, and licked him in the face as if to thank him for all the help and kindness he'd given to her. As the cow's old rough tongue licked him across his face he immediately woke up. Not only did the cow wake him up but she almost scared the daylights of him. When he opened his eyes, and saw the cow standing over him he was startled at first when he saw the big animal.

Joe finally realized the cow was just thanking him so he got up from the ground. The cow even let him pet her because she was use to people at the dairy milking her, and feeding her everyday. The cow's little calf finally managed to stand up, and it took one step then fell to the ground. The little calf got back up on its wobbly little skinny legs, and just stood there trying to get its balance. The mama cow went over to the little calf, and licked it in the face. Then the little calf started nudging its mother hunting for some milk. As it turned out the calf was a little girl calf.

Joe walked over to the little calf, petted it then said, "I got to go little girl." He petted the mama cow, and said, "Take care of your little girl, little mama." Joe headed back towards the fence, but climbed under it instead of trying to go over it. He didn't want to get hung up in the fence again.

Joe then started to leave to go on his way to town once again. He hoped he didn't have anything else happen on his way in. Well, he did make it to the café okay. As he got to the café he saw that it was jammed pack full of people again. He went on inside to find him a seat to sit at so he could get a bite to eat before he went into town. Joe saw Runt coming over to his table to take his order. When she got there she asked him what had happened to him. He told her it was a long story. She took his order then told Joe she would be back to hear his story when she got everyone situated at the other tables. He told her to take her time because he wasn't in a hurry.

Joe went to the bathroom to wash up his hands, and to use the bathroom because he hadn't went all day. He looked at himself in the mirror, and saw that he had a big long red stripe across his face. He couldn't figure out what it was on his face. He hadn't scratched himself in any way that he could remember. Joe washed his face and hands after he used the bathroom then went back and sat at his table. Runt had set his tea on the table while he was gone. He sat down then started drinking his good cold glass of tea. He was sure thirsty, and his stomach was beginning to tell him it was time to eat because it had began to growl again.

As Joe sat there at his little table waiting for his food to arrive he thought about the old cow and her little calf. He wondered what would have happened if he hadn't been there at that moment to help her get free from the wire she was tangled up in. It seemed that Joe was in the right place at the right time this time. He felt pretty proud of himself at the good deed he had done for the day, but felt like a wuss because he passed out.

Well, he finally got his jumbo hamburger, fries, baked beans, and cole slaw. Now he could chow down, and enjoy himself for a while. After Joe had almost finished his lunch Runt came over to his table to see if he needed anything else. He told her he was okay right now, but he did want to take a big glass of tea to go when he was ready to leave.

She told him she wanted to hear what he'd been up to lately because she hadn't saw him in a while. Joe told her he'd been doing a little fishing, and he'd even had Loretta Ann out to eat dinner with him when he cooked up the fish he had caught. Runt told Joe "You go boy." then he smiled, and told her they were just good friends. Runt laughed, then told him, "Yea, we know." Joe told her about how he'd helped the cow out that was in trouble today. She told him that not many people would have stopped to do what he did. She told him that was very kind and humane of him to help like he did.

Joe told Runt he was meeting Loretta Ann today so she could show him what store to buy his cell phone from. He told her that he was taking Loretta Ann out to eat later on in the evening at a little restaurant around the lake. Runt told him she knew the restaurant he was talking about because she goes there to eat with her family once in a while. She told him she always ate the oysters and shrimp there because they were really good.

Joe told her he wasn't sure what he would have until he saw what they had on their menu. He told Runt he just hoped the food was as good there as it is here at her little café. She told him he would like the food there to. Joe finished his lunch then paid for his meal so he could get on into town. It wouldn't be much longer until he had to meet Loretta Ann, and he had to go buy another pair of shorts or pants because the ones he had on were tore up. He told Runt he'd see her later on. She told him to hurry on back when he got the chance. He almost forgot to get his big cup of tea to go. He wanted to have something to sip on during his wait for Loretta Ann.

Joe made it into town a little earlier than he expected so he took his time when he went in to buy himself a pair of slacks. He bought a new shirt while he was there because the one he had on had dirt all over it. When he paid for his clothes then got permission from the manager to change his clothes before he left. He left the store then went to the post office to wait for Loretta Ann. As he arrived at the post office he went to the pay phone to call and let her know that he would be there waiting for her. Loretta Ann still must be at work because her answer machine picked up again. Well, he left her another message telling her he was at the post office, and he hoped to see her soon.

Chapter twenty seven

The Pistol Phone

As he sat waiting at the post office, here came Loretta Ann driving up right on time. It was 4:oo right on the dot. Joe followed her in his car to the phone shop. The phone shop wasn't too far from the post office. As they pulled up in front of the shop they parked their cars then went inside to look around. They walked all over the store looking at many different kinds, colors, and shapes of cell phones. Joe saw one that caught his eye. He picked it up then asked Loretta Ann what she thought of it. The cell phone was shaped like a pistol. She told him that it looked like the real McCoy all right. She told him it might not go pow pow, but she told Joe that it might just fool some one into thinking it was a real pistol. There was a carrying case that came with the pistol phone that looked like a real holster.

    He walked around the phone store, but didn't see any other phones that he liked. Joe paid for his cell phone and case at the counter where the salesman was. He asked the man to set his phone for him so he wouldn't have to do it. Joe wasn't sure he could set it right anyways. The man told him it was ready now, and all that he would have to do was turn it on and dial the number he wanted to call. He thanked the man for setting his phone, and told the man he just hoped he could get used to using the cell phone.

    Joe and Loretta Ann left the phone shop then went to eat dinner at the restaurant close to the lake. Loretta Ann ordered catfish to eat. Joe thought he'd try some shrimp and oysters to eat. While they were waiting on their meals to get cooked, they began talking about the crazy week they each had. Loretta Ann said it had to get better because it couldn't get any worse.

Joe asked her what she'd be doing this Friday, and she told him she had Friday off, but she had to work Saturday. She told him she'd like to go over to Ft. Pierce to the beach when she had the whole weekend off. He told her he'd like to go to, but she would have to show him the way over there.

Joe told her they would go to Lake Placid on Sunday if she would like to, and they could mess around over that way to see all the sights in the little town. He was a little familiar with Lake Placid especially the tall tower there, but he didn't go into details with Loretta Ann. He had been embarrassed enough from the elevator incident.

Joe told her they would get up early to go over there so they would have the whole day to drive around the little town. She told him to call her to let her know what time they would leave later on. He told her he would call her later on before he went to bed. Loretta Ann told him she enjoyed the evening very much. Well, they finished their meals and now it was once again time for them to go. Joe told Loretta Ann he enjoyed it and they would have to go out again sometimes. She told him that was a date.

Well, Joe thanked her for all her help in getting him situated with a cell phone. Loretta Ann told him now you don't have any excuse not to call me. He told her he didn't have to have any excuse to call her, but she'd probably get tired of him because he would be calling her all the time. Loretta Ann told Joe not a chance. Well, since each one had driven their own car, they parted company each one going their separate way.

Loretta Ann drove on back to her house in town. However, Joe had about 23 miles to drive before he would reach his little tent in the woods. He didn't seem to mind though. He had plenty of time to get there anyways. He was driving back to camp just as happy as a lark. He had a real good day today. Everything seemed to go like clockwork. So we can chalk another one up for Joe.

Chapter twenty eight

Joe's Broke Tooth

Joe was heading out of town when he spotted a little ice cream parlor. It had a drive by window and he couldn't resist stopping to get him an ice cream to eat. Since he didn't have any dessert at the restaurant he would have one now. Joe ordered himself a large hot fudge sundae with extra walnuts to eat. He sat in the parking lot in his car, and ate his sundae. He was in a hurry to get back to camp so he could call Loretta Ann on his cell phone before she went to bed. Joe was eating his ice cream sundae so fast it was a wonder that he didn't get choked on the walnuts. He was really chomping down on the walnuts when all of a sudden his tooth broke. Joe only had a couple bites more left of his ice cream sundae then it would be gone. Well, he didn't want to throw it away because it tasted so good so he tried to eat the last little bit that was left. That was the wrong thing for him to do because as soon as the cold ice cream hit the broken tooth it sent instant pain to Joe's tooth. He had to stop eating the ice cream then because he was in so much pain. He was in so much agony he could hardly think straight.

Well, Joe knew he had to find something to stop his toothache. He threw away the rest of his ice cream then went to a little convenient store to buy some toothache drops. He would be in a lot of pain if he couldn't find any.

Well, Joe was lucky because the little store had one box of toothache drops left on the shelf. He bought the toothache drops then headed on his way to his little camp so he could get himself doctored up.

Joe would have to suffer with the toothache until he got back to his camp. As he was turning off of the main highway going to his camp his pistol cell phone started ringing. It was none other than the sweet Loretta Ann. She asked him if he was at his camp yet, and he told her he was getting close to it. Loretta Ann told him to call her back when he made it to his camp because it wasn't good to drive and talk on a cell phone. She told him she didn't want him to have a wreck trying to talk to her while he was trying to concentrate on his driving. He told he would call her back shortly then said good-bye and hung up his phone.

As Joe turned into the road leading into his camp he suddenly stopped his car because right there in front of his car stood a big buck deer. He couldn't believe his eyes at what he was seeing. The deer was really big, and had a big set of antlers. He thought how beautiful of an animal the deer was. He sat in his car watching the deer eating some grass. The deer didn't seem to pay any attention to him at all. Joe blew his car horn, and this startled the deer. The deer darted off into the woods running away with his white tail sticking straight up in the air.

Since it was dark he knew that he had to get a campfire burning so he would be able to see what he had to do in his little camp. Joe stopped his car then went over and started building a campfire before he called Loretta Ann back. He put some toothache drops on his aching tooth then went and sat down in his little chair so he could sit and relax while he talked to her. He took his little pistol phone out of its holster that he was wearing on his side. He decided now was the time to call her.

He dialed Loretta Ann's number, and it came up on the little face on the phone screen. Joe sat there and waited for her phone to ring, but it wouldn't ring. Well, he dialed it again and waited for her phone to start ringing, but it just wouldn't ring for him. Well, he got up and started to walk to a different spot around the camp. Joe had remembered what the man in the phone store had told him about how sometimes the phone wouldn't get out in certain areas.

Well, his phone had a dial tone as clear as a bell, but he couldn't seem to get his Loretta Ann on the phone. He was beginning to get a little perturbed. Now you know Joe is a patient man, but I guess he doesn't have that much patience if something tries to interfere with him trying to contact his Loretta Ann.

Joe went to his car to get his cell phone manual. He read the manual for several minutes to make sure he wasn't doing anything wrong on his phone. Well, as it turned out he was forgetting to hit the talk button. That was the reason why he couldn't get her phone to ring. Joe thought out aloud, you have to mash the talk button dummy. When he did this he was like a kid with a new toy because Loretta Ann's phone commenced to ring.

He waited patiently for her to answer the phone, but he was let down when her answering machine picked up, and said for him to leave a message. Joe was disappointed when he didn't get to talk to his Loretta Ann. Especially, when he called her for the first time on his phone. Well, anyways he got to hear her voice on the phone from her message. He left her a message that he would call her again later on.

Joe knew she was at home when she had called him earlier. She told him she always went to bed by 10:00 p.m. She told him she had to get up so early to go to work that's why she turned in early for bed. Joe would just have to keep trying till he reached her by phone. Surely she would be home sooner or later. Well, he waited for another 35 minutes then he dialed her number again. This time Loretta Ann answered the phone in person. He wanted to talk to her about going to the Water Park in Sebring on Friday. It was a new attraction that was called Wet Willie's Water Park. Joe was sure she would go, but he wanted to make sure before he got his hopes up. When she picked up the phone it just about tickled him to death when he heard her say hello.

Joe was glad that it was Loretta Ann that had answered instead of her answering machine. He told her that he had been trying to call her, but he just got her answering machine instead. She told him that she had to go to the store to buy some milk for her coffee in the morning. She also went to the post office to check her mail since she hadn't done it earlier today. Loretta Ann asked him what was he was doing at his camp right now? He told her he was sitting by the campfire he had built waiting for his toothache to go away. She asked him how come his tooth was hurting, and he told her he'd stopped at the little ice cream parlor to get him an ice cream sundae. He told her he was eating some of the walnuts in it, and his tooth broke off. Joe told her he bought some toothache drops from the little store in town, and had put some on his tooth when he came back to his camp. He told her his toothache was almost gone now.

As Joe kept on talking to Loretta Ann he had completely forgot about his toothache altogether. It seemed that she was good medicine for him. He hadn't given his toothache anymore thought since he started talking to her. Maybe the toothache drops stopped the toothache pain, but we won't know for sure will we? Oh well, at least his pain is gone so that is a good sign. Joe would have done almost anything to stop his tooth from hurting like it was. Well, since his tooth had quit hurting he began to tell her about the Water Park over in Sebring. Joe told her he had talked to a man that had worked over there at the park when it was being constructed. The man was named Harry that had been talking to him about the Water Park. Joe had met the man when he had stopped in at the little café in town earlier during the week. The man had started talking to him when he went into the café to grab him a quick bite to eat. Harry had told him that he'd worked there for five years, but he'd have to find another job since the park was completed. Harry told him that he was considering a job offer that was made to him to help at the park. He had told Joe he didn't know if he would like that kind of job or not. He had told him he guessed that he could try it to see if he would like it.

Joe told Harry that he had only had one job since he had been out of high school. He told Harry that he had worked at the same job so long that he didn't know if he could work any place else or not. He told Harry that he did put in some job applications since he had been in Okeechobee. He told him that he really liked it in Okeechobee, and he would like a change if he found a job similar to his. He told Harry he thought he could adjust to a new job if he did find one.

Joe had told Harry about his camp at the Prairie. He told Harry he was staying at the Wildes camp until he had to go back to Virginia. Harry had told him he knew the Wildes very well. He told him he had known them for many years because they all grew up together in Okeechobee. Joe told Loretta Ann that Harry had told him he was raised in Okeechobee. Joe told her that he told him he'd met a girl named Loretta Ann, and she was from Okeechobee to. Loretta Ann was flattered when Joe told Harry that he'd met her. He told her that Harry had laughed and told him it was a small world after all. He told Joe he had known Loretta Ann all his life since they were from the same town.

Joe didn't tell Loretta Ann that Harry told him that she didn't have much to do with anyone, and that she stayed mostly to herself. He told her that Harry knew her friend May Day, and had told him that she looked out for her. Harry told him the same thing that Loretta Ann told him that May Day didn't have any family left in Okeechobee. As he told her what Harry had told him it made her feel good that people knew she took care of May Day. She told Joe she always made sure that the little May Day got to town, and she made sure that she was okay.

She told Joe that he must have had quite a conversation with Harry at the little café in town. Joe told her he'd invited Harry to come out to the camp if he had the time. She told him she had known Harry all her life, and he was a good person to know. She told Joe he would probably come out to see him at his camp because Harry did a lot of camping himself. She told him if Harry told him about the Water Park then it must be a nice place to go to. She told Joe if he wanted to go this Friday then they would take a trip over to Sebring. She wanted to know what time they would be leaving to go over there, and he told her they might as well get an early start so they could spend the day over there.

Well, as he talked to Loretta Ann he made another mistake. He had got up out of his chair to get him a cold bottle of water to drink because he had gotten a dry throat from talking so much. He hadn't given his tooth one thought at all. He turned up the bottle of cold water, and once he got a mouth full of water he thought holy cow my tooth. He developed an instant toothache once more. Loretta Ann knew that he was in agony by the way he was carrying on. She told him she would call the dentist for him tonight if he wanted her to. Joe told her that maybe he would be able to make it through the night then he'd call the dentist to see if he could get an appointment to have his tooth fixed the next morning. He told her he would put some more drops on his tooth then he'd go to bed.

Chapter twenty nine

Dr. Wayne Bojangles

Joe asked her if she knew a good dentist in town that would see him tomorrow, and she told him she knew one that Runt's dad had been going to. Loretta Ann told him she would find out who the dentist was, and would call him back first thing tomorrow morning. Joe thanked her for helping him find a dentist. He told her he would sure go if he could get an appointment.

She told him she never went to the dentist, but she knew she needed to. She told him she wasn't too fond of any doctors that had needles. Joe told her he hoped he could get an appointment with the dentist, or maybe get worked in even if he had to wait. She told him there were several dentists in town so he should be able to get in to see one of them.

Loretta Ann told him she would call Runt at her house right now instead of waiting until morning. She told him she would call him back in a few minutes, and he told her he'd be waiting. Loretta Ann called to see if Runt was at home, and she was. Runt asked her what had she been up to lately? Of course Loretta Ann had to fill Runt in on every detail about her and Joe. She told Runt about him breaking his tooth and that he needed to see a dentist. She asked Runt if she knew the name of her dad's dentist. She told Loretta Ann she sure did because she went to him to have her teeth cleaned and fixed when she needed it done. Loretta Ann asked if he was a good dentist, and Runt told her he was the best in town that she had been to the others, and she liked him the best out of them all.

Runt told her to hold on and she would give her his telephone number so she could call him. She told Loretta Ann to call him tonight because he always answered his calls. She told her that was why he was such a good doctor because he is so dedicated to his profession. Loretta Ann told her thanks so much for her help. Runt told Loretta Ann anytime, and for her and Joe to come see them at the café when they were out that way. Loretta Ann said she would be stopping in soon. They each said good-bye to each other then Loretta Ann called Joe back with the information she'd got from Runt. She told him the dentist's name was Dr. Wayne and gave him the dentist's phone number. Joe asked what the dentist's last name was, but she told him everyone just called him Dr. Wayne. She told Joe she thought his last name was Bojangles.

Loretta Ann told him she knew he had a dog by the name of Bojangles, and that's why she was sure his last name was Bojangles. Joe told her that was an odd name to be a person's last name, but he'd heard people that had a nickname of Bojanles many times before. Loretta Ann told him he could probably call Dr. Wayne tonight, but Joe told her he would wait until morning because he hated to bother anyone at night. She told Joe she was sure the doctor wouldn't mind if he wanted to call him.

She told him that Dr. Wayne had another profession also, but it had started out as a hobby. She then started telling him how everyone came about calling Dr. Wayne, "Bojangles the Groomer." Joe asked her why they called him a groomer when he was a dentist. She told him that Dr. Wayne had gone hunting one time many years ago by himself in Colorado. As Dr. Wayne was walking along in the woods he found an old sheep dog that was almost dead. The old dog had a rope around his neck that had got hung on a log in the woods. The rope was already chewed into and was very short, but had managed to get the dog tangled up on the log. Apparently someone had the dog tied up, and he had managed to chew the rope into and got away. Then unfortunately he became tangled up in the woods.

Dr. Wayne got the rope loose then took his pocketknife and cut the rope off the dog's neck. The old dog was in bad shape, but he managed to lick Dr. Wayne's hand. This I guess you could say was the only way the dog could thank Dr. Wayne for his help. After Dr. Wayne cut the rope loose, he noticed that the rope had made a deep gash in the old dog's neck. He picked the old dog up, and carried him back to his camp so he could try to doctor the poor animal. He had some medicine you could use for cuts on human beings, but didn't know how it would work on the dog.

Well, Dr. Wayne told the old dog it surely couldn't hurt him anymore than he was already hurt. After Dr. Wayne doctored the old dog up he took his pocketknife out, and started to cut off the old dog's shaggy, matted, hair that was full of sticker burrs and knots. The old dog's hair was so long over his eyes that the dog couldn't even see at all. Dr. Wayne thought no wonder the dog got hung up on the log because he couldn't see where he was going.

Well, the good doctor kept cutting the old matted hair off in different spots on the old sheep dog. Little did he know he was creating a design that would be the beginning of his new hobby when he went back home? One thing Dr. Wayne observed while he was trying to groom the old dog's hair was that the old sheep dog was beginning to enjoy the trim he was getting. After he had finished grooming the dog he was fascinated at how the dog looked. It was as if the dog had been transformed into a new one.

Dr. Wayne drove into town to see if anyone knew who owned the old sheep dog, but they didn't know who the dog belonged to. Since the dog had no collar on it would be hard to find the owner. He thought to himself that no one needed an animal if they were going to keep him tied up on the end of a rope all the time. While the good doctor was in town he bought some dog food for the dog then he carried him back to his hunting camp in the woods. He started calling the old dog by some names to see if he would come to any of them. The only name the dog seemed to pay any attention to was the name of Bojangles. He told the old dog he could have the same name as his since Bojangles was the name the dog responded to.

Well, Dr. Wayne stayed and hunted for another week then he returned home again. Since he had taken the dog into town with him several more times and couldn't find his owner he ended up taking old Bojangles home with him. He carried Bojangles everywhere with him. It was as if the two of them were inseparable. When Dr. Wayne went on hunting trips he always carried Bojangles along to. Old Bojangles turned out to be quite a good hunting dog believe it or not. He did have a good life with Dr. Wayne because he lived 12 more years after Dr. Wayne brought him home to stay with him. Old Bojangles passed on one day to the dog heaven in the sky. Dr. Wayne was real attached to Bojangles, and never got another dog after Bojangles passed on.

Loretta Ann told Joe the whole story how Dr. Wayne became to be known as Bojangles the Groomer. Once he had made it back off of his trip with the old dog he'd found it was then everyone looked at the dog's unusual haircut. Dr. Wayne's haircut on old Bojangles had caught everyone's eye when he brought the dog home with him.

Everyone began to ask Dr. Wayne questions of what had happened to the dog, and who had cut the dog's hair like that. Once he started telling his story about the old sheep dog then to Dr. Wayne's surprise he began receiving phone calls asking if he would groom their dogs hair like he had groomed old Bojangles hair. It didn't take long after his story got around about old Bojangles that everyone wanted to get him to groom their dogs just like he had groomed old Bojangles.

Dr. Wayne had no experience at all when he started grooming everyone's dogs in town, but the more dogs he groomed the better he became at his grooming profession. Dr. Wayne always told anyone that came to him to have their dogs hair groomed that he wasn't a professional groomer, but no one seemed to care because they just liked the strange unusual looking haircuts Dr. Wayne could come up with.

He had so many requests for him to groom their dogs that he'd built up a good clientele of people that kept coming back each month for him to groom their dogs. Since dentistry was his number one profession he had to slow down on the hobby of grooming so many dogs. He only took on so many to groom each month, but the people that had their dogs groomed by him also became his patients at his dentist office. It was as if he was becoming somewhat of a celebrity in his little hometown of Okeechobee. Dr. Wayne was always talked about, but only in a good way.

Joe was really enthused by the story Loretta Ann had told him about Dr. Wayne. He told her he would call her in the morning when he got to go to the dentist to have his tooth fixed. He told her that if he had to he would wait all day long to get in to see Dr. Wayne. Joe had already taken a liking to this man and had never met him yet. He told her that anyone that was that kind to an animal had to be a good person.

Well, Joe and Loretta Ann talked a little while longer then told each other goodnight because it was getting very late. She told him she had to go to bed so she could get her beauty sleep. He didn't say anything else to Loretta Ann except goodnight and he'd call her tomorrow. He knew she was a good person, and that's what made her beautiful inside and out.

Joe went on to bed after he drank the bottle of water through a straw he'd found in his car. Joe knew as long as the water didn't hit his broken tooth he would be able to drink water until he got it fixed. He also carried a bottle of water to sit by his little cot so he wouldn't have to get up during the night as he always did. He was asleep in no time at all, and his toothache had gone completely away. Joe's toothache medicine had done the job in getting rid of his toothache. He didn't get up anymore that night. Maybe the toothache drops had helped him to sleep so peacefully since he'd put drops on all his teeth to make sure his mouth was numb so it wouldn't hurt him anymore that night. He rested really well during the night until the next morning.

Chapter thirty

Appointment At The Dentist's

Joe woke up early the next morning. He started getting ready in case he got an appointment with the dentist. Joe waited until eight o' clock then he called Dr. Wayne's office and told them what had happened to his tooth. He asked if he would be able to see the doctor today, and the lady in the office checked with Dr. Wayne to see if he could see Joe. As it turned out Dr. Wayne was able to work Joe in so he could see him. Joe called Loretta Ann and told her he had managed to get an appointment to see Dr. Wayne. He told her that if he was still in town by the time she got home from work that he would come by and see her. She told him to call her to make sure she was at home. Joe told her he was going to go on to town because the dentist said he would work him in early so he could get his tooth fixed.

After he finished talking with Loretta Ann he drove to town to the dentist's office. Joe found it without any problem at all. Joe parked his car in front of the office then went inside. After he got signed in he sat down in the waiting room and began to read a magazine. Joe was a little nervous, but he knew that he had to get his tooth fixed and that is all there was to it. Well, he had to wait until several people had got to see the dentist then he finally got to go in to see Dr. Wayne.

Joe was told to sit in the big chair, and Dr. Wayne would be right in to fix him up. He sat in the dentist chair looking out the glass window that was in front of the chair. He saw some squirrels running back and forth across the top of the roof on the building next to Dr. Wayne's office. He watched the squirrels as they ran back and forth carrying what seemed to be nuts in their mouths. Joe thought it was comical that the squirrels were such busy bodies.

Well, his thought about the squirrels soon ended because in walked Dr. Wayne. He greeted Joe with a big smile, and asked him how he was feeling. He told Dr. Wayne he felt fine, but he had a broken tooth that needed fixing. Dr. Wayne told him to open his mouth so he could check his teeth. Joe opened his mouth so wide that you could have put a whole grapefruit in it. Dr. Wayne took his little dentist tool and began to tap each one of Joe's teeth. He asked Joe if he had any problems with any of his other teeth other than the one that was broke. He told Dr. Wayne he never had any of his teeth to bother him because he always took care of them.

Dr. Wayne told him he wished everyone took care of their teeth because it would save them a lot of pain in the long run. Well, Dr. Wayne asked Joe if he was allergic to any kind of medicines, but he told him not that he knew of he wasn't. Well, Dr. Wayne checked his broken tooth and told him he would be able to fill the tooth so he wouldn't have to pull it out. He told Dr. Wayne that was okay so go ahead and do what he had to do.

Well, he sat there in the chair after Dr. Wayne had given him a shot to numb his mouth. Joe had to wait a few minutes for the shot to make his mouth go numb so he wouldn't feel anything when the doctor had to start drilling on his tooth. It didn't take too long for the shot to have its effect on him. His mouth was so numb he couldn't feel anything at all. Matter of fact he was drooling all over himself and didn't even realize it.

The nurse came back into the room and handed him some kleenex tissues so he could wipe his mouth. Joe tried to talk to her, but couldn't because his tongue was even numb. Dr. Wayne came into the room again, and asked him if he could feel anything when he started to drill on his tooth. He could only shake his head no because he was too numb to speak. Dr. Wayne talked away to him while he was filling his tooth. All he could do was to nod his head at Dr. Wayne.

Well, it didn't take Dr. Wayne long, and he had him all fixed up once more. He told Joe to call him later on to let him know if his tooth bothered him or not. He shook his head yes to Dr. Wayne then shook his hand before he left his office. Joe paid the lady up front in the office then left to go back to the Prairie. It was too early for him to go by Loretta Ann's house. His whole face was still numb so he didn't want to stop anywhere until he got his feeling back. Joe looked at himself in the mirror, and noticed his tongue was sticking out of his mouth. He had to stop at the red light in town, and as he looked around he saw a lady looking at him sort of funny. He noticed the lady in the car at the red light next to him was looking at him. All of a sudden she stuck her tongue out at him. He knew the lady probably thought he was sticking his tongue out at her, but it wasn't him doing it on purpose. It was the medicine that had him out of control.

Joe took off from the red light in such a hurry that it caused his old stationwagon to squeal its tires. He didn't know his old car even had enough power to do that. Well, as it happened he had to try to explain his situation to a policeman that happen to be parked on the side street at the red light. The policeman had heard Joe squeal his car tires. He knew he was in trouble now, and knew he would have a heck of time trying to talk to the policeman. As the policeman walked up to the side of his car he asked Joe to see his driver's license and registration. He handed him the papers that he asked for. The policeman told him to get out of his car. Joe did as he was told to do by the policeman.

The policeman asked him what he was doing in Okeechobee, and he tried to tell the officer. The officer thought he was drunk by the way he was talking. He told Joe to walk in front of his car and put one foot in front of the other one. He did this without any problem. The next thing the officer had him to do was to blow in the Breathalyzer machine. Well, this was a problem for Joe because he was so numb he couldn't blow in the machine at all. All he could do was to slobber on the Breathalyzer machine. He was so embarrassed he could hardly stand it.

Well, the officer asked him what was the matter with him, but Joe could only do hand signals trying to show the officer he'd just got his tooth fixed. He motioned to the officer for a pencil and paper so he could write out a note for the officer. The officer understood this and gave him a pencil and paper. Joe wrote that he had just left Dr. Wayne Bojangles office because he had to have a tooth fixed. He wrote that his face and mouth is numb so that's why he can't talk right.

Once the officer read Joe's note he let him go because he told him the medicine probably had an effect on his driving. He asked him if he would be okay to go home by himself, and Joe shook his head yes. He took his licenses and papers then left to go on his way back to the Prairie. He waved at the officer then drove off.

It was later on in the afternoon before he got the feeling back in his face. He stayed at camp because he was afraid to try to go anywhere else. After Joe had all the feeling return to his mouth he fixed himself something to eat and drink. It was getting about time for Loretta Ann to get off work so he thought he would call to see if she had made it home yet. Well, he was just fixing to hang up the phone because the answering machine would be picking up anytime. Before he hung up he heard her saying hello on the other end of his phone. She asked how his appointment turned out at the dentist's office. He told her he had to get his tooth filled so it wasn't hurting anymore. Joe told her he liked Dr. Wayne because the dentist didn't hurt him at all when he was fixing his tooth. She told him she had heard he was a good dentist.

Joe told her about the episode at the red light, and he didn't think she would ever stop laughing at what had happened to him. He told her that the policeman probably thought he was a mad dog at the way he was drooling all over himself. Loretta Ann told him he had better start taking a pen and paper with him when he had to go anywhere at all. He told her he guessed he might as well because you never know what will happen next.

Joe asked Loretta Ann how her day went, and she told him it

was just a typical day at work, and nothing out of the ordinary happened today. She told him she didn't have as much excitement as he had in his life. He told her he hoped no one had his luck because they would be in bad shape if they did. Loretta Ann told Joe if he didn't have all the excitement like he had he would probably be bored to death. He laughed at her, and told her he probably would.

Chapter thirty one

Wet Willie's Water World

Well, Joe started talking to Loretta Ann about the Water Park in Sebring again. He asked her if she was ready to go to Sebring this Friday, which was only two days away. She told him she would be ready to go anytime that he was ready to go. She told him she wished she could get off the whole weekend, but it was her turn to take that shift so someone else could have off a couple of days. She told him she didn't mind though because when it was her turn she would have 3 days off to.

He told her some more information about the park in Sebring. She told him that she had heard a little about the park, but didn't know where it was. Joe told her that they would leave early Friday morning so they could be sure to find the park so they could have enough time to enjoy themselves and not have to be in a hurry. She told him that sounded good to her.

Joe told Loretta Ann that the park would probably be easy to find since it was a new attraction. She said that Sebring wasn't that big of a town so they would find it okay. She was glad that he had asked her to go with him to the park. They talked to each other until midnight. They were talking about what they would do at the park.

Joe asked her if she wanted to eat breakfast before they went to the park, and Loretta Ann told him she would like that. Well, they finally said goodnight to each other. He told her he would see her soon. Loretta Ann told him she would be waiting. The two of them were really excited about their trip to the Water Park. The next two days would probably drag by so slow and seem like an eternity to them. Well, at least the date was on and they both had somewhere to go instead of just staying home and moping around the house. It's a wonder that either one of them got any sleep at all the next couple of nights because they both were so keyed up. However, they both managed to sleep through the nights okay.

Joe did have a dream about Loretta Ann, and it was such a sweet dream that he didn't want to wake up from it the next morning. Yes sir, Joe Macoochee was star struck with this fine young lady. Here he is in Okeechobee supposed to be enjoying his vacation on a camping trip. Oh well, I guess since he is enjoying himself what the heck. I guess he can have his cake and eat it too as the saying goes. What can I say except that Joe and Loretta Ann seemed to be a permanent fixture together?

Well, the big day that they had been waiting for had finally arrived. Joe and Loretta Ann were to go to the new park in Sebring called "Wet Willie's Water World." The two of them were both ready to go at the crack of dawn. They were excited about the day ahead that they would be spending together. They stopped at a restaurant in Sebring to eat breakfast before they went to the Water Park. They were both so excited that they could hardly eat any breakfast at all.

When they left the restaurant to find the park it wasn't that easy to find afterall. They had to stop three times at different places to get directions of how to get there. They did however manage to get there early before the park even opened up. Joe and Loretta Ann weren't too familiar with the little town of Sebring, but they would soon find their way around it okay because they were there the whole day.

The two of them went into the park as soon as it opened its gates. It was a nice morning with a cool breeze blowing and the clouds were just a little overcast. Maybe for once Joe would have a normal day. Well, the gates opened up for everyone to enter the park so in they went to start their day at Wet Willie's. He paid for their entry fee to get in. Loretta Ann was going to pay her way, but Joe told her to put her money away because it wasn't any good here. She looked at him sort of strangely, but finally it registered in her head what he meant by it.

Joe saw a water ride that looked like a barrel lying on its side that you had to sit in. He asked her if she would like to go on it, and she said sure why not? It went through a dark tunnel then it started to spin around and around. Loretta Ann started laughing so hard that she could hardly hold herself upright in the seat. Joe sat in his seat not saying too much while he was spinning out of control. He wasn't use to riding on rides that much, but before the day was up he didn't have any problems going on them all. Loretta Ann took him on every ride there in the park several times. She was a completely different person there at the park. She was having herself one heck of a great day. Joe had got into it himself because he had someone to enjoy the day with. The both of them were having the time of their lives.

He was laughing at Loretta Ann because she was so funny the way she laughed. The two of them were having so much fun they were acting plum crazy. They were acting like two kids at the park. After they got off the water barrel ride that they had rode for the fifth time they got on a type of swing that swung them up and down and around and around. By the time they got their feet back on the ground they were a little drunk from all the swinging around on the swing. They decided that they would take a break from riding the rides for a few minutes. They had been going wild getting on one ride after another, but they couldn't help themselves.

Joe and Loretta Ann went to sit under a big tree at a

table to rest for a while. He asked her if she would like something to drink, and she told him she would like to have a soda to drink. Joe saw a drink machine a few feet from where they were sitting at so he walked over to it to buy them a drink. He put in 50 cents to get a drink, but the machine kept his money and wouldn't give him a drink. Well, he put 50 cents more in to see if he could get a drink this time, but the machine kept his money again. Well, Joe tried the third time to get a drink from the machine and got one this time.

Once again he put enough money into the machine for another drink, but the machine kept his money again. Well, this time Joe hauled off and kicked the machine so hard that it almost tipped the drink machine over backwards. Luckily enough it fell back into its place. He was glad of that because he didn't want to get into trouble about the drink machine.

As it turns out though the drink machine spit out a can of soda. He took the drink from the machine then started to go back over where Loretta Ann was sitting. Just about that time the drink machine spit out another can of drink. He took the can of drink thinking that he had really gotten his money's worth by now, but it didn't happen that way because the machine kept giving drink after drink after drink. He was stacking the drinks up in a little pile next to the machine. Boy he was getting embarrassed because there were a lot of people stopping, and watching him at the drink machine.

Joe ended up stacking up about 40 drinks or more before the machine quit spitting them out. He politely took his two drinks then went to sit down with Loretta Ann at their table. He was trying to act coy because he was so embarrassed about what had happened. Loretta Ann thought that it was comical about the machine going crazy, but Joe didn't think so because he felt like a dummy. Anyway, they drank their sodas then walked around the park before they went on anymore rides.

They were just having a grand old time together. It seemed like the two of them were just like two peas in a pod you could say. They rode many more water rides in which they both got drenched from the water splashing all over them, but it was nice since the day had warmed up so much. They both looked like two drowned rats by the end of the day. Well, as it was getting late they knew they had to return back to the little town of Okeechobee.

Joe and Loretta Ann talked a mile a minute on their way back to Okeechobee. They both told each other how much they had enjoyed the day at the park. Well, they arrived back in town and Joe took Loretta Ann by and bought her a drink before he took her back home. She had to get up in the morning to go to work so he knew he wouldn't stay at her house very long.

He was tired from his day at the park, and so was Loretta Ann. Neither one of them would have to have anyone to rock them to sleep. By the time their heads hit their pillows they would probably be out like a light. Well, it turned out to be a good day for the two of them at last. Joe dropped her off at her house when they left the little dairy queen where he bought her a drink.

He told her that he would see her the next following Friday morning so for her to be ready to rock and roll. She told him she'd be sitting D.O.R. which meant dead on ready. Neither one could hardly wait till Friday got there so they could see each other again. They were both really keyed up about going to the beach the following weekend. Joe told her he'd better be getting back to camp. He hoped he would be able to find it okay since it was so dark. They told each other good night then Joe left to go back to his camp.

Well, it was getting dark and he wanted to get back to his little camp before it got too late. He wanted to start him a campfire before he went to bed. That way he might be able to smoke the mosquitoes out some more. It seemed they left the camp when he had a fire built. Joe left the main road to turn onto the other paved road that headed towards the camp. He still had to find the dirt road to turn off on. He wasn't sure he'd be able to find it tonight because it was so dark.

Joe knew it turned to the right, but he hadn't seen a sign yet. He drove another 15 miles or so then he came to a dirt road that turned to the right. He was sure this was the right road to turn on, but as it turned out it was the wrong road. As Joe drove along he tried to see if he saw any familiar surroundings, but that was almost impossible because of the dark.

Well, he kept driving on until he saw a sign that had Blue Brothers Harvesting Co. Well, he turned onto a road that he thought was the road to the camp. As it turned out he ended up at a metal gate. Joe knew he had taken the wrong road. As he started backing out onto the dirt road again so he could go back in the direction he'd come from he saw some trees with some orange things on them. He got out of his car, and walked over to where the trees were at. It just happened that the trees were orange trees, and they were full of oranges.

Joe pulled about 10 oranges then put them into his car. Well, nothing has it, but about that time a truck pulled up behind his car. He was worried then because he figured he'd get into a lot of trouble for picking the oranges. Joe walked over to the truck because he saw a big man getting out of it. The big guy asked him what he was doing there on his road. He told the man he was going back to his camp at the Prairie, and had taken the wrong turn he guessed.

The big guy introduced himself to Joe. He told Joe his name was Blue Hopper. Joe then told him his name, and reached to shake the man's hand. Blue shook his hand, and squeezed it pretty hard when he shook his hand. Joe thought he was in trouble if the man got upset with him being on his property. He was just a pip-squeak compared to the big guy Blue. Blue saw the oranges in his car. He asked Joe if he picked them from the tree by the gate. Joe said yes sir I did. He thought to himself, "Well, Joe Macoochee this is where you go to jail." He was really surprised when Blue told him he would like those oranges because they were real sweet when he ate them. He told Joe to get him some more if he wanted to as long as he was going to eat them himself.

Joe offered to pay Blue for the oranges, but Blue told him that was okay not to worry about it. He told Blue he was down on vacation from Virginia. Blue told him he had some kin people up in

Virginia, but he didn't know what town they were in because he hadn't heard anything from them in years. Joe told him he really liked it in Okeechobee because it was so different from the place he lived in.

Blue told him he had lived in Okeechobee for thirty-two years, and had went into the orange grove business. He told Joe it seems that if anyone comes to Okeechobee they get the little town in their blood, and even if they leave they seem to always come back to stay. Joe told him he could understand why. He told Blue he was camping at the Wildes camp at the Prairie, and Blue told him he knew them very well. He told Joe he ate at their café two or three times a week.

Joe told him that was his favorite little café he'd found to eat at. Blue told him they had pretty good food there. After they had talked a while longer Blue told him he'd have to turn around to get back on the right road to go where he was headed. He told Joe to go back to the highway take a right then go 8 more miles then turn on the road that had a little sign that had Peavine Grade on it. That was the right road to take. Joe thanked Blue for the oranges and the directions back to his camp. Blue told him he would be seeing him around.

Well, Joe did find the road okay, and it was exactly eight miles to the Peavine Road. He was glad his speedometer worked so he went exactly the right mileage. He could hear loud noises in the dark as he turned on the dirt road towards the camp. Joe thought how spooky it seemed to be in the pitch-black dark of the night. As he drove along slowly he saw the road that he had to turn on to go into the camp. Boy, he was relieved to be back at his little camp once more. It seemed to Joe that he was at his little home away from home when he was there at the camp.

He made sure he parked his car not too far from his little tent. After he got out of his car he went over to the woodpile to gather up wood for his campfire. Joe always put plenty of wood on his campfire because he wanted to keep his fire going during the night. He knew all the wood was wet from all the rain so he decided to pour some gas on the oak wood to help get it started easier. Joe struck a match then threw it on the oak wood that he'd saturated with gasoline. When he threw the lighted match on the gas he realized he'd poured too much gas because it exploded when the spark hit it. The combustion of the fire went varoom, and almost knocked him down from the gas exploding. Boy, it's a wonder something worse didn't happen. As you know, it seems that if anything could happen to one human being it would have to happen to Joe Macoochee.

    Joe did get a big fire built, and it seemed to get rid of the mosquitoes he saw flying around earlier. The mosquitoes didn't like to be smoked out so they'd disappear until the smoke went away which would be when the fire goes out. He took out a couple of the oranges from his car to eat before he went to bed. He sat down in his little chair by the fire, and peeled one of the oranges. He ate the orange and couldn't believe how good it tasted. It was deliciously sweet, so he couldn't resist eating the other one.

    Joe washed his sticky hands when he finished eating his oranges, and then he sat back down by his campfire. Well, as he sat in his little chair he started to think about the cell phone he'd bought. He hadn't used one that much before so he decided to check his phone out to see what all different features were on it. Everyone else he knew had one so he might as well have one to. He learned how to bring up the menu to find what he needed on different types of information on the phone. It didn't seem all that complicated to use after he got used to using it. Joe however did know how to call Loretta Ann without any problem at all. His finger knew where to do the dialing when he was to call his sweet thang. He had no problem at all doing this feature. He was like a trained robot when it came time to call her.

Chapter thirty two

Joe's Dark Boogery Night

Well, Joe lay his cell phone on the piece of wood next to his chair. He had his fire built, and the flames were blazing high as he sat back in his little camp chair. He was so comfortable in his little chair that he just laid back in his chair and propped up his feet. As he sat there he couldn't hold his eyes open any longer. Joe went fast to sleep without any trouble at all. The only thing was that he didn't have enough wood on the fire so that it would burn all night long like he had wanted it to do.

He was sleeping so sound that he didn't wake up until 2:00 a.m. he probably wouldn't have woke up then, but the mosquitoes were biting him so bad that they caused his legs, hands, face, and arms to sting and itch like crazy. When Joe awoke in the dark he didn't know where he was at. He was disorientated. It was so dark that he couldn't even see his hand in front of his face.

Joe knew one thing for certain and that was he would have to find his way to his little tent somehow, somewhere in the dark. The mosquitoes were eating him alive. He was afraid to try to get up in the dark to try to find his way to his tent. He was afraid that if did get up that he might get lost in the dark, or that he might fall over something and get hurt.

Well, as it went Joe sure couldn't keep sitting there in his little chair the rest of the night or he would have to have a transfusion from the mosquitoes eating him up. Well, he knew it was time for him to get up right then no matter what happens. He knew he would have to be very careful since he didn't even have his flashlight to use.

As he stood up from his chair he extended his hands and arms out in front of him. Joe thought maybe by doing this he would be able to feel his way around better. It was at this moment that he thought he knew how a blind person felt by not being able to see. Joe envied a blind person that was able to motivate about without anyone helping them. He knew he'd never be able to get around by himself if he ever lost his eyesight. Well, at this moment he was blind as a bat because it was pitch black dark and he couldn't see anything at all.

Joe started to walk forward a little then he came to a complete stop because he had no inkling of an idea where he was at there in his little camp. All he knew was that he had just left his little chair he was sitting in, and now he didn't know what direction he was heading in. All he could do was just stumble around in the dark. As he did so, he began to notice all sorts of different sounds. He wished he had a stick or something so he could use it to hit the ground to check what was in his way.

Since Joe had no stick to help guide himself along he just had to make the best of it. Well, he kept walking along in the dark. He finally found something in the dark all right. It was a big tree of some kind and he ran smack into it. He could feel vines or some kind of shrubbery all over the tree. He didn't know what he had gotten into, but whatever it was it had thorns and they were sticking him. He ended up getting tangled in whatever the vines were. He could feel the thorns scratching his arms, legs, and his face each time he moved.

It took Joe a little while, but he did manage to free himself of the vines, or whatever it was that had hold of him. He sure hoped that he didn't grab hold of a snake there in the dark, or he might end up hurting himself trying to get away from it. As he walked a few steps away from the tree he walked right into another bunch of bushes that had a lot of vines in them. He was once again tangled up in some very thorny vines that were sticking him like a bunch of big needles. He couldn't see them, but right at this moment he felt like a pincushion.

Joe only wanted for daylight to get there in a hurry. It was still a very long time until morning would come. Finally, once again he got freed from all the vines. This time when he started to walk around again he went into a different direction. He didn't know what direction he was going in, but it didn't matter he just went. He didn't know if he was going north, south, east, or west. He knew he just had to try to find his little tent or car so he could quit wandering around in the dark woods.

Tired out from wandering in the woods all night Joe Macoochee went to sleep against a log

He took a few more steps then he stumbled over something and fell flat on his stomach. Joe felt around with his hands trying to make out what he'd fallen over. It seemed to him that he'd fallen over a log. It was big so it could possibly be a fallen tree but he wasn't for sure. Joe leaned against the so-called log so he could think of what he should do next. The ground was very hard so he pulled himself up and sat on a smooth spot on the log. He felt like a bump on a log. He couldn't believe the predicament that he was in right now, but with the luck he had it wasn't anything out of the ordinary.

Joe sat there on the log trying to get his bearings, but he was a lost puppy right now. He thought he would try crawling on his knees, and maybe he wouldn't get into any trouble that way. He knew he couldn't just sit on the log the rest of the night because it was too hard, and there were too many mosquitoes around for his comfort. He decided to sit back on the ground because it was a little softer than the log. Joe sat there trying to picture in his mind how he had placed everything in his camp, but only came up with a dud.

Well, he was getting ready to start crawling on his knees when he felt something bump his shoe. Joe jumped when he felt whatever it was bump him. He knew there was something there with him now, and he was no longer by himself. He knew there was a creature of some sort next to him in the dark. He just didn't want to move because he was afraid he might upset the creature, and cause it to bite or attack him.

Well, whatever it was it began to push at his feet. Joe sure hoped it wasn't a dangerous animal because he would be unable to defend himself in the dark. He sat still as he could trying to play dead so maybe the little animal would leave, and go elsewhere. The little night creature began scratching his legs like it was trying to dig a hole. Joe tried to sit still. He was getting very nervous, and it wasn't easy at all for him to sit still.

Lost in woods Joe Macoochee sleeping with head on log.

Finally, the little creature climbed up into his lap. He froze from fear. The little animal seemed liked it weighed as much as a medium sized dog. The little creature climbed up on his chest, and stuck its nose against Joe's face. He couldn't sit still anymore. He grabbed hold of the little animal and slung it away from him. The little animal made a growling noise. Joe couldn't figure out what kind of animal had crawled up on his lap. Whatever it was it had a hard nose and a hard shell that pinched his hands when he threw it off of his lap.

He just hoped the thing ran away after he threw it to the ground. He still had to find his camp in the dark, and he didn't want to tie up with that thing again. Joe still had to crawl around on his knees another two hours before he finally managed to find his tent. He was a happy camper then because he found his flashlight, and now he could see how to get around his camp. Joe went to his car then cranked it up. Since the mosquitoes were so bad he just sat in his car and ran his air-conditioner for a little while. He knew he couldn't run his car all night because it would run hot. Before he went into his tent he turned his car lights on to see if there were any little creatures hanging around the camp, but he didn't see anything. He guessed the creature took to the woods once again, at least that's what he hoped for.

Joe found his bottle of rubbing alcohol so he rubbed some on his mosquito bites to keep them from itching. After he finished putting the alcohol on himself he thought he would go to bed. He had given it some serious thought about sleeping in his car, but he knew he couldn't let some little creature scare him that bad. So off to bed he went. Joe knew he couldn't worry about every little thing because if he did he wouldn't be able to finish up his vacation camping out in the woods. Besides he didn't want to ruin his vacation because it was okay so far.

Joe Macoochee sitting on log thinking things over.

He looked at his watch. It was almost 4:00 a.m. it wouldn't be too long before daylight, but he wasn't going to get up early like he had planned to do. Since he didn't get much sleep he planned to sleep later that morning. Joe lay down on his little cot. He seemed to be real tired, but he knew it was because he hadn't got much sleep during the night. It didn't take long at all for him to go back to sleep again. He was sleeping so sound that he began to snore. He started snoring so loud that he woke himself up.

Well, I guess it just wasn't meant for him to get much sleep, but he could be lazy tomorrow if he wanted to. Joe finally went back to sleep, and he didn't wake up until 9:30 a.m. When he woke up he felt well rested when he did get up out of bed. He got up to go outside to see if he could see any signs of what might have been in his camp last night. All he saw was some holes dug in the ground, and he had no idea of what it could have been. He was sure glad the animal hadn't bit him.

Joe saw the place where he had sat down on the ground by the log. It was quite a long ways from his tent. It was amazing to him that he didn't wander farther into the woods and get lost. He walked around the trees and saw all the spots where he had been. He had just about made it around the whole camp, but fortunately he made it safely back to his tent.

Chapter thirty three

The Port-o-let

Found port-o-let hid in the woods Joe Macoochee so tired he falls asleep in the doorway.

Joe had made his way to the far edge of the woods that night because he saw the vines he'd pulled down from the trees that he had got tangled up in. He thought that he was a lucky man this time. He knew he didn't want to fall asleep in his chair again unless he had a flashlight tied to his hip. He started walking back towards his camp when he noticed something behind the big old oak tree at the edge of the woods. It had green colors on it. As he walked up to it he saw it was a little building of some sort. He walked up to it and opened the door. He could hardly believe his eyes. It was a little port-o-let which is an outside toilet.

Joe couldn't believe he hadn't seen it there in the woods. It was so well camouflaged that he'd been there camping all this time and using the woods for his bathroom. He felt real dumb, but he sure didn't see the well hidden port-o-let there in the woods. Well, this would really be nice now because he wouldn't have to go to the woods taking the chance of getting snake bit when he had to use the bathroom. He had his own facility out in the middle of nowhere. It was just like being uptown with Charlie Brown.

Joe was starting to get a little hungry so he fixed him some breakfast on his little camp stove. He drank almost a whole pot of coffee that he'd made. He hadn't planned to do too much today except maybe to romp through the woods to see if he could find a good pond close by to go fishing in later. He could really use some relaxation, and when he went fishing that was just what he did. He just sat back and relaxed while he enjoyed his sport.

Joe looked at his arms and legs. He had scratches all over him that was probably from the vines. He saw that his legs had red dots on them that looked like the measles, but they were from the mosquito bites. This was the second time he had been attacked by the hungry mosquitoes. He couldn't afford to get bit many more times because he wouldn't have any blood left for the little bloodsuckers. He went to his car and looked at himself in the mirror. It was shocking at what he saw. His face was dirty and he had mosquito bites so bad that it looked as if he had some sort of a disease of some kind. After he saw how dirty his face was it didn't take him long to get cleaned up. Joe shouldn't have worried about it though because he was camping, and you don't have to be a Mr. Clean guy when you're roughing it in the woods. He cleaned up his little kitchen once again then went on his hike.

It was a nice day today. It wasn't hot yet, but at the time it was pleasant. Joe was getting accustomed to the weather here, but he still hadn't got over the weird thunderstorm that had come from nowhere. He wouldn't ever get accustomed to any kind of thunderstorms or tornado weather because it made him too nervous. One thing for sure if he stayed here in Okeechobee for very long he would have to get accustomed to a lot of different things. He seemed to be adapting very well so far.

Joe was ready to get on with his day and enjoy it. Before he left to go on his hike he made sure he carried a canteen of water with him this time. He didn't want to take the chance of being thirsty again because he knew it wasn't safe to drink any other water especially out of ponds or canals.

Joe hadn't walked too far from camp before he found a pond. It wasn't a real big pond, but he knew he would be able to catch fish in a pond that size because they don't have much of anywheres to get away from you when you are fishing for them. Also, they don't get that much to eat in a pond unless they have someone feeding them.

Joe knew if the pond wasn't fished in much, he might have the chance of catching a big fish. He was proud of the fish he had caught in the river and at the lake. He was beginning to turn out to be a good fisherman since he had been down here. Joe had done well on his fishing trips so far. Well, he started to walk on his little hike into the woods. He looked at his watch to see what time it was because he only wanted to walk around for 2 or 3 hours then he'd go back to camp, and fix his lunch. Maybe later on today he might just take a ride into town to pick up a few more items he needed to get.

Chapter thirty four

Poison Ivy Itch

There was so much that Joe wanted to do while he was here in Okeechobee. He just didn't know what he wanted to do the most of first. He was having a wonderful time on his vacation even if he had run into trouble along the way, but what the heck that's what made it challenging. Well, it had started to warm up pretty good now. He was beginning to break out into a sweat, and he hadn't been walking that long. As he walked along he felt his arms and legs begin to itch. Joe began to scratch his itch, but it didn't help any. He thought it was because the sun was coming out, and it was getting hotter. He decided to head back to his little camp.

He would come back later on one day, and fish in the little pond he'd found today since he knew where to go. If it wasn't too late when he came back from town he might come fish a little while because it would be cooler. Well, he made it back to his camp. He took a wash cloth, and wet it from the water out of the pump. It seemed to help his itching a little bit, but as soon as he dried his arms and legs off they started itching all over again. He couldn't figure out why he was beginning to itch all over his body now. He'd never had anything like this before except when he had the chicken pox when he was a little boy.

Joe took some alcohol and rubbed it all over himself to see if it would stop his body from itching. Well, when he put the alcohol on his itch it set him on fire because he had scratched himself raw. All he could do was to get under the cool water of the hand pump to try to make the burning stop. Boy, he didn't know what to do now because he had never had something like this to happen to him before. He started itching again so bad that he could just imagine what a poor flea bitten or mangy dog felt like when they had to scratch their itch. This itch he had was driving him crazy. He knew he had to get some medicine for it so he could be at ease. Well, he thought he'd better get on into town to the drugstore to see if he could find something to stop the itching. He would ask the pharmacist if he had anything for an itch. Surely there would be something at the drugstore that would give him some relief. There just had to be something he could buy to help him quit itching. Joe got ready then he grabbed him a bite to eat which was only a sandwich.

He left his little camp then headed to Okeechobee to seek help at the drugstore. He sure hoped that maybe someone would be able to assist him in some way. It didn't take him but a few minutes till he came to the little town of Okeechobee. Of course, he was driving faster than he usually did because he was in such agony from itching from whatever he had.

Joe made his way to the drugstore in town without any problem. He knew his way around the town pretty well now. He parked his car in front of the little drugstore then walked inside. He saw the pharmacist filling out medicines in the back of the store. As he walked up to the counter he waited for the man to wait on him. Joe stood there looking at his arms. He noticed that they were beginning to have blisters all over them. He was beginning to get worried now.

Finally, the man came over and asked him what he could help him with. Joe told the pharmacist that he had developed an itch, and he didn't know what it was or where he could have gotten it from. The man asked him if he had got into any kind of spray or chemical. Joe told the pharmacist that he hadn't been into anything he knew that would hurt him or anything that he was allergic to. He told him that he was camping in the woods, and had a bunch of mosquitoes bite him. The pharmacist told him mosquito bites wouldn't cause him to have blisters like he had coming up on his arms.

The pharmacist laughed then asked Joe if he had got into any type of vines while he was in the woods. He told the pharmacist about his little episode the other night. He told the man that he had got lost in the dark and had got entangled in some bushes and vines with thorns. The pharmacist told him that he had the symptoms of poison ivy.

The pharmacist knew when he saw the blisters on his arms that it wasn't from the mosquitoes. Joe told him the blisters had come up a few hours ago. The man asked him if he had any on his legs. He rolled up his pants legs, and his legs were full of blisters to. The man told him he had some salve that he could buy. He told Joe to use the salve and if the rash hadn't left or gone away in the morning he should see a doctor.

Joe thanked the pharmacist then he left the drugstore. He took the salve he'd bought at the drugstore, and when he got to his car he read the directions so he made sure he used it like he was supposed to. He sure wanted to get rid of his rash in the worst kind of way. So far as he knew he wasn't allergic to anything so maybe it would help him get rid of the itch.

Joe thought he'd go to a café in town to eat him a bite of lunch then he would go back to his little camp so he could doctor his rash. He was itching so bad he could hardly stand it. He knew he had better hurry up and get himself doctored. If he kept scratching himself he wouldn't have any skin left to doctor. Well, he had to stop and find a bathroom to go to so he could put the medicine on his rash. He was itching so badly that he couldn't wait till he made it back to his camp. Once he got the salve opened he rubbed it all over his poison ivy then he felt more at ease. What a relief the medicine was to his itching.

Chapter thirty five

Coot's Place

Well, Joe drove on the other side of the little town to find the café he had saw the other day. He remembered the name because it sounded so different. As he drove along he saw the little place. It was called Coot's Place. It wasn't a very big café at all. There were some motorcycles parked out front along with some trucks. He parked his car, and went into the little café.

As he walked inside he noticed some men playing pool. There were six pool tables inside the café. People were playing pool on them. Joe had played pool a few times, but he wasn't a pool shark that was for sure. He walked by the people playing pool, and went over to a booth in the corner of the café and sat down.

Joe noticed the little café looked something like a sports bar. It had a big t.v. screen on the wall by the bar. It was a neat little place. He noticed that the menu was on the table so he picked it up to see what he wanted to order for his lunch. He was really hungry right about now, and he wanted something good to eat.

Joe couldn't believe the different meals that were on the menu. This little café had probably 100 different choices to choose from. He kept looking over everything that was on the menu, but just couldn't decide what to order to eat. He thought that there was just too much to make up his mind up about to eat. There was anything from cooter (turtle), frog legs, gator tail, fried turkey legs, chicken, or just about anything you could even think of that you wanted to eat. There was even beef tripe on the menu. In case you don't know what beef tripe is it is the stomach of a cow. You fix a batter and fry it in hot grease until it is golden brown and crunchy then you have got something good to eat.

There was a little dark haired waitress that came over to Joe to get his order, and she greeted him with a howdy-howdy, and a big old smile. He told her hello, and started talking to the waitress. He asked her what was the house specialty. The waitress which by the way had Coot written on her shirt told him everything on their menu was the house specialty. Joe asked her if she was the owner, and she told him she was the one and only.

Coot asked him if he was new in town? He told her he was just vacationing for a while at the Prairie. He told Coot that he really liked Okeechobee, and might consider moving down here if he could find a good job. He told her he had been in Okeechobee a few weeks, and he was enjoying his stay very much. He told her that he was camped out at the Prairie right now. Coot told him they had a lot of people come to Okeechobee to camp out and go fishing at the lake.

She asked him where he was staying at, out at the Prairie? He told her he was staying at the Wildes camp. Coot laughed, then told him that was her mom and dad's camp that he was staying at. He asked her then you and Runt are sisters, am I right? She laughed again, and told him "Yelp, Runt's my sister." He told her he knew she looked like someone he knew, but he had not figured it out yet. He told Coot that he ate out at the Lonesome Dove all the time, and it was his favorite place to eat.

Coot told him that her sister was a good cook, and that her brother Bubba was also a good chef. She told him he would get to eat some of Bubba's cooking because he was the chef here at her place. He asked her how many brothers and sisters she had? She told

Joe there were four girls and one boy. She had another sister named Tabitha, and one named Jamie. She told him that Jamie helped her at the café along with her brother Bubba. She told him that she had opened her little café when she graduated from high school. Joe asked her about her other sister Tabitha.

Coot told him her sister Tabitha was the president of the bank here in Okeechobee. She told him that her sister had worked there so many years at the bank that she had made the president there. She told him that her sister had worked very hard to get where she was at. Coot told him that all her hard work had paid off though. Joe told her that it was a small world after all. Well, she told him I had better take your order or you'll be starved to death. Joe laughed, and told her you sure got that right. He started off by ordering a glass of sweet tea to drink. When she brought it back to him he gave her his order. He ordered the wild man's plate. It had cooter (turtle), gator tail, frog legs, catfish fingers, and it came with cole slaw, potato salad, baked beans, and hushpuppies. When he got his plate of food he couldn't believe his eyes. The plate was stacked up so high with food that he knew he couldn't eat all of it. He just thought he would get him a doggy box, and carry some back to camp with him to eat later on.

Well, as it turned out he ate every single morsel of food on his plate. When he started eating, the food was so good that he couldn't stop eating until everything was gone. Coot came back to his booth and asked him if he wanted anything else to eat or drink? He told her he would probably have to be carried out when he got ready to leave to go back to his camp. Joe told her that everything was delicious. Coot thanked him, and told him he had better try some of their gator pie, but he told her he just couldn't eat another bite. He told her he would try some of the gator pie the next time he came in.

Well, Joe sat there in his booth watching the people play pool. The little café was beginning to get crowded so he got up to pay for his meal at the cash register. He saw Coot coming to the register to take his money for his meal. She told him to hurry up and come back now, and he told her he'd see her soon.

Joe noticed a newspaper on the counter by the cash register, and asked if it was for sale? She told him it wasn't for sale, but he could have it because she had an extra one so he could keep that one. Joe told her thanks, and took the newspaper with him to read later on. He had wanted to look at the land ads to see how much property there was for sale in Okeechobee. He told her to give his compliments to the chef because the meal was very good. She told him to wait a minute then he could tell Bubba the chef himself in person.

Coot went into the kitchen and Bubba came back out with her so he could be introduced to Joe. He shook Bubba's hand and told him he sure could cook a mean meal. Bubba told him thanks, and he's glad that he enjoyed it. He told Bubba he had met all his family except his sisters Tabitha and Jamie. He told Bubba and Coot he hoped he could meet them before he went back home. He told them that all of their family seemed nice. They told him once again to be sure to come back again before he went back home.

He told them he would be seeing them again. He told them they really had a nice café. Joe then told them good-bye, and he'd see them later. Just as he started to leave to go out the door a young blonde haired girl was coming into the café. It was Jamie coming to work. Coot told him to wait a minute before he left because she wanted him to meet her sister Jamie. He looked at her kinda of puzzled because she had told him Jamie wasn't there at the café yet. He then realized the girl he'd opened the door for was Jamie Coot's other sister. She introduced her sister to Joe, and told her that Joe was staying out at their parents camp at the Prairie.

Jamie smiled and told him she was glad to meet him. She told him not to hurry off, but he told them that he had to get back to camp. Well, he left the little café to go back to his little camp out in the woods. He thought of how many people he had met since he had been in Okeechobee, and so far all of them were very nice. Joe was thinking about the Wildes family, and how lucky they were to have such a big family. He wished he had brothers and sisters, but he was his parents one and only number one son. He guessed once they saw him they didn't want anymore. Now, I'm just pulling your leg because they would have had a house full of children if it had been meant to be. He was a good kid growing up, and he was never any trouble at all. I guess since Joe was an only child you could say he was well protected, and for that he was blessed to have parents that cared so much.

Chapter thirty six

Back at Camp Prairie

Joe once again was at his little camp. He was sort of thirsty from eating his lunch so he got himself a soda to drink. He poured it over some ice into a mug he'd brought with him on his trip. He forgot to bring the lid that went to the mug, but the mug kept his drink cold anyways because it was insulated. He thought he would lie on the little hammock to take a little nap. He was so lazy right now because he'd eaten another big meal, and he was filled to the gills again. He took a few more gulps of his drink then sat it on the ground next to the hammock. He was very content at this moment. Joe was resting so peacefully on the little hammock.

Today had turned out to be such a beautiful day. The breeze was blowing ever so gently through the trees. The tree limbs were moving just enough so that the leaves were making a soft rustling sound as the limbs swayed back and forth from the gentle blowing breeze. Right now Joe was living the "Life of Riley" again. He heard several owls making their hoot owl sounds. He even saw them flying around in the trees. They seemed to be trying to figure out what he was I guess because one of them flew and landed on a tree limb over his head. The owl didn't seem to be scared of him at all. The owl just seemed very curious at the man lying in the hammock. The owl just sat there on the limb looking him over very carefully.

The owl started to hoot at him, and then Joe tried to make a hoot owl sound back at the owl. The owl sat on the limb overhead looking down at him. The owl kept turning his head from side to side as Joe made the sounds. The old bird probably thought that Joe sounded like a sick owl because he wasn't making the hooting sound very good at all.

Finally the old bird flew away to the other trees where the other owls were at. He probably went to let the other owls know about the strange creature in the hammock. As Joe watched the trees swaying back and forth his eyelids got so heavy that he couldn't hold his eyes open any longer. Well, as it happens Joe was sleeping peacefully once again.

The owls flew back in the tree over Joe's hammock once more. They sat there fluffing up their feathers and cleaning themselves like all birds do. They made some more hooting sounds, but he didn't wake up. The owls couldn't seem to budge him at all since he went to sleep so they flew away farther into the woods.

Joe Macoochee was sound asleep right now without any cares at all. He slept probably an hour then he woke up. He picked up his mug to drink his soda to get himself wide-awake again. For some reason he was still thirsty. He always ads salt to everything he eats so that's probably why he couldn't get enough to drink.

Joe was gulping down his drink and as he got to the bottom of his glass he could see something in the bottom of his mug. Well, whatever it was it didn't look too good. He finally realized that it was bird droppings that fell into his mug from the owls that had been sitting overhead on the limb. He didn't want to think of what he had just dranked because he had a weak stomach.

Well, Joe had just realized he hadn't itched at all since he had left the café. He thought the salve had done the job on the poison ivy. Little did he know, but the salve would only last a few hours then it would be itch time again. He knew one thing, and that was he had never itched so much in his entire life as he had with the poison ivy.

Joe knew he'd have to be more careful about what kinds of bushes and vines he got into. He looked around at his little camp, and saw what a mess it was in so he started to tidy it up. After a few minutes he had his camp organized once again. Well, he thought he would call Loretta Ann later on in the evening to see what she had been doing. He loved it in the woods, but he was a little lonely there by himself not having anyone to talk to during the day.

Joe decided to take his little pan bath while it was warm. He didn't want to take one at night because it was cooler. He took his bath, and changed into some different clothes because his other ones were pretty dirty. He played his car radio for a while to listen to the news. There wasn't much happening on the news so he turned his radio off. He was getting a little restless so he messed around his little camp some more.

He got out his playing cards then started to play solitary again to pass the time away. Joe played cards until dark and actually beat the king quite a few times. After he tired from playing cards he ate a can of boiled peanuts, and snacked on some peaches. Since it was getting pretty late now he decided he better call his sweet Loretta Ann. Well, he didn't have any luck trying to call her so he just went on to bed and called it a day.

He made up his mind to get up in the morning and cook something there at the camp. Joe had been on the go all day long so he was ready to get some rest. He drank a bottle of water because he couldn't handle anymore soda. He went on to bed without a care in the world. The wind had picked up and was blowing a lot harder than it had in the afternoon. He hoped he wouldn't have more bad weather tonight. Joe went to sleep almost as soon as his head hit his pillow. He didn't even get up during the night at all because he was tired from his day. He just wasn't accustomed to all the physical activity he'd been involved in lately. Joe woke up early the next morning. He looked at his watch and it was only 5:15 a.m. so he dozed back off to sleep.

When he got up the next morning he washed his face the first thing to start with. Joe wanted to get himself awake so he could get motivated enough to move. So after he washed his face and combed his hair he then brushed his teeth. He didn't like to brush his teeth much, but always did because that was his father had taught him to do when he was a little boy. His dad always told him to take good care of his teeth or he wouldn't be able to eat. Since he was just a little boy his father's word stuck in his mind from that day on. Joe loved to eat so he made sure he took very good care of his teeth. He was still half-asleep, but he always brushed his teeth the first thing in the morning so he wouldn't forget. He had to rinse the toothpaste out of his mouth, and instead of laying the tube of toothpaste on the table he stuck the tube of toothpaste in his back pocket. Joe also rinsed his mouth out with some mouthwash so his yuk mouth would be no more. Well, he had finished grooming himself so he was ready to face the music you could say.

Since it was early he decided to get himself a little something to eat. He always tried to eat a little something even though he wasn't that hungry. Joe fixed a pot of coffee on his little camp stove and had a little cake to eat. When he finished eating his cake he decided to take something out of his cooler. He did this so it could thaw out so he could fix it for lunch later. He didn't really know what he wanted to eat for lunch. Since he had just finished eating he didn't want to think of food at that moment. That's like the old saying goes, "Don't buy groceries on an empty stomach, or you'll buy the store out." The other saying is, "`Buy groceries on a full stomach then you won't buy so much," and there's a lot of truth in that to. I've been there and done that you could say. Since Joe didn't have an appetite right then he just reached in his cooler and pulled out the first thing he got his hands on.

He ended up taking out some chicken he had in his cooler. It would take a long time for it to thaw out before it could be cooked. Joe would wash the chicken once it was thawed out then he could prepare it to cook. It would be ready to cook in a couple of hours. He thought about trying to cook on the open campfire but changed his mind. He might end up turning everything upside down so he'd better stick to grilling on the grill.

Joe stayed around his camp that day since he didn't have to go to town for anything. He gathered up some more wood to burn at night when he built his campfire. He enjoyed the outdoors more than he did indoors. He had messed around camp all that morning fixing his little camp up so he would have everything in place. He looked at his watch, and it was 11:30 already. He accomplished most of the things he needed to do around his little camp. He always liked to be as organized as he possibly could be, but what the heck he didn't have any set time limit to do anything. Well, it was time for him to get everything ready to start cooking again.

A couple of hours had passed by since he had put the chicken in water to thaw out. Joe checked to see if the chicken had thawed out so he could put it on the grill to cook. The chicken was now ready to be marinated to cook. After he finished marinating the chicken he decided to put it on the grill. He was going to cook grilled bar-b-que chicken, bake a couple potatoes inside tin foil on the grill along with some green beans. He started to cook some pork and beans, but changed his mind because he didn't want to be gassed up for his date when he saw Loretta Ann. Every time he ate pork and beans he stayed too windy for at least 4 days. So he decided to play it safe and not eat any porkers today.

While he was waiting for the food to cook on the grill he decided to get out his deck of playing cards again. Joe took his little canvas chair to sit in while he played cards at the little wooden table. He started playing solitary once more, but soon tired of playing cards. While he was waiting for the bar-b-que to cook. He was trying to find something to do to kill time. He just ended up walking around his little camp because he didn't want to leave his food unattended like he did once before. That one time had taught him to keep his eyes on his cooking or it could turn out to be a disaster. He checked on the food on the grill, and it was cooking slowly like good old bar-b-que should be cooked. His mouth began to water when he started to smell the fumes of the bar-b-que. He could hardly wait till the food finished cooking, but that's what he'd have to do because he sure couldn't eat it raw. Joe fixed up his little table with napkins, paper plates, and forks so he could dig in as soon as the food got cooked. He had eaten a skimpy breakfast, and he was beginning to get hungry now. He guessed it was because he kept smelling the food cooking on the grill, and that's what made him so hungry.

Joe would be the first one to the table to eat. Of course, since he was the only one there he would be the last one up from the table to. I know I'm getting to be a wisecracker am I not? It was another hour before he finally sat down to eat his lunch. Boy, it was worth the wait because it tasted so good. He ate so much bar-b-que chicken that he felt like he was going to bust wide open. Joe had gnawed the chicken bones so clean that they wouldn't have been worth throwing them to the dogs. Matter of a fact a dog would have been insulted if he had thrown him the chewed up chicken bones. He sat there just enjoying life in the woods after he had finished his meal. He was letting his food settle I guess. That's better than saying he was just too lazy to move. We know which part it really was though.

Joe Macoochee looking at BBQ grill

Joe Macoochee checking out BBQ grill

Chapter thirty seven

Resting In The Hammock

Joe finished drinking his coke then headed for the little hammock hanging between the oak tree and the tall cabbage tree. He thought he'd just take a little catnap for a while. I reckon he needed the rest since he had his belly full. Afterall, he was entitled to a crazy lazy vacation if that was what he wanted. He had worked hard to get the vacation time he so much deserved.

As he sat down carefully on the hammock swing he lifted his leg up to help him get balanced so he could lay back onto the hammock. As you guessed, Joe wasn't very coordinated at all. He fell over the other side of the swing and hit the hard ground with a loud thud. It's a wonder he didn't bust wide open from all the food he'd ate for lunch, but he stayed together that time. Joe hit the ground so hard that it actually knocked the breath out of him. When this happened he had to lay there on the ground for about 10 minutes in order to get himself together to try it again. Joe managed to get his breath back again, and he managed to get onto the hammock the next time. He was very careful because he didn't want to fall down again on the hard ground. Joe still had the tube of toothpaste in his back pocket. He had forgotten to take it out and put it back with his toothbrush and grooming stuff. The toothpaste exploded in his back pocket when he fell flat on the ground out of the hammock. He had no idea that the toothpaste had got all over the back of his shorts. Well, Joe not realizing anything had happened to his clothes was in for a surprise later on.

Joe lay there in the hammock swing looking up into the trees, and there were the squirrels again running and jumping from limb to limb in the tip-top of the trees. He enjoyed watching the little creatures running around in the treetops. The little squirrels scurried around in the trees like Joe scurried around on the flat ground. He loved watching the wildlife running about all over the place. He thought how well balanced the little squirrels were as they jumped from tree to tree. He wished he could be as balanced as the little squirrels, but he knew that was impossible. He wasn't well balanced at all as a grown man because he was such a klutz, so couldn't you imagine him as a squirrel?

Joe lay there in the hammock swing quiet as a mouse. He didn't like to move around on the hammock too much because he had fallen out several times because of his balance not being very good. He still didn't give up trying though, and you can say that's what I liked about him. He just wasn't a quitter, and that was good. Joe growing up without any brothers or sisters to help him along learned he had to make judgments on his own as a child. If he did something he wasn't supposed to then that meant he would have to face all the wrong consequences alone. When he had to face his dad that was enough punishment for him. His dad always tried to steer him in the right direction, and to teach him right from wrong. Joe was a normal guy with only good thoughts in mind.

Joe thought to himself that he could just lay in the little hammock, and never get up. He knew he shouldn't have eaten so much, but it was too late now. He'd overstuffed himself once more. He was trying to let all the food he'd

Joe Macoochee dead to world sleeping in hammock swing

Joe sleeping in the hammock swing

Asleep in hammock. Joe Macoochee gets some rest

eaten settle down because he could hardly move. He was just enjoying himself while he could. He knew now what he'd missed all these years by not getting out and enjoying life more. He knew he wouldn't just stay home and work on his vacation anymore. That's what he usually did each year when his vacation time came around. Joe always found enough stuff to do to keep him busy when he was at home. Matter of fact he worked harder at home when he was off than he did at his job. He made up his mind from now on he would enjoy his vacation time to its fullest. He had the best time of his life since he'd been here in Okeechobee so he knew next year when he got his vacation he wouldn't be hanging around the house that was for sure. He thought everybody could start calling him "Wandering Joe" because he would be on the road again.

I guess Joe had a case of layzidus right now if you know what I mean. His eyes were getting real heavy, and he couldn't hold them open any longer. He had as you guessed it went to sleep again. He seemed to be sleeping a lot during each day especially after he ate. Boy, he was sleeping so hard that he began to snore. He sounded like he was pulp wooding with a chain saw. Man, I'm telling you that Joe was sawing some logs. Of course, that's a figure of speech just like everyone uses here in Okeechobee. It was so peaceful there in the woods. He looked like he was in "Hog Heaven", as he lay there in the hammock asleep.

The wind was blowing a little today, but some bad looking clouds began to move in again. It sure looked as if it was going to be another day of bad weather. The day had started out pretty as a picture, but you never can really tell what old Mother Nature has got in store for you. It started to thunder a long way off, but you could still tell by the rumbling sound that the bad weather was on its way.

Even with the sound of the thunder and lightning far off in the distance, and the wind blowing harder Joe didn't wake up. He kept sleeping very peaceful in his little swing. Joe at that moment didn't have a care in the world. He was just enjoying his sleep. His swing began to move a little because the wind was starting to blow much harder now. It was beginning to sprinkle rain, and this woke him up from his sleep. He was somewhat in a stupor because he was stumbling around about to fall. If anyone saw him this way they would think that he was drunk or either drinking. After he got his bearings once again he realized bad weather was approaching.

Joe ran over to his car and moved it to the little clearing close to his tent because he didn't want anymore tree limbs to fall on it. He wanted to be able to get into his car out of the weather if it got too bad. He remembered the stormy night he been through, and he wanted to be prepared this time.

Joe couldn't believe that the weather had gotten so bad since he'd dozed off to sleep. He hurried quickly from his car to his little tent. He sat there wondering if the same stormy weather was back again. He wasn't sure if he should go back to his car, or if he should just stay put where he was at. Well, he just remained inside his little tent to tough it out. As it turned out the rain and wind didn't take long to pass over. As the weather became calm again so did Joe.

Joe's fire had gotten rained out, but he would light up another one when it got dark. He couldn't see any use in building another fire now since he wouldn't be cooking anymore today. He did make sure he rounded up a lot of wood for later on when he lit the fire back again. One rule he had developed since his camping out was to keep his fire burning all night if at all possible. This way he felt a little safer when he could see, and when he had to get up during the night.

Joe decided to give Loretta Ann a call to see if it had rained any in town, and to see what she had been doing. Loretta Ann told him it hadn't rained at all in town today. He told Loretta Ann he'd had some good old bar-b-qued chicken

Joe Macoochee fell out of hammock and hung toe in the netting of the hammock

he'd grilled today. He told her he had eaten so much that he almost made himself sick. Loretta Ann laughed and told him it must have been really good if he almost foundered himself like that. She told him she only had a couple of tube steaks for her lunch with some fried potatoes. He asked her what kind of an animal did a tube steak come from, and she laughed. She told him it was just another name for a hot dog. Joe then said, "Oh, I guess I haven't ever heard a hot dog called that before."

Joe felt like he was kind of dense sometimes, but it was a different place he was in right now. He hadn't gotten use to all the slang terms that he'd heard the people using, but before he goes back home I'm sure he will. He didn't ask anymore questions after he'd embarrassed himself. If he did have anymore questions to ask he'd do it at another time.

Joe told Loretta Ann he'd be glad when they got to go to the beach. She told him she could hardly wait. Loretta Ann said she sure hoped the weather would be okay. Joe told her that maybe it would turn out to be a nice weekend when they went to the beach. Well, Joe and Loretta Ann told each other bye for now. He told her he'd talk to her later on. She told him okay, and she would call him back when she came back home from town. He told her he'd keep his ears open for her to ring his bell.

Well, Joe started back doing his little task of picking up firewood. After he finished he sat down to relax and drink a cold bottle of water. After all, he'd worked up a thirst from the little bit of work he'd done. As he sat there drinking on his bottle of cold water he began to think of what they would do the weekend when they finally get to go to the beach. He was really looking forward to spending that day with sweet little Loretta Ann.

Joe couldn't believe how fast the days seemed to fly by so quickly. He had plenty of sick time built up at his job, but had never used any of it. He was thinking that if worse came to worse he could always get an extended vacation if the need be by using some of his sick time up if he had to, but he didn't want to have to play sick when he wasn't.

Joe was about to go to the port-o-let John to take his nature break because it was getting that time of day when he always took his constitution. He was sure glad that Donald & Shirley had a potty port-o-let to go to when you had to use the bathroom. Now he wouldn't have to go to the woods anymore thank goodness. Since there was a bathroom there he no longer had to worry about hiding in the bushes either, especially when he was using the bathroom. He didn't like the idea of getting caught with his pants down like he had in the tower elevator in Lake Placid.

Well, nothing else would have it, but his sweet Loretta Ann called him back like she said she would on his cell phone. She asked him what he was up to now, and he didn't really want to tell her what he had to do. He sort of spoke to her in a low voice, and told her had to use the John. Loretta Ann couldn't hear what he said so she asked him again what he was doing. Finally he said out loud I've got to go to the John, and into the John he went with his cell phone. She told him she didn't want to disturb him if he wanted to call her back later. He said that was okay, and he kept on talking while he was busy at everything else he was doing. Besides, he could just sit a spell and chill out while he was taking care of business. He asked her what had she been doing since he talked to her earlier? She told him her day had been a bummer because it seemed nothing went her way at all today. Well, Joe told her he must be rubbing off on her because his days hardly ever went right. She told him we've got something in common then don't we Joe. Joe said yea, I guess we do Loretta Ann.

Joe told her I'm counting down the days because we only have a few more left. You know it will be here before we know it Loretta Ann. She said I'm really looking forward to going, and he said he was looking forward to it to. He told her we'll carry something to fix some sandwiches out of, and carry us plenty of drinks and water so we don't get thirsty. Loretta Ann said that sounds good to me. He told her that his time was going by too quickly. She told him it sure was, and before he knew it his vacation would be over.

Joe told her about putting in his resumes in the other day at some offices there in town for a job. She asked him if he was serious about moving to Okeechobee. He told her he was really thinking seriously about it because he really loved it down here in Okeechobee. When he told her about his decision she could feel her heart speed up from excitement. She told him she believed he would really love it down here. He told her he knew he would like living in Okeechobee because it was his kind of town.

They had already made their plans to go to the beach this coming weekend because Loretta Ann had the whole weekend off. Joe told her since they were going to the beach this weekend they would have to go to another amusement park before he went back home to Virginia. Loretta Ann said that would be nice. She told him she would really miss him a lot when he did go back home. He told her that was "Ditto" for him also.

Well, as it was beginning to get late Loretta Ann told Joe she would call him tomorrow when she got home from work. He told her he'd be out there somewhere, and she had his number. She laughed then told him she didn't mean to disturb his important business. He told her that was okay because he liked talking to her anytime and anyplace. As they said their good-byes for the night, Joe left out of the John to head for his bed. He grabbed him a bottle of water as he usually did to take to his tent to sip on during the night in case he got thirsty. He did that so as not to have to get up to wander around outside at night.

Joe did build another campfire so he could smoke off some of the mosquitoes that were buzzing around already. As much wood as he put on the fire it would take all night for it to burn out. He hoped it wouldn't rain again and put his fire out. He made sure everything was in check before he made his way into his little tent for the night. As he entered his little tent it seemed that everything was okay.

Chapter thirty eight

The Prisoner Capture

Joe went into his tent then crawled underneath his cover on his little cot to retire for the night. He seemed to be tired, but he didn't seem to know why because he hadn't done that much at all today. He thought he was getting a little on the lazy side because he hadn't been working like he usually did back at home. He got comfortable on his little cot then went to sleep. His campfire was still blazing up high during the night. It was burning so bright that it lit up his whole camp, and you could see real well even if it was dark.

Joe was sure sleeping a sound sleep until he was awakened by a noise of something or someone walking around outside his tent. He was sleeping on his side so he could see the campfire, and all around his camp without any problem. He heard the noise again and wondered what it could be. No sooner than the thought had run through his head that Joe saw something that sent cold chills down his spine. He was so scared that he couldn't even move at all. Joe kept looking outside of his tent at an image that was bent over his campfire doing something.

Joe began to think about the Satscwatsh Runt had told him to keep an eye out for. Oh, Lord what could he do now? He kept watching the image of whatever it was, and one thing for sure he wished it would leave. As He lay quietly on his cot watching, he figured out that it was a man eating something by his fire. The man by the fire was dressed in an orange suit. It was at that moment that an alarm went off in his head. He realized it was the escaped prisoner that had broken out of the big house correctional institution a couple of days ago. He was so alarmed that he couldn't think straight at all. What in the world should he do if the man came inside his tent? He was paralyzed from fright, and he wasn't sure what step to take next.

Joe didn't know if he should play like he was asleep, or if he should try to sneak away from under the side of the tent. He didn't want to make any noise at all because the prisoner might hear him then he would be in real bad trouble then. Right now he just knew he was in a bad situation any way that he looked at it.

The prisoner was eating like he was starving to death. Joe thought that he probably hadn't eaten anything since he had escaped. He lay there as quiet as a mouse, but the time finally came when the prisoner looked around at the tent where he was at. He could have just died at that moment when he saw the prisoner glaring in his direction. He could see the face of the man from the fire burning so brightly. He thought how mean looking the man appeared to be. He knew the man had finished eating because he threw his plate into the fire. Joe held his breath too scared to even breathe. He peeked out of his eye because he was going to act like he was asleep. He hoped that if the man thought he was asleep that he wouldn't bother him, but that was just wishful thinking on his part.

As the escaped prisoner walked towards his tent Joe's heart began to pound so hard that it felt like it was going to beat out of his chest. He still didn't make a move to do anything at all. He was trying to play possum you could say. Joe could see the man getting closer to his tent. As the prisoner got to the door of his tent he stopped there to see if there was anyone inside. He still remained motionless, and held his breath.

He thought for sure the prisoner was about to leave, but then his worst nightmare began to happen. The man opened the door, and walked inside his tent. Joe's blood felt like it had run cold. He knew he had to be ready to do something real quick like. He wasn't going to make the first move because he wanted to see what the prisoner might do next. Afterall, the radio said the prisoner was considered dangerous. He wasn't sure how strong he would be against the man anyways.

The prisoner bent over towards him, and when he did this Joe came alive. He wasn't about to be killed by the prisoner without putting up a good fight. Joe couldn't take the pressure any longer of having to play like he was asleep.

He grabbed the escapee around the neck in a bulldog style fashion. When Joe did this it caught the prisoner by surprise. This caused the prisoner to fall down on top of him. It was at this moment that both of them were fighting hard to get away from each other. Neither one really wanted to find out what the other one was capable of doing.

The prisoner pulled at Joe's hair trying to get loose, but he held on tight to the prisoner's neck too scared to let go. He feared for his life right at this moment, and as it was, anything goes. The prisoner began to hit Joe with his fists, but then Joe bit the prisoner on his ear. The prisoner let out a scream that sounded like a panther, which sounds like a woman screaming.

The prisoner starting trying to get to his feet. As he finally managed to stand up he started pulling himself and Joe out of the tent towards the campfire. Joe saw that he was getting near the fire so he lunged to the side to throw the man off balance. He made a very smart move when he did this because the man lost his balance, and fell on top of his canvas camp chair. As he fell on the chair his leg got caught in between the metal legs, and then the chair folded closed on his leg. The man was somewhat trapped. The man was crying out with pain because his leg was getting mashed from the chair legs.

Now it was time for Joe to take this matter into his hands. His only reaction that he could think of at the time was to knock the prisoner out, and that was just what Joe Machoochee did. Joe socked the man so hard that he put the man's lights out temporarily. The prisoner was out cold right now so he had to act fast. Joe was so nervous that his mind could hardly function right now. As he tried to think of what to do next after his technical knockout with the escapee, he came to his senses. Man, I have got to get this man tied up before he wakes up. Right as that thought occurred he took his knife then cut off the nylon cords from Shirley and Donald's hammock swing.

Joe turned the prisoner over on his belly then he managed to tie up the prisoner very securely with the nylon cords. He tied the escapee's hands behind him, and tied the man's feet together real tight. He had tied the prisoner up so fast that he could have won a calf tying contest even if he had to bulldog it first. Joe surprised himself at what he had just been able to do. As a matter of fact the police would probably have a hard time trying to untie the knots out of the nylon cord to release the prisoner. He had tied about fifty knots to make sure his prisoner wasn't about to get loose again.

Joe dragged the prisoner over to the little port-o-let John, and put him inside of it until the law could get there to pick the man up. As he managed to get the prisoner inside the port-o-let he sat the man's feet into the hole of the toilet. This way with the man's hands tied behind him, and both feet tied hanging over inside the toilet hole he wasn't about to go anywheres at all unless it was down. By meaning down that meant he would fall down into the toilet hole only to be wedged real tight. He was sure the prisoner was smarter than that.

Joe closed the door then drove his station wagon right against the door of the port-o-let. This way he knew the prisoner wouldn't get out of the port-o-let at least not out the door. He felt safe now so he called the sheriff's office from his cell phone, and told them he'd captured the escaped convict that had broken out of the big house. It's a shame that he couldn't have fooled the prisoner with his pistol phone, but he didn't have time to even think about that. Joe gave the sheriff's office directions to his camp where he was at. The police told him the man was considered to be very dangerous, so be sure to keep his eye on him. He told the sheriff's office he had the man tied and locked up in the port-o-let John. The officer that he spoke to laughed when Joe told him the part about the port-o-let. The officer told him they would be there immediately.

Joe sat on the hood of his car until the county police got there to take over the situation. He wondered what time it was getting to be because it wasn't daylight yet. He looked at his watch, and it was 3:49 a.m. in the dawn hours. Joe mumbled to himself that he never knew he had it in him. Well, what he meant by that was he never knew he was man enough to put up such a fight the way he did with the prisoner. He was pretty proud of himself right about now.

The sheriff's deputies arrived in a short time. The highway patrol and guards from the prison were close behind the county officers. Joe had never had such excitement happen to him in all his entire life. Here he was 41 years old, and it seemed like everything in the world was starting to happen to him now. Maybe that was what he got from living such a sheltered life. The sheriff's deputy told him he could come down to the sheriff's office in the morning to give them the rest of the information they would need for their report that had to be filled out.

Joe thanked all the deputies for coming to his rescue so quickly, but really he had everything already under control. He told the officers he would see them later. The officers delivered the prisoner back to the big house behind bars where he belonged. The prisoner would be there many more years since he managed to break out of prison.

Joe finally got his nerves calmed down once more. He checked to see what the prisoner had got into. The only thing out of place was the lid was left off the food he'd cooked earlier. He was really lucky that something worse didn't happen to him. Joe had the "Good Man" on his side that was for sure. He knew he should go on back to bed to try to get some sleep, but he wasn't sure he could even close his eyes after all his excitement. Well, he drank himself a bottle of water then went back to his little tent to try to sleep once more. It was only a few minutes before he went sound to sleep. He didn't wake up anymore that night. Joe got up the next morning then brushed his hair, teeth, and got groomed for the day ahead. He started to fix some breakfast to eat, but after his rough night last night he decided to stop by the "Dove" to eat. He wanted to tell them the news of what had happened to him.

Chapter thirty nine

The Sheriff's Report

Joe put everything back in its place once again at his camp then headed out to the "Dove." He had to go to the sheriff's department to go over the reports the sheriff's deputy had started filling out last night about the escapee. He didn't want to go to the sheriff's office down at the jailhouse, but he knew it was his duty.

Joe drove into the parking lot at the Dove. He got out of his stationwagon, and went inside to get him some good old breakfast. Everyone greeted him as he walked through the door. Joe was happy to see everybody there. They told him they heard about his wrestling match with the prisoner. Runt told him she was glad he was okay. She asked him what did Loretta Ann have to say about all his excitement. He told her that he hadn't spoken to Loretta Ann yet, but he was planning to call her before too much longer.

Joe sat down at the counter on a stool to give Runt his breakfast order. He ordered the Macho Man breakfast to eat. Runt asked him if he felt macho this morning? He laughed then told her he was just starving for some food. He told her he guessed it was because he worked up an appetite after his wrestling match. She told him that had to be it. She went in the kitchen to fix his breakfast. Joe went over to a booth, and sat down to wait on his breakfast. He sure felt tired this morning. He felt like he didn't have any energy at all. Runt brought his big glass of orange juice out to him. She told him it would be a few minutes then his breakfast would be ready to eat. Joe thanked her then said, "I'm so hungry that I could eat the knots out of a hobby horse." She laughed, and said my dad has the same saying as you. Joe said, I guess that saying has been around for many years because my dad used to say that when I was a little boy growing up in Virginia.

Runt went back into the kitchen to bring Joe his breakfast. The toast popped up out of the toaster as soon as she walked through the kitchen door. She got the butter and jelly and the big plate of ham with all of its trimmings then carried it out to Joe. She told him if you eat all this breakfast, then you can be sure to call yourself a Macho Man. He told her he bet he could put a big dent in it. Once he got started eating on it he ate all the big breakfast. Joe ate like he was starving to death, but of course he wasn't. He finished his big breakfast then paid Runt at the cash register.

He told her he had to go fill out the report at the sheriff's office. After he finished that he was going back to the Prairie, and wasn't going to do anything but lay back and relax. Joe told her that he had a date with Loretta Ann to go to the beach in Ft. Pierce this weekend. She winked her eye at Joe, and said, "Way to go Tiger."

Joe felt his face turning red so he was in a hurry to get out of there. Runt told him good-bye, and to behave himself. He said good-bye to her then he left. Little did he realize it, but he still had the toothpaste tube in his back pocket. If he had known this he could have changed his shorts before he came into town. He didn't even know that he had left the toothpaste in his pocket, and that it had got squooshed out of the tube when he had fallen out of the hammock swing. His rolling and tumbling with the prisoner had finished mashing the toothpaste tube completely dry.

Poor Joe was walking around with the toothpaste all over his rump and didn't even realize it. He had walked into the sheriff's office and he had noticed that people were staring at him. He noticed a couple of people starting to laugh when he passed by them. He didn't know what was going on, but he knew it had to be something about him because people seemed to be acting strange towards him. He gave the sheriff's department all the information he could on what had happened at the camp when he captured the escapee. They told him that it was a miracle that he hadn't gotten hurt by the man. They told him the prisoner had already killed an old man and woman down in Miami, and that he was a very dangerous man. The deputy told Joe it took them several months in Miami to finally catch the man and try him for the old people's murders. After he was caught he was sent to the big house here in Okeechobee after he was found guilty at his trial. The prisoner was serving a life sentence without parole.

Joe was just happy that his ordeal with the prisoner was over. That is one part of his life that he still couldn't believe. He didn't even know he was that strong, but he guessed when you were scared enough you can do just about anything. He finished helping with the police report then left on his way back to his camp at the Prairie. Joe decided today that he was going to ride around to look at the property at the Prairie to see what was for sale. As he drove back to the north part of the Prairie towards the State Park he noticed there was a lot of land for sale. The park had many acres that adjoined the Prairie, and it was all for sale.

Joe wanted to see if he could find a parcel with a lot of trees. As he drove back in the direction of his camp he saw a five-acre tract that was for sale, and it had a lot of big oak trees and cabbage trees on it. There was a sign with a phone number on it so he wrote the number on a piece of paper. He would call later on to see how much they were asking for the land. He thought this was a real pretty wooded area.

As Joe kept driving around he thought about the job resumes he'd filled out and turned in to the offices in town. He was thinking seriously about maybe trying to move down to Okeechobee. He knew it would cost a lot, but if he could get the job it would be worth it to move down to Okeechobee. Joe loved the little town plus he'd met so many new friends here. Also, he might be in the prospect of having a serious relationship with his new female friend Loretta Ann. He seemed to be taken in by her.

Joe thought he would call her later on in the afternoon to see what she was up to after she got off work. He might just go into town and hang around a while. He'd been staying in the woods most of the time, but he had been enjoying himself at the little camp he had made. He had several things he needed to do in town, and today would be just as good as the next one to do his errands.

Joe came upon another piece of property for sale. He stopped at this one then got out of his car to walk over to look at it. Boy, this was quite an extra pretty spot to him. It had all kinds of trees on it. He walked on into the wooded hammock to see if it would be a suitable spot to put a home. It was even nicer that he could expect because it had a pond at the edge of the tree hammock. The pond was probably half of an acre. It looked to him like it was a natural pond not a manmade one.

Joe started thinking of his weekend coming up. Today was Wednesday, and he and Loretta Ann were to go to the beach in Ft. Pierce early Friday morning. That was only 2 days away. He was so glad that this was the weekend that she had Friday, Saturday, and Sunday off. He knew one thing for sure, and that was that he was ready to go. He stopped thinking of Loretta Ann because he couldn't keep his mind on what he was supposed to be doing. At this moment he was supposed to be looking for property that was for sale.

Well, Joe did manage to take down quite a few phone numbers. He planned to call them to inquire information on the property that they had for sale. He pretty well covered all the roads at the Prairie looking at the property for sale there. He drove on back to his little camp to call the numbers he'd taken down about the property for sale. He started calling, and he reached everyone that he'd called except 2 numbers. It could possibly be that the people weren't in from work yet. Joe could call them back later. He had asked about the selling price on the property, and it wasn't a bad price for the land. He told the people that he talked to that he would get back to them, and thanked them for all their information.

Joe would have to figure out if he could still keep his expenses around the same bracket here as he has them in Virginia. He sat down in his little canvas chair to think what all he'd have to do in order to move from Virginia to Florida. It was quite a long ways to relocate, but there are people that move farther distances.

Joe went to get a drink out of his ice cooler. He was real thirsty today. He guessed it was from the heat because it was probably 98 degrees today. He was pretty use to the weather if it didn't get much hotter then he'd be fine. He liked the heat, but he sure didn't like the thunder and lightning storms that he'd been in a couple of times this past week. He was thinking over his prospect of how to go about everything so he could get moved down here. He wanted to buy a piece of property at the Prairie if he was able to get everything in order. He had been saving his money for a long time, and he probably had enough to buy an acre or two. He would like to buy some land down here so if he wanted to go camping again he would have a place to go to. He loved the outdoors, and this was one vacation he'd remember as long as he lived.

Joe started figuring out his expenses he'd had at home. He didn't have hardly any bills except for the usual ones everybody has. He made pretty good money at the job where he worked at now. Of course, he had been there for many years. He was the only one that had remained there since he got out of high school. He is quite a dedicated employee. Joe had saved a little nest egg up, and he had invested some money in the stock market. He had thought at one time of putting his stock money into savings because the stock market wasn't doing too well at times. He wasn't a big spender so that was one thing that was good. Joe always looked ahead to the future. He knew that one-day that he might get married, have a family and he would have to be able to support them. He seemed to always be planning ahead.

Well, it was getting that time of day that Joe was to eat his meal. He thought he'd do some grilling, but felt a little lazy about now. He had plenty of other food he could eat instead of having to fire up the hot grill. He ended up fixing himself a ham and cheese sub sandwich along with some potato chips to eat. Joe could open up a can of something to eat later if the little meal didn't fill him up. After all it was just too warm to eat a big meal. Joe didn't eat big meals at home so there wasn't much reason to change here at the camp. Joe did eat a lot more at the Dove than he ate at home. He guessed that was because the food was so much better at the café than it was at his home. Joe could cook somewhat, but one thing for sure is that he wasn't an entrepreneur. Oh well, he managed to get along so far.

Joe had thought of going fishing, but decided to just lie around camp. As a matter of fact he got sleepy, and took a long nap. It didn't do any good for him to get his beauty rest because he would never get enough sleep to help him out in the looks department. He was just getting rested up for his trip to the beach. He wanted to be rested up and full of energy so he could stay at the beach all day swimming with Loretta Ann. He was just counting the days, hours, minutes, and seconds until he and Loretta Ann could be on their way to the beach. He hoped they could enjoy the surf or waves or whatever. Just as long as he was with his Loretta Ann he knew he could probably enjoy a hurricane.

Chapter forty

Old Man Dan

Joe awoke from his sleep when he heard someone saying hello is anybody there. There was an old man that had been looking for his property he'd bought at the Prairie. He was on the right street, but he was on the wrong lot. He asked Joe what the lot number was at his lot, but Joe told him he didn't know. Joe told him that he was just down on vacation, and the camp belonged to the Wildes family. The man told him he knew them because his lot was just on the other side of theirs. The man told him that most everyone called him Old Man Dan. He told Dan he was Joe Machoochee from Spicey Town, Virginia. Joe asked Old Man Dan if it would be okay for him to call him Dan? The old man said that was okay. Joe respected his elders, and really didn't feel comfortable calling them by their first name. He'd rather call the man Dan if he must, but he couldn't bring himself to call him Old Man Dan even if it was a nickname.

Old Dan told him he'd bought the property he owned in 1965, and he had been there only a few times. Old Dan told him that's why he was lost because it had been 7 years since he'd been in Okeechobee. His property had grown up so much from all the trees and shrubbery, and that's why he couldn't find it. Old Dan lived in Lake Placid. Joe told him he was in Lake Placid a week or two ago. Joe told Old Dan he really liked the muriel paintings that were painted on all the store building's walls. Old Dan told him the man that painted the pictures had a God given talent. He told Old Dan it was a pretty little town.

Old Dan told him he was born in Sebring, but moved to Lake Placid when he was a little boy. He told Joe his daddy had an orange grove there, and a packing house. The company was the first one that was built in Lake Placid. It was an old company, but it was still in operation. Old Dan told him his family sold it to a man that owned other companies all over Florida.

Old Dan told him his daddy used to have some beehives in his orange grove too. He told Joe they had some of the best honey you could ever eat. He told him it was orange blossom honey, and it was so good that it would melt in your mouth. Joe told Old Dan he'd eat clover honey, but never the orange blossom flavored kind. He told the old man he'd got strangled on honey one time so he didn't eat it much. He told the old man he thought he was going to cough himself to death. Old Dan laughed, and told him he did the same thing. Old Dan told him I still eat my share of honey though. He told Joe he loved to eat it on a good hot biscuit with his breakfast. Dan told him that honey was good for you to eat.

The two of them talked for another hour or two before Old Man Dan left. Old Dan told him he would see him before he went back to Lake Placid. Joe told him to stop by and see him anytime he wanted to. He told Old Dan he would go to see him later on today if he was going to be around for a while. Old Dan told him to come on over he'd be glad to have his company.

Old Dan went over to his lot to see how much it had grown up. The weeds had taken over his little road that went into his place, but he drove his pick up truck right on through the weeds without any problem. Old Dan wanted to build a house out there on his lot one day, but was too old to live so far out of town due to his health. So Old Man Dan and his wife would have to remain in town in Lake Placid to live. Old Dan liked it out in the country, and would love to live here on the Prairie.

Joe walked over to his place later on to visit with the old man for a while. He told Old Dan he sure had a pretty place, and wished he could find one like that. Old Dan told him he had considered selling his land because he never got to spend any time out there. Joe told him to let him know if he ever decides to sell it because he'd be interested in buying it from him. Old Dan told him he'd be the first one he'd let know if he did sell it.

Joe asked him if he had any children, and he told Joe he and his wife never had any children because she wasn't able to have any. Joe told him he wasn't married yet, but hoped he would be one day. He told Old Dan he was the only child, and all his parents had died. He told him his mother had died when he was only a few years old, and his dad raised him by himself. Old Dan told him he really enjoyed talking to him. He told him he'd like to have had a house full of children, but he guessed it just wasn't meant to be.

Joe asked him if he needed help with anything at his lot, but he told him not right now. Old Dan said he might be over the following week to clear some of the underbrush from under the trees. He asked Joe how much longer did he have before he had to go back to work in Virginia. He told him he had several more weeks then he'd be leaving to go back home to the drawing board once again.

Joe told him he'd met a girl he really liked that was born and raised in Okeechobee. He told Dan her name was Loretta Ann, and she was a nice girl. Old Dan told him son you better go after her and not let her get away because life is too short. He told Joe he had been married to his wife for 51 years, and it seemed like only yesterday that they'd got married. Dan told him they'd been together so many years that each one knew what the other one was thinking all the time. Joe thought that it was really nice for the little old man to think so much of his wife.

Joe told him that he guessed he'd go back over to his camp to cook something to eat. He told Dan he was welcome to eat when he got something cooked. Old Dan told him thanks, but he had to get on back to Lake Placid. If he stayed gone too long his wife would be worried. Joe told him to stop by if he came over to Okeechobee next week, and Old Dan told him he would probably bring his wife with him the next week so he could meet her before he went back to

Virginia. He told Dan to be careful when he headed back home. He told Joe he always took a short cut so there wasn't much traffic on it. Joe asked him if he had a telephone so he could get his phone number? Old Dan said why sure, and if you have a phone then give me your number and I'll call you up sometimes. They swapped phone numbers with each other, and then Joe left and went back to his little camp.

Joe went to his camp to fix him something to eat. Joe really didn't want to cook so he just opened him a can of spaghetti and meatballs. He ate the spaghetti then opened up a can of fruit to snack on. He had a can of sliced peaches, and they just hit the spot. As Joe sat at his little table finishing up his peaches he thought about the old man. He thought it was sad that Old Dan never had any children. It seems that the people that want children can't have any, and the ones that don't want or need children have them. Joe thought that Old Dan would have made a good father. He liked Old Dan because he reminded him a little of his dad. He sure missed his dad very much, and what hurt so bad was that he didn't have any other family. Well, maybe he would have a family one-day of his own.

Well, Joe was going to hang around camp all day, but changed his mind. He needed to go buy a few groceries that he was out of so he'd do it today. Joe sat there watching the little redbirds flying around the camp. They were feeding on the corn on the ground that had been scattered by the other animals. He could have sat there all day watching the birds and squirrels playing about, and eating out of the feeder.

The country life sure agreed with Joe Macoochee because he didn't have a care in the world right now. He just sort of blended in like cheese on grits I guess you could say. He just loved the plain and simple life, and I guess that is really the way to be. He got up to go to town to do his little bit of shopping. As he drove out of the woods towards the highway he noticed the bears roaming through the bushes near the dirt road he was on. Joe hoped that they wouldn't go to the highway because it would be sad if they got on the highway and got killed. They were such beautiful animals.

Chapter forty one

The Mad Boar Gator

Joe was making his way on to the main highway. As he drove along he had thought about the dream he had about Loretta Ann the other night. On his way into town he thought he'd call to see if she was at home. He dialed her number, but only her answer machine picked up. It seemed that every time he called her that the old faithful machine did its job.

As he hung up his pistol phone he looked ahead in the road in front of him and saw an alligator crossing the road. Boy, the gator must be 9 or 10 feet long. Matter of fact he had to slow down to let the gator go across the highway. It was the time of year that alligators travel to find a mate. Joe of course had no idea what the gator had on his mind. A male gator is meaner than a woman with P.M.S. is and during the mating season an alligator will catch you in a heartbeat.

Joe looked in his rearview mirror to see if anyone was coming, but the coast was clear. Since he didn't see any traffic coming either way he kinda did something stupid. He commenced to go towards the gator and began to make noises to get the gator's attention. Little did he know, but the gator was paying full attention to him already.

Since Joe was excited about getting a snapshot of a live alligator he kept walking closer and closer. The alligator was already mad at the world as it was. When he finally got close to the gator's side he then snapped the gator's picture with his flash camera, and that was when the boar gator came alive. Now that's a figure of speech and it didn't mean the gator was dead. It just meant the gator was about to become a ferocious reptile. The big gator whirled around and ran straight towards him. The gator threw his tail over his back. When Joe saw the alligator do this he figured out real quick like that he was in trouble, and had probably teed the gator off. When the alligator does this movement he can run as fast as a horse on his 4 feet. He looked the gator in the eye, and knew he was in trouble. Joe snapped another picture of the gator, and this was when the gator gave him a run for his money. Joe turned and ran as fast as he could because at this moment he had to run for his life or pay the consequences.

He managed to run and jump on the hood of his car, and if he hadn't been able to do that he would have been in big trouble. Joe was bouncing around on the top of his car hood. He couldn't think of what he should do next because he was so scared. If only he could have got inside his car he would have felt safe. He felt like a sitting duck on top of his car.

The alligator was highly ticked off because he even tried to climb up on the hood with him. When the gator tried to climb on the hood Joe jumped on the top of his car, and that was the highest spot left to get away from him. He was lucky he was able to get up there because that was the safest place for him to be right then. The gator couldn't climb up on the hood because he was so big and bulky. The gator sat there looking at Joe making a hissing sound with his big mouth wide open showing him his big white teeth. Here he was in the middle of the highway cornered up by a big gator, and no one was there to help him. He began to yell at the gator clapping his hands, and stomping his feet. The noise made the big gator move away a little. The gator was truly mad because he even snapped at the front tire of his car. When his big teeth bit the tire it made his tire go flat. The gator's tail hit the side of Joe's car door, and put a small dent in it. The gator had the notion that he wasn't going to let Joe get away from him so somehow the big reptile managed to squeeze underneath his car. The gator had one intention right now and that was he'd just lie under the car, and wait for Joe Macoochee to come down from his car then he'd put the bite on him. When he saw the gator go under his car he thought he was in for it now. He wondered," how in the world am I going to get into my car with the gator waiting to make me his next meal?" Really, that was a good question. He would have to be very careful.

Joe saw a semi-truck coming up the road in the other lane. He started waving his hands, and motioned for the trucker to stop. Well, the truck driver did stop to see if he needed help. When he told the truck driver he had a big gator chase him on to his car then the gator bit a hole in his tire the trucker drove off shaking his head. He thought Joe had lost his mind, or he was hallucinating on something. Well, Joe was left alone again except for his big gator friend under his car. He thought he would try to climb down and get into his car, but when he made a move to try to do this then the gator hissed and raised up under the car. The gator was so big Joe was afraid the gator would turn his car over.

Well, it happened that 5 more cars came up behind him only to go past without stopping. They thought that Joe was crazy stopped in the middle of the road jumping up and down on the top of his hood. Little did they know what kind of terrible predicament he was in right at that moment. He sat down on his hood and lay back against the windshield of his car. He lay on the hood wondering what he would do if no one stopped to help him. Joe hit the side of the car to see if the gator would do anything, and he made a growling noise. It was as if he were waiting so he could put the bite on him for sure.

Joe wondered why he always got in such predicaments like he did. The only thing he could figure out was that he must have a curse on him. Just about that time his pistol phone began ringing. He knew that it was Loretta Ann because she was the only one that had his phone number besides Old Dan. Oh, what am I going to do? Well, his nerves weren't going to take much more. It was then and only then that he made up his mind to do something about the situation. As the saying goes, "A man has got to do what a man has got to do."

That's when he did what he had to do. Joe kicked his front windshield out so that he could get inside of his car. It was already cracked from the limb falling on it so it wasn't hard to break it on out. As soon as he got the windshield broke out he climbed into his car very carefully. He sure didn't want to cut himself anywheres from the glass. Joe sat down in his car seat then started his car motor up. Once he did this he felt the gator start to move around a lot under his car. He then put his car in gear to make it move, but it wouldn't budge at all. The big gator had moved into a position in which he had the rear end of the car lifted off the ground.

The gator had the car where it couldn't get any traction with its tires off of the ground. He revved up his engine, but the gator had him in a predicament. Joe took his pistol phone then called Loretta Ann. He told her what was happening. As he was talking to her on the phone another car came up and stopped to see if he needed help. There was a lady and a man in the car. The lady started to ask him if they could help in any way, but he looked at her with the pistol phone in his hand holding it next to his ear. The lady told her husband to hurry up and get out of there because the man was going to shoot them or himself.

Joe tried to stop them from leaving, but he couldn't get out of his car to tell them what was happening. He told Loretta Ann about his problem, and she told him not to go anywheres, and she would call the game commission so they could help him. She told him she would come on out to see if she could be of help to him. Joe sure wished someone would come by to help him before the game wardens got there. He was embarrassed enough without having them see him sitting there with a broke windshield, and with a big gator under his car. Sometimes he felt like he could crawl through the eye of a needle.

It wasn't long before Loretta Ann got to the scene with Joe. He told her not to get out of her car at all. She stayed in her car like he asked her to do. She did park her car behind his, and turned on her flashers so no one would run into the back of his car. Since there was hardly any traffic that didn't seem likely to happen. He could have very easily turned on the flashers on his car, but he was so shook up right now he probably didn't even remember his name.

Well, it was a few minutes more before the game wardens showed up. When they did arrive they pulled off to the edge of the road onto the grass. They walked towards Joe, but he told them not to come any closer because there was a big gator under his car. One of the game wardens looked under the car, and when he did this the gator growled a real long growl. The game warden jumped up and told the other one that they would have to dart that big gator. He told the other game warden to bring his dart rifle to him.

When the game warden loaded his dart rifle he aimed it at the gator so he could tranquilize the reptile in order to be able to handle him. The man darted the gator in his leg, but it wasn't strong enough to knock the big gator out. After 3 tranquilizers darted into the gator it finally worked. The gator was under the car in a deep sleep, and now was the time for them to get in gear and capture the gator. The game officer that was in charge told the other man to bring him a rope from the truck.

The officer took the rope, and slipped one of the loops over the front foot of the gator. He then tried to pull the gator from under the car, but he couldn't move the gator an inch. The gator was so huge that he was complete dead weight knocked out like he was. Well, the officers put another loop over the gator's other foot and head this time. Both of the men tried to pull the gator from underneath the car, but they weren't strong enough to pull him out because he was so big.

Joe was still sitting in his car waiting to get out. He finally asked the officers if it would be okay from him to get out of his car so he could help them. They told him to get out of his car real easy and quiet like. Joe did as they told him to do, and he walked over to where the officers were at then asked if he could help them pull the gator out from under the car. They all tried once more to pull out the gator, but they just didn't have enough manpower.

Joe walked over to the side of the road where Loretta Ann was standing. She was talking to a man that had come up and started talking to her. He turned out to be a newspaper reporter. Joe introduced himself to the man. The reporter introduced himself as Big John Barton. He asked Joe all about the alligator. Joe told him that the gator was crossing the highway, and he had to stop to let the gator go on across. He then told the reporter that he'd never seen an alligator that big in the wild before except at a park or zoo. He told the reporter he got out of his car to take a picture of the gator, but soon saw that was a bad idea. Joe told the reporter that the gator didn't like this picture taking business so he chased him to his car then got underneath it. The reporter told him that he was a very lucky man because it's the time of year that alligators are very aggressive. They will attack you for no reason at all. This is the time of year that the alligator travels around looking for his mate. Joe just laughed then told the reporter that was probably why he was trying to attack him because he was in a bad mood already.

As time passed, a crowd of people began to gather at the scene. They parked their cars along the side of the road, and walked over to where the officers were at. The people were asking all kinds of questions, and they were beginning to get in the way of the officers doing their jobs. The game warden that seemed to be the boss told the other officer to call for more help. He told the officer to have the other men bring a floor jack so they could lift the side of the car up in the air. Maybe this way they would be able to get the gator out from under the car.

As the crowd began to get larger the game wardens told the people they would have to step back out of the way. The people did as the officer asked. They were all a little curious I guess about the gator underneath the car. Well, the other officers arrived with the floor jack, and some more rope to tie to the gator so they could pull him out. Well, they did manage to get the gator from under the car this time, but he was too much weight for them to pick up. As a matter of fact they had to get a larger trailer in order to haul the giant reptile.

The officers measured the gator's length, and it was the biggest one that had been caught so far in Okeechobee. The gator was 17 feet and 11 inches long. Everybody was amazed that the gator was so big. The gator's head was almost 4 foot long lacking 3 inches. No doubt about it, but this gator was one big sucker.

Joe asked the game warden what would happen to the gator. He told him that most definitely this gator would be taken to an alligator pond at the Green Gator Farm over in Lake Placid. He told Joe they had a big farm they raised gators at over there, and the public could pay to walk through the farm to look at the gators. The officers were sure they had the largest gator that had been caught so far in Okeechobee, perhaps in the State of Florida. They just hoped the big gator would make out okay in captivity with all the other gators. He would probably make out just fine. As big as he was he would probably be considered as "Boss Gator." He would probably have plenty of gator girl friends there.

Well, the officers wanted to get the alligator loaded into the trailer after they had him all tied and taped up securely. They had a wench built on the top of the trailer so they managed to get him loaded into the trailer easier than thought possible. There was a lady that came over to Joe, and asked if he was very scared. He told the lady he was scared when the gator ran after him trying to catch him. She told him the gator looked like a dinosaur. Some of the people that had stopped had never seen an alligator before. Some had only seen them on television.

After the alligator was caught and put inside the trailer they all looked at the big boy. Some took pictures of the gator because they were amazed at how big he was. The crowd slowly began to dwindle away, and all that remained at the scene was the reporter, Loretta

Ann, Joe, and the game wardens. They all posed for the reporter as he snapped their pictures for the newspaper.

Well, Joe was sure glad that this ordeal was over. He had been in Okeechobee only a couple of weeks, and he had managed to get into all kinds of predicaments. If he went home and told everyone what all had happened to him they would think he was crazy for sure. As the gator was being hauled away to his new home Joe thought he would go to the Dove eat lunch, and then just go back to his little camp. Maybe if he did this he could manage to stay out of trouble. Joe had to change his tire before he left, and he also had to get another windshield put in his car when he made it to town.

He asked Loretta Ann if she wanted to join him for lunch, but she told him that she had to get back to work. She told him she would call him later on. He left after the game wardens gave him a long lecture about messing with the animals in the wild. The game warden officer told him he could have been seriously hurt by the alligator. He told them he meant no harm, but he has learned his lesson the hard way.

Joe left then went by the Dove to get him something to eat and drink because he was overdue on his meal. As he pulled up to his favorite little café there was a lot of people there again today. It was busy just about all the time, or at least it was when he went there. As he walked in the front door someone noticed him and yelled out, "Here comes the Gator Man." Joe's face turned red because he was blushing. He said, "Yelp, the Gator Man has arrived" then Joe snapped his jaws together a couple of times. When he did this everyone at the café broke loose and started laughing again.

Joe walked over to a little booth, and sat down waiting for Runt to take his order. Well, she came out to his table to get his order. She came towards him laughing with her arms extended out in front of her making the sign of a gator opening and closing its mouth. Joe knew he would never live the gator ordeal down.

Runt was giggling her head off. She asked him, "You like to live on the wild side don't you?" Joe just grinned his big old grin, and told her he liked to live dangerously. She told him there were several different people that had stopped in, and they each had a different story that they told her about the gator. She told him that she liked the little lady that had told her the gator looked like a dinosaur. Joe told her he had met that lady because she had told him the same thing about the dinosaur. Runt told him, "At least you didn't let the big one get away." Joe just snickered then didn't say much of anything else.

Runt asked him what he'd like to eat today. The man sitting behind him heard her ask Joe this, and then he made the comment that Joe would probably like gator tail to eat. When the man made that remark everyone broke down into a fit of laughter again. It seemed everyone there was having a good time laughing at all the jokes that were being thrown in his direction. Joe told Runt that he guessed he would be the talk of the town now. She told him that everyone liked him, and that's why he was getting picked on. She told Joe she was out of gator tail, but they had about everything else to eat.

Since he hadn't eaten a big breakfast he told Runt he guessed he'd have the Macho Man breakfast today. Everyone in the little café said, "Way to go Joe." Well, as it went it seemed that he was becoming somewhat of a celebrity. Of course, he was eating up every bit of attention he was getting. As he sat waiting for his breakfast to be prepared he thought how nice it was to be kidded and picked at. Back home at the office where he worked it seemed that everyone was always on pins and needles. Down here in Okeechobee the atmosphere was really different for him. It was a much better atmosphere to him, and it wouldn't take much to get use to it.

When Runt brought out his breakfast she asked him if he was going to be able to handle the big Macho Man breakfast by himself. The little old lady sitting at a nearby table told Runt if Joe could handle that big gator he can handle anything. Then the little old lady smiled and winked her eye at him. Well, Joe ate every bit of the food on his plate. He guessed he'd worked up an appetite at doing nothing. He finished drinking his tea then went to pay for his breakfast at the cash register. The man that was sitting behind him while he was eating his breakfast told Runt that Joe's breakfast was on him. The man told him he hadn't had a good laugh like that in years.

The man reached his hand out to shake Joe's hand then told him his name was Tony Gee. Joe thanked the man for buying him his breakfast, and told Tony he was glad to meet him. He told everyone at the café that he'd see them later. At that moment the little old lady chimed in, "See ya later alligator, after while crocodile." Joe smiled at the little old lady then walked on out the door. He was going to go into town, but changed his mind, and went on back to his little camp. He decided to do his shopping another day. Joe decided to go fishing instead. He had such good luck the other day that he thought today would be a good day to go especially after the way his day had went so far. He was afraid that if he went into town there's no telling what he might get into, and he had about all the excitement in one day that he could stand.

Chapter forty two

The Old Gator Turtle

Joe got into his old stationwagon then headed back towards the Prairie. He knew one thing for sure that he wouldn't stop for anything heading on his way back to his little camp. Joe had enough excitement for a day. Matter of a fact he'd had enough excitement for a month or two. Joe was just glad that this day was almost behind him.

When he got out of his car at camp he went straight to the little spot where he had his poles and fishing tackle at. He then loaded all his fishing tackle into his stationwagon, and went on his merry way fishing again. Maybe his day would turn out to be a good one after all.

Well, Joe went down to the river bridge to see if he could catch any fish again. He put all his tackle besides his chair so he wouldn't have to get up out of his little chair once he sat down. He baited all his fishhooks on his poles then just sat back waiting for the fish to start biting.

It was a pretty hot day today. It was about 96 degrees, but it was a little cooler in the shade of the bridge. Joe sat there in his little canvas chair thinking how lucky he was that the big alligator hadn't caught him. He knew now not to bother any gators because he had the experience at the park he visited on his way down to Florida, and then the gator episode today so he had learned some valuable lessons about alligators. That one lesson being that he could have easily become mincemeat for the gator.

Well, Joe waited and waited, but he still hadn't had a single fish bite. He thought he probably wouldn't catch any because his day had been a total bummer so far. One thing for sure he wasn't about to give up though. One thing for sure is that Joe Macoochee was not a quitter. Sometimes the light looked mighty dim at the end of the tunnel, but he never gave up on what he did. He always kept on persevering I guess you could say.

Joe saw his little cork start to bob up and down in the water. He sat up in his chair not making a move to pick up his pole off the ground until he was sure that the fish was getting a good bite on the bait. As he watched his little cork start to move farther toward the middle of the river he took his pole and set-up on the hook, and had the fish hooked on his line. It seemed like a good-sized fish, but he wouldn't be able to tell until he had him brought in.

When Joe got the fish reeled in it was a big old catfish. This excited him pretty much because he didn't think he would catch anything at all for a while. Well, as it went he baited his hook up again then tossed it back into the river. No sooner had he just leaned back in his chair then he managed to get another bite on his hook. This time he grabbed his rod and reel up and hung into something else. Joe knew whatever it was that it was gigantic because he could hardly move his rod at all. Instead his line kept spinning off of his reel. He thought that he was going to lose all of his line off of his reel because the drag just wasn't holding whatever it was on his line.

Joe fought to wind in the line on his rod, but every time he could get his line reeled in a little bit then whatever it was on his hook would swim right back towards the middle of the river. He had begun to work up a sweat fighting with the thing on his line. He knew one thing for sure, and that was he was not about to give up, and let this big thing get away. The only way he would stop fighting to pull in the thing on his rod was for the line to break.

Joe had 30 pound test line so it wouldn't likely break that easy. Well, as he kept up his fight with the fish, or whatever he had on the end of his fishing line, it seemed to be tiring itself out. This made him happy because whatever it was it was about to whip him. Joe now turned the table on the fish or what was on the end of his pole. He now almost had the line reeled in so he was about to find out what he had hooked on the end of his line.

Well, Joe thought that he must have some kind of killey monster on his line. After he managed to get his line in it turned out not to be a big fish afterall. He had just caught a big gator turtle. It was the biggest turtle he had ever seen in his life. The gator turtle weighed about 15 ponds or more.

Joe looked at the big gator turtle, and thought how ugly he was. The big turtle had green slimy looking grass all over his thorny looking shell. Joe thought he was so ugly that the turtle looked plum prehistoric. The turtle had to be very old from the way he looked, and from the big size of him. The next thing that he had to contend with was to try to get the gator turtle off of his hook. Joe knew that this wasn't going to be an easy task to do. He and the turtle were both tired at this moment. The old gator turtle lay still on the ground as if he was trying to recuperate.

Joe had plum tuckered the old turtle out bringing him into land. If you looked at the turtle you would kinda feel sorry for him because it was as if his pride was broken from being caught. Well, Joe moved real slowly towards his tackle box to get his little flimsy pair of pliers so he could remove the hook from the turtle's mouth.

Joe's little pliers were so flimsy that they weren't really worth keeping, much less worth throwing away. Well, either way he had to remove the hook from the turtle's mouth. He pulled the turtle closer to him, and was thinking to himself that he'd better be real careful with this ugly sucker. He was worried about the turtle biting him with his big old mouth. Joe had always heard the saying since he was a little boy, that if a turtle bit you that it wouldn't turn loose until it thundered. He sure wasn't ready for that to happen to him.

Joe managed to grab the hook with his pair of pliers, but he also pinched the turtle's mouth at the same time by accident. Well, when he did this the old gator turtle really came alive. The gator turtle had managed to get rested since he had been lying still on the ground for a while. The old turtle was giving him another good fight, but this time he was on the ground. The old turtle opened his mouth wide open and then snapped at his hand. Joe knew he had better watch the turtle very carefully because he was making a hissing sound like he was very mad. All he wanted to do was to unhook the turtle and let him go, but the turtle didn't understand this so he put up another good fight with him. He sure had himself a handful this time because the turtle fought a lot harder than he did when he was in the water.

Well, Joe was in another predicament now because he hadn't figured out how he was going to be able to get the turtle loose from his hook since he had made the turtle mad from pinching his already sore hooked mouth. The turtle was turning and twisting trying to get away from him. You can't blame the turtle from being mad because it was bad enough to be hooked on a fishing line, but it was worse getting pinched in the process with a pair of pliers.

Finally, he got the hook loose from the turtle's mouth. The turtle turned away from him and tried to escape. Joe not thinking grabbed the old gator turtle's thorny tail. He knew he had made a big mistake when he did this. Joe was holding onto the gator turtle's tail, but soon learned to let go of it. He saw the turtle's big jaws open up, and he knew he had the gator turtle mad enough to eat him up. The turtle just whirled his whole turtle shell around, and as he did this he bit at Joe's hand.

Joe saw that he had better let the turtle go, and he had better do it in a hurry. His hand got scratched by the turtle's claws, and also by the turtle's thorny tail. He backed away from the turtle quickly, and watched as the big old gator turtle made his way back into the river.

He told the turtle to go live a long life because he knew the turtle had been around for many years because he was so big.

Joe didn't know if he wanted to fish anymore or not because he sure didn't want to catch the turtle again. He did eventually fish another hour or so after his ordeal with the turtle then he went back to his camp. Joe had caught five more fish to go along with the catfish he had caught. He decided to head back to camp to clean his catch of the day. He would put the fish on ice then cook them the next day for his lunch.

As Joe mosied back to his car, he got the wits scared out of him. He had walked right up on a big black indigo snake lying in the grass next to the path he was walking on. You couldn't tell who got scared the worse Joe or the snake. Anyways the snake made a quick exit, as so did he. Joe high stepped it around to the other side of his car, loaded up all his gear and fish then went back to his camp. He had quite an unusual fishing trip today. One thing for sure he was glad that it was over with because of the turtle incident.

Well, he knew it was time for him to eat because his stomach started growling. He ended up fixing himself a hot dog with chili and onions on it. He ate some potato chips and pickles along with his little meal. After he had eaten the one hot dog he fixed himself two more before he got filled up. Joe ate like he was starving to death. It must have been all the energy he had to use up when he was fishing.

If he kept on eating a lot like he had been doing lately he would have to go on a diet when he got back home. Joe covered the chili up with a paper towel so he could eat the rest of it later on. He still had a couple of hot dogs left that he had cooked in the pot.

Right now Joe just wanted to sit down and relax in his little canvas lounge chair. He was feeling a little lazy and sleepy just about now. As he sat in his little chair taking life easy he started thinking about their trip to the beach this weekend. He was going to call Loretta Ann to make sure she was still going to be able to go. Joe couldn't believe that the weekend they were planning to go to the beach in Ft. Pierce was finally here. He could hardly wait until the day got there, and now since it was so close he was getting nervous about going.

Joe sat day dreaming about what they would do when they did go to Ft. Pierce. He was very excited about going, and so was Loretta Ann. Joe was counting down the days, hours, minutes, and seconds until they would make it to the beach. It was only a couple of days until they would be leaving on their way. He decided to wait until he came back from town to call Loretta Ann. She probably wasn't home yet anyways. He checked everything at his camp to see what all he needed to pick up when he went in.

He left to go on his way to town to pick up some drinks and lunchmeat so that they could make them a sandwich if they got hungry. Joe would do his errands today so he wouldn't have to wait until the last minute. He didn't want to use up his precious time that he could be spending with his sweet Loretta Ann. He finished his errands in town that he had to do so he started on his way back to his camp. As he was starting to leave town on his way back to the camp he noticed a movie theater that he hadn't seen before. He thought that he might ask Loretta Ann to go to the movies with him before his vacation got over.

Well, Joe managed to arrive back at his camp safely once more. He separated all the beach food so he could pack most of it in the car. He had to put the lunchmeat on ice to keep it cold until his little refrigerator got cooled down. Joe finally got off of his wallet and bought one for the beach trip. The little refrigerator operates off of a car battery. He plugged it into the cigarette lighter to see if it would work. To his surprise it got cool really fast. Joe thought it would be a penny saver because he wouldn't have to buy so much ice now and worry about it melting away all the time. At least he could keep all of his stuff good and cold. He would check on the little refrigerator later on to make sure it got cold so he could put the lunchmeat in it along with some drinks and water. It had a long plug in cord so he could put it in the back of his car.

Joe finished all his packing for the beach so he went walking through the woods instead of staying on his hammock today. He knew he needed to get out and do some walking because he had slacked off the last few days and had been lazy. He walked down to the little pond to see if he could see any animals around it, but all he saw were some wild ducks swimming there today. As soon as they spotted him they flew off in a hurry. He had hoped to see the otter he'd seen the last time he was there, but the otter was nowhere in sight today. He walked back towards the camp, but as he got close he walked on past it. He thought he would go look at Old Man Dan's lot next door. He walked up the little road that was almost grown up from all the weeds and bushes. As Joe walked through the wooded hammock he saw all kinds of birds flying around in the top of the trees. He noticed that there were a lot of butterflies fluttering around and wondered why the birds weren't catching them to eat. Maybe the birds were living off of the berries he had seen on some bushes there in the woods. It was strange how everything seemed to live together here in the woods. It seemed that all the little creatures were contented with each other. Joe thought that Mother Nature had been good to all the animals here at the Prairie.

Well, it was getting late so he walked back to his camp. Joe grabbed himself something to munch on because his appetite was back again. He went to his car to get himself a book to read. He loved to read whenever he got the chance, but here lately he hadn't been reading at all. Joe found his book, and sat down in his little chair to read for a while before it got too dark. He found that reading a book was very soothing to him, and he seemed to rest better at night when he read some before he went to bed. Well, he read until it got too dark to see the small writing in the book.

Joe built his campfire as usual then he sat down by the fire, and called Loretta Ann. She asked him what he'd been up to today, and he told her all that he had done. She told him she was already packed for their trip to the beach. She asked him if he was ready to go, and he told her he was ready to go when they had first started making plans. Loretta Ann laughed at him because he was funny at the way he said things. She knew that he had to be one of a kind.

She told him to be sure to call her when he left his camp the morning they were to go to the beach because she wanted to make sure that she was up. Of course, we know that neither one of them would probably get much sleep the night before because they were so wound up to go. After they talked for a little while longer they said goodbye to each other then they both called it a night.

Joe had gone to bed but he was restless all night long. He could hardly go to sleep because he kept thinking about the beach trip with Loretta Ann. He just hoped everything would go okay, and that they could have a good time together. He finally told himself that too much couldn't go wrong just going to spend the day at the beach then he dozed off to sleep.

He woke up the next morning early. Once he got out of bed he fixed something to eat for breakfast. Joe knew that tomorrow was the big day that he and Loretta Ann had been waiting for so long to get here. It would only be a few hours until they would be on their way to Ft. Pierce. He was more nervous that a cat on a hot tin roof. He knew he had to calm down some or he would be a total wreck by the next day. He made up his mind that he was just going to stay at his camp today. He would just take it easy and try to calm his nerves down by reading his book. Joe took his book and went to the hammock to read some more. He just lay back and enjoyed his book for the rest of the day. He did stop to take a break so he could call Loretta Ann that afternoon to remind her tomorrow was the big day. Anyone would know that she wasn't about to forget that day at all. It was such an important day to Loretta Ann just like Christmas time is to most people. Now that's what I call an important day.

Joe would call Loretta Ann at lunch to tell her about the little refrigerator that he'd bought. He got her on the phone before she went to lunch. Loretta Ann told him that was really nice of him buying a refrigerator for them to use. She thought Joe was a very thoughtful person in many ways. That was just the way he had been brought up during his childhood. You can say that his father raised him right I guess. Joe told her he'd call later on so she wouldn't miss her lunch hour. As Joe hung up the telephone he checked on the little refrigerator once more and it was forming ice inside the freezer so he knew it would work just fine.

Joe wasn't planning on doing anything else today except to make sure that he had all the beach food packed up. He didn't want to leave anything at camp that he would need for their little day at the beach. He wanted everything to go just perfect for them. The wind had started to blow pretty hard now and he just hoped it didn't blow up a rain. With his luck it would probably rain then they wouldn't get to go on their beach trip. Joe decided to take himself a nap then he'd have to call Loretta Ann later on. Well, he piled up in the hammock once more being careful as he could be. He didn't want to fall out of the hammock and knock the breath out of himself again. Well, believe it or not he made it on to the hammock without losing his balance that time. He thought that he would just snooze a few minutes before he got on the telephone again.

Joe's nap turned out to be a few hours. It was so comfortable there in the little hammock that he couldn't resist the long sleep. Joe was sure sleeping hard when he suddenly woke up. He knew that he was supposed to call his lady friend and he had almost slept too long. As he went to get out of the hammock he got his big toe hung in the netted holes of the hammock. He had taken off his shoes before he lay down so they wouldn't tear the netted holes of the hammock. Maybe if he had left them on then he wouldn't have got himself into another predicament.

Here we go again, poor Joe was in agony now because he couldn't get his toe loose from the netting. The next thing that happened was that he fell to the ground still tangled up in the hammock netting. Boy, his toe was sure hurting bad now and starting to turn a dark purple color. He didn't know how he would get loose because every time he tried to reach up to grab hold of the hammock to pull himself up he would lose his grip and fall back to the ground again.

Joe just lay still on the ground for a minute trying to think of how he should handle this situation. While he lay on the ground he spotted a small rock that had a sharp looking edge on it. It was almost out of his grasp but he kept stretching himself out on the ground as much as the hammock would allow him to do. Finally, he had the rock in his had. Now all he had to do was to lift himself up and hang on to the hammock long enough to cut the netting loose from his toe. This was quite a chore for him to do this because he had gained a few pounds that were now getting in his way. It took Joe about ten minutes before he freed himself from the netting of the hammock swing. His toe looked bad and it was numb from the blood circulation being cut off so long. He kept moving and rubbing on his toe to get the feeling to come back in which it finally did. That was a good sign for Joe because it could have been much worse. He could have wound up losing his toe or he could have hung there tangled up until someone had found him.

Joe got up to go call Loretta Ann before it got too late. He had told her what had happened to him and she couldn't help but laugh even though she knew it wasn't funny. The two of them liked to have talked each other to death. It got to where they acted like they hadn't talked to each other for a long, long, time. I guess they were really getting attached to each other and they had to make up for lost time. It was getting late, so once again Joe and Loretta Ann bid each other farewell. He told her he would call her first thing in the morning to see if she was up. You can bet your sweet bippy that Loretta Ann wouldn't have any trouble at all in getting up that morning. She had been waiting for this moment to get here, and she wasn't going to let anything mess it up. Once again they turned in for the night so they could get up early, and be on their way to the beach the next morning.

Chapter forty three

Trip To The Beach

Well, the day had finally come that Joe and Loretta Ann were going to the beach together. This was the day that they would have some fun in the sun. It was early Friday morning so he called Loretta Ann to see if she was ready to go. It was 5:30 a.m. and it was early, but they both had gotten up at 4:30 a.m. they had been waiting for this day to come for quite a long time. They were both more excited than a couple of kids going on a trip to Disney World.

Loretta Ann told him that she was sitting dead on ready, and he could come pick her up whenever he was ready to go. Joe had packed everything he thought they would need for their little day at the beach. He even loaded up a couple of his little camp chairs so they would have something to sit on. He just wanted to be prepared for his day at the beach.

Joe started up his stationwagon then on his way he went to Loretta Ann's house. He drove faster than he normally did when he had to go to town to get supplies. We know why he was in such a hurry without having to put 2 and 2 together. He was just so excited that today had finally come that he was beside himself.

Joe played his car radio on his way into town. As he was cruising along he was listening to the weather report. The weatherman was saying that the day would be in the high 80's with no chance of rain in sight. Well, he thought that maybe the day would turn out to be a perfect one for him and Loretta Ann while they spent the day at the beach. He wanted his date with Loretta Ann to be another perfect one like the one at the Water Park.

Joe could hardly wait till he made it to her house because he was so excited. When he made it to the little town of Okeechobee he stopped at a gas station to top off his gas tank so they would have plenty of gas to drive around on after they left the beach.

Well, Joe finally made it to Loretta Ann's house. When he pulled up in her driveway he saw her sitting on her doorsteps waiting to be picked up. She had a beach bag sitting on the ground next to her. It looked like she had it packed with enough stuff to stay gone for a week. She had made sure she was ready to go when Joe got there. He got out of his car to open the door for her to get in. She told him thank you, and he told her she was quite welcome. You see he had very good manners. That was another thing that his dad had taught him, and that was to be polite and courteous. Joe was a very polite young man, and he always respected his elders as well as other people. He always said, "yes sir and no sir, and yes mam and no mam," to his elders. Nowadays it's rare to hear anyone saying that to their elder folk. Well, he walked over to pick up her beach bag to carry it to the car. He couldn't believe how heavy it was when he picked it up. As he walked to the back of his car to put the bag inside he tripped on a rock that was in the driveway. Joe fell against his old battlewagon. Luckily, he managed to grab hold of the door handle before he fell and hit the hard ground which was a shelled driveway. After he loaded up the beach bag he did manage to get into his car without anything else happening to him.

Loretta Ann asked him if he was all right, and he told her yes that he guessed that he just had two left feet. He noticed that she was as excited as he was as he got in his car. They both were smiling at each other like two chesser cats. Loretta Ann said a big good morning to Joe, and he said a big good morning back to her. He cranked up his car then looked at Loretta Ann and asked her, "Are you ready for this?" She told him I sure am, and that was because she had been waiting for this day to get here ever since they had planned to go to the beach.

Well, he started backing out of the driveway. They were about to be on their merry way to Ft. Pierce. As he started going through town he asked her if she would like to stop and eat some breakfast before they got on the road to Ft. Pierce. Loretta Ann told him no thanks because she wasn't much on eating early in the morning, and he said he didn't care to eat early either. However he did stop at a little drive-thru café to buy himself a cup of coffee. He asked Loretta Ann if she cared for anything to drink, and she said she would drink some orange juice. He paid for the drinks then started to pull onto the highway once again to go to Ft. Pierce.

Joe had to ask her which way they had to go to get to Ft. Pierce. She showed him the road that they would have to take. As they were leaving Okeechobee he notice how lit up the little town was that early in the morning. He saw how everyone had to get up early to go to work. That reminded him of being back home having to get up real early to go to work.

Since it was still dark they could take their time going to Ft. Pierce. They had the whole day so they didn't have to be in a hurry. They finished drinking their beverages, and then they began to talk away to each other. They acted like they hadn't seen each other for a year or two.

Joe and Loretta Ann were talking so much to each other that they hadn't even realized that they had made it to the town of Ft. Pierce. Now that is what I'd say would have to be an interesting conversation, or it was that they were merely tuned out to the rest of the world.

Joe told Loretta Ann that she would have to guide him along to the beach. She told him she knew exactly which way they had to go. She told Joe to turn left on U.S. Highway 1. He did as he was instructed to do. As they proceeded on their way up the highway he told her that this town was a lot different than Okeechobee. She told him the buildings were much different because they were close to the beach, and years ago that was the style of the houses.

Well, he saw a sign that showed the way to the beach so he turned onto it and followed the signs. They had to go over a bridge that was real high up in the air. Since Joe was afraid of heights this made him real nervous to have to drive over it. He knew one thing for sure and that was he could have never helped to build this tall bridge. If he worked outside he'd have to have a job that let him keep his feet flat on the ground. He could only work in a tall building if it was enclosed around him. Joe didn't want her to see how scared he was so he kept talking away to her. He told her he wasn't much on high places. He told her didn't like to be that high in the air. Loretta Ann told him that the height didn't bother her at all. She told him that she had always wanted to try bungy jumping. She had seen it done on the television and thought that it looked like fun. He told her that he wouldn't bungy jump for a million dollars. She told him that he could go with her sometimes to try it. Joe just looked at her like she had lost her mind or something. As they reached the top part of the bridge his eyes looked as if they would pop out of his head at any moment. He just kept holding his breath hoping he'd soon be off of the bridge. As they reached the flat highway again he breathed with a sigh of relief. Joe was glad to be back on level ground again.

Well, they finally made it to the little park at the beach, and he drove to a spot and parked the car. They got out of the car and walked through the park to see what all was there. They saw some bar-b-que grills and tables next to the inlet. Joe told her that was a great spot to have a picnic. He saw people fishing all along the inlet near the walkway that led out to the ocean. Joe and Loretta Ann decided to walk out on the walkway that was called the Jetties. They noticed that the fish were biting because they saw several people pulling fish in on their poles. Boy, Joe wanted to be there right along with the rest of the people at that moment, but he didn't bring any poles. They walked all through the entire park then went for a walk along the beach.

They walked up and down the beach for a couple of hours just watching the waves roll in and out. Joe asked her if she would like to go swimming, but Loretta Ann told him that she didn't bring a swimsuit to go swimming in. He told her he didn't have one either, but they could go to a shop and he'd buy one if she would like to go into the water. She asked him if he knew how to swim. He told her that he could swim pretty fair. The truth is that Joe wasn't a very good swimmer at all. He could probably dog paddle enough to save himself and that was about it.

As they were walking down the beach Loretta Ann started telling him how she had to save her cousin one time while they were swimming in a lake. It was a nice sunny day and Loretta Ann and her cousin went wading in the lake. It was a big lake and wasn't real deep around the edge of the lake so she and her cousin kept wading out farther and farther into the lake. The water was up to their chest and they were enjoying themselves just splashing around.

They were having so much fun that they hadn't really paid any attention to the dark clouds that were rolling in over the lake. Well, the wind started to pick up and blow causing the lake to get rough. As it got rougher they were trying to come back into shore, but the waves were starting to go over their heads. Loretta Ann's cousin couldn't swim much at all so she had to put her cousin on her shoulders to try to carry her in towards the shore.

Loretta Ann was about to drown herself staying under the water so long trying to walk into the shore so she had to let her cousin back into the water. She told her cousin to hop up and down in the water, and to catch her breath each time she came up out of the water. Loretta Ann did this to make sure her cousin would be okay because she was going in to shore to get help. Her cousin listened to her and did as she was told to do. She had learned to breathe in air and hold it until she had to come back up again. Loretta Ann's cousin kept on bouncing up and down like she was instructed to do.

She didn't want to leave her cousin by herself, but knew she had to get some help immediately. As she hugged her cousin good-bye she told her she would be right back, and to be sure she kept hopping up and down till she got back. Well, it only took Loretta Ann just a few minutes until she made it to land again.

As she got out of the water she started to run towards a lady lying in a lounge chair sunbathing. As she approached the lady she asked her if she had a spare tire she could use for a few minutes. The lady asked her what she needed it for and Loretta Ann told her real quickly about her cousin out in the lake. She ran over to her car and opened the trunk to get the tire out for Loretta Ann. The lady asked her if she was sure the tire would float in the water, and Loretta Ann told her that it would. The lady told her to be careful, and that she would call for help. It was then that Loretta Ann headed on her way back into the lake to get her cousin.

She finally managed to get the tire into the water. Once she put the tire in the water it started to float and that made it easy to push it along in the water. The water was getting deeper and deeper. The waves were getting higher and higher and Loretta Ann was beginning to get worried because she could see no sign of her cousin at all. She was getting very scared now.

Loretta Ann started to yell out her cousin's name, but still she couldn't hear or see her cousin. Loretta Ann started crying and began to pray that she would be able to find her cousin alive. It was about 10 minutes more that Loretta had to keep yelling for her cousin, and then she heard her cousin calling out for her. That was one of the most beautiful sounds that she had ever heard. Loretta Ann kept going in the direction towards her cousin's yelling, and finally she saw her cousin's head bobbing up and down out of the water. Boy, that was the best sight that she could have seen.

As Loretta Ann grabbed hold of her cousin's hand she pulled her to the tire so she could hang on, and all the two of them could do was hug each other and cry. Now they could float safely back to shore. They didn't care how long it took as long as they were both together again, and had the tire to carry them to safety.

The two of them held on to the spare tire and both kicked their feet to try to propel themselves into shore. The wind was still blowing hard so they had to just float around hanging on to the tire until the bad weather storm blew by. As the lake calmed down once again they began to dog paddle themselves towards the shore. The wind had blown them farther out into the lake. It was about an hour before they finally made it to shore. There were people gathering at the lake to get ready to go out to rescue them. Everyone started yelling and clapping when they saw the two tired girls dog paddling in on the spare tire coming to shore. Loretta Ann and her cousin thanked God that they made it back safely. When they reached the shore they were 2 tired young ladies.

    Loretta Ann and her cousin were greeted by the concerned people, and that made them feel good that people really cared about their lives that could have been easily taken away by them drowning in the big lake. From that day on Loretta Ann and her cousin never went swimming again unless they had some kind of floating raft or inner tube to keep them safe. Since her cousin wasn't that great of a swimmer she started taking swimming lessons, and turned out to be a good strong swimmer.

    That was one day that the two girls would remember till the day they die. That was a horrible experience that taught them how precious life is, and how you could be gone in the twinkling of an eye. They learned how quickly one can be taken away if you're not careful. The two girls thanked the lady for the loan of her spare tire that helped save her cousin's life. The lady told the girls that they were very welcome. She also told them that they had someone watching over them to guide them back safely. They went on home after that incident and rested up just glad that everything turned out okay. From that day on each one just took each day at a time, and enjoyed each day as it came. Loretta Ann and her cousin knew now that how you spent your time was very important to, because time waits on no man, woman, or child.

    Joe told Loretta Ann that was a very brave thing that she did by saving her cousin. She could have very well lost her life, but unselfishly she put her life on the line to save her cousin's. As he had listened to her story it made him see how good a person Loretta Ann was. He knew there was something special about her right from the start.

After they started walking back to the park she told him if he wanted to go swimming they would. She told Joe she would like to have a tube or some kind of raft to float on while she was in the water. He told her they would find a shop to buy them each a swimsuit then he would find some type of raft so they could float around in the water. They left the little park then found a swimsuit shop only a block from the park. They went inside and tried on several suits then bought a couple suits so they could to go back to the beach again.

As Joe came to a gas station he had an idea. He stopped then went inside to see if they had any inner tubes. It turned out that they had some tubes so he bought two of them. He bought one for Loretta Ann and one for himself. Joe had the man at the station to air the inner tubes up in the back of his car. The man did as he instructed him to do. He thanked the man then he and Loretta Ann left the gas station to go back to the park at the beach.

When they got back to the park he told her they would grab them a bite to eat before they went swimming if she wanted to. She told him that sounded good. He parked his car by one of the tables so they could sit and enjoy their lunch while watching the boats coming in and going out of the ocean. Joe took the lunchmeat out of the little refrigerator and put it on the table so they could make themselves a sandwich to eat. He had potato chips, pickles, and more food for them to snack on. The drinks were ice cold that he got from inside the refrigerator. He knew that was one thing he'd bought that would come in handy to use if he ever went camping again.

After they finished eating their lunch they waited for an hour before going into the water to swim. They got out their swimsuits so they could put them on. Joe and Loretta Ann found the park bathrooms then they went inside and changed into their swimsuits. Loretta Ann had brought a towel in her beach bag in case they had to sit on the ground. She thought they were going to have a picnic so she had even brought a tablecloth to use. Instead they just ate off the bare table which was fine.

As each one came out of their bathroom you could see their faces start to turn red. They both were bashful being in a swimsuit. Well, Joe saw how bashful Loretta Ann was so he decided to get her mind on something else so she wouldn't be so shy. He told her they would have to get the inner tubes out of his car first before they went swimming. She was glad to help him with the inner tubes. The only thing was that they had a hard time getting the tubes out of the back of his car. The man had put so much air in them that they were wedged in the back of his car. Joe and Loretta Ann pulled and tugged on the inner tubes for a few minutes. He told her to sit on the tubes so he could see if he could pull them out that way. Well, after a long hard battle getting the tubes out of the car they finally managed to pull them out. Before he managed to get them out of his car things looked kind of dim for a while. Joe thought that if worse came to worse he would have to let some of the air out of the inner tubes. He didn't want to have to do this because he didn't have any way to air the tubes back up. Anyway they had their tubes now so they headed towards the beach.

Chapter forty four

Floating Far Away

Well, it did turn out for the best because Loretta Ann and Joe made it into the water with their tubes. She had her tube around her waist holding onto it as they walked into the water. They walked out farther into the deep water so they would be able to float on their tubes. The water was nice and warm. The water was real salty as Joe found out real quick like because he tried to climb on the top of his tube and fell into the water. He couldn't believe how the salt-water burned his eyes. There for a moment he was blinded because he couldn't open his eyes. Finally, after a few tries of hopping on to his tube he actually made it, and now he just wanted to lay back and float on his big tube. Loretta Ann did the same as Joe, and now they both were just relaxing in the sun as they floated around in the ocean. They both were taking in the good old warm sunshine, and enjoying their day at the beach.

Joe and Loretta Ann were like two peas in a pod. They were really enjoying each other's company at this moment. Here they were all alone in the ocean without a care in the world. Time was just floating right on by like they were on their inner tubes. Joe told Loretta Ann this was like living the Life of Riley, and she agreed with him 100%. He asked her if she came to the beach very often, and she told him that she didn't like to go by herself.

Loretta Ann told him that she often went to the movies, and once in a while she would try her luck at going fishing. She told him that she went fishing with her friend May Day sometimes, but they hardly ever caught any fish. She told him that if she caught her limit she was doing good. She told him that her limit was only 3 fish if she was even able to catch them. Joe laughed at her when she told him this. He told her that she must not be holding her mouth right. Loretta Ann told him she guessed she wasn't.

Well, the two of them were having so much fun that they hadn't realized they had been floating on the tube for a couple of hours already. They hadn't even paid any attention to the changing tide, and how it had carried them a long ways off shore. When they did finally notice they had floated away from the shore they knew they were in trouble now. Matter of fact they couldn't even see the shoreline because they were so far out. They couldn't see any sign of land at all. They couldn't even see the trees off in the horizon. Loretta Ann was almost at the point of panicking, but she wanted to stay calm if at all possible. Joe told her not to worry that they would be okay as long as they stayed together.

He told her that maybe a boat would come by soon and then they could catch a ride back to shore. At least he was sure hoping for one to come by. It would take 6 hours or more before the tide changed to go back into the shore. Well, one thing that was good, and that was they were stranded together and not all alone. The tide was going on out and there was no telling where the two of them were going to wind up at. They would have to just go with the flow until they found land or until they got rescued if you get my drift.

Since Joe had been down in Florida he had wanted to get a suntan so he could have that tanned look when he went back home from vacation. Well, as it was turning out he would have plenty of tan because right at this moment he was already sunburned from the few hours they had been on their tubes. Joe already had the burnt red lobster look. Neither Joe nor Loretta Ann even thought to get any suntan lotion to put on before they went in swimming. I guess it was all the excitement that had made them forget. Joe and Loretta Ann both would be cooked and sizzled sealed if they had to stay out in the sun too much longer because they were too white to get so much sun at one time.

Well, since there was nothing to do except to try to make the best of it Loretta Ann told Joe they would sing some songs to try to pass the time by. Well, the first song as you would guess was, "Row, Row, Row, Your Boat." I guess just about every kid had learned that song at one time or another. They laughed and sang probably 20 songs or more before they tired out from singing.

It was beginning to get late in the afternoon and still no one had come to their rescue. They were beginning to get a little worried now because people got lost at sea all the time. Joe told Loretta Ann they should try treading the water with their hands and arms in the opposite direction that their tubes were floating. They did this for a while, but they weren't getting anywhere fast. Joe slid off his tube into the water because his legs were trying to cramp up on him. He was hanging onto the side of the tube when he felt something brush against his leg in the water. It took him less than 10 seconds to get back on his tube.

Loretta Ann asked him what was the matter, and he told her he felt something hit his leg in the water. Joe was nervous after this happened to him. As they floated along on their tubes they began to see fish start jumping out of the water all around them. Joe asked Loretta Ann if she knew what kind of fish they were, and she told him they were probably some kind of baitfish. Well, he picked up on the word baitfish in a hurry. Joe knew there wasn't anything for him and Loretta Ann to do except lay back and watch the fish jump around in the water. One fish jumped over Loretta Ann's tube startling her causing her to scream out. Joe thought this was funny so he laughed at her and told her it was only a fish. The next thing that happened was that 3 fish jumped over him in which one smacked Joe right in the face. When this happened Loretta Ann went into a fit of laughter. She asked Joe if he saw the fish coming, and then laughed that much harder. He started laughing at how she was laughing because it was so funny to him. After a while they both quit laughing at each other because their sides ached so badly from all the laughter.

Joe asked her if she knew why the fish kept jumping around so much, and then she told him something was probably trying to catch the fish to eat them. She told him that barracuda, dolphins, sharks, and many more fish feed on the small baitfish. After she told Joe about the fish, he then saw a fin poking up out of the water. This was when he yelled out shark, shark, and almost scared Loretta Ann out of her wits.

Joe was beginning to panic now. Loretta Ann told him to be real still and not to move because sharks will bite you if you thrash around in the water. Joe asked, "What are we going to do?" She told him, "Just be still, don't move, and to quit talking" so he did as Loretta Ann had told him. He took her advice very well because he was too scared to move anyways. Joe was so scared that it seemed his heart was going to beat out of his chest. He was more scared right at that moment than he had been when he was fighting with the escapee, and the alligator.

Well, the shark swam closer to Joe and Loretta Ann's tubes. Joe was beginning to hyperventilate and Loretta Ann noticed this right away. She told him to breathe deep and slow. Joe did as he was told. He then held his breath as the shark swam even closer to them. They both lay motionless on the inner tubes too scared to even bat an eye.

Well, there were several more fins that popped up out of the water. They began to circle slowly around Joe and Loretta Ann's tubes. One even bumped Joe's tube several times, but he didn't move an inch. He wished at that moment that he could walk on water, but that wasn't about to happen either. Loretta Ann could already feel the sharks' teeth, and hadn't even been bitten yet. The sharks had been circling around them for several minutes, but it seemed liked hours. The sharks started to swim away quickly now because some dolphins began to chase them away from Loretta Ann and Joe. The two of them were relieved at last.

Neither one of them could actually believe what was happening to them. They were glad that the dolphins came along to chase off the sharks. Dolphins hate sharks and will kill them if they get the chance. It's like dolphins are the protectors of the ocean. They have saved many peoples lives throughout the years of mankind. The dolphin is usually a friendly mammal, but some have been known to be aggressive at times.

Joe noticed that Loretta Ann had a piece of nylon rope tied to her inner tube. He told her to hand it to him so he could tie her tube to his so they wouldn't get separated from each other. Well, just about that time she felt something nudging her tube and it started to move. This at first scared her, but when she saw it was only a dolphin she just sat still. The dolphin pushed their tubes along in the water for a little ways then he swam on off with the other dolphins so he wouldn't get left behind.

Well, it was peaceful once again and Loretta Ann and Joe knew they had to try to figure out something to help them out of their situation. They both knew that the sun set in the west so that is the direction they should start paddling in. That would be the direction the tide would go once it changed again.

Well, they couldn't believe that no one had come looking for them. They couldn't believe they hadn't even seen a boat at all. Here they were lost in the middle of the ocean with nothing to drink or eat. Both of them were saying their prayers that they would be found before it was too late. Joe and Loretta Ann knew the tide was changing because the water was beginning to flow swiftly in the opposite direction. They just held onto each other's hand, and floated in the direction of the changing tide. After about 2 hours they saw waves going up and down. They sure hoped that the ocean wasn't going to get rough because the waves looked dangerous to them. Well, as it happened Joe and Loretta Ann were going back in the right direction, but going to a different place than they had started from. Little did they know how close they were until they finally saw some trees and land? Thank the good Lord they could see land. Well, they started to paddle their inner tubes as fast as they could.

Chapter forty five

Home On The Island

It was a miracle they had made it back to land. Joe and Loretta Ann were 2 happy people at this moment. They pulled their inner tubes behind them not even noticing how tired they both were. They just knew how happy they were to be safe again. As they went ashore they knew they were in a different place. They had no idea at all where they were at, but they knew they were glad they weren't in the shark-infested waters of the ocean anymore. They went and sat on the ground trying to figure out where they were. Wherever they were, one thing for sure is that they were now stranded.

Joe noticed a tree that looked like a fruit tree so he got up and walked over to it. It was an orange tree and it had a lot of fruit on it. Joe picked some of the oranges then went back to where Loretta Ann was still sitting. He told her to have an orange since they hadn't had anything to eat or drink since lunch. They ate a couple of oranges each then they went to see what else they could find. They found an old building that had almost fallen down. There was an old shed that was in the trees behind the old house. It was protected from the weather somewhat because it was in fair shape. Loretta Ann and Joe went inside the little shed once they managed to get the door opened.

They looked all around the shed to see if they could find anything they could use in case they weren't rescued. There were some old pots, plates, and coffee cups. They even found some cooking utensils and silverware. At least they could set up housekeeping with what they had. They walked through the woods looking to see if they saw anymore houses or maybe some people. As they walked all over the little island they had landed on, there were no houses or people to be found at all. So this meant that Loretta Ann and Joe were all alone on the island. They were on an island, and they didn't even know which one it was. It could have been deserted for years, and they might never be found at all. At least they were safe right now for the time being.

Well, it was starting to get dark so they knew they had better try to fix them a place to bed down for the night. They found an ax in the shed then went to cut some limbs from a tree to make a place to lay on. They tried to find some wood to see if they would be able to try to start a fire. Well, they didn't manage to start a fire the first night because they couldn't get the sticks to burn as they tried rubbing them together. They ate the rest of the oranges Joe had picked then they went to bed since they didn't have any lights to see by. They would have to just make the best of it. Maybe they would find some way to try to get help tomorrow. They said goodnight to each other then went to bed on the limbs they had cut. They had made their beds under some trees since it was a cool breezy evening, but soon realized that it was in the wrong place.

During the night the wind started to blow hard. It started lightning and then it started to rain. Here they were right in the middle of the bad weather. Joe and Loretta Ann managed to find the shed when the sky lit up from the lightning. It leaked in many places in the roof, but they did find a spot that wasn't leaking so that was where they stayed. They had got so sunburned from being in the sun all day that the rainy weather wasn't chilly to them at all. They were so tired that they went back to sleep not waking up until the next morning.

When morning came Joe and Loretta Ann got up trying to get their bearings. They finally realized that they were still on the island that they landed on the day before. They both said good morning to each other. They knew since they were down to their bare necessities, which were their swimsuits. This meant that they had to find some sort of covering to make them some clothes out of. If they didn't find some covering for their bodies they would totally get fried from the hot sun.

The first thing Joe and Loretta Ann decided to do was to start looking around the little island for food. They found some more fruit trees so at least they would have some fruit to eat. As they walked towards the center of the island they noticed that the elevation was getting higher.

As they walked on they began to go up some rock formations that were almost as big as a mountain. When they reached the top of the rocks they could see all around the island. It was a spectacular view from up there. They even saw a big ship out in the ocean, but it was a long way off. They knew they had to build a fire some way or another. Joe had an idea, but he wasn't sure if it would even work or not. He had it in his mind to take some rocks and hit them together to make them spark enough to catch some leaves on fire. Joe had seen that done on a program on television before. He would try almost anything once. It couldn't hurt to try that was for sure.

He also thought about making some kind of S.O.S. signs on top of the rocks. Joe and Loretta Ann headed back to the little camp they had made to see what they could come up with. She told him they might try hanging their inner tubes up on some poles. They would have to cut down some trees to get the poles, but it might just work if an airplane happened to fly over and see the tubes hanging in the air on the poles. Well, they first cut down a couple of tall skinny trees to get the poles they needed. They trimmed off all the limbs and leaves so they had 2 smooth poles. Once they were finished with the poles their next project was to get a fire started.

They chopped up some pieces of old dried wood they found

next to the old shed. It was just luck that they had found any dry wood at all after the rain they had last night. Joe managed to scrape off some thin shavings from the wood. The thin shavings would start burning easily if they were able to get the spark they needed from the rocks. Joe then took 2 rocks and began to hit them together. He did get them to put off some sparks by hitting them together, but still couldn't get them to spark enough to make a fire.

Joe and Loretta Ann cut down a couple more skinny trees to make some more poles out of because they might have to use them later on. They knew they had to get a camp built in case they were stranded very long on the island. The ax Joe was using was very dull, but it got the job done. He was thankful to have it because he wouldn't have been able to cut the trees with his bare hands. When he finished he had 2 more smooth poles. He told Loretta Ann they had better fix their S.O.S. signals out of the tubes first. Now came the chore of carrying the poles to the top of the rocks. That was where Loretta Ann became a lot of help to Joe. She grabbed one end of the pole and Joe grabbed the other end. Between the both of them they made it up to the top of the high rocks without any trouble. They still had to make one more trip up to the top of the rocks with the other pole. After Joe and Loretta Ann tied the tubes to the poles with the nylon cord, they managed to get the poles stood up between some rocks so they wouldn't fall down on the ground. The tubes were flapping around on top of the poles, and you couldn't help but notice them moving.

Joe and Loretta Ann returned to the little place where they had cut up the other trees. Now they were getting ready to set up housekeeping so they began to patch up the little old shed because they had decided to make it into their camphouse. They put some limbs on the top of the little shed that he'd cut off of the trees he'd made into poles. This should help stop the rain from coming into the little shed so bad. It didn't take them very long to get this done so they knew they had a lot more things to do before night came again. After Joe put the finishing touch on the little camphouse shed he told Loretta Ann they were going to have to get things all fired up. She looked at him with such a funny look that he told her he was talking about building the fire. Loretta Ann smiled then told him that's right.

Joe took the 2 rocks that he'd found and tried to spark them off again. He beat and beat the 2 rocks together, but finally gave up. This was when Loretta Ann decided to give it a try. She had the little shavings in a pile on the ground. She started to beat the rocks together, and got them to put off some big sparks. Loretta Ann had the rocks putting off sparks that you wouldn't believe. Joe just didn't know what to think about this. He thought that maybe she would be able to get the fire going because he just didn't have the touch it seemed. After she tried this for a few minutes and couldn't get the fire to burn she stopped, and just sat there like she was in a deep thought. Loretta Ann started hitting the rocks together again, and this time she blew air on the sparks that fell onto the wood shavings. Bingo, this time she got a fire started. Joe couldn't believe his eyes. They quickly gathered more leaves that were under the trees that hadn't got wet from the rain. They put some wood little by little onto the fire, and soon had a big blaze going. Joe and Loretta Ann did a little dance around the fire because they were both happy to have the fire going. They knew now that if they caught some fish or something else they would be able to have a hot meal at least.

Joe told her they needed to get up a bunch of wood to lay by the fire so they could keep it going all the time. He did at his little camp at the Prairie when he was there all day. He told her maybe someone would see it burning then they would be found. Joe and Loretta Ann sat down to rest a little while before they did anything else. They just sat on the ground talking about the adventure they'd had so far.

Loretta Ann asked him if he thought that his car would be noticed since it was at the park all night long. He said they probably had checked it out, but no one knew him because he wasn't from Florida. Also if they tried to contact anyone they would have to break into his car to check his drivers licenses to find out any information. Since he was on vacation he wouldn't be missed at all.

Well, Loretta Ann wouldn't be missed until Monday since that was the day she was to return to work. She would be missed if she didn't come to work because she never missed a day's work for any reason. Even if Loretta Ann was sick she always managed to do her work. It just looked like they were stranded until someone saw them on the island. If Loretta Ann was gone too long her friend May Day would call the law. May Day always looked out for Loretta Ann and Loretta Ann always checked on May Day because she had no one else to depend on. The other possibility would be if Runt heard the news that Loretta Ann hadn't went to work and couldn't be found then she would be able to help the police because she was the only one that knew that Joe and Loretta Ann were going to the beach. Surely, they would be found soon.

Well, Joe told Loretta Ann that he was going back up on top of the rocks to check on the inner tubes on the poles. He wanted to make sure they hadn't fallen over. He told her that maybe they would be seen and then maybe help would come. He told her that they could pick some of the oranges he'd found then he'd go up on the rocks to check the poles.

They started walking to the orange tree when Loretta Ann saw a mango tree that was full of mangoes. She told him that at least they would have something to eat while they were on the island. Loretta Ann climbed up high enough in the mango tree that she was able to pick some of the mangoes, and tossed them to the ground. They gathered up some of the oranges and mangos then carried them back to their little camp. She asked Joe if he wanted any of the fruit to eat, but he told her he would eat some when he came back from checking on the inner tubes on top of the rocks. She told him she'd wait for him at the camp then she'd eat later on also.

Joe climbed back to the top of the formation of rocks. He was tired from the climbing, but he didn't stop to rest until he went back down. While he was on the top of the rocks making sure the tubes and poles were secured tightly, he noticed a big bird diving into the water. He thought at first that the bird was hurt, but then saw the bird surface to the top of the water again. As the bird came up out of the water he saw a big fish in the bird's mouth. He couldn't believe how big the fish was that the bird had caught. Joe then got an idea of what they could do to get some food to eat. As he went back down the rocks to the camp he looked for a limb that could be made into a spear. Joe was actually going to see if he could spear some fish so that they would have something to eat.

Joe found a long slender piece of branch that he'd cut from one of the trees. He took his little ax and began to strip all the bark and knots off the branch. Once he finished doing this he put a point on the end of the branch thus making it into a homemade spear. It was really limber and lightweight so he shouldn't have any trouble throwing it at all. Joe took the rest of the nylon string that was left from Loretta Ann's tube then tied it to the spear. He wanted to be able to catch the fish if he did accidentally spear one. He didn't want the fish to get away with his spear so that's why he wasn't taking any chances.

Loretta Ann told him he'd better eat some mangos and oranges or he would get hungry and lose his strength if he didn't eat. She had a large pile of mangoes stacked up for them to eat whenever they felt like eating. She asked him if he wanted a mango, but he told her he didn't want one right now because he was fixing to go fishing. Loretta Ann started eating her a mango then followed him down to the water to watch him try to spear some fish.

Joe walked out into the water, but didn't see any fish at all. He stood real still hoping that one might swim by. Well, it happened that one fish did swim by, but when he tried to spear it the fish took off like a scalded dog. Joe waited and waited, but he saw no more fish. He started to wade back to shore when he spotted a crab in the water. He moved towards the crab slower than a turtle. Joe then carefully aimed his spear and threw it at the crab. Believe it or not he speared the crab. It was a big blue crab, but he would have to catch more than one to be able to have a meal.

Joe was proud of himself that he actually managed to spear the crab. Loretta Ann got all excited and started clapping her hands and applauding his catch. As she clapped her hands together her mango went flying through the air. Oh, well she could always get another mango to eat later on, but right now she was more interested in Joe's hunting for fish and crabs. Joe threw the speared crab onto the beach then went back into the water to try to catch something else for them to eat.

Well, as it went his patience and persevering paid off because he ended up spearing a total of 8 crabs and 2 fish. They went back to the little camp they made. Joe cleaned the fish and crabs then he strung the crabs and fish on a stick. He cooked the crabs and fish over the fire they had built earlier. They ended up have a seafood meal that day afterall. Loretta Ann really enjoyed her meal because she was smacking so loud that Joe could hardly eat his meal because he was watching her eat. He had accomplished getting food that day, but they didn't know how long they would be there on the little island so he might not be as lucky the next time.

Joe was just hoping that they would be rescued soon because him and Loretta Ann didn't have any clothes to wear except what they had on, and that was just their swimsuits. They didn't have any food on the island except the fruit, and whatever he would be able to catch out of the ocean. Surely someone would be able to see their inner tubes on top of the poles, and as long as they had wood to burn maybe someone would see the smoke coming from the little island. Joe and Loretta Ann had found a lot of wood to burn they just had to make sure that during the night that it didn't go out.

They finally finished eating their meal. They started to talk about trying to get some palm fronds from the palm trees to make them a hat. Maybe they could also make some type of clothing so that they wouldn't get anymore sunburn. As it was, they both were red as beets from all the sun they had received. Being around the salt-water didn't help out either because they weren't able to wash off the saltwater residue.

Joe and Loretta Ann went through an old trunk they had found inside the little shed. It had some clothes in it that looked like they were 50 or 60 years old, but right at that moment they didn't care how out of style the clothes were. Joe found an old pair of pants that were so big that he had to cut a vine off a tree in order to keep them up. Loretta Ann found a dress that was so long and baggy that she could have made 2 dresses out of the one dress for herself. They both laughed at each other, but soon began to realize again that they were stranded on the island for how long they didn't know.

Joe told her they would have to take the little pots they had found in the old house and boil some of the ocean water to get the salt out so they would have some to drink. She told him that was a good idea, and then they both went to work on that little project. He told Loretta Ann after they got some water boiled that they would walk over the island again to make sure it was deserted. He told her that there might be someone on the other side that they hadn't seen earlier. She told him okay. After they finished boiling the water they set out to explore the little island again.

They had walked so long that it seemed like they had been gone for hours. They walked through a bunch of trees that looked like a jungle because it was so thick with trees and underbrush. They saw some birds on the island, and were surprised to see what kind they were. As they got closer to the birds Joe noticed that there were parakeets, canaries, and 2 big parrots up in the trees. Apparently the birds had made the island their home. On islands in the ocean it was normal to see birds of their species because they live in the wild before they are caught and sold in stores. Many birds were carried to different places by hurricanes and bad storms.

Loretta Ann thought the birds were so beautiful because of their colors. It could also have been seeing them in the wild that really made it so nice to. He told her about how he had seen some pink flamingos in a cow pasture one day when he was heading to the Prairie. Loretta Ann told him she had seen some flamingos in a pond in a field a time or two herself. She told Joe they probably flew away from the Jungle Park that was once in Jupiter. There used to be monkeys, birds, alligators, snakes, and many more animals in the little Jungle Park, but unfortunately people quit visiting the little park so it closed. Joe told Loretta Ann it was a shame that little places had to close because of different things moving in drawing the interest of people away to newer attractions. Loretta Ann said, "Yes that's a sign of progress, but it's the little people that made the country what it is today." If it hadn't been for the little people working that the big boys I'm sure wouldn't be where they are today. Joe said that's the truth, and it makes a lot of sense.

Joe and Loretta Ann had walked a very long way from their camp, and had seen no sign of another human being at all. They decided to go back to camp because they wanted to keep their fire going, and if it went out they might not be able to get it fired up again. It was very important that they kept the fire burning. If they had a fire they would be able to cook anything they caught for food to eat. They also could have warmth at night in case it turned out to be a cool night.

Chapter forty six

The Sound Of The Waterfalls

Well, Joe and Loretta Ann saw some different rock formations that they hadn't noticed before. They climbed up on them to see what they could see from the top of the rocks. It was an unbelievable sight to see. The water was so pretty and crystal blue that it looked as if it were a scene from a fairytale movie. The view below on the island of all the trees was also spectacular. As they stood on the top of the rocks admiring the beautiful scenery they heard a trickling sound. Joe told Loretta Ann that it sounded like running water. She told him that there was no way running water could be on the island. He told her they would check to see what the sound was.

Well, as it turned out it there was water flowing over the edge of the rocks. They climbed down the rock formation to the other side of the rocks to see what the water was flowing into. When they found the running water it turned out to be a small waterfalls. The waterfalls had made a pond from the falling water. There's no telling how many years the waterfalls had been there. There was a steady flow of water coming from the top of the rocks. They found a cave at the bottom of the little waterfalls.

This was simply amazing to Joe and Loretta Ann. They walked over to the little cave and looked inside, but didn't go in because it was so dark. Loretta Ann put her hands under the running water of the little falls and tasted the water. She was astonished by what she had discovered. The water from the waterfalls wasn't salty at all. She told Joe to drink some of the water, and he was a little hesitant at first because of his ordeal at the Prairie. He tasted the water and couldn't believe it wasn't salty tasting. He told her they would bring their pots there to the falls and get some water to carry back to camp.

Joe and Loretta Ann hurried back to the little camp. They were happy as two little larks at what they had found. They had to put a bunch of wood on the campfire because it was beginning to burn out. He told her they would have keep putting wood on the fire because they wanted to be sure someone could see their smoke so they could be found. The other wood was burning up fast since the wind was blowing so hard. They would look for more wood after they had a bite to eat. Since they didn't have a big supply of food they each had to settle for a fruit meal. Joe and Loretta Ann ate a mango and an orange before they went back to the waterfalls to get some water. Once they got enough water back to the camp, they started to look for big pieces of wood for their fire.

At least they could survive if they could just keep fruit, water, and catch food from the ocean to eat. She told Joe they had to have a guardian angel looking out for them. He agreed with Loretta Ann, and told her he was glad they did have one. As they headed back to get some water they heard an airplane engine. They both ran to the top of the rock formation where Joe had put up the poles that had the inner tubes hanging from them. The plane had already flown out of sight by the time they reached the top of the rocks.

They were both out of breath by the time they reached the top of the high rocks so they sat down to catch their breath again. Being disappointed as they both were, each one got up to head back down to the camp once they had got rested. They took the pots to the waterfalls, and filled them up with the fresh water. Once they reached the camp again they put the water under the shed to keep anything from getting into it.

They both sat down under a palm tree and began to talk again about the things they needed to do on the island while they were occupying it. They both agreed they needed to make a fire on the top of the rocks high up in the air where the poles were at. Joe told Loretta Ann that they might have to separate at night to make sure that each one could keep each of the fires burning. Loretta Ann wasn't sure about being alone on the island at night. In the daytime she could at least see what was around her. Joe told her if she was scared to stay by herself then he would just get up at night and check on the fire on top of the rocks.

Loretta Ann told him she would help him keep wood on both of the fires because she wanted to help as much as she could. He told her okay then they started to gather up a lot of wood and carry it up on top of the rocks for the fire. Well, everything went okay until Joe slipped on a rock and fell down hard on his rumpus. He thought he had broken his tailbone, but it turned out he just got bruised up a little bit. Joe walked funny for a while, but soon recovered from his little accident.

He took one of the big pieces of burning wood from the campfire then went back up on the rocks and started the other fire. They had plenty of wood on the fire so it could be spotted a long way off. They should be found in no time at all because of all the smoke coming from the little island. They knew they would be okay as long as they stayed close to each other so as not to get lost. You couldn't separate them if you tried I don't think.

Neither one of them really knew that much about survival techniques, but they were learning. Joe had watched enough survival shows on television to help out some. Loretta Ann didn't get the chance to watch television much so she was mostly a newcomer on camping. Well, they finished up the work they had to do then rested for a short while. Joe later on walked down to the ocean to try to spear some fish and crabs again. Loretta Ann stayed underneath the palm tree while Joe went spear fishing. She was tired from her day's work on the island. She dosed off to sleep and was really resting comfortably.

Joe in the meantime was alone in the water waiting patiently for something to swim by so he could try to spear it for their supper. Well, he threw his spear at a fish and a crab, but this time he missed them both. Joe was just about to give up on his spear fishing for the day when he just happened to see a big stingray. He wasn't too sure if he should try to mess with this funny looking creature or not. He knew he would probably lose his spear if he did manage to spear the big stingray. Joe no doubt would have a big fight on his hands. Well, he made his throw at the stingray, and bingo he hit the stingray. The stingray did like any other animal would have done. It took off in the opposite direction once the spear hit him. Joe and the stingray weren't fighting with each other. They were both just fighting to survive you could say. The stingray was swimming for his life, but it turned out that Joe was a bigger fighter than he was. Joe had been flopping in and out of the water trying to catch the stingray for their food for almost an hour. This fight had given him plum out, but he wound up with another meal for him and Loretta Ann.

Joe was tuckered out once he dragged the stingray to shore. He looked like a tired half-drowned rat that had just escaped a flood. Joe looked at the stingray and wondered how in the world that was he going to clean this animal so they could eat him. Well, he picked him up very carefully and walked over to the spot where Loretta Ann was sleeping under the palm tree. He held the stingray over Loretta Ann and some water fell off the stingray onto her face. When this happened it woke her up from her sleep. Not only did this wake Loretta Ann up, but it also scared her so badly that she screamed to the top of her lungs when she saw the stingray Joe was holding over her. He didn't mean to scare Loretta Ann, all he only wanted to do was to show her his catch of the day. Once she got calmed down again, she asked him how he would be able to clean the stingray, and he told her he wasn't sure how, but he'd find a way.

Well, Joe looked in the old house to see if there was any

kind of tools he could find that would be of use to him in cleaning the stingray. He didn't find anything in the house, but he did find a blade of some sort in the old shed. With the blade he managed to get the hide off of the stingray without much trouble. Loretta Ann found a little rusty spoon that she cleaned up enough to use. She took the spoon and dug the meat off of the stingray in little chunks. After they had all the meat from the stingray then they began to thread the little chunks onto some sticks Joe had managed to skin clean and smooth. They cooked the stingray over the open fire. They had so much meat cooked it would feed them for several meals, but it would spoil if they didn't eat it because they had no way to keep it refrigerated. They didn't have any seasonings to put on the meat while they cooked it, but it sure tasted good anyways.

Joe told her he would use the leftover meat to chum up more fish when he went spear fishing for their next meal. She told him she would have never thought of that at all. They both took their plates they found in the little shed filled them up with the stingray and then went and sat by the fire and ate their meal. Each one was thankful to have a meal to eat. Loretta Ann told him if they had to stay on the island very long they wouldn't know how to act once they reached civilization again. Joe laughed then told her that he was sure it wouldn't be hard for him to adjust back to civilization at all.

Joe finished eating before Loretta Ann so he walked back up on top of the rocks to check the fire to see if it had enough wood on it. As he made it to the top he could see the fire was still burning and it had plenty of wood on it. He stood on top of the high rocks looking out at the sea. He stood there thinking about how lucky they were to have landed on this island. It could have been much worse because they could still be on the tubes floating out in the ocean. Oh well, he thought things could be much worse than what they are right at this moment. Matter of fact he really felt safe on this little island instead of being in the water with all the sharks and other creatures. Out there he was expecting to be a meal for some ocean creature at anytime.

He made his way back down the rocks to the camp again. He told Loretta Ann the fire was burning okay up on the rocks, but they would have to check on it before they turned in for the night. She told him the meal he cooked was good. He told her it was unusual but at least it was filling. He talked about how he had speared the stingray, and Loretta Ann was of course was all ears when he told her his story. The day was sort of breezy, but it was nice.

Joe told Loretta Ann that they would walk down to the cave tomorrow if she felt up to it. She told him sure she'd like to see what was in it. Anyways she wanted to bathe in the waterfall since she hadn't been able to take a bath since they had been on the island. Joe told her they would take a lighted piece of wood if they could keep it burning long enough so maybe they could see what was inside the cave.

The two of them didn't do much for the rest of the remainder of the day. However they did scratch the days they had been on the island on the trunk of a tree. This way they would be able to keep up with the day of the week plus keep up with how many days they were on the island. Since this was only the second day on the island they were doing okay.

Joe asked her if she was homesick and Loretta Ann told him all she missed at home were her friends there and little May Day because she had no one to look after her that much. Since she had no family Loretta Ann always watched out for her all the time to make sure she was okay, and had a way to go buy her groceries and pay her bills when she needed to.

She told him that Runt carried May Day around with her sometimes when she wasn't busy. Between the two of them May Day would be well looked after. He told her that he sure missed his dad because he was always with him all the time, and since he passed away it was like he had lost part of himself. Loretta Ann told him she knew how he felt because not having family around was like being alone all the time. She told him she guessed that was why she enjoyed working so much because she could pass the time by that way. He told her he was into his work all the time, and he was sure that was what kept him going. He told her he was glad he had come to Okeechobee for his vacation though because it was a different time for him. Loretta Ann told him she was glad he came down to Okeechobee for his vacation to. She told him he was quite a character. Joe didn't know where to take that as a compliment or a cut down, but he knew Loretta Ann hadn't acted like the type of person to cut anyone down. So he just took it as a good compliment on what she had said.

Well, Joe and Loretta Ann just lay back taking life as easy as they could since they had no other choice in the matter. They talked about each other's life, and had told each other so much about themselves that they felt like they had known each other forever. It had been a while since they had eaten lunch so they ate some more of the catch of the day which was the stingray. After they finished eating they both walked up on top of the rocks once again to check on the fire to see if it had enough wood on it. They had to put more wood on the fire, and then they stood on top of the rocks looking at how beautiful the evening was. The ocean breeze was still blowing inward towards the little island. Joe told Loretta Ann that he would miss the little island once they were rescued. She told him she would miss it too, but her miss would really be that they would be returning to the everyday way of life. It wasn't that bad, but this was so much different being alone with Joe. It was as if they were the only two people in the whole universe being there on the little island. Well, they both went back down to the little camp, then called it another night.

They had made it through another day on the island stranded in the middle of nowhere. At least that is what it seemed. They couldn't see land so it seemed like they were really isolated completely. They had worked hard all day so the two of them didn't talk much that night because they were both tired. After they had said goodnight to each other they both went right off to sleep. They had decided to sleep under the old shed since it was in better condition than the old house. It was out of the weather, and at least they did have a roof over their heads. The little island was their safe haven for right now.

Well, Joe got up once during the night because he knew he had to check the fires to make sure they still had enough wood on them. He didn't want the fires to go out because he had high hopes someone would pass by and see them burning. He had to put wood on the fire on the top of the rocks. It had burned almost all the wood up but he had plenty more to go on it for the time being and they would have enough to get them through until the next morning.

He kept standing on the top of the rocks high up in the air. It was very peaceful there on the rocks. Joe just stood there looking up at the starlit sky. It was so clear that it looked as if it were a city lit up with a million lights. He looked across the ocean hoping to get a glance of a ship passing by, but he didn't see any lights at all except what was in the sky. He saw a shooting star falling from the sky, and he made a wish on it. Of course, we can probably guess what he wished for. He sat down on the hard rocky ground, and just sat there thinking of the last couple of days. This had been a very different experience for him to because here he was alone on an island stranded with a woman named Loretta Ann.

Joe knew someone had to be looking for them, but he was just wondering how long it would be until they would be found. He knew they could make some type of raft that would float the both of them, but he didn't want to go back into the ocean to maybe take the chance of going farther away than they were already. If they stayed on the island at least they did have a shelter and food right now. They had water from the falls that they could drink and they also could use the water to bathe with, so they were somewhat like Adam and Eve, just the two of them all alone on the little garden island.

Joe thought that he and Loretta Ann could see what existed in the cave that they had found. He thought tomorrow would be okay since they didn't have any pressing appointments they had to go to. If the cave looked safe then maybe they would have another place to go to in case there were any hard rain and windstorms that they needed to be sheltered from. The little shed they slept in didn't look like it could stand much more bad weather. There's no telling how old the shed was though, because it was manmade from old rough wood that was probably cut right off the island. Joe sat a few minutes more listening to the waves as they crashed onto the rocks below then he went back down to the little camp. He went back to sleep, and didn't wake up until the next morning.

    Loretta Ann got up before Joe, and had gone walking along the beach. She couldn't believe she was stranded on an island. That was something you usually see in a movie, but it was happening to her in real life. She was glad that she had Joe with her and that she wasn't by herself because that would be awful lonely. She was glad they had floated to the island that had trees on it because it could had been a bare island, then they would be in the bad weather without any protection at all. They were in a bad situation, but they could be thankful for what they had because it could be worse.

    Loretta Ann waded along the water and started to pick up seashells. She saw something star shaped so she picked it up. It was a starfish, and she had never seen one right out of the ocean before. She took it along with the seashells back to camp to show Joe what she had found. Joe hadn't ever seen one fresh out of the ocean before so this was new to him to. Of course, he had seen pictures of them when he studied biology, but that was only in a book at school. Loretta Ann put the starfish back into the water after she had shown it to Joe because it was still alive. Well, one thing about this trip it sure wasn't boring at all. Matter of a fact it was totally different from what Joe and Loretta Ann were used to altogether. Oh well, they were making the best of it along with learning new things they hadn't ever had to know about before. You could say they were having a learning experience at this time.

    Joe and Loretta Ann ate a mango for their breakfast that morning. The mangoes were very tasteful. Loretta Ann was the last one to finish eating. Joe noticed after she had finished eating her mango that she had some of the mango strings in her teeth. He wanted to tell her, but wasn't sure how to go about telling her in fear he might hurt her feelings. Well, instead he asked her if she was ready to go check the cave out. She responded by giving him a great big old smile, mango strings and all. They made sure to put some more wood on the fires when they left their little camp. The fires were burning okay so far so they went on their way back to the waterfalls and cave.

Chapter forty seven

The Giant Lizard

Joe told Loretta Ann he would carry a piece of the burning wood from the fire so that they might get to see inside the cave with the lit piece of firewood. They struck out towards the waterfalls where the cave was at. As they approached the waterfalls they stopped dead in their tracks, and didn't move an inch. There at the waterfalls drinking some of the water was a big lizard. This was just too much for Joe and Loretta Ann to believe. It was actually more than the two of them could comprehend at all. They looked at each other as if to say what the heck is it? They knew one thing for sure, and that was that they didn't want any part of the lizard. Loretta Ann clapped her hands together, and when she did this, the lizard looked up and saw them. The lizard didn't seemed threatened at all by Loretta Ann and Joe.

He told Loretta Ann if he didn't know better that he'd swear they had landed on an island lost in time. She laughed at what he said, but she assured him that they were on a normal island. Joe told her he had heard of lizards living on islands near Hawaii, but he knew they hadn't floated that far from Ft. Pierce. She told him the lizard could have been someone's pet, and they might have turned him loose on the island. Many people let their snakes go into the wild because they get too big to care for, and some people get tired of taking care of them, which is sad in a way. She told him she had seen on television where people actually flushed baby pet alligators down the toilet, and the sewers wound up being their permanent home. Joe told her that was a cruel thing to do to any animal. He told her if he had any animals like that he would carry them to a zoo to see if they would take them especially after they had been used to people taking care of them.

Joe and Loretta Ann started walking towards the lizard, and the closer they got to him he decided to shy away from them. Well, this put them at ease knowing that the lizard was just as scared of them as they were of him. They went to the cave underneath the waterfalls, and tried to see inside. It was very dark inside. Joe and Loretta Ann walked into the cave. He was holding the piece of burning wood that served as their torch at the moment. He moved it around close to the wall of the cave to try to see what it looked like, but it was such a dim fire that it didn't serve their purpose.

They came back out of the cave because it was too dark to see anything. As they stood in the opening of the cave entrance they heard a loud eerie wailing sound. Joe got goosebumps, and the sound made the hairs stand up on Loretta Ann's arms. They both came outside feeling spooked a little from the sounds they had heard. Joe told her before they went into the cave again that they would have to get a better light to see by. She told him that was one thing for sure.

Loretta Ann and Joe walked up to the top of the waterfalls to see where the water was flowing from. Much to their surprise there was a small artisan spring that the water came from. It was able to flow without being pumped because an artisan spring or well flows from pressure. This little place seemed to amaze them both. They just stood there watching the water flow from the springs and fall over the top of the rocks thus creating a waterfall. The little pond below was a little catch basin for some of the water, but the rest just flowed through the cave and was wasted to salt-water. It was such a pretty sight to see. As the sun hit the spraying water falling into the little pond below it looked like a rainbow of many different colors.

Joe noticed some of the birds from the trees had flown over to get some water to drink from the little pond. It seemed that the little pond was the main stopping place for the little animals to get a drink of water. It might be the only water that is drinkable on the island he thought. Well, he and Loretta Ann started walking on a little trail they found leaving in a different direction away from their camp. They hadn't even thought about catching anything to eat for their lunch for that day. They still had a lot of mangoes to eat, which would make for a slim meal in case they didn't catch anything to eat later on that day.

They just got off of on a different track today. They were more in an exploring mood now, and hadn't thought much about anything else. It was such a pretty day that they just couldn't resist walking around and about the island. They walked for hours all over the island looking at the different places they hadn't noticed the other day. It seemed so different today for some reason. It could be because Joe and Loretta Ann were becoming so ammuned to the little island. They spotted another bunch of big rocks on the island so they climbed up them to see what was on them.

As they made it to the top of the rocks they were overcome with the beautiful view. It was different from the view on the other rock formation where they had their fire burning. They could see the smoke from both of the fires they had burning so that was a good sign that someone else might see it too. Joe told Loretta Ann that in a way he would hate to leave the island because it was so pretty. She told him she hadn't seen any place as pretty as the little island before and he told her he agreed with her completely.

While Joe and Loretta Ann were admiring the new spot they had found they saw an airplane fly by not too far away from them. They both got excited and started waving their hands and arms. They both were yelling to the top of their lungs, but of course they were not heard at all. He told her he hoped the distress signals on the beach would be seen. He told her they could find more rocks to make words out of and place them on this side of the beach so they could be seen by a passing plane from the air.

Loretta Ann told him they needed to do that before they went back to the camp. She saw a ship a long ways off. She had spotted the boat because she could see smoke coming from its smokestack. She told Joe that she guessed that's what it was called because she didn't know that much about boats or ships. He told her not to feel bad because he wasn't up on his history on boats either. He told her that they couldn't be too far from civilization if the boats and airplanes continued to come by. Loretta Ann told him that's exactly what she was thinking when he said that. Well, one thing for sure and that was it seemed Joe and Loretta Ann seemed to be pretty compatible with each other and probably didn't even realize it.

Well, Joe and Loretta Ann returned to their camp like two happy tourists off of a tour. They had to add some wood to the fire at the camp so he told Loretta Ann he would go up on the high rocks where the other fire was burning and add some wood to that fire also. He told her when he got back they would do some spear fishing if she wanted to so they could have lunch. She told him she would be ready to go when he came back down.

Joe walked up to the top of the rocks. He had to put more wood on the fire again. The next time he would have to carry some more wood up to the fire on the rocks because he had used the last bit of wood on the fire. He met Loretta Ann at camp then got his spear so he could try to catch their lunch once more. The two of them set out to catch their lunch. Loretta Ann told him that she would work on some more signals and put them a little farther down the beach from where she had put the first ones she had made. She told him they could never have too many signals that was for sure. She told him he could try to catch their food so he said, okay then he waded into the water.

Loretta Ann managed to find some good-sized rocks, and in no time had the distress signal made on the beach. She had made the words "HELP and SOS" hoping that someone would see them. As Joe stayed and kept trying to spear their lunch Loretta Ann walked up on top of the rock formation to see if she could see the letters she had made on the beach. They showed up real clear from the top of the rocks so they could be seen clearly up in the air from an airplane. She started back down to the beach where Joe was spear fishing. As she made her way down the rocks she slipped and fell. Luckily, she didn't hurt herself, but she did scratch her legs up pretty bad. Loretta Ann seem to have Joe's luck of being clumsy.

Loretta Ann went back to the beach and watched Joe as he threw his spear and brought in a fish. He noticed her legs all skinned up and ask her what happened to her. She told him she tried to break dance she guessed and then she laughed. As she sat there watching Joe she thought about their incident on the inner tubes out in the ocean. She thought about the sharks swimming around them, and it gave her the willies because they could have been the sharks' meal. Once again she was very thankful they had landed on the island.

Joe caught another fish and it took him a long time to bring this one in because the fish was bound and determined it wasn't going to be a meal ticket, but the fish ended up being their meal afterall. Joe caught three crabs then came out of the water so he could clean the fish and crabs. He was getting the hang of the spear fishing down pat like he had been doing it for years. He was really enjoying the spear fishing because it was like he was in primitive times. I guess that you could say they were except they had a head start by being born later on in history. Since they were in the civilized world they knew much of what was needed to have to survive unlike the primitive man that never had the pleasure of any luxuries of the present day life.

Loretta Ann and Joe had it made on the little island compared to the primitive man. Well, the two of them went back to camp to eat their lunch once they got it cleaned and cooked. Joe was pretty good at preparing a cooked meal now even if it was only one thing at a time. Neither one of them complained about having to eat so much fish because they were glad to have anything to eat.

After they ate their meal they had to carry up wood to the top of the rocks where they had their fire built so they could keep it burning night and day. After they took up all the wood they needed for the fire they went back to the camp.

Later on they went to the waterfalls to bathe. Both of them needed to take a bath because they hadn't been able to take a bath unless it was in the salt-water. Since they found the fresh-water they could be more hygiene about themselves. Loretta Ann stood under the water falling from the rocks. She told Joe the water was fine. Well, he decided to join her under the falling water, and as he started to get under the falls to join Loretta Ann he hit a slippery spot on the rocks then fell into the water hole. Loretta Ann thought it was hilarious that Joe had slipped down. It took Joe by surprise at first, but since he didn't hurt anything he just lay back and relaxed in the water.

Loretta Ann kept laughing at Joe, and she asked him how was his trip? Joe told her it was a quick trip. She just couldn't stop laughing at him so he knew he had to have his laugh to so he got out of the water then grabbed hold of Loretta Ann and threw her into the waterhole. Poor Loretta Ann looked really surprised when he threw her into the waterhole. It wasn't deep so they both were safe there. Now Joe laughed at Loretta Ann because she really looked pitiful with her hair all wet and stringy. Since they had no brushes or combs to use their hair looked a mess. Loretta Ann's hair was in knots, and Joe's hair was really shaggy looking. It would make anyone feel sorry for them because once they did get back to civilization they probably wouldn't be able to get all the knots out of their hair with a fine toothed comb.

Well, the two of them didn't have a care in the world right at this moment because they were having so much fun they had forgotten all their troubles. They both started pushing each other into the waterhole just having a lot of fun monkeying around. Soon both of them tired out from all the playing, so they got out of the water then went back to their little camp. Once they made it back they both lay back on the little beds they had made out of the tree branches. They were just drying off in the sun. Joe and Loretta Ann were both getting tanned from being in the sun so much. They didn't have on a full wardrobe of clothes so they would get their share of sunshine each day. The clothes they had found in the little shed were too hot to wear so Joe had cut some palm fronds to make them some clothing to wear over their bathing suits. The palm fronds kept some of the sun off of them so they wouldn't get completely cooked by the sun.

    Joe told Loretta Ann they needed to find something to make some SOS words out of on top of both of the rock formations. Loretta Ann told Joe she had thought of the same thing because the more signals they had the more of a chance someone would be able to know they needed help. As they finished drying off from the sun Loretta Ann and Joe set out to find the stuff to help make their other signals. They had found everything they needed in a few minutes. They had found some coconuts that had fallen from some of the trees. Joe wanted to try to open one of them so they could eat it, but he couldn't break them open. Maybe he would figure out a way to do that later on.

    Joe and Loretta Ann carried the coconuts up to the top of the rocks, and made their signals for everyone to see. It would just be a matter of time. They both were tired now because they had been climbing up and down the rocks along with all the walking they had done today. Both of them agreed to call it a day when they made it back to camp. They just sat back and ate some mangoes and oranges and didn't do anything else for the rest of the day. Once again they had accomplished what they had set out to do. Joe and Loretta Ann were just enjoying each other's company while they were relaxing. Joe asked Loretta Ann what she planned to do once they got back to Okeechobee, and she told him she guessed she would probably go back to her daily normal routine. He told her that he was going to call some of the people about the property for sale at the Prairie because he wanted to buy some of the land before he went back to Virginia.

Loretta Ann starting telling him that she was going to move out of Okeechobee one day. Joe asked her real quick like why she was going to move away from Okeechobee. She laughed then told him she was going to move out into the country away from the middle of town. He was at ease then because Loretta Ann didn't know it, but he was getting upset that he might not get to see her again if she moved away. He told her he was glad she wasn't moving out of town because he would miss seeing her when he came back down to Okeechobee.

She told him she was tired of living in the city because it was so noisy at times, and it was so peaceful out in the country. She told Joe she couldn't have any kind of animals because they had certain restrictions in the city limits, and that's why she'd like to live out in the country. Joe told her that's why he liked it away from the city too. He asked her where she thought she would like to live out in the country, and she told him it would probably be out north of town. He told her she would like it at the Prairie because it was very quiet except for the sounds of the animals in the woods. Loretta Ann told Joe it was nice out that way, but it was a long way to have to drive back to work. He told her that he drove a lot farther than that each day to work, but he had done it for so many years that it didn't bother him at all.

Well, it was getting late now so they had to go check the fire on the hill again to make sure it was still burning okay. They had carried some wood up for the fire earlier so they would put plenty on the fire so it would burn all night long. They stayed only a few minutes on top of the rock formation then they came back to turn in for the day. Neither of them had to be rocked to sleep either because they were two tired puppies.

Joe didn't even wake up during the night to go put more wood on the fire, but the wind hadn't blown that hard during the night so they hit it lucky once more. Joe was so tired that he snored so loud that Loretta Ann was about ready to knock him in the head, but she knew how tired he was because she was exhausted herself. She just ignored him the best she could then she went back to sleep. Joe and Loretta Ann both slept late the next morning.

The two of them woke up about the same time, but neither one was in a hurry to get up. Joe told Loretta Ann if they didn't get rescued in another day or two they would have to start thinking of some way to leave the island to find their way back to Ft. Pierce or back to civilization. She told him that as long as they had some way to survive they had better stay put on the island where they would be safe. She told him if they went back out into the ocean there's no telling where they might wind up at, and they would be back in the ocean with all the sharks again. He told her he really didn't want to go back out into the ocean again, but they would have to do something so they could be found.

Well, they walked to the beach to catch more food to eat. This time Joe got a little worried because he didn't see anything at all swimming in the water to catch for their meal. He told Loretta Ann that maybe if they walked farther around the island they might have better luck in catching something to eat for their lunch. Well, their luck did change because the water current was flowing in a different direction. The current wasn't moving that fast where he usually did his spearfishing so they found out that they couldn't depend on one spot to supply them with the fish they needed.

Joe lucked out by catching several fish and another stingray for their lunch. Loretta Ann helped him clean the fish and stingray once they went back to the camp. It didn't take that long to cook the fish because they didn't cook the stingray. After they finished eating they went back to the beach and tried to bait up some crabs with the raw meat. They would cook part of it later on once they caught some crabs. Joe took the raw stingray and threw it in the water where he was standing really still. Sure enough he managed to catch a dozen crabs. They took their catch of the day and returned to camp. Joe found an old pot that was in the old shed then put some water in it after he washed it out. He put the dozen crabs into the pot of water to save for their lunch the next day.

Loretta Ann asked him if he was going to eat any seafood when he got back home, and he told her it would probably be a long time before he did. He told Loretta Ann when he did get back to civilization again he was going to the Lonesome Dove and get one of their big jumbo cheeseburgers with all the trimmings on it. Joe told her he was going to eat a big order of fries along with some baked beans, and a big order of that good old cole slaw that Runt makes from scratch. Loretta Ann told him she would join him for lunch so be sure to let her know when he was ready to go once they made it back home to Okeechobee. He told her that was a date, and he would even come pick her up if she wanted him to.

Loretta Ann told him that's one reason she was really looking forward to being at home again, and that was to get some good old fashioned home cooking. He told her it would be nice to get back to Okeechobee so they could enjoy the luxury of civilization. Joe told her it was okay on the island, but he would be glad to get his regular clothes back on again. He told her that if he had to keep running around in his swimsuit much longer he might not get accustomed to wearing regular clothes again. Loretta Ann laughed at what he said, but told him she was sure he wouldn't have any trouble getting use to his regular clothes once he got back into them again.

Loretta Ann told him she has really enjoyed the time on the island even if it has been a little rough. Joe told her he had some wild times on his vacation, and no one will believe him when he goes back home and tells them about all the things he'd done while on vacation. He told her he didn't mind it on the island except seeing the big lizard they had seen the other day. Joe said by the way I wondered where the lizard got off to? Loretta Ann told him she hadn't even thought of the lizard until he mentioned it just now. He told her he had thought of the lizard several times, and it was always at night. He told her that since they had the fire burning at night he wasn't worried too much because lizards are probably scared of the fire. Loretta Ann told him he was probably right about the lizard being scared of the fire at least she hoped so.

They kept talking about all the things they wanted to do when they got back to Okeechobee. Well that is, if they get rescued from the island.

She told him they would go to the movies when they got back if he would like to go. Joe of course, said yes that he'd like to go watch a good movie because he hadn't went to one in many years.

Loretta Ann told him she went to a movie more than any other kind of recreation because she could sit and relax while she enjoyed the picture. She told Joe at home she turned the television on, but was always busy doing things around the house so the television just watched itself. Joe told Loretta Ann that was the way he did at home because he just couldn't sit still very long to watch television. He said he just couldn't make himself become a couch potato. Loretta Ann laughed, and told him people often asked her why she was so hyper, and she told Joe she always told them she guessed she had worms that's why she couldn't be still. He told her that's what his dad always told him when he was a little boy that he must have worms because he was always on the go.

Joe started asking Loretta Ann about the lake in Okeechobee. He asked her if she had ever gone fishing in the lake on a boat, and she told him only a couple of times. She told him that she went fishing at the mouth of the Kissimmee River by Okee-Tanti. Joe said that's where we ate at the Chobee Seafood Restaurant isn't it? Loretta Ann told him yelp that's it. She told him that she went fishing with her friends that had a big pontoon boat. He asked her what was a pontoon boat, and Loretta Ann described how they looked then he remembered seeing one that looked like what she was describing. He told her he had seen one at the lake one day while he sat and watched some people skiing in the water.

Loretta Ann asked Joe if he had ever water-skied, but he told her he hadn't ever tried to do that. He told her he was too uncoordinated to balance himself on two pieces of wood. Loretta Ann told him it wasn't that difficult to do. She told him she went skiing with the same friends, that had another boat that they used to pull water skiers with. She told Joe it took her three times to get up on the skis, but she managed to ski as long as it was going in a straight direction. She told him she tried to turn to go in a different direction, but went head over heels and drank about half the lake up. She told him she hated getting water up her nose because she felt like she was drowning. He told her he guessed he would just stick to floating on an inner tube for his excitement. She told Joe she had all the excitement she could stand for a while the last couple of days. He laughed and told Loretta Ann she had that right.

Joe and Loretta Ann were still talking away when they heard something that sounded like a boat motor in the distance. Both of them jumped up at the same time, and ran in the direction of the sound they had heard. They couldn't see a boat, but they knew it had to be a boat by the way it sounded. Well, they both said at the same time, let's go on the top of the rocks to see if we can see anything from up there. Away they went running like they were in a foot race with each other. By the time they reached the top of the rocks both of them were so out of breath that they had to sit down. As they sat there listening to the sound it seemed to be getting fainter.

Joe stood up to look to see if there was anything in sight, but he saw nothing at all. All he could see was the waves rolling into the shore. Joe told Loretta Ann he knew that had to be the sound of a boat engine and Loretta Ann said it sure sounded like one to her too.

Joe and Loretta Ann stayed on top of the rocks looking out to the sea hoping they would see a boat come into sight, but there was not a boat to come their way today. They saw some seagulls flying overhead. That was the first time any gulls had been around them since the one ones they had seen flying overhead at the beach in Ft. Pierce. They watched as the birds circled around them. The seagulls started to dive into the water catching little fish to eat. It probably was baitfish because they looked like minnows in the bird's mouths. Joe told Loretta Ann he wished he had good eyesight like a bird because he could have seen if the sound they heard was a boat or not. Loretta Ann told him she knew that the seagulls usually followed fishing and shrimping boats when they went to sea because they were sometimes lucky when the fishermen cleaned their catch at sea. Most of the big boats usually carried their catch in to the fishhouses to be cleaned. Some fishermen just sold their fish in the rough. When Loretta Ann said this, Joe had to ask her what she meant by fish in the rough, and she told him it was when they sold the fish whole without cleaning them. She told Joe they didn't get as much money per pound like they would if they had cleaned them.

He asked her if there were any fishhouses in Okeehobee, and she told him there were two in Okeechobee that had been there for many years. Loretta Ann told him that Lake Okeechobee was known for its abundant fishing. She told Joe people not only used it for fishing, but also used it for duck hunting and recreation as well. She told him the catfishermen sold their fish to the local restaurants as well as shipping them off to other retailers. She told him that the fishermen also fished for cooter. Joe asked Loretta Ann what a cooter fish looked like, and Loretta Ann burst out with laughter at what Joe had asked her. She told him that was what the fishermen called a soft-shelled turtle. Joe felt a little dense, but what the heck he wasn't ever around anything like he had been here in Okeechobee. It was a new environment to him altogether.

Joe was amazed with how much knowledge that Loretta Ann knew about the wild life of Okeechobee. He had never in his entire life met anyone like her. She was quite a gal. Joe had taken a liking towards Loretta Ann since the first time he had met her. The two of them were in a bad situation, but they were still hitting it off good. It seemed like they were made for each other.

Well, Joe started putting some wood on the fire that had been burning for days now. He asked Loretta Ann if she was ready to go back to camp, and she told him she guessed she was. She told him she was going to pick some more fruit once she made it back down from the rocks. He told her he would help her with the fruit picking if she wanted him too. As they climbed back down the rocks they went to the mango tree, and picked some big mangoes then carried them to camp. They stacked them in the little shed so they wouldn't be bothered by any varmits. Joe told Loretta Ann they might as well get some oranges then they would be stocked up for a few more days.

As they walked through the trees to go pick some oranges they both stopped dead in their tracks. There in front of them once again was the lizard they had seen drinking water at the waterfalls. They stood silently watching as the big lizard ate some of the oranges that had fallen from the tree. They watched in amazement at the lizard as took his front feet and clawed open the oranges to eat them. Joe told Loretta Ann he hoped the lizard was a vegetarian, and didn't like to eat meat because he didn't want to be an item on the lizard's menu.

Well, Joe and Loretta Ann waited patiently watching the lizard eat the oranges. Once the lizard ate all that he wanted he walked slowly back into the little wooded jungle. This was the opportunity for them to pick their oranges without having to worry about the lizard bothering them. They decided to pick a lot of oranges to carry back with them because they wanted to avoid meeting up with the lizard as much as possible.

Once they got back to camp Joe told Loretta Ann he was going to gather some more wood for their woodpile. He was restless today for some reason. He just had to keep himself doing something to occupy his time since he had so much time on his hands. He told her he thought he'd go up on the rocks and sit for a while to see if he could see anything in sight.

Loretta Ann decided to go for a walk on the beach by herself since Joe was keeping himself busy with other things. She walked a long ways from camp looking out at the crystal blue ocean. As she walked along the beach she would stop from time to time and try to think of some way for them to be rescued. Loretta Ann was hoping that it would be soon that they would make it back home safe and sound. She knew that May Day surely had to miss them in

Okeechobee because she was always saw Loretta Ann or talked to her everyday. She knew May Day would call the law if she didn't hear from her soon.

Loretta Ann ended up walking around the entire island. Joe was waiting at camp when she finally made it back. He told her he was worried about her, and told her not to wander off like that again because something could happen to her. Loretta Ann told him she had only walked along the beach around the whole island, and hadn't walked through the woods. She told him that he should walk around the island to see how different it looked on the other side. She told him there were a lot more trees on the other side than there were here at their camp. Loretta Ann told Joe she saw a lot more rock formations on the other side of the island too.

He asked her if she could see the smoke from the fires from the other side of the island, and she told him she could see the smoke very well. She asked Joe if there was a way they could build a raft to leave the island on? He told her they could build a raft, but it would take time to do it. He told her he didn't know how safe it would be to ride a raft out in the ocean since they had no idea which way they would have to go. He told her he wanted to get back to Okeechobee to, but maybe they should wait on the island until someone finds them.

Well, Joe and Loretta Ann would have to make the best of it on the island, but as they say there's no place like home. They would have to just wait patiently, and do the best they could under the circumstances.

Well, it was very warm today on the little island. It looked like rain was forming off in the distance. At least they would be out of the rain because they had put some of the palm fronds over the little shed so that the rain wouldn't get inside of it. Since Joe and Loretta Ann had been on the island they had pretty well kept busy fixing up their little camp so they could feel pretty much like they were at home.

Joe decided it was time to cook the rest of the stingray he had saved to eat later. He didn't want it to ruin so he cooked it for them to eat for their supper. Joe checked to see if the crabs were still alive that he had caught, and they were still crawling around in the pot of water he had put them in. Loretta Ann took three of the mangoes they had picked and peeled them so they could eat them with their meal. Since there wasn't a lot to choose from she told Joe they could pretend the mangoes were baked potatoes they were eating for supper.

Another day had just about gone by. They were lucky once more being able to have a meal to eat. Joe told Loretta Ann that they would scout the island again the next day if she wanted to. He told her he wanted to check the cave out again to see if they could find anything that could be of any use to them in the cave. Loretta Ann told him that maybe they could build a fire close to the cave, and that way they would be able to keep a torch burning for a light so they could see inside the cave. He told her that they could try to build a fire inside the cave. He told her since they had the fire all they had to do was get enough wood to make a big fire with.

Loretta Ann told him that she didn't know if they would get smoked out of the cave once they made a fire inside or not. He told her that if there was enough ventilation of air going through the cave then the fire should burn okay. He told her that if there was no air coming in and out of the cave then the fire wouldn't burn, and it would smother itself out, and they would get smoked out for sure.

Well, they finished eating their stingray and their pretend baked potatoes, and by this time it was too dark to do anything else. It was really dark tonight, and the wind had begun to pick up and blow much harder than it had since they had been on the island. Loretta Ann told Joe it looked like they would have a rainstorm before the night was over. He told her that he hoped it wasn't bad as the one he had went through at the camp at the Prairie. He told Loretta Ann he wasn't sure if he was going to survive that night or not. Joe told Loretta Ann they would have to find something to put over the fire to protect it from the rain. If a hard rain came then they would be out of luck in the fire department. He told her they might not be as lucky as they were the first time in getting the fire started again. Joe told her if they had real bad weather they might have to try to find their way to the cave.

Loretta Ann told Joe she didn't like bad weather at all because her family had the roof blown off their house many years ago by a tornado. She told him she was just a little girl, but she has always remembered that bad storm. Joe told Loretta Ann that the weather up in Virginia wasn't bad except for the cold during the wintertime. He told her they didn't have tornadoes or hurricanes in the part of Virginia where he lived at. He told her they had storms closer to the coastal part, but not inland where he was at.

Well, Loretta Ann and Joe knew they had to keep a fire burning somehow so they had to really think of something to come up with fast. They got some wood and piled it in a little pile underneath the shed. Joe had to figure out a way to keep the fire from burning the roof of the shed. Joe soon managed to overcome that problem. He found a big round saw blade that looked like it was off a sawmill saw. The blade was leaning against the shed partially covered up by sand and tree leaves. He managed to get the blade out then very carefully dragged it underneath the shed. Joe propped the big blade up at an angle so the blaze of the little fire they made didn't catch the shed on fire and burn it down. Joe took the pot he'd had the crabs in and built a small fire inside of it. This way he would be able to transfer the fire to a different place if he had to as long as he didn't burn himself. Well, Joe managed to do something else right without hurting himself or anyone else. He was really becoming a camper for sure.

Well, Joe and Loretta Ann made it just in time because as soon as they finished with the fire it started to pour down rain. The wind blew so hard that they were worried that the little fire would be blown out from the wind. Well, so far so good they were managing to keep dry under the shed. Well, the storm was bad enough as it was, but it had to start lightning and thundering along with the wind and rain. Joe told Loretta Ann it looked like they were in for a night of bad weather from the storm. She told him maybe it would pass over soon at least she hoped it would.

Loretta Ann was starting to get cold from the wind blowing off the rain. Joe told her to come over and sit by him in the corner of the shed. It was warm there in the corner of the shed, and much more comfortable Loretta Ann thought sitting next to Joe. Well, the bad weather had set in for the night. It finally stopped raining the next morning. After the weather had gone Loretta Ann and Joe went up on the top of the rock formation to see if they could see anyone out in the ocean. They thought since it was such a bad storm that if anyone had got caught in it they might have came closer to the island to stay and weather out the storm. As it went there was still no one in sight.

Joe and Loretta Ann started back to their camp to see if they could find some wood that wasn't too wet to burn. They wanted to get a fire built again on the rocks so maybe someone would accidentally see it burning, and see their distress signals. Joe and Loretta Ann got their big fire going once again so they put the one under the shed out. It was a good thing they had built it because they wouldn't have ever gotten the damp wood to burn from all the rain that had fallen on the wood outside in the woodpile. It was a good thing that they had stockpiled the wood underneath the little shed out of the rain. They had a heck of time getting the fire started again on top of the rocks because the wood was too damp to burn. After they carried some of the dry wood up they got everything under control again. They had a nice big fire burning once again.

Chapter forty eight

The Cave Explorers

Well, it was still too early to cook lunch. Neither Joe nor Loretta Ann was hungry so they decided to set out to go to the cave at the waterfalls. When they got to the waterfalls they started to gather wood so they could try to make a fire inside the cave. Joe found a big log, but had to get Loretta Ann to lend her muscles so they could get it to the cave. Once they got everything in place at the entrance of the cave they returned to their little camp to bring some lit firewood back to the cave. They made it back to the cave with the burning wood, and started the fire at the cave. Now they had three fires to tend to, but as long as they could find wood they would be okay.

The fire burned okay at the cave. It had enough air flowing through the cave so it didn't try to burn itself out. Joe and Loretta Ann stood in the entrance of the dark cave trying to see what was inside of the cave. Well, the fire started to burn higher, and it began to light the cave up so you could see real well inside the cave. Loretta Ann walked a little ways inside the cave not really sure if she should or not. Joe picked up a stick out of the fire, and walked closely behind her. The fire flickered on the cave walls making it look spooky inside the cave. It was already spooky to start with not knowing what might be inside the cave.

As Joe and Loretta Ann walked farther into the cave something made a screeching noise then flew over their heads. It turned out to be a big bat, and it almost gave them a heart attack. Joe told Loretta Ann there's no telling what is inside the cave. She told him that they would never find out what is inside the cave unless they explored it inside. He told her that she was braver than he was. Loretta Ann saw the fire reflecting on what seemed to be a water passage. It must be a little cove that gets water inside the cave when the tide comes in. Joe saw something next to the cave wall. He couldn't believe his eyes. He thought his eyes were playing tricks on him. He showed it to Loretta Ann, and she couldn't believe her eyes either. As it turned out there was a little rowboat that was leaning on its side against the wall. Joe knew someone had to have put it there in that position against the cave wall. Joe and Loretta Ann walked over to it and checked it out. The little boat was in good shape. It was an old homemade boat that must have been there for many years. Maybe the people that lived in the old house had made the boat to use so they could get back and forth to the island.

All that Joe could think of right at that moment was to drag the little boat out of the cave to inspect it to see if it was floatable. It was very heavy to be such a small boat, but they managed to get it outside the cave. Loretta Ann told Joe if it floated, the little boat could be the meal ticket off the island. Joe agreed with her, but told her they would have to make some oars so they would be able to paddle the boat. She told him that she would kick the water with her feet if she had to so that she could make the little boat move in the water. She sounded bound and determined at that moment to get back to civilization.

Joe checked the little boat inside and out. It looked to be very sturdy so the next step was to put it in some water to check it out to make sure it didn't leak. Joe told Loretta Ann to grab hold of the bow of the boat, and he would take the back of the boat to see if they could slide it to the little waterhole where they had taken their baths. As they put the boat into the water they both held their breath hoping there wouldn't be any leaks in the bottom of the boat. As the boat seemed to float okay Joe saw one small leak in the side of the boat that was in the water. He told Loretta Ann that he would find a way to fix it so it wouldn't leak. He marked the spot where the leak was at then they pulled the boat back out of the water.

He told Loretta Ann he would be back in a few minutes then he returned to their camp so he could get some kind of tools to work with. Joe got his blade that he had been carving with, and then got a heavy object to pound wood with. He was excited about the boat they had found in the cave. Joe knew now they had some hope of getting off the island. He knew he would be able to make the oars for the little boat because he used to carve things out of wood when he was a little boy.

Joe was very lucky that he had a dad that taught him so much when he was growing up. His dad had bought Joe a little pocketknife when he was eight years old, and he had taught Joe how to whittle things out of pieces of wood. This was another good trait that he kept with him all of his life. Well, Joe walked back to the cave where he had left Loretta Ann with the boat. He told Loretta Ann to help him look for a hard piece of wood so he could make the boat oars out of it. It took a while because they had already gathered most of the wood up for the campfires. He finally found a big piece of wood that he could make the boat oars from.

Joe started to chip away at the wood with the blade he had found. It would be a tedious job to get the oars made, but he was bound and determined to get them made. It was way past time for them to eat their lunch, but Loretta Ann and Joe only had one thought on their minds now. It was to get the boat ready to float, and also to get the boat oars made. Joe managed to get one made that day, but would have to wait till the next day to finish the other one. It was hard trying to get the wood whittled down with the blade, but he had managed to succeed okay so far.

Joe took a piece of the carvings from the oar he had made, and managed to pound it into the crack that was leaking on the side of the boat. Once he finished doing this he told Loretta Ann they might as well go fix their lunch so they could eat. The day was passing by rather fast. Joe told Loretta Ann they would eat the crabs he had caught for their lunch. She told him that sounded good. Once they cleaned the crabs they boiled them in the little pot of water. The crabs sure were tasty Joe thought. Both of them were very hungry so they ate every morsel of the crabs he had cooked.

Loretta Ann told Joe they should finish making the other boat oar since they were finished eating. He told her he would work on it a little later on. He told Loretta Ann he needed to go check the fire on the rocks to see if it was burning okay. Joe did have to add some wood to the fire because it was burning low. They were lucky to get it burning again after the rain they got the night before.

Joe came back to camp where Loretta Ann was, and asked her if she was ready to go back to the cave to work on the boat oar. Loretta Ann told him that she was ready to go anytime that he was. The both of them walked to the waterfalls where the cave was at. Once they got there they started whittling away on the other piece of wood. Loretta Ann helped Joe so they managed to get the last oar made quicker than the first one. He told her that they would put the boat in the water at the beach tomorrow. This way he could be certain the boat was worthy to ride in.

Loretta Ann told Joe she had faith that the little boat would make it okay in the water. He told her they would leave it in the water for a few hours to make sure it was leakproof, and then they could make plans to leave the island. Loretta Ann was anxious as she could be. She could hardly wait till tomorrow came. Joe and Loretta Ann went back to camp so they could figure out what they needed to carry with them in the little boat. They wouldn't be able to carry a big load because the boat was so small.

He looked at the water container that the drinking water was in. He knew he would have to make a brace of some sort so the water wouldn't turn over in the boat and spill out. Joe then thought how he would build a little box to put some fruit in so it wouldn't get scattered in the bottom of the boat. He told Loretta Ann about the idea he had, and she told him they could make a bottom for the inner tubes then they could float them behind the boat, and carry some stuff inside of them.

Joe told Loretta Ann that was a good idea. Then they went back to the top of the rocks to get the tubes. Then they pulled some vines from the trees and wound them around and around the inner tubes making a bottom something like a net. Joe got more excited with each step that they managed to accomplish. Soon they would be ready to set sail. Once Joe thought about setting sail another thought came into his mind. He thought about making some kind of sail so that the wind could help push them along whenever they got too tired to row the boat.

Well, as they say, "Rome wasn't built in a day." They could get up earlier tomorrow morning and start to work on the sail for the boat. Joe and Loretta Ann took a break from their work. He told her he was going to eat some fruit, and asked her if she cared for anything to eat. Loretta Ann told him she believed she would eat a mango. Loretta Ann loved mangoes and could eat them all day long. Joe liked his oranges a little better than the mangoes because they were easier to eat. Well, Joe noticed Loretta Ann eating her mango in a hurry. He asked her if she wanted him to fix her another mango to eat, but Loretta Ann told him she would eat an orange next. The fruit seemed to hit the spot. Joe ate a couple more oranges then he washed his hands because they made his hands so sticky.

After they finished their break they started getting more stuff ready for their little boat. Joe and Loretta Ann knew they wouldn't be able to carry much in their little boat, but they had to be sure they had enough water to drink. They had to take something to eat along with them, but the only thing they really would be able to take was some fruit. When they set sail they wanted to be sure they had everything that wasn't very perishable. Joe told Loretta Ann they needed to pick some of the greener fruit so it would last longer for their trip. He told her they didn't know where to go once that they headed out to sea again so they needed to be prepared the best they possibly could.

Joe and Loretta Ann started talking about what they would have to do once they left the island. He told her if they could catch the wind blowing in the opposite direction of what brought them to the island they might have the possibility of going back the way they came. Joe knew it was a slim chance, but they had no other choice so they had to try it. Maybe if the current pulled them away they might get lucky, and hit the changing tide just right. This way they would be able to get back to the beachline in Ft. Pierce or maybe somewheres close. They knew they had floated for several hours before they landed on the little island. It would really depend on the tide, and the length they had to stay in the water.

Well, the day had once again come to an end so Joe and Loretta Ann had to stop on their project until morning. They sat around the campfire talking until they ran out of things to talk about. Joe and Loretta Ann told each other goodnight once again, and off to sleep they went. Joe went to sleep only to start dreaming about being on the sea in the little boat. He dreamed they were far out to sea when all of a sudden the little boat developed a leak and started filling up with water and began to sink.

Joe went down with the sinking boat, and started sinking himself. He began to swallow a lot of the salty ocean water, and at that point in his dream he woke up gasping for air. The dream was so real that Joe was actually coughing because he thought he had swallowed a bunch of water. He had the awful feeling that he had almost drowned.

Loretta Ann woke up when she heard Joe coughing. She thought something was wrong with him, but soon found out it was only a dream. Loretta Ann told him to relax, and not to be so nervous because they would make it back okay. Joe was glad it was only a dream because he didn't want to even think about the possibility of drowning. He was expecting to live a long healthy life because he still had a lot in his time to accomplish.

Well, Joe tried to go back to sleep, but had a hard time doing so after his dream. As he lay there looking up into the clear starry sky he thought of many things they still had to do before they left the island. Joe was wide-awake now, and wished it was daylight so he could be working on the boat. He knew they would have the inner tubes to fall back on in case the boat didn't make the trip, but Joe just couldn't forget about the sharks that had paraded around them several times. Oh well, that was the chance they would have to take, and he knew it.

Joe finally started to get sleepy, and did manage to get a few more hours of sleep before morning came. He felt like he hadn't slept at all, but once he got up he was fine. Loretta Ann asked him what did he want to do first, and he told her they would eat a bite of breakfast. Of course, it would have to be fruit because that was all they had to eat at the moment. Joe was going to go spearfishing for their lunch later on, but wanted to work on the boat for a little while first.

Once they ate their breakfast of fruit Joe and Loretta Ann started on what they had been working on the day before. They both were glad to see the boat hadn't leaked any while it was in the water. This made Joe feel really good when the little boat didn't leak because of the dream he had. Joe and Loretta Ann managed to get one of the smaller poles for their sail put in place. It was hard to do this since they had no hammer or nails, but they managed to use the vines after they twisted enough of them together to support the little sail pole.

Well, they did get everything finished on the little boat that day. All they had left was to get the food and water ready then they could set sail on the high seas once again. Joe told Loretta Ann that it was time for him to see if he could catch them some supper to eat because they had let lunchtime go by since they had been working on the boat. She told him she would help him catch something to eat if he needed her to help. Joe told her she could come along if she wanted to because he could always use a helping hand. So on their way they went down to the beach to catch their food.

Chapter forty nine

The Fish Smokers

Joe and Loretta Ann tore the fish up today. They speared 37 fish in no time at all. Joe told Loretta Ann he hoped she was fish hungry. Loretta Ann got a thought in her head, and told Joe about it. She asked Joe how could they smoke some of the fish? Joe stood in the water trying to think of a way to rig up something so they could smoke some of the fish since they had so many. Joe told her that was a good idea, and if he could manage to fix a smoker of some sort then they would be able to take some smoked fish along with them when they left the island.

Joe told Loretta Ann to help him carry the fish back to camp so he could clean them, and get them ready to eat for their lunch. As he cleaned the fish one by one he got an idea that he was sure would work. He told Loretta Ann he had seen a picture on television one time about some natives in Hawaii that had smoked hogs in the ground in a hole in the sand. He told Loretta Ann that might just work with the fish if they tried smoking them in the ground like the natives did.

Well, they dug a hole in the ground and put some of the burning wood in the old pot down into the hole. They took some of the palm fronds and laid them on top of the wood.

When they put the palm fronds on the bottom they placed the fish on top on the palm fronds then covered the top of the fish with more palm fronds. Joe told Loretta Ann it would probably take 3 or 4 hours for the fish to get smoked good enough for them to eat. He put the other fish on the sticks over the open fire, and it didn't take long until it was cooked and ready to eat.

Joe and Loretta Ann kept close to camp because they didn't want the fish to burn up in the hole in the ground. They had finished the boat so all they had to do now was get the inner tubes packed up with all the fruit they had picked to carry with them. They would have enough to eat for several days on the open sea. That is, if they didn't happen to have any bad luck. Joe and Loretta Ann would be ready to set sail in a couple of days. They were both excited about getting back to Okeechobee, and getting their lives back to normal once again.

Well, Joe and Loretta Ann ate the fish they cooked over the open fire. The fish were a different kind, and they tasted really good. Joe told Loretta Ann that they should be really smart because they had eaten so much fish. He told Loretta Ann he had always heard that fish were a brain food. He told Loretta Ann that if they were he should eat them every single day. She just laughed at what Joe had said because he was always coming up with something that could trigger her tickle box, and make her laugh even if she didn't feel like laughing.

Joe checked on the fish smoking in the ground to see if they were okay. The fish were just smoking along fine so now they had learned some other way to cook now. He told her the fish that were being smoked had been cooked in a ground oven, and that was the news report from the chef. She told Joe that he was turning out to be quite a good chef afterall. He told Loretta Ann thank you mam, and smiled real big at her. She had just made his day by telling him that he was a good chef.

The smoked fish were smoked enough so Joe took them out of

the ground oven then he and Loretta Ann wrapped them up in some of the green palm fronds. This kept them from getting flies and bugs on them. He told Loretta Ann they would get an early start the next morning so they could start packing the little inner tube rafts with their food. He told her they would carry some water in the boat, and put some in a container in the little tube rafts also. Today would be their last day to do anything on the island because the next day they would have to get everything ready to go the following morning so they could set sail.

Joe asked Loretta Ann if she would like to walk around the island one more time before they left it, and she told him she would love to go around just one more time. Loretta Ann had grown to like the little island, and told Joe she would miss it in a way. He told her he knew just how she felt. Well, they walked all the way around the little island one more time. Then they walked back to visit the waterfalls and cave one last time also. Joe and Loretta Ann just stood silently looking at the pretty waterfalls filling the little pond underneath it. They walked into the entrance of the cave, and they could no longer see the fire burning inside. The two of them were very fortunate to have found the little boat inside the cave. It was as if the little boat had been waiting for them to get it out of the cave so it could be used to get them home once again.

Yelp, Joe and Loretta Ann both were sort of sad right now because they knew they would probably never see the little island again. Joe and Loretta Ann finally left their little special place then went back to their camp. The little camp was also a special place to them because it had sheltered them from the storms, and had been their place of rest. Well, Joe and Loretta Ann both double-checked their supplies to make sure they had everything ready to start packing the next morning. Everything was in tact so they just spent the rest of the day enjoying each other's company. They decided to walk up on top of the rocks, and take one more final glance at everything up there. It was so peaceful on top of the rocks with the wind blowing ever so gently through their hair. Loretta Ann told Joe she hated to leave the island in a way, but knew they had to make it back home somehow to let everyone know they are alive and well.

Joe told Loretta Ann he has enjoyed every single day on the island with her. She told him she had enjoyed every moment on the island too. Well, Joe and Loretta Ann looked out at the waves of the ocean rolling in and out one last time. They soon would be riding the waves in the ocean going on their journey to try to make it back home. They came down from the top of the rocks, and stayed at their camp. The day had passed by so quickly today, and they decided they had better get all the rest they could before they started on their journey at sea.

Joe and Loretta Ann just lay back and took off the rest of the day as if they were tourists lying around on vacation. Soon it would be dark so they would have to turn in for the night anyways. Joe did put more wood on the campfire to keep it going until they were on their way off the island. They still had to cook their food so that was why it was so important to keep the fire all lit up. They did want to eat their last meal before they left the island. Also Joe wanted to make sure the big lizard wouldn't come close with the fire burning in case he was lurking nearby.

Loretta Ann asked Joe if he wanted a mango to eat. He told her he guessed he would eat one if she was going to have one. They both sat back eating mangoes, and drinking some of the fresh-water they had stored in the containers. It would have been nice to have a big old glass of tea right about now, but you can't have everything in life.

Joe and Loretta Ann talked about what they should do if they started having rough weather while they were in the little boat out in the ocean. They knew it was a good possibility that they wouldn't be found, but they both agreed that was a chance they had to take. Well, it had gotten so dark they knew it must be getting late so they both went to bed so they would be able to get up early. Each one said a prayer to help them make it safely back home.

Joe and Loretta Ann both rose up early the next morning. It wasn't quite daylight yet. So they started gathering up the things they needed to carry with them on the journey back home. Joe started to check each item to make sure it would be feasible for them to carry it on the trip. He just wanted the stuff that would last several days on the trip. He told Loretta Ann the main thing he wanted to have was plenty of fresh-water so they wouldn't become dehydrated from the sun beating down on them.

Loretta Ann asked Joe when did he think it would be the best time to try to set sail off the island? He told her they would watch the tide to see when it started to change, and then they would set sail. They were a little hesitant about leaving the little island because they knew what kind of dangers lay ahead. Joe checked the inner tubes bottoms they had fixed out of vines to make sure they would be strong enough to carry each load. They took all the inner tubes and put them on the shore so they would be at the boat the next morning.

Once morning came they would only have to put the rafts of fruit and water into the ocean behind the little boat. However they would have to be very careful or the rafts might turn over when the waves come crashing into the beach. It would be easier said than done. Joe told Loretta Ann he would catch their lunch early today then they would gather a little extra fruit to add to what they already had on hand. Loretta Ann asked him what were they going to put on the menu for lunch today, and he told her they would probably have blue crabs or fish. Loretta Ann told Joe well, I guess we do need the fish don't we? Joe told her the fish hadn't made them smart enough to stay put on the island. She told him it made us smart enough to get the boat ready for sail so I guess the brain food fish has worked in a way.

Joe laughed at her little remark, but he still had a funny feeling about taking on the whole ocean again.

Joe took his spear then headed down to the water to catch their lunch once again. He wanted to be sure to carry his spear with him just in case he got the chance to catch some food at sea. The only thing with catching fish in the ocean was they would have to eat it as sushi unless they let the sun bake it.

Joe had made it to the water and had speared 2 fish by the time Loretta Ann got there. Loretta Ann asked Joe how was the fishing today? He told her he had only caught 2 so far. She told him he would have to hold his mouth right then he would catch a lot of fish. Joe told her that had to be it, he just wasn't holding his mouth right. Loretta Ann watched Joe as he caught several more fish for their lunch. After they caught enough fish they returned to camp to do the usual thing and that was to clean and eat the fish.

Joe had the fish ready to eat and on the fire cooking in no time at all. He had developed an appetite today, and ate till he was about to burst open from eating so much. It was as if Joe was eating his last meal. After he ate all his fish he ate 2 mangoes and 3 oranges. After he ate the fruit he was in misery. He told Loretta Ann he was going to take a little nap. She told him to go ahead and get some rest.

Loretta Ann decided to take a walk while Joe took his nap. She would take herself a little nap when she got back from her walk. Joe told her to be careful and not to get lost. She told him that she might get lost by going around the island in a circle. Loretta Ann struck out walking towards the shoreline. As she walked along she thought how lucky they were to have landed on the island. It had been their little home away from home. Loretta Ann felt a little happy and a little sad today because she knew everything would get back to normal once they reached their home again. At least she hoped to make it back to her home. She sure didn't want to end up in another strange place.

Loretta Ann saw a flock of birds fly overhead. They

looked like pelican birds. She knew pelican birds usually stayed close to shore to feed for fish. As she watched them fly by she kept watching in the direction they were flying. Loretta Ann thought it was strange that they didn't stop and feed close to the island. She began to think that maybe her and Joe were closer to land than they realized, but couldn't be sure until they left the island to find out.

Well, Loretta Ann finished her walk around the little island. When she got her back to camp she got her some water to drink then lay down to take a nap like Joe. Joe was still sleeping so she didn't bother to wake him up and tell him about the birds. She must have been tired because she dozed right off to sleep.

The weather was so comfortable today that anyone could just rear back and relax without any trouble. Loretta Ann started to dream about the island. She dreamed they were living in a big house on the island. The island had other people on it so they weren't the only ones there. She dreamed they had a zoo with all kinds of animals in it. Loretta Ann and Joe had to watch out for the big lizards because they were meat eaters, and they were always trying to catch the animals in the zoo and eat them. Her dream seemed so real that it scared her so bad that she woke up yelling. At the sound of Loretta Ann's yelling Joe woke immediately from his nap. He asked her what was wrong, and she told him she just had a dream.

I guess it was their nerves bothering them both because of the following day that was coming up. Joe got up since he was disturbed from his nap and went to get him something to drink. He asked Loretta Ann if she wanted anything to eat or drink, but she told him no.

Loretta Ann and Joe started carrying on a conversation with each other again. They talked about how everyone would be surprised to see them once they made it home. She told him she hoped she still had her job when she got back, and Joe told her she would still have her job so not to worry. He told her he had to check on the status of the resumes he had put in at some of the offices. He told Loretta Ann he had heard from one of the offices already. He just hoped they would wait for him to get back to check with them on it.

Loretta Ann asked him if he was really serious about moving to Okeechobee, and Joe told her he had been giving it much consideration. She told him she was sure he would fit right in perfectly in her little town. He told her he had become very fond of the little town, and of some of its special people there. Loretta Ann smiled real big at Joe then told him how nice.

Well, the day was such a pretty day that Joe couldn't resist going for a walk in the woods. He asked Loretta Ann if she would like to go along with him, and she said sure I'd like that. Well, the both of them ended up at the little waterfalls once again. They both couldn't help it they just liked this little special place on the island. They walked over by a tree close to the waterfalls and sat on the ground. Joe and Loretta Ann leaned against the tree just sitting there listening to the sound of the waterfalls.

Loretta Ann told Joe they would be leaving their Paradise Island tomorrow. He said in a way I hate to go, but we have got to try to make it back home. Loretta Ann told him she knew it because they had people there that depended on them. Joe picked up a little sharp rock, and began to carve his name on the tree trunk. He gave the rock to Loretta Ann so she could carve her name on the tree trunk, but she wasn't strong enough so Joe took the rock then carved Loretta Ann under his name. He also carved the words "Paradise Island of Joe and Loretta Ann." This made Loretta Ann blush a little, but she still had a big smile to go along with her blushing. They sat there by the waterfalls almost the remainder of the day. When they got up to leave they stood there a few more minutes just looking at their little special place then they turned and walked away not saying anything to each other. As they arrived at camp once again Joe asked Loretta Ann if she wanted anything to eat, but she told him she didn't care for anything just then.

Joe was like a walking stomach because he had to peel him another mango and orange to eat. He wanted to keep himself occupied so he wouldn't think about the big day tomorrow, but it didn't work. He had all kinds of nervous energy, and the closer it got to leaving the island the more nervous he became. Loretta Ann had noticed how nervous Joe was and she knew deep down inside that she was just as nervous as he was.

Well, he told Loretta Ann they'd get up early again the next morning in case she wanted to eat something before they started on their journey. She told him she didn't know if she was going to eat before they left because she didn't want to get seasick on the water. He told her they should try to eat a little something so they wouldn't be too hungry.

Chapter fifty

Preparing To Leave The Island

It was just a matter of a few hours until they would be on their way out to the open sea in an effort to reach their destination. The day had once again come to end so Joe and Loretta Ann said goodnight to each other then went to bed. That night both Joe and Loretta Ann couldn't sleep much because they kept thinking about leaving the island tomorrow morning. They had all sorts of thoughts running through their heads. They had to be wondering what lay ahead of them once they set sail tomorrow. Once they set sail they would be on their own when they left the little island and headed out to sea.

Joe finally went to sleep but tossed and tumbled most of the night. He was so restless that by the time he woke up the next morning he couldn't even tell he'd rested at all. Loretta Ann woke up pretty chipper, and greeted Joe with a big good morning. He told her good morning then got up and started putting everything into the boat and rafts. He asked Loretta Ann if she was ready for this, and she told him she was as ready as she could possibly be. Joe said, "Me to."

Well, they finally got everything packed and ready to go. Joe looked at Loretta Ann then he told her what he needed her to do. She listened very carefully because he was telling her they would have to be very careful getting the little boat out past the waves rolling in. He told her that once they got out far enough they'd have to get inside the boat very carefully so as not to turn it upside down. Joe told Loretta Ann, "Well, Loretta Ann this is it." Loretta Ann knew it was time to go, and she and Joe started wading out into the water side by side pulling the rafts and boat out farther and farther into the water. The water seemed to be calm at that moment so it must be getting time for the tide to change again. Sometimes it took so many hours for the tide to change back, and they both were hoping to be far enough out so they didn't get washed back to shore.

The little rafts were floating okay in the water behind the boat. Joe helped Loretta Ann to get inside the boat then he got in very carefully so as not to tip the boat over. They both looked at each other as if to say I hope we're doing the right thing. Well, there was a little breeze starting to blow, which was a good thing for Joe and Loretta Ann. They could get more windspeed if the wind blew their little sail, which they had opened up. It was blowing enough to help them see how their little boat would handle pulling the rafts behind them.

Joe and Loretta Ann had floated out far enough now from the island that they could no longer see it in sight. It was as if the little island had disappeared, and never existed at all. Well, Joe kept looking in the boat to see if he saw any leaking spots, but so far so good. Loretta Ann saw some birds flying towards them, and it made her think of the pelicans she had saw the day before that flew over her at the island. She told Joe about it and told him they should watch the direction the birds fly in.

Finally at last Joe and Loretta Ann were well on their way. Joe and Loretta Ann didn't know where they were at to start with since they had gotten stranded on the island. They tried to calculate how far they were from Ft. Pierce because they had landed on the island before it had got dark the day they had got lost. Joe told Loretta Ann they had to watch the sunset because the sun always sets in the west in the United States. He told her if they were on the right tide they should be okay. He told her he thought they were going the right way because the boat was pulled away from the island so that had to be a good sign.

   Loretta Ann told Joe they might hit it lucky enough to see someone in a boat or maybe an airplane. The little boat and rafts were being blown along with ease from the wind. The wind seemed to be blowing harder now than it was when they had left the island. The little sailboat was just sailing along on the deep-blue sea. They watched for the horizon, but still couldn't see anything but water. The sun was beginning to get warmer now because it was getting close to noon. They talked about their adventures on the island. Joe told Loretta Ann he was glad they made it off the island, and that everything had went smoothly so far.

   Loretta Ann was laid back taking in the sun when she saw an airplane high up in the air. She jumped up so fast that she almost tipped the boat over on its side. Joe told her the plane was too high in the sky to even see them. She told him she just got excited at seeing the plane. She told him she just wanted to get rescued so bad that she could hardly stand it. Joe told her they would have to keep calm and be patient. Loretta Ann told him she had no doubt in her mind now that they couldn't be that far from Ft. Pierce. She told him if they kept cruising along like they were now maybe they could reach landfall by night. He told her when it got dark maybe they would be able to see the city lights if they were close enough to land.

   Joe was getting a little hungry so he got a mango out of the raft. He asked Loretta Ann if she wanted one to eat, but she told him she would have an orange to eat instead. They floated along in the little sailboat eating their fruit like they didn't have a care in the world. Well, at that moment they didn't have any cares in the world. All they could do was just sit it out, and that's what they did.

   Loretta Ann asked Joe if he would peel her a mango to eat because she was still a little hungry herself. He did as she had asked and peeled her a mango. Loretta Ann was enjoying her mango so much that she was smacking away on it and hadn't even realized at how much noise she was making eating her mango. Joe tried to look the other way so he wouldn't start laughing at her. She noticed Joe starting to smile, and she asked him what was so funny? He told her nothing, but he couldn't hold a straight face. Loretta Ann thought Joe was losing it because he was smiling about nothing.

Well, Joe noticed that Loretta Ann had mango all around her mouth, and he had started to smile again. She asked him again what was he smiling about? Joe told her that he wasn't trying to make fun of her, but she had mango all over her face. Loretta Ann looked over the edge of the boat into the water. She could see the reflection of herself in the water and saw the mango all over her face. She was a little embarrassed, but she told Joe that was just her make-up. It was at this moment that they both started to laugh. The two of them just couldn't seem to stop laughing. They were both laughing so hard that their sides and stomachs ached from all the laughter. Loretta Ann had tears in her eyes, and Joe had tears of laughter rolling down his cheeks. It looked as if Joe Macoochee was actually crying, but he wasn't.

Chapter fifty one

Stormy Weather

Well, it was getting on in the afternoon now, and the sky was becoming cloudy. The rain clouds had started to move slowly overhead. It seemed the clouds just popped up out of nowhere. The wind had started to blow much harder than it was earlier in the day. Joe and Loretta Ann knew they would probably be in for the ride of their life if the weather got any worse. The clouds were really dark, and they were the big heavy cumulus ones. When these kinds of clouds come about you can bet there will be a lot of rainfall from them. Joe and Loretta Ann had already talked about what they would have to do if a bad storm came up while they were in the little boat.

Joe had told her they couldn't panic because that would only make things worse. He told her if they happened to get capsized they would have to hold on to the rafts so they could stay afloat. Well, it wasn't but a few minutes then the rains came pouring down. Both Joe and Loretta Ann were worried that the little boat would sink from all the rain that was falling into it. The rain came down in droves, and the wind had the little boat rocking and reeling in the water. They started to dip some of the rainwater out of the boat with the water container that held their fresh-water to drink. They didn't want to throw their water away, but it was either they dip the water out of the boat or take the chance of sinking in the ocean.

The rain came down hard for about an hour, and then it just drizzled out after that. Both Joe and Loretta Ann were glad the rainstorm had passed by so quickly. Well, the little storm had carried the boat a long ways from the little island. Joe and Loretta Ann were making good time and didn't even know it. As they were sailing along more calmly now they both began to breathe with a sigh of relief that they made it through the storm okay.

Joe threw the last bit of water he could dip up out of the bottom of the boat. Joe then told Loretta Ann he hoped they didn't have to go through another one of those storms again. Loretta Ann said she hoped they found land soon so they could get their feet back on the ground. Joe told Loretta Ann he hoped they soon would hit land to because he was just a land lover himself. He told her if he went swimming anymore it would probably be in his bathtub or maybe a swimming pool. Loretta Ann told Joe, "I hear that." She told him she wasn't a duck or a fish so she knew she was staying on shore from now on.

Joe and Loretta Ann were both laid back taking it easy now since the storm had went away. They were floating along in the little boat carrying on a conversation with each other when they heard the noise of some sort of engine. Loretta Ann asked, "Joe did you hear that, and he told her he heard it." They sat real still barely breathing so they could be sure it was an engine that they heard. They both were looking all around them in all directions to see if they could see anything in sight. All of a sudden Loretta Ann let out a holler that sent chills down his spine. It was such a loud sharp pitched sound that it got next to Joe. Anyone would have thought that Loretta Ann was in extreme pain by the way that she hollered out.

Joe soon saw the reason why Loretta Ann was yelling out like she was. He to began to whoop and holler right along with her because there not too far away was a fishing vessel. They were jumping up and down in the little boat with excitement. They knew the people on the fishing vessel had to see them. Neither one of them stopped waving and hollering because they wanted to make sure they were seen. Once they saw the fishing vessel turn in their direction and start coming their way they sort of settled down.

Joe and Loretta Ann hugged each other's neck because they knew now they would be rescued for sure. They were so overcome with joy that they began to wave and yell at the fishing vessel again. Loretta Ann started to shiver with excitement as the vessel came closer to them. Joe couldn't believe they were finally going to get back home to Okeechobee. It wouldn't be much longer then Loretta Ann and Joe would soon be on their way back home.

They waited patiently as the big vessel came close to them. They saw the crew on the fishing vessel waving at them. Loretta Ann and Joe started to clap their hands when the fishing vessel came to a stop in the water close to them. Loretta Ann and Joe paddled their little boat on up next to the big vessel. Once they made it alongside the fishing vessel the crew helped Loretta Ann and Joe out of their little boat and onto the fishing vessel. Loretta Ann and Joe hugged everyone's neck and thanked all the crew for saving their lives.

The captain of the fishing vessel came out to greet Loretta Ann and Joe. He asked them if they were okay or if they needed any medical assistance, but she told him they were both fine. The captain asked them if they were the 2 people that had been missing from Ft. Pierce, and Loretta Ann told him yes that they were the missing links. The captain of the fishing vessel told them they still had search parties out looking for them. He asked Loretta Ann and Joe what had happened, and they told him the long dragged out story about how they had been carried away by the tide.

Loretta Ann told the captain how they had found the little island, and how they had stayed on it until they found the little boat in the cave. She told the captain once they fixed the little boat they had no choice, but to leave the island so they could try to find their way back home. She told him they weren't sure if they would make it back or not, but they had to take the chance. The captain told her they had probably landed on Pirate's Island. The captain told them the little island had been deserted for many years now. He told them they were lucky to have made it on the island because it used to have a lot of sharks that stayed close to it feeding on the fish that swam up close to the shoreline.

Joe told him the fishing was good there on the beach because he had to spear food for them to eat everyday they were there. Joe told him about the encounter with the sharks when they were floating in the ocean, and how the dolphins had run them off. The captain told Joe they had to have a guardian angel with them.

Once the crew got Joe and Loretta Ann's boat tied up to their fishing vessel they headed back into land. The captain radioed to the coast guards that they had picked up the 2 missing people and that they were both okay. The crew of the vessel asked Joe and Loretta Ann if they wanted anything to eat or drink, but they both only had some water to drink. They were too excited about being rescued that they couldn't have eaten anything if they had wanted to. Well, Joe and Loretta Ann stood up on the bow of the boat looking ahead of them hoping soon to see land. It took the fishing vessel around 3 hours to make it back to the inlet of Ft. Pierce.

Chapter fifty two

Back To Civilization

Well, they could finally see land and civilization again. Loretta Ann and Joe saw a bunch of people standing on the inlet waving and yelling out to them. This made Loretta Ann and Joe feel real good because people cared enough to help them. As they got closer to the dock they could see people lined up and down along the shoreline waving at them too. They saw a t.v. van parked where the crowd of people was at. Loretta Ann and Joe knew they would be one of the main topics on the nightly news. She told Joe she guessed they would be the talk of the town when they got back to Okeechobee. Joe told Loretta Ann that he had already hit the news a couple of times already since he'd been in Okeechobee. He told her he reckoned he'd wind up being a celebrity before it was over with.

Well, as soon as the crew got their little boat and rafts anchored up they told Loretta Ann and Joe they guessed they would be on their way back out to sea. Joe asked the captain how much did they owe him for bringing them into shore, and the captain told them they didn't owe him anything.

Loretta Ann asked the captain of the fishing vessel what his name was, and the captain told her to just call him Captain Bill. They thanked Captain Bill and his crew for coming to their rescue, and told them if they were ever in Okeechobee to be sure to look them up. Loretta

Ann gave the captain her name, phone number, and address in case he made it to Okeechobee. The captain and his crew waved goodbye to them as they set out once more to go fishing.

As Joe and Loretta Ann started to walk up to the place where the crowd of people were at they saw a man with a camera mounted on his shoulders coming towards them. The cameraman introduced himself to Loretta Ann and Joe as Oscar Widman. He asked them if he could ask them some questions about their being lost at sea. They told him it was okay so he gave them an interview that made it on the late nightly news, and also aired the next morning on the world and local news on t.v. Yelp, sure enough Joe and Loretta Ann had hit the big time news. They would be seen on t.v. back in Spicey Town, Virginia because Oscar had taken their pictures along with the interview. Joe just hoped no one at work had seen the news because he would never hear the end of it from everyone he worked with.

After Oscar had got the interview from Loretta Ann and Joe, he asked them if he could treat them to dinner. They told Oscar he didn't have to buy them dinner, but he told them it would be an honor for him to be able to do that for them. Both Loretta Ann and Joe agreed for Oscar to buy them dinner. They told him they wanted to get a shower first and get their regular clothes on before they left, and Oscar told them to take their time. Joe and Loretta Ann got their clothes from the old stationwagon that was still parked in the same place it had been for several days. It was a miracle that everything was still in tact on Joe's car, but the park was very well looked after so that's probably why no one messed with anything.

After they had gotten their clothes they went to the showers to bathe. The water was cold, but it felt so good to be able to shower in a normal way again. Joe and Loretta Ann were both sunburned so they didn't mind the cold shower at all. As the 2 of them finally finished showering they came out one by one to a still waiting crowd. Once again the people applauded Loretta Ann and Joe then told them good luck, and they were glad they made it back home safely. They thanked everyone for their kindness. Joe and Loretta Ann got into his stationwagon and followed behind Oscar's news van to a restaurant to eat dinner.

Chapter fifty three

Oscar Buys Dinner

Joe, Loretta Ann, and Oscar all went inside the restaurant, and were seated in a booth by a window that overlooked the water. Oscar asked them if this booth was okay, and they told him it was fine as long as they could look out the window and know they were on land and not in the water. They sat talking with each other until the waiter came to take their order. They ordered their drinks first, and then ordered their meals once their drinks were served. All of them had sweet ice tea to drink. Joe ordered the all you can eat fried chicken, and Loretta Ann ordered a thick and juicy steak. Oscar ordered himself the catfish special all you can eat. Loretta Ann and Joe just looked at each other and smiled because they knew they weren't going to eat fish today.

It didn't take long until they had their meals to eat. Once everyone started eating no one said another word until they had finished. Joe ate thirds instead of seconds, and Oscar had seconds on his catfish because he couldn't eat anymore. Loretta Ann ate her steak along with her order of vegetables and baked potato then she was full. They thanked Oscar for their dinner, and he told them they were very welcome.

Loretta Ann asked Oscar how long had he been a news reporter and cameraman, and he told her he'd been one for over 17 years. She told him she bet it was an exciting job to be on top of the news all the time. He told her he had seen many different news events during his time of being a news reporter. Oscar told them a story about how he was doing a news report on a car accident and how it turned out to be a strange news report. It was a real bad wreck, and the police were trying to get everyone out of the wrecked vehicles so they could be taken to the hospital and be treated. The amazing thing that happened next was when Oscar heard a noise coming from one of the wrecked cars in which everyone had been taken out of it. Oscar went over to the car where he thought the noise was coming from, and discovered that someone was trying to call for help from inside the car trunk.

Oscar told the police officer at the scene of the accident that he heard something that sounded like a person trying to call out for help. As the police officer had one of the wrecker men pry open the trunk lid of the car they were amazed at what they found. Inside the car trunk was a woman that had been tied up and gagged with a handkerchief over her mouth. Boy, the lady was one lucky lady because if Oscar hadn't heard the muffled sounds she'd made then she might not have been found at all. If he hadn't been there at the right time she might have ended up dying in the trunk of the wrecked car.

Well, as it turned out the lady had been kidnapped and her car hijacked by the 3 men. They threw her in the trunk, and went in a hurry to get out of town when they had the wreck with another car. The 3 men were immediately taken into custody at the hospital then carted off to jail until they had their trials. Once they got their sentences they would go to prison where they would remain for many years to come or maybe for the rest of their lives.

Oscar told them he'd been given a reward from the family, and the police department gave him an award for doing a good job and being so alert and observative. That year Oscar also received another award for the best t.v. news reporter of the year.

Well, Loretta Ann and Joe told Oscar it was a privilege

to meet such an important person, and thanked him for buying their dinner once again. Oscar told them it was his pleasure and privilege to meet them and to be able to spend the time he had with them. He told them thanks for their interview, and to be sure to watch the late night news because they would be on it.

Loretta Ann told Oscar that she lived in Okeechobee, and if he was ever over that way for him to stop in and see her. Joe told Oscar he lived in Virginia, and was down on vacation right now. He told Oscar that if everything went like he wanted it to he would be a Florida resident one-day. Oscar wished them both good luck, and they had wished him the same. They all shook hands then went on their way.

Chapter fifty four

Welcome Home Party

Well, Joe and Loretta Ann had started out of Ft. Pierce to head home to Okeechobee. They were both tired from their ordeal. Neither one said much at all on the way back home. Joe had made it back to the big bridge that he hated to drive over, but this time he didn't seem to pay it any attention at how high it was this time because he was so tired. It was about 9:30 p.m. by the time they made it back to Okeechobee. As they drove into the edge of town they had a surprise waiting for them. There in front of them hanging all the way across the street was a sign that read "Welcome Home" Loretta Ann and Joe.

They were so surprised at what they saw, and both were so happy to be welcomed home in such a manner. People were waiting for them just like they were at the inlet of Ft. Pierce. They knew Oscar had to have had something to do with the welcoming home party because he was the news reporter. Anyways they were greeted once again, and this time it was by their hometown friends.

It was at this moment in Joe's life that he'd ever felt such a warm welcoming home. Joe knew he was accepted as one of the hometown folks here in Okeechobee. At the moment Joe had made his mind up that he was going to return for good one day. It was quite a turn out for the little town of Okeechobee.

Little May Day was there along with Runt's family and Granny Hetty waiting on them to get back home. They all went to Coot's place, and sat around telling everyone about what had happened to them in the ocean and on the island. Everyone sat there listening to all the details of their adventurous story. Once they heard everything that Joe and Loretta Ann had done while they were away they all had something to drink then, and made a toast and gave thanks for their safe return home.

Joe and Loretta Ann told everyone thanks for the welcoming home party, and thanks for being such good friends. They then left to go to Loretta Ann's house. Joe walked Loretta Ann up to her door, and she asked him if he wanted to stay the night there, but he told her he would go on out to his little camp so he could check to make sure everything was still there.

Joe told Loretta Ann thanks for the good time at the beach, and she also told him thanks for the good time to. She also told him thanks for keeping her safe. Joe told Loretta Ann he would call her tomorrow to see how she was doing. She told him she would be waiting to hear from him. Joe then left Loretta Ann's house and drove back to his little camp at the Prairie.

Well, Joe stopped at the little country store that was close to the Prairie so he could have something to drink later on and also to pick up some ice. Once he got there everyone came up to him and started shaking his hand. They told him they were glad to see that he made it safely home. They told Joe they had seen the news on t.v. and were so glad that nothing bad happened to him and Loretta Ann. He told them he was glad to be back home here in Okeechobee. He told them he would see them later that he was going to go to his little camp and call it a day. Joe told everyone goodnight at the little store then he left to go back to his camp. He put his merchandise into his car then he drove on to his camp. Joe was finally back at his camp. It seemed to him that he was at home. It was sure good to be back there again Joe thought. As the saying goes there's no place like home, and right now the little Prairie camp was his home sweet home.

Well, Joe put away his ice so it wouldn't melt then he drank himself a bottle of water. Joe went to bed after he finished his water because he was completely exhausted from his day. Joe knew Loretta Ann would probably have to go to work tomorrow, and he felt sorry for her because he knew she was tired completely out. Joe went to bed and slept like a baby. He was glad to be back at his little camp. Well, Joe and Loretta Ann were 2 lucky people, and they knew it. They would have a story to tell their children one day if they ever got married and had a family.

Well, once again it was morning, but Joe didn't get up early because he was still tired out. Joe couldn't believe he was back in Okeechobee again. He even pinched himself to make sure he wasn't dreaming. He couldn't lay there any longer so he got out of bed, and fixed himself one heck of a breakfast that morning to eat. He fried himself some potatoes, and opened a can of corned beef hash, and also fixed some pan-fried toast to go with it. After he ate the potatoes, hash, and toast he ended up cooking some grits. Believe it or not Joe ate every smidging of food he had fixed. He ate it like food was going out of style.

Chapter fifty five

Joe's Big-Mouth Bass

Joe thought he might go fishing today to see if he could still catch them on a fishing pole. He drove down to the Kissimmee River Bridge, and began to do the same old routine of fishing. He took his little chair and fishing tackle out of his car, and made himself comfortable in his chair. Joe had to use some cut up hot dogs because he didn't have any live bait to fish with. As he put his last pole in the water he sat back in his easy chair to catch some fish. Joe had done pretty well with a spear, but the water was really clear at the ocean. Here in the river the water was dark so you couldn't see anything in it. He didn't care how dirty looking the water looked because he was back home.

Joe sat in his chair just enjoying life. He was so thankful just to be alive. He hadn't realized how precious life is until he saw how dim the light could be at the end of the tunnel. Joe knew now how short life could be. He and Loretta Ann could have been goners a couple of times when they were in the ocean. Joe noticed his fishing pole was starting to get a nibble on his line. He sat there being quiet and still as a mouse.

Joe just waited till the cork started to move on farther out into the river. Once it started pulling the slack out of his line Joe pulled back on his pole and hung into the fish. Well, he had his first fish for the day. It was a speckled perch, and a good-sized one at that. Joe didn't think he would catch anything with the cut up hot dog, but he did. He baited his pole up again and tossed it back into the river. He just sat back in his chair waiting for the next one to bite. It wasn't long at all until Joe hung another fish. This time it seemed like it was a whopper. He had to fight with this one a few minutes before the fish gave up so Joe could pull him in.

This fish wasn't a keeper because it was a big old garfish. Joe knew the garfish was just a trash fish, but he just couldn't take the fish's life so he threw the garfish back into the water. The fish he kept would be ate so he wouldn't be taking their life for nothing because they would become a meal for him to eat. Joe had eaten plenty of fish, but he still enjoyed catching them. Joe waited for another fish to bite his hook, but it was a long time before one did decide to bite his bait once more. Well, this time Joe caught a big fish. It was a big mouth bass, and he almost had a fit when he pulled up the fish to the top of the water and saw how big it was. He fought a few minutes with the big bass, but finally brought the big fish in.

When Joe caught this fish he immediately put the bass into a bucket of water. The other fish he had put on his fish stringer. Joe grabbed up all his fishing tackle, poles, and little chair then headed into town to have his fish weighed at the little tackle shop down by the lake. Joe took the bucket with the big bass he had caught and carried it inside the tackle shop to see how much his fish weighed. The lady inside the store said hello to him. He introduced himself to her. She had remembered him coming into the store to buy bait before.

The lady introduced herself to Joe, and told him her name was Martha Jane. Joe took the fish out of the bucket and hung him on the hook on the scales. Joe had caught a bass that weighed 14 pounds 12 ounces. Martha Jane told Joe that was the biggest fish that had been caught and weighed in her shop in over 2 months or more. She told him no one was catching bass that big anymore. She asked him if he was going to have his big fish mounted, and he asked her if there was anyone there that could mount the fish for him. Martha Jane told him that there was a man named Shorty in town that everyone got to mount their fish for them. She told him he was pretty reasonable on his price on mounting fish.

Martha Jane gave the directions of how to get to Shorty's place. He went there as soon as he put his fish back into the bucket of water. Joe went to Shorty's place, and he was in luck because Shorty had just pulled up in front of him in an old pick up truck. He looked at Shorty and knew why everyone called him Shorty. Shorty wasn't a tall man at all if you know what I mean. He was sort of in between I guess you could say. Well, Joe told him he had a big fish he had caught a little while ago, and took him to show him the fish in the bucket in his stationwagon. Shorty told him that was a nice big mouth bass and asked Joe where he had caught him at?

Joe told him he caught the fish in the Kissimmee River. Shorty told Joe the big fish would make a great mount. Joe asked how much it would cost to have the fish mounted, and Shorty told him it would be about $65.00. He told him that was okay to go ahead and mount his fish for him. He asked Shorty how long would it take, and Shorty told him it would be at least 5 or 6 days before he could pick the fish up because he wanted the fish to be dry enough to move him so he wouldn't get damaged.

Joe asked him if he needed to pay him up front before he mounted the fish, but he told Joe he could pay him when he came to pick up his fish. Joe told him thanks then he shook his hand, and left to go to the Lonesome Dove. Joe had ate a big breakfast, but he'd been craving one of those big juicy jumbo cheeseburgers that Runt made. He drove on out to the Dove to grab him a bite to eat. There weren't many people there when he first got to the little café, but it wasn't long before they started flocking in.

When Joe walked inside the little café he received a loud hoop and holler from the people that were there eating their lunch. Joe had grown accustomed to being greeted that way when he went there to eat. It was because he had always been in a situation that everyone had heard about, and they had to greet him like that. Joe was well known in Okeechobee now, and he had only been there for a few weeks in the little town. You just couldn't help to like Joe Machoochee because he just had something about him that sort of made you drawn to him.

Joe sat at one of the booths in the corner, and waited for his order to be taken. As he sat there looking at the menu he noticed Runt and Dee Dee coming out of the kitchen with something in their hands. It was a cake they had made that had a little island scene on the top of the cake. There were little toy palm trees, a toy man, and a toy woman that had been put on the top of the cake. Joe felt his face burning so he knew it was red from being so embarrassed.

He read the writing on the top of the cake and it read, "Joe and Loretta Ann's Island." Joe told them thank you for the cake. He told them he wanted to show it to Loretta Ann before he cut it to eat. They told him to be sure that he let Loretta Ann help him eat it. He told them he would be sure to do that. Well, Runt asked him if he wanted his big glass of sweet tea, or had he started drinking something different since he was on the island. He laughed and told her he still drank and ate the same thing since he was back home again. Joe gave her his food order which was the jumbo cheeseburger, french fries, baked beans, and that good old cole slaw Runt made from scratch.

Joe told Runt and Dee Dee about the big bass he had caught today, and told them when he could pick it up from being mounted that he would bring it by for them to see it. There was a man sitting across from Joe that overheard him telling the girls about the big bass he'd caught. He told Joe his name was T.J. and he used to fish on the Kissimmee River all the time. T.J. told him he had caught some real big fish out of the old river. T.J. told him he used to catch the big black catfish that usually could be caught in the month of May. He told Joe he had caught one many years ago that weighed 101 pounds. He told Joe it took him almost 2 hours to get the fish tired out enough so he could gap him, and bring him in to shore. T.J. told him he had pictures of most of the fish he had ever caught in the old river. He told Joe that was the good old days.

T.J. told him if he ever caught another one that big he would be out of here because the next time he might not be lucky enough to catch the big fish. T.J. told Joe that instead the big fish might catch him. He told Joe as big as the old catfish was that there might be some of the fish's relatives waiting for him to return again. He told Joe he sure didn't want to meet up with them. Joe laughed at what he had told him. Joe told him about his incident in Ft. Pierce and he told Joe that he didn't go in the ocean unless it was in a big boat. He told Joe he had a fear of sharks so he kept his distance from them.

Joe's food was being brought out to him so T.J. told him that it was a pleasure to have met him. He told Joe he would see him around sometimes. Joe told him see ya later then when T.J. left and Joe didn't waste any time at all eating on his big jumbo cheeseburger and other food. Joe ate like he was starving slap to death. Joe couldn't remember how good those big old burgers were until he took his first bite. As soon as he tasted the first morsel his memory came back real fast. Well, he finished off his meal, and Runt asked him if he wanted any dessert. He asked her what kind of dessert did they have today, and she told him they had homemade peach cobbler that was made from scratch. He told her he believed he would have a bowl of that then he would have to quit because he was about to pop right then.

Runt went into the kitchen and came back out with a big bowl of hot homemade peach cobbler topped with vanilla ice cream. Joe's mouth began to water as he started to eat the cobbler. He knew he shouldn't eat so much, but he was back home here in Okeechobee so he had to make up for lost time. He finished his cobbler then went to the cash register to pay for his meal. After he paid for his meal Runt gave him the little town's newspaper, and told him to be sure to read it. She told him to be sure to let Loretta Ann see the cake they had got for him and Loretta Ann. Runt put the cake back into its cake box, and handed it to Joe and told him to be careful with it.

He told the girls the food was delicious as always, and he would be seeing them again soon. They told Joe good-bye, and not to get lost again. He told them he wasn't taking his feet off of land for a long time. He told them thank you for the cake again then he went back out to his camp. Joe was happy as a lark right now. As he left the Dove he decided to call Loretta Ann at work. It should be almost time for her to take her lunch break. He dialed her work number, and asked to speak to her when someone answered the phone. They told him to hold a minute please.

Well, it was only a few seconds until Loretta Ann came to the telephone. She said, hello, and then Joe asked her, "Did ya miss me?" Then Loretta Ann laughed because she knew it was Joe. She told him yes that she missed him because he wasn't there when she got up this morning. He asked her if she was okay, and she told him she was fine and glad to be back home. Loretta Ann asked him what had he been up to today, and he told her all about his good fishing trip at the river. Joe told her how much the bass weighed that he had caught, and she got all excited when he told her all about his good luck at fishing.

Loretta Ann told him she was fixing to go on her lunch break, and asked him what he was doing right now. He told her he was just fixing to head back to the Prairie so he could clean his other fish he'd caught. She told him to come have lunch with her if he wasn't in too big of a hurry to get back to his camp. Joe told her he did have something he wanted to show her. She asked him what it was, but he told her she would just have to wait and see what it was. Joe asked her where she was going to eat lunch. She told him she was going home for lunch today. He told her he would be there before she could snap her fingers.

Well, Loretta Ann couldn't believe that he had beaten her home. He was sitting on her doorsteps waiting for her to get there. She asked him where he'd ate lunch, and he told her at the Lonesome Dove. Loretta Ann told him she thought that was probably where he ate at. Loretta Ann told him to come on in, as she unlocked the door to her house. She asked him if he cared for anything to drink, but he told her he couldn't eat or drink anything else. Joe told her he'd be right back. He went to his car and got the cake Runt had made for him and Loretta Ann. When she saw the fixtures on the top of the cake she was overwhelmed. She loved the little island with the palm trees, and 2 people on it. She was really surprised when she saw the writing on the cake that read "Joe and Loretta Ann's Island."

Loretta Ann told him to leave it up to Runt to come up with something like that. She was always up to some kind of mischief. She told Joe that Runt was a very mischievous young lady, and she always loved to get one over on you. Joe asked her what she meant by that, and she told him Runt loved to play cupid and matchmaker a lot, and play tricks on people all the time. She told Joe that was what everybody loved about Runt because they never knew what she would come up with. There was no way of telling what would happen next that was for sure. Loretta Ann fixed herself a ham and cheese sandwich, and drank a coke. She tried to get Joe to eat something else, but he told her he was still full. He told her he might eat a small piece of cake, but that would be it.

He did eat a small piece of the cake that Runt had given to him and Loretta Ann. They hated to cut the cake because it was so cute, but they did. Each one of them ate the cake, and made sure they ate every morsel that was on their plate. Well, it soon was time for Loretta Ann to go back to work. She told Joe she would put the cake in the box so he could carry it back with him to his camp. He told her to keep the cake there at her house because the ants would probably get into it at the camp. She told him she would wrap him some up in tin foil if he wanted to take some with him, but he told her to keep it or put it in the freezer because it would keep for a long time if it was frozen. She told him okay then put it in the refrigerator for the time being.

Well, they were getting ready to go their separate ways one more time until they had the chance to get together again. Loretta Ann returned to her job place, and Joe returned to his little campsite. He had told her to call him when she got off work, and they'd catch up on all the news. Loretta Ann told him she probably would get home at 5:00 today so she would call him then. She told him good-bye, and Joe said, "I'm out of here, see ya Loretta Ann."

Joe stopped by the store before he went back to his camp. He bought some more groceries for his camp. He had been craving some junk food so he stocked up on it also. He ended up buying some bananas, and a big watermelon to eat. Well, he was going to go broke from buying so many groceries. I guess he was glad to be able to have the nice things in life once more.

As he started on his way out of town he noticed the welcome home banners were still hanging across the main street of Okeechobee. He was so glad to be back. It was still hard to believe that he and Loretta Ann had been stranded like they had, but it had really happened. Joe made it to his little camp and unloaded all the groceries he'd bought. After he finished doing that he took the newspaper Runt had given to him, and started to read it. Of course, there was a picture of him and Loretta Ann on the front page of the newspaper. There was a nice newspaper article that had been written by Oscar Widman. He was the news reporter that had bought them dinner, and had done the interview with them in Ft. Pierce. Joe chuckled as he read the article about them being stranded, and he was wondering if Loretta Ann had seen the paper yet. Well, he would ask her when he talked to her later on today.

Joe didn't do anything much today except go for a walk in the woods. He'd walked around through the woods longer than he'd expected to because it was so pretty out there in the woods that he'd lost track of time. After he finished his walk he fired up his little camp stove to fix himself a little bite of supper. He fried up some sausages he'd bought, and fixed some pork and beans to go along with them. Joe had worked up an appetite from all the walking he'd done I guess. He ate his supper then he went to his favorite hang out spot at the camp, which was the hammock swing. He lay down in it very carefully, and thought to himself he would have had it made if he'd had his hammock on the island. There were all kinds of trees he could have hung it from on the little island.

Well, Joe had put his cell phone on his phone charger inside his stationwagon, and if it rang then the car horn would blow. That was another phone feature that he let the man at the store put on his phone for him. It didn't cost that much for him to get it hooked up, and it only took about 10 minutes for the man to connect it up for him. He thought he would take a little cat nap until he heard from Loretta Ann. Joe went to sleep, and started to saw logs again. He snored so loud that it's a wonder he didn't run off all the wildlife that was there in the woods. Well, he was sleeping very soundly when all of a sudden his car horn started to blow. Joe jumped up suddenly, and wham he fell to the ground. It took him a minute or two to get his bearings, but then he realized it was his phone making his car horn blow.

After Joe made it to his car to get his phone he answered it with a big hello. Of course it was Loretta Ann on the other end of the phone. She called him back just like she said she would. She wanted to know what took him so long to answer his phone, but he didn't get into telling her about how he had fallen out of the hammock. He thought she might think him to be very lazy, if he told her about him just lying around so much.

She started telling him about how everyone at work had been asking her all kinds of questions today. She told him that she was about talked out from all the questions. Well, he told her he had to ask her something to, and Loretta Ann asked him what it was? He asked her if she'd got the newspaper today? She told him she usually bought one everyday, but hadn't got one yet. He told her to be sure to get one because there was an article in the paper about them. Joe told her it was an article written by their friend in Ft. Pierce. Loretta Ann told him she had recorded the late night news for him because they were also on it. She had wanted to surprise him but since he had told her about the article in the newspaper she had to tell him about the news she had recorded for him. He asked her if she had the weekend off this week? She told him she would be off on Friday and Sunday, but had to work this Saturday. She asked him what he had planned?

He told her he was wondering if she would like to take in a movie if she wasn't busy doing anything. Loretta Ann told him they'd go either day that he wanted to. Joe told her they would go to Coot's Place and eat lunch before they went to the movies if she would like to. She told him she would really enjoy that. After they talked some more they decided to go to the movies on Friday.

The two of them talked for about an hour more then they told each other they would see each other Friday. Joe told her he would pick her up about 11:30 a.m. if that was okay. She told him she'd be waiting on him. Well, since today was Thursday I think that's why they both picked Friday to go to the movies. They wouldn't have to wait so long like they would if they had waited for Sunday to get there. Well, Joe and Loretta Ann didn't talk to each other until the next day when he called to see if she was ready to go to the movies.

He told her he would be there shortly so not to go anywheres. Loretta Ann laughed, and told him she wasn't going anywheres yet. Joe drove to Loretta Ann's house to pick her up. He didn't even fix himself any breakfast to eat so he was starting to get hungry. He had drank a soda, but that was it. He got ready and drove into town in no time at all. That was because he was going to Loretta Ann's house and he wasn't going to waste any time going to pick up his hot date. It was such a pretty day today, and it would be even a better one once he and Loretta Ann got together to spend the day with each other.

He picked Loretta Ann up at her house then they went to Coot's Place to have lunch. As soon as the two of them came into the café they were greeted by Coot, Sissy, and Bubba. They told Loretta Ann and Joe they were glad they made it back home safe and sound. Joe and Loretta Ann told them it was good to be back. Coot asked them if they wanted to sit at a table or at a booth? He told her he would like to sit in a booth by the window if it was okay with Loretta Ann. Little did he know, but Loretta Ann would have sat on top of the table if he had wanted her to. That was how attracted to him that Loretta Ann had become.

    Joe and Loretta Ann seated themselves in the booth by the window. Coot told them what the special of the day was. They had lima beans and rice, mustard greens, sliced tomatoes, corn, green beans, and cornbread. They had a choice of meats to pick from which was baked chicken or meatloaf. Joe told Coot that sounded really good. He ordered meatloaf with lima beans and rice, sliced tomatoes, and cornbread. Loretta Ann ordered the baked chicken, lima beans and rice, corn, and cornbread. As they were drinking their glasses of tea that Sissy had brought out to them Joe asked Loretta Ann what kind of movies did she like to watch? She told him she liked just about any kind of movie.

    Sissy and Coot brought out their plates of food. Lo and behold, it was heaped up on the plates about 3 inches high. Joe saw all the beans he had to eat, and wasn't too sure if he should try to eat that many, but once he tasted how good they were he couldn't help himself. Loretta Ann's plate had just as much as his, but they did manage to eat every bit of the food piled up on the plates. Sissy came over to see if they needed any more tea, and if they cared for any dessert. They did drink another glass of tea, but declined from eating any dessert.

    He told Sissy the meal was very delicious, and he couldn't eat anything else. He asked for the check because he and Loretta Ann wanted to be on their way to the movies to see what was playing today. Sissy brought the bill to them, and he paid it and told Sissy to keep the change, which was a $10.00 tip. She told them thank you, and to come back again. Sissy told him and Loretta Ann that there was a good scary movie on they'd probably like. Bubba had just come from the kitchen to tell them good-bye. Coot and Sissy told them to behave, and Joe told them they would because they were going to see a movie. He told them he hoped they wouldn't get into any trouble there.

Loretta Ann was just standing there not saying a word as usual, but she was smiling like a chesser cat. She told them she would see them all later on. Loretta Ann went to Coot's Place at least twice a week to eat. It was usually when she went to lunch when she worked.

Chapter fifty six

Scary Movie At The Theater

Joe and Loretta Ann left the little café then went to the movies to catch a matinee. As they walked up to the theater they looked at the different displays of different movies that were showing today. Loretta Ann saw the scary movie display she had heard everyone talk about. It was a good scary movie from what everyone had described to her.

She asked Joe if he was able to watch scary movies, and he told her yes. He told her he watched them on t.v. sometimes. She suggested they go see the scarey movie called "The Creeper of the Woods." Joe bought their movie tickets then they went inside the movie so they could get a seat. He asked Loretta Ann if she wanted a drink or some popcorn, but since she had just eaten lunch she didn't want anything just yet.

Finally the movie started, and everyone in the theater had gotten quiet. The movie was about a girl named Mary that lived in an old two-story house by herself deep into the woods. The girl was in her early thirties, and had no family left since someone had murdered her father a little over a year ago. They never found out who it was that had murdered her father because he was such a nice man. Mary still hadn't been able to go anywheres much. She just stayed to herself, and lived all alone in the big house.

Mary used to sit on the old porch that went all the way around the old house. She had seen someone watching her one day from the edge of the woods in a long black cloak. It scared her so bad that she never sat on the porch again. Mary had become a highly nervous person now. She had gone to the doctor with her problem, and her doctor had prescribed her some strong nerve pills, and some potent sleeping pills to help her sleep. Mary didn't like to take any kind of drugs because she was afraid that she might become addicted to them.

Well, the movie went on telling about her life as a little girl, and how it had been a normal one. She had one sister and one brother, but they had got lost in the swamp that was on the other side of the woods. The two children were never found so everyone figured they had gotten into the quick sand and went under. Their footprints had stopped at the edge of the swamp. Maybe one had fallen into the quick sand, and the other one tried to help, then fell into the quick sand to.

Mary didn't know it, but someone wanted something that her father had, and would do anything to scare her away or even kill her for it. The movie had some parts that would keep you on the edge of your seats. It had so much suspense in it that people were screaming out from fright. The movie had Joe nerved up pretty good because Loretta Ann reached over and grabbed his arm, and he just about jumped out of his seat. Well, after the movie was over he and Loretta Ann went outside to go do something else. He asked her if she wanted a drink and popcorn now, and she told him she'd have one if he did. Well, Joe had to have something to wet his whistle with after that movie because he had a dry mouth after watching the scary movie.

They took their drinks then started walking to the car. Someone that drove by them screamed out real loud causing Joe to lose half of his popcorn, but he still had enough to eat. He asked Loretta Ann what did she want to do now?

Chapter fifty seven

Hike On The Dike

Loretta Ann told him that the only thing she could think of was to drive down to the lake and see what was happening there. That sounded like a good idea to Joe so down to the lake they went. When they got to the lake there were a few people fishing on the pier. Joe and Loretta Ann got out of the car and walked out on the pier for a few minutes then they walked along the edge of the water feeding some of the popcorn to the seagulls and blackbirds. One time they threw a few pieces of popcorn to the few birds there and then they saw a bunch more flying in to get a handout to. The popcorn was gone in a hurry with all the birds that had gathered there now.

Loretta Ann asked Joe if he felt up to taking a hike on the top of the dike? He said he was ready and willing so let's go. They talked about how pretty the view of the lake was from the top of the dike. As they walked along they saw people cruising all over in boats, and fishing a long ways out in the lake. Loretta Ann told him the dike went all the way around the lake that was 36 miles wide and long. He knew the lake looked really big when he first saw it. They had walked 5 or 6 miles before they had realized it. They were enjoying the time they had spent together today.

Loretta Ann thanked him for taking her to lunch and to the movies. He told her she was quite welcome, and he was glad they had got to go. Joe's shoes were starting to hurt his feet so he took them off and walked barefoot for a while so he could give his feet some relief. He hadn't walked twenty feet from the spot where he had taken off his shoes when he ended up stepping into a patch of sandspurs.

Joe yelled out when he stepped into the sandspur patch. He scared Loretta Ann when he did this. He was in agony at that moment with all the sandspurs that had stuck into his feet. Loretta Ann saw what he had done, and told him to be still and she would help pull them out of his feet. He couldn't stand up any longer because every time he moved a little the sandspurs would go deeper into the bottom of his feet. Well, the situation didn't get any better because when he sat down on the ground he sat on some more sandspurs that got in the seat of his pants.

Loretta Ann told him it would sting when she pulled the sandspurs out, but it couldn't be helped. Joe asked Loretta Ann what kind of sticker bushes the sandspurs were. She told him that they were just a trash weed that grew where the soils were sandy. She told him she had forgot that he wasn't from around here because everyone knows what a sandspur is surely. He told her that they didn't have any sandspurs back in Spicey Town, Virginia.

She told Joe she was sorry about not telling him about the sandspurs, but Joe told her that was okay because now he knew what they were. If he had been by himself he might just have shedded a tear or two, but with Loretta Ann being there he had to stand up to his ego. Finally Loretta Ann got all the sandspurs out of his feet so he could put his shoes back on. Once he stood to his feet the embarrassing part came. He had no choice but to let her pull the sandspurs out of the seat of his pants. Finally the pain and embarrassment was over. He thanked Loretta Ann several times about coming to his rescue and being his nurse.

It was getting late in the afternoon so Loretta Ann and Joe started to walk back to where the car was parked. He told her that he had to stop by the office that had told him to check back in with them about the job application he'd filled out. He told her that he thought about it a lot the last couple of days, and he had made his mind up that he was going to move to Okeechobee if he found a job before he went back to Virginia. Boy, Loretta Ann lit up like a shining light at what Joe had just told her. She hadn't thought he was too serious about moving down here to Okeechobee because she didn't want to get her hopes built up only to be let down.

Well, Loretta Ann was walking on cloud nine at that moment. She was one of the happiest girls in the world. Her Joe wasn't going away afterall to stay. He noticed how perked up she seemed to be, and he thought he had a good idea why she was that way.

Joe and Loretta Ann drove to the office that had told him that they had an employee moving back to Pennsylvania. They went inside to see if the job had become available yet. So happen the job would be available for Joe in three weeks. The boss man asked him if he thought he would need more time than that, but he told him he would leave to go back home in a couple of days so he could give them two weeks notice that he would be moving. Joe and the man shook hands, and the man told him welcome aboard, and he would see him in three weeks. Loretta Ann knew Joe had to go back for a little while so he could get everything packed up to move down here. She asked him if he was going to rent a place in town or stay at the Prairie for a little while? He told her he would try to find a place before he went back to Virginia.

Well, they went to get a paper out of the paper box so they could look to see if there was anything for rent. There were several apartments for rent, and three houses that Joe told her that he would check on to see how much they were and where they were at. She told him she could help him look for one when she got off work tomorrow if he needed her help. Since she knew the area so well they would surely be able to find a place for him to move into.

They left the office where Joe had stopped to check on the job. They drove around town, and found two of the houses that were for rent in the newspaper. He and Loretta Ann got the key from the landlord, and went inside to see what the houses looked like. They were both in good condition, so he took the name of the landlord in case he decided to give them a deposit on one of them. One house was at the edge of town, and the other one was around the lake. He told Loretta Ann he really didn't need a 3-bedroom house for himself, and he knew he wouldn't ever have company down to spend the night. She told him he would have a lot of storage room though if he had a lot of things that he had to bring down.

Joe told her that was something he never thought about. He did have a lot of stuff to move down from Virginia to Okeechobee. He told her he would have to rent a big truck to haul his stuff down to Okeechobee, and pull his car behind the truck. Well, they went back to Loretta Ann's house. Joe got out and went inside for a little while talking things over with her about what he had in mind to do about the moving situation. She told him he could stay at her house if he wanted to until he got situated into an apartment or house. He told her she was very kind, but he wanted to find a place to get settled into so he wouldn't have to move but one time.

Loretta Ann told him she would help him when he needed her to. Joe told her he would be calling on her a lot to help him if she didn't mind. Loretta Ann sure didn't mind at all. Well, Joe left her house to go back to his camp. He told her he was going to pack up most of his stuff he had brought down except his tent, and he would have to pack it up last. He told her that he guessed he would leave to go home early Sunday or Monday morning. Loretta Ann told him to come by her house, and she would fix him dinner before he went back to Virginia. Joe told her if it would be okay he would give her a raincheck, and let her fix him dinner when he came back to Okeechobee in about 3 weeks. She told him that it was a date, and she was going to hold him to it.

Joe waved at Loretta Ann as he drove out of her driveway. She stood there smiling and waving back at him. He had only been a couple of blocks from Loretta Ann's house, and he was missing her already. Loretta Ann went back inside her house, and right now she felt like she had lost her best friend. I guess she was more wrapped up in Joe than she had really realized.

Joe stopped by the Lonesome Dove to let Runt and everybody know he was leaving in a couple of days just in case he didn't get by to see them. He told Runt he wanted to get a big sweet ice tea to go in case he didn't get back by there. He went to pay Runt for the tea, but she wouldn't take his money for it. She told him it was on the house, and to enjoy it. Joe thanked her for the tea, and told her it surely would be enjoyed, and he meant every drop of it. He told Runt and Dee Dee he'd see them when got back in 3 weeks because he was moving to Okeechobee to stay for good. They told him to have a safe trip home and to be sure to come see them as soon as he got back to Okeechobee.

As he walked out of the door at the Dove he saw 2 young blonde-haired boys skateboarding on the pavement. Joe saw Bubba outside showing them how to ride their boards. He had on his chef hat and apron and was flying through the air like a big bird. Joe thought that it looked like fun, but knew he would never have been able to skateboard because he just wasn't coordinated enough. He knew he could pull off a good crash if he tried it so that's why he just stayed on the ground on his feet.

Bubba saw that Joe was fixing to leave so he and the 2 boys went over to talk to him. Bubba introduced the 2 boys to Joe and told him their names were Mann Mann known as "Turdhead" and Chase known as "Hot Rod." Bubba told Joe they were his nephews, and they came out to see him all the time. The 2 boys looked up to Bubba as their hero. Joe told the boys they were doing a good job at skateboarding, but to be careful and to listen and learn from their Uncle Bubba. Joe told them he would see them when he got back to Okeechobee because he was leaving to go back home. He told them he was moving to Okeechobee so he'd see them a lot. Bubba and the boys told him goodbye and that they would see him when he came back.

Joe got into his stationwagon and started leaving out the driveway of the Lonesome Dove. As he drove away he could see the boys still skateboarding and doing their tricks on their skateboards in the rearview mirror of his car.

Joe took his tea and drove slowly back to his camp at the Prairie thinking things through about the big step he was fixing to take. As he drove along he weighed every option against the other one, and of course it was to go ahead and move down to Okeechobee as soon as possible. Joe was very happy today because he thought he had made a good decision for his future. As he looked at it, he really liked Okeechobee and the people here. Most of all he had found him someone that he was very attracted to, and he thinks she feels the same way. So there might be something wonderful about to happen in his life once he returns to the little town of Okeechobee.

When Joe made it to his camp he called Loretta Ann, and told her he would miss her when he went back home. Loretta Ann told Joe that's ditto for her too. He told her he might leave early Sunday morning, but he wanted to come by to see her before he leaves. She told him to call her and let her know when he'd be there. He told her that the sooner he left the quicker he could return. She told him that was a good thought. Well, he told her he was going to do what packing he could do then he was going to rear back and take it easy for a while. That was exactly what Joe did because he wanted to lie in the hammock one more time and just lay there listening to all the birds, and different sounds that came from the animals and woods. It was time for him to get ready for bed since nightfall had come.

Joe built a campfire before he went inside his tent to go to sleep, once he built his fire he sacked out for the night. Joe was kinda happy and kinda sad, and he sure hated to leave that was one thing he knew for sure. Joe just lay in his little tent thinking about the great day that he and Loretta Ann had together all except the sandspur incident. It was worth it as long as he was with Loretta Ann. Joe finally went to sleep. During the night he was awaken by the sounds of a wild hog squealing somewhere in the woods close by. He hoped the hog would stay his distance because he didn't want to have to get up out of his comfortable little bed. The hog must have gone in the opposite direction because Joe didn't hear him anymore that night.

Well, the night passed, and it soon was morning again. Joe could hear turkeys gobbling in the woods this morning. It was really foggy at his camp so maybe that was why they were out making so much noise because they were lost in the fog. Joe got up to get everything going for his day, but it was so foggy he couldn't see in the front of him so he just sat down by his little fire in his little canvas chair. Joe waited till the fog lifted then he made himself some breakfast on the little campstove. After he finished eating everything he had cooked for his breakfast Joe then cleaned up the dishes and little campstove, and packed it into his stationwagon. He would pick something up to eat in town if he went in today. Well, it was Saturday, and he thought he would go fishing one more time before he went back home. If he caught any fish he would just throw them back into the river, sort of a catch and release method like you see the big boys do on t.v. Well, he caught 22 fish today, but let everyone of them go back into the river. He had fun catching them, and that was one of the main things.

Well, Joe dreaded the trip of going back home tomorrow, but knew he had it to do. Well, he thought he had better get on back to camp, and make sure everything was loaded up to take off early in the morning. After he pulled his poles out of the water he just sat back and enjoyed watching the ducks and coots swimming in the river. While Joe sat in his little chair he saw a big alligator swimming across the river. He had to be at least 10 feet long. He didn't move at all he just sat watching the alligator until he finally swam out of sight.

Joe drove back to his camp to see if he had completed everything that he had needed to do before leaving in the morning. Sure enough he had everything organized pretty good. Joe just couldn't pinpoint it, but it seemed that he was forgetting to do something. He thought and thought, but nothing came into his mind. Oh well, he told himself it must be nothing if I can't remember it.

Joe went to the little country store that was close to his camp to fill his car up with gas so he wouldn't have to do it in the morning. The first thing he had to do the next morning was to pack up his tent and bed, and then he would go by to see Loretta Ann so he could be on his way. It was almost time for lunch, but he just fixed himself a sandwich out of some canned Spam and ate that for his lunch. Joe had always been a Spam man ever since he was a little boy. He just loved the flavor of his Spam sandwich after he got it all heaped up with all the trimmings. After he fixed his sandwich he had one big enough to feed 3 people, but it was just a snack for him. He would do the same thing for his supper unless he got something at the store to eat. It was 3:30, and it wouldn't be much longer until Loretta Ann got off work.

Joe would wait until 5:15 to see if Loretta Ann was going to call him then if she didn't he would call her. Joe decided to take one last walk through the woods, and by that time Loretta Ann should be home. Joe walked about a mile from his camp, but headed back to his camp because it wouldn't be too long until it was dark. Well, it was 5:30 so Joe called Loretta Ann. She didn't answer the phone so Joe left a message on her answering machine to be sure to call him.

It was about 6:30 when Loretta Ann called Joe. She told him she had to carry May Day to town to buy her some groceries again. Joe asked how May Day was doing, and Loretta Ann told Joe she was okay, and everything was back to normal once again. Joe told Loretta Ann he was leaving in the morning around 6:00 a.m., and he asked her if that was going to be too early for him to come by her house to see her before he leaves? Loretta Ann told him she would be waiting to see him because she gets up early most every morning anyways.

The two of them talked and talked, and hated to tell each other goodnight, but they soon had to because it was getting so late. Joe told Loretta Ann he would see her in the morning so goodnight and sleep tight. Loretta Ann said goodnight to Joe then hung up the phone. Joe didn't sit up late that night because he wanted to be rested up good for his trip.

Well, it was morning again, and it was time for Joe to head home from his vacation. It was 5:00 in the morning, and Joe knew he still had to pack up his bed and tent. Once he did that he put out the campfire he'd made the night before. Joe took one last look around the little Prairie Camp then got into his stationwagon to go to Loretta Ann's house. He called her to make sure she was up, and believe it or not she had got up at 3:oo to make sure she would have some food cooked and fixed up for Joe so he would have something to eat while he was on the road back home. It was sort of a picnic lunch she had prepared for him. That was a nice thing for her to do for Joe. Well, one thing for sure she wanted to make sure that her Joe didn't go hungry before he got back home to Spicey Town, Virginia. Loretta Ann was sure hating to see Joe go back home.

Chapter fifty eight

Farewell Loretta Ann

Well, Joe made it to Loretta Ann's house. He got out and went inside to bid her good-bye, and had got a surprise because Loretta Ann had breakfast waiting for him to eat. Joe sat down and ate breakfast with Loretta Ann then he told her he'd have to be on his way. Loretta Ann gave Joe the other food she had fixed up for him to eat as he drove along on his way home. Well, the time was here, and he hated to tell Loretta Ann good-bye just as bad as she hated to say good-bye to him. He thanked her for fixing his breakfast, and for the food he was carrying with him on the road home.

Loretta Ann walked Joe out to his car. He put the food she had cooked inside his car. Then Joe turned to Loretta Ann, and pulled her up close to him and gave her a big long kiss good-bye. Loretta Ann thought she was going to faint. She had never been kissed by a man like that before. Well, Loretta Ann and Joe both seemed to be seeing stars right about that moment. Joe then told Loretta Ann he would miss her and he would be back soon. Loretta Ann told him to call her while he was on his way home, and to be sure to call her when he made it home. Loretta Ann told Joe to be safe, and hurry back to her. She had let that slip out before she thought about what she had said. Joe smiled really big at Loretta Ann and told her he would return. He hugged her then he got into his stationwagon and drove on his way back home.

Joe left Loretta Ann's house and drove on his way to Virginia. As Joe was driving on his way back home he just couldn't stop thinking about his moving trip to Florida. Joe thought of all the things that he had done while he was on vacation. He knew it was something that he'd remember for the rest of his life. He thought about the incidents of the mad boar gator, the beach, the old cow having her calf, and the big ugly turtle he had caught on one of his fishing trips, and also the big mouth bass he'd caught. Joe all of a sudden had a memory flash that came back to him on what he had forgotten. It was his big mouth bass fish that he had left at the taxidermist's shop to be mounted.

Joe pulled over to the side of the road to call Loretta Ann, and ask her if she would mind picking his fish up for him. He dialed her from his cell phone, and got her on the second ring. She was all excited that Joe had called her already. She asked him if everything was okay, and Joe told her yes, and he was about to leave Okeechobee County. He asked her if she could get his fish from Shorty the taxidermist, and he would send her a check for the amount if she could do that for him. Loretta Ann asked Joe when was the fish supposed to be ready to pick up, and he told her in a couple of days.

Loretta Ann told him she would call Shorty, and explain to him what had happened, and she would be glad to do that for him. Joe told her thanks, and told her he would call her again once he got closer to home. Joe ended up calling her a couple of more times on his way back. He called her again as soon as he pulled into his driveway at home. He told her the food she fixed him just hit the spot. He told her once he got everything took care of up there he'd be back. In the meantime Loretta Ann and Joe would keep in touch by long distance until he made it back to Okeechobee.

Joe Macoochee was a very lucky man that seemed to have

everything going right for him at this stage of his life. We wish him well with all of the things that he wishes to accomplish in his lifetime. We also wish Joe and Loretta Ann many more good times together, and maybe possibly a bright future ahead of them together.

Written: by Shirley Ann Wildes
P.O. Box 1146
Okeechobee, Florida 34973
(863) 763-4400

P.s. I hope you enjoyed reading volume one about Joe Macoochee and Loretta Ann. I hope to get my book published one-day and to keep it in its slang form.

Joe fell off the spillway. Almost fell into the water.

About the Author Shirley Ann Wildes

I live in my little hometown of Okeechobee. Being a people person I rarely meet a stranger. My hobbies are dirt track stock car racing with the fellers. Wish I could race the big brown truck just one time. I'm trying to write crazy funny books keeping them in my own slang wording.

I work in the septic tank industry and could tell you stories that would probably curl your toenails. I'm always joking around. Guess you could say, "I'm just full of malarkey." It's good to laugh whenever you can.

"Peace be to all." "God Bless America."

Summary About; "Joe Macoochee's Wild Camp Out Adventures"

While traveling on vacation Joe Macoochee has some hair-raising experiences. Stopping at a state park in Ormond Beach he tries helping a fisherman but only causes him to lose his big fish.

Going to an amusement park he falls off the shuttle train. Trying to enjoy his day he rode the attractions only having more bad luck.

Arriving in Okeechobee he meets new friends and a special girl named Loretta Ann. They go to the beach, a movie, and have a bar-b-que at his camp.

Many strange events happen during his stay camping out in the woods at the Prairie.

BVG